Violence and crime in nineteenth-century England

Why does violence seem to haunt modern civilization? Can violence "speak," and if so, what can it tell us? Where do our attitudes toward violence come from?

This book examines these questions by considering a critical period in the evolution of attitudes toward violence. Using the English experience, it explores the meanings of violence through an accessible mixture of detailed empirical research and a broad survey of cutting-edge historical theory. It critically investigates the concept of the "civilizing process" and asks readers to rethink their own views of violence.

Nineteenth-century social upheaval changed attitudes toward class, gender, suffering, public space and state power, leading to new understandings of violence. Adherents of emerging "civilized" views confronted a "customary" mentality with different views of violent behavior. That encounter saw the "invention" of violence as a social problem that was seen to threaten a nascent culture of refinement. The author critically examines this process, and the customary mentality of violence is given particularly close attention. The complex and dynamic interactions between civilization and custom are revealed through topics such as streetfighting, policing, sports, community discipline, and domestic violence. Although customary notions eventually faded, this book shows how the nineteenth century established enduring patterns in views of violence.

Violence and Crime in Nineteenth-Century England will be essential reading for advanced students and researchers of modern British history, social and cultural history, and criminology.

J. Carter Wood received a Ph.D. in modern British history from the University of Maryland, College Park, where he also taught as a visiting lecturer. His work has appeared in the journal *Crime, History & Societies* and he was a contributor to *Comparative Histories of Crime* (2003). He lives and works in Germany.

Violence and crime in nineteenth-century England

The shadow of our refinement

J. Carter Wood

LONDON AND NEW YORK

First published 2004
by Routledge
2 Park Square, Milton Park, Abingdon, Oxfordshire OX14 4RN

Simultaneously published in the USA and Canada
by Routledge
711 Third Avenue, New York, NY 10017

Routledge is an imprint of the Taylor and Francis Group, an informa business

First issued in paperback 2015

© 2004 J. Carter Wood

Typeset in Baskerville by Taylor & Francis Ltd

British Library Cataloguing in Publication Data
A catalogue record for this book is available from the British Library

Library of Congress Cataloging in Publication Data to follow

ISBN 978-0-415-32905-7 (hbk)
ISBN 978-1-138-01021-5 (pbk)

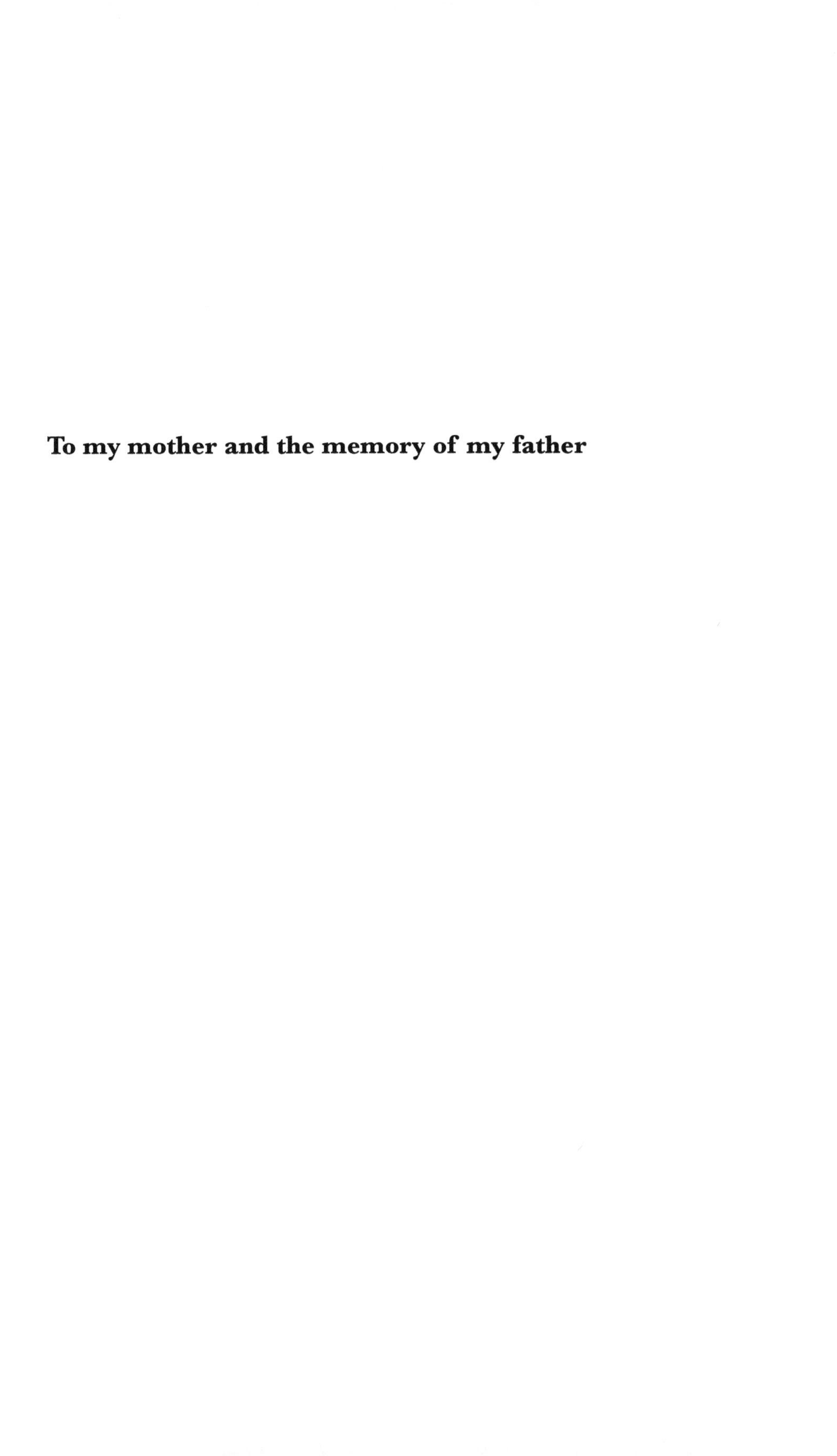

To my mother and the memory of my father

Contents

Preface

I began researching this book with an interest in the way that the boundaries around appropriate social behaviors change and a fascination with the phenomenon of violence itself. When one looks closely at the history of any type of human activity – from the intricacies of table manners to the way that societies define acceptable violent or sexual acts – the instability inherent in the most seemingly "natural" of social activities becomes apparent. Highlighting these trends can be a difficult project, as the researcher is likewise working from a position within the inherited accumulations of cultural norms. The imperatives of academic writing, with their assumption of dispassionate distance and authority, can also serve to conceal the way an author is positioned in relation to his or her subject. However, one's location in the midst of the present cultural context occurs only because of an uncountable series of highly contingent circumstances, and our perspectives on the past are inevitably affected by our own social and individual situations. Thus, it might be useful to make a few brief remarks about my own approach.

First, I find criminality to be simultaneously one of the most useful lenses on culture and society and one of the most volatile of human notions. More than three decades of English criminal history have emphasized the ways that "the law" is not merely a self-contained institution subject only to its own rules and trends. It is unquestionable that its internal workings are vitally important to understanding its development, and work done along these lines is essential to the project of criminal history. However, law is only one of the social institutions that set the boundaries between the acceptable and unacceptable, and these lines are continuously contested and shifting. Although I rely heavily upon sources created by the practice of law, my approach is more broadly cultural and located at the point at which law, popular cultures and violence interact.

Second, when beginning the present work, I faced a choice between doing a wide-ranging general survey or a narrowly focused local study. In opting for a more general appraisal of attitudes toward violence, I have faced certain advantages and disadvantages. The key advantages are the opportunity to identify and analyze large and influential trends and to engage with a variety of secondary literature on violence. The main disadvantage, of course, is that, in delineating general currents, significant regional and local variations might have been missed. In no way do I claim that the present work serves as a comprehensive statement about attitudes toward violence in the nineteenth century: in conceptualizing a topic as broad as violence, I have had to draw lines regarding what will or will not be brought into view. Furthermore, anyone who has looked at the records of a large number of violent events (or who has experienced violence) can likely attest to the apparent individuality of those occurrences. Yet, none of us think about or react to violence in a vacuum, and the attitudes we apply to experience derive from more general cultural currents, including many that we may remain unaware of. I believe that I have been able to identify the dominant contours of the English cultural mind in regard to interpersonal physical aggression at a particular state of historical development. Looking more closely at regional or local contexts might have revealed specific differences, but I suggest those variations would recognizably have been rooted in the general themes sketched out herein. Another goal has been to delineate models and conceptualizations that are relevant to contemporary discussions about violence. The study of violence in England is a relatively young field, and I hope that my analysis will be useful in giving attention to the way violence is narrativized; exploring the influence of ritual and custom on behavior; and establishing the connections among violence, identity and space, both historically and in the present day.

Third, as other scholars of violence have noted (both in writing and in discussions I have had with them), one becomes very accustomed to justifying what often appears to others as a morbid interest in a disturbing topic. However, in my efforts to understand violence – for instance to argue that it sometimes "made sense" in opposition to the common view that it is always "senseless" or merely an inchoate, animalistic behavior – I do not suggest that it is a more desirable alternative to non-violence. Like most people, violence features prominently in my pantheon of fears, and there are no doubt some personal motivations in attempting to grapple analytically with the subject itself. I believe that my engagement with the topic of violence has been fruitful and, while I think that the issue of violence can never be "solved," further investigation across all intellectual disciplines (both in the sciences and humanities) has the potential to demystify our conflicted relationship to it. The study of violence, after all, goes to the center of both the social and psychological aspects of the human condition.

As a technical note, much of my evidence comes from handwritten sources, often hastily written, and I have made every effort to present them in a format that makes them clearer without overly altering their original form. In quoting such sources, I have added or changed some original punctuation, spelling and capitalization in order to improve their readability and clarity.

Acknowledgements

A project such as this inevitably (and happily) becomes a collaborative endeavor despite the fact that only one name appears under the title, and I have been fortunate in the many people who have assisted me during the past several years. Initial appreciation must go to the Department of History of the University of Maryland, College Park. The department exhibits a high level of intellectual innovation and rigor in its faculty and among its graduate students. My thinking on many topics has been a beneficiary of that atmosphere, and I hope that a palimpsest of several years of seminars, independent study and hallway conversation is visible in the chapters that follow. I am no less grateful for financial support in the forms of a graduate fellowship, two research grants and a travel grant for conference participation. In reference to my time at Maryland, I owe particular professional and personal thanks to Richard N. Price, Richard F. Wetzell, Alison Olson, Marvin Breslow, Douglas Bristol, Amy Masciola, and Scott Ickes. I also thank the secretaries and support staff of the department, who are among the very best I have ever known.

I was greatly assisted by the staffs of the Public Record Office and the British Library, where the bulk of my research was conducted. They provided consistently helpful service, and their dedication to the stewardship of the national record makes work such as this possible. I give personal thanks to my family for their financial and emotional support at crucial stages of my work and to the Davé family in London for the accommodation and friendship that I serendipitously enjoyed during part of my research. Sections of this work – in particular from Chapters 3, 6 and 7 – appeared in a different form as "Self-Policing and the Policing of the Self: Violence, Protection and the Civilizing Bargain in Britain" in *Crime, Histoire & Sociétés / Crime, History & Societies*, 2003, vol. 7, no. 1, 109–128. I am grateful to Droz, Genève-Paris for permission to reproduce that material.

Many readers have commented upon various aspects and fragments of this project as it took form. Their analysis, criticism and enthusiasm have made it far better than it otherwise would have been. The late Marvin Rosen, whom I met while an undergraduate at Northern Illinois University, was the key inspiration for my decision to pursue historical study and offered many helpful suggestions and extraordinary intellectual support. I also wish to express particular gratitude to John E. Archer, Victor Bailey, William Beik, Andy Davies, Anna Davin, Barry Godfrey, Rohan McWilliam, Jessica Walsh, Cassie Watson, Martin Wiener and Chris Williams for comments on various aspects of this project and thank the History Workshop Seminar in London and the Victorian Studies Reading Group at the Johns Hopkins University in Baltimore for hosting presentations of mine that helped move my thinking forward. I am grateful for the assistance of my editing team at Routledge for their professionalism and support and to four anonymous readers who provided constructive criticism of my original book manuscript. Of course, any errors or awkwardness that remain are my sole responsibility. I must separately thank Anja Müller-Wood, who has influenced this project, my work and my life in ways that are beyond counting and to an extent that continues to amaze me.

Finally, and without employing a cliché involving the words "best" and "last," I wish to acknowledge the advisor who supervised the dissertation out of which this book emerged. My decision to study crime arose out of an independent study with him during my early days at the University of Maryland. Subsequently, he has unfailingly provided inspiration, advice and criticism in a spirit of patient respect and good-humored personal regard. For his scholarship, influence and friendship, I thank James S. Cockburn.

Introduction
Casting shadows

The issue [of understanding crime] takes us beyond amassing criminal statistics and cataloging elite fears about a disintegrating social order.... Yet one avenue toward understanding how crime modernized must be to set the question in the wider context of how the personal comportment, psychological framework, and expectations about interpersonal interactions of individuals altered.

J. A. Sharpe[1]

It will be necessary to construct a history of what happens in the nineteenth century and how the present highly-complex relation of forces – the current outline of the battle – has been arrived at through a succession of offensives and counter-offensives, effects and counter-effects. The coherence of such a history does not derive from the revelation of a project but from a logic of opposing strategies.

Michel Foucault[2]

The specter of violence haunts modern life. It is an evocative, recurrent phenomenon that both fascinates and horrifies. Today, violence is generally seen as something to be banished as much as possible from daily life, and contemporary European societies have largely succeeded in creating pacified public spheres within which the incidence of physical attack is, by historical and international standards, relatively low. In fact, this has become a point of European pride often contrasted with more "dangerous" places in the world such as the United States. At the same time, however, violence is always lurking "out there": statisticians report how many people are assaulted, raped or killed every day; press accounts of violent crime and war are ubiquitous; and violence's literary, celluloid, video and sporting forms are extremely popular entertainments. Some vague sense that violence might suddenly erupt into our lives at any time is regularly present, and the notion that a propensity toward it is inherent in the human psyche is widespread. The tensions between these contradictory aspects of violence – repugnance and allure, absence and omnipresence – have contributed to violence's cultural importance. As Carolyn Nordstrom has written,

There is a curious irony in the popular epistemologies that surround violence in the west. Violence is presented as something both integral to the

> human condition and as antithetical to it. ... It is cast as the excessive, the abnormal, the other, and yet as intrinsic. We are taught to ascribe tremendous power to violence, and then to fear that power to the extent that we seek to remove it from "our worlds," from those places where we live our lives. We seek to tame it.[3]

Although "taming" violence might seem to be a natural or obviously sensible reaction to physical aggression, it is instead the result of a historical process. Violence and its "place" in society have been viewed differently in other cultures or by people of our own cultures during earlier eras. For example, Michel Foucault has examined the creation of new discourses of crime and delinquency in which the origins of Nordstrom's "curious irony" can already be glimpsed. As he notes, in the late eighteenth and early nineteenth centuries an enormous mass of "crime stories" developed

> in which delinquency appears both as very close and quite alien, a perpetual threat to everyday life, but extremely distant in its origin and motives, both everyday and exotic in the milieu in which it takes place. Through the importance attributed to it and the surfeit of discourse surrounding it, a line is traced round it which, while exalting it, sets it apart.[4]

Violence – like poverty – is often considered a more or less eternal problem. However, while we may always have violence, we do not always have the same violence: its meanings are continually fluctuating, and an "economy of violence" is a complex nexus of custom, law, economics, ethnicity, politics and psychology.[5] As a result, the study of violence involves larger issues such as the relationship between social structure and individual psychology, the tensions between law and custom, the creation of new discourses of power and the tendencies and contradictions of the "process of civilization." In combination, these issues are at the heart of this book, which examines historical patterns in attitudes toward violence through the example of nineteenth-century England.

While there were many specific factors that shaped the history of English violence, a consideration of the English past also highlights more general tendencies, relationships and configurations in the formation and maintenance of mentalities of violence. Although the following chapter introduces my main analytical interests, some words on the location of this study within English historiography, a clarification of its empirical basis and a summary of its themes are perhaps useful. As an initial aside, I have chosen to examine *English* rather than *British* violence. While I believe that many of the trends I identify could be found in Wales, Ireland and Scotland, their differences would have muddied several issues and made delineating general patterns even more difficult. After all, regional variations were pronounced even within England. Thus, I have supplemented my main evidentiary materials from southeastern England with primary and secondary sources referring to other regions and pointed out variations where I have been able to find them. Fortunately, there is an expanding amount of work on the history of violence in Wales, Ireland and Scotland that is able to do justice to the specificities of those cultures.[6]

Violence has become a distinct topic in English historiography through the histories of crime, the criminal law and political protest. Beginning in the 1960s, studies of crowds and "mobs" delineated elements of a "moral economy" and ritualized group violence.[7] Statistical studies of crime developed in the 1970s and raised frequent debates about the extent to which crime had risen or declined and the impact of other sorts of social data on crime rates.[8] At that time, much of the historiography dealt with property crime, and a spirited debate ensued regarding law and capitalist power as well as the validity of the concept of "social crime" – the notion that crime could be viewed as a form of social protest.[9] During the 1980s, violent crime increasingly received more focused study, leading to an extended discussion of historical trends in violence based largely on homicide rates.[10] Although the amassing of quantitative data had raised important questions and pointed toward tentative conclusions regarding rates of violence, subsequent work in the 1990s and beyond began to augment predominantly quantitative approaches with more qualitative investigations into the "social meaning of violence."[11]

This raised a salient point: to posit a level of violence tends to assume a constant definition of what "violence" is. However, violence does not have a consistent measure – like a barometric reading – that can explain its cultural relevance over time. For instance, levels of concern about it may have only a tenuous link to its actual prevalence in a given society or era. Furthermore, attitudes toward violence often mediate other issues such as concerns about social change or disorder, instabilities in gender relationships, standards of self-control and behavior, or the creation of new structures of authority. In asking questions about how and why violence was contoured in a particular way or what it meant to those affected by it, one must go beyond the tempting solidity of the "level" of violence and enter a far murkier world of interpretation and cultural analysis. A relatively recent commentator suggests that "in our analysis of people's propensity for killing ... we should concentrate on the mode in which aggression was expressed and the extent to which different modes were socially accepted or rejected."[12] These are central issues in the present study, as the illumination of such qualitative themes has much to say about the historical forces that shape attitudes to violence and the reasons why violence has assumed its currently conflicted cultural status.

One point that I wish to emphasize is the way that collective attitudes toward violence are actively created and maintained. Those processes work through a mixture of conflict and compromise among social forces and assume various historically specific configurations. In nineteenth-century England, I believe that the most important dynamic (but certainly not the only one) was the interaction between two dominant mentalities of violence. One I label "civilized" (representing an emergent culture of middle- and upper-class refinement that idealized rationality and self-restraint) and another I call "customary" (originating in an older social context, legitimating direct physical confrontation, appealing to less restrained notions of propriety and becoming associated with the poor and working-classes). "Civilized" thinking on violence became dominant by the end of the nineteenth century, largely through seeing older cultures of violence as a "shadow" of new, "refined" standards of behavior. The meanings behind these labels and the outline of their interactions are introduced in the following chapter and shape the rest of this book. However, first some word is due as to the sources and methods that have framed my research and writing.

Sources to illuminate the "civilized" mentality are relatively numerous: moral reformers had the platforms of law, press and pulpit to express their views; the state debated and changed laws and issued government reports; and an increasingly literate middle-class audience read a growing number of journals and magazines that shaped the culture of refinement. Crime and violence became a major topic of literature, journalism and opinionated prose at this time: murder was a "staple" of nineteenth-century popular fiction and the reporting of homicidal violence was a key element in the development of the popular press.[13] I have examined published sources that were part of this culture of refinement, particularly books, pamphlets and articles concerned with nineteenth-century social problems, in order to discern patterns in the ways that "civilization" was defined. New kinds of rhetoric accompanied changing institutions and legal practices related to the issues of violence and social disorder. "Custom" expressed itself with greater difficulty but, I suggest, with no less coherence. Evidence of customary views does exist in printed sources, particularly those related to forms of violence with cross-class appeal such as traditional prize-fighting. Since customary views were rooted in what had once been more widely shared norms, the traditions of the eighteenth century can be examined as one of the ingredients of nineteenth-century customary thought. Contemporary investigations into the conditions of working-class life, although biased, can shed light on the customary views against which civilization was defining itself. As customary views increasingly became the province of the working classes and poor, recovering glimpses of them becomes more difficult and requires far more piecing together from various clues. The archives of English crime are a major source of these clues. Much of my evidence comes from the records of the criminal courts, particularly from the assizes, the circuit courts that perambulated through the counties on a regular biannual schedule to, among other things, try serious crime. Assize records, quantitatively and qualitatively, are valuable sources on crime. I have examined depositions (witness statements) relating to violent crime from the early 1820s to the early 1870s in the records of the Southeastern (or "Home") Circuit. Other depositions, from the London Central Criminal Court and from the Court of King's Bench ("Queen's Bench" under Victoria) have also been consulted on a less systematic basis. Finally, as the next chapter discusses, I suggest that the performance of violent acts themselves can be read to tell us something of the social roles they played and the mentalities that lay behind them.

The seven chapters that comprise the body of this work are organized thematically. Chapter 1 elaborates my main conceptual questions and theoretical framework. It begins with a double-sided consideration of the relationship between "speech" (taken broadly to include writing) and violence. First, narratives were (and are) central to the ways that people deal with the experience of violence. However, individual narratives about violence are not free-floating and independent, instead they interact with cultural stores of knowledge about and attitudes toward violence that I refer to as "mentalities" of violence. The second side of this relationship is my suggestion that violence itself can function like a language: violence "speaks," putting cultural attitudes into physical forms. Its linguistic structure also makes it readable, articulating notions of power, authority, dominance, gendered identity, community or familial discipline, and recreation. Of course, not every act of violence adheres to the culturally legitimate "rules"; nonetheless, violence remains fundamentally coherent overall. Various rhetorical shifts, reforming efforts and state-building drives – the nineteenth-century "civilizing offensive" – dramatically altered the boundaries of acceptable violence and narrowed its social legitimacy. Here, various conceptual approaches to these issues, particularly those associated with Norbert Elias and Michel Foucault, are introduced. While not dismissing the power and success of the civilizing offensive, I suggest that the influence and importance of counternarratives to civilizing progress should not be underestimated.

Chapter 2 focuses upon "civilized" thinking on the issue of violence. As part of a long-term process of emerging "sensibilities," the first decades of the nineteenth century saw the "invention" of violence as a social issue, and new narratives classified "civilization" in opposition to the presumed "savagery" of the working classes. Although the refined classes were often distanced from the experience of violence, it became a significant theme in the literature and journalism aimed at them. One of the purposes of this literature was to create a new middle-class identity demarcated by its strident opposition to "brutality": a didactic literature of pain contributed to the construction of the refined individual who was taught how to react to violence. However, civilization was an ambiguous and flexible construction that did not dictate an absolute cessation of violence, and there were many limitations on the extent to which humanitarianism shaped the civilized mentality.

Chapter 3 begins the process of examining the "customary" mentality of violence. Customary attitudes had roots in pre-industrial England, where physical aggression was more widely tolerated and there were fewer differences between upper- and lower-class behavior: the legitimate display of aggression was part of a shared culture that (relative to the nineteenth century) accepted violence as a legitimate form of expression. Amicable relations and pleasure seeking could turn quickly to aggression and hostility and back again, "brutal" entertainments were widespread and physically retributive violence was common in both community life and state punishment. Disciplinary power was diffuse, granting widely dispersed authority to use violence in the maintenance of social norms. As state authority and social integration developed, such violent "self-help" was increasingly suppressed and the cultural force of Victorian respectability began reshaping working-class life. However, the underlying structures of the customary mentality – physical retribution, autonomy and discipline – remained significant organizing principles for attitudes toward violence well into the nineteenth century.

Chapter 4 takes up a particular sort of violence – ritualized fistfighting – and traces its interactions with recreation and dispute settlement. A traditional form of prizefighting emerged as a popular sport in the eighteenth century and, despite increasing state suppression, remained so for much of the nineteenth century. The civilization of pugilism brought a new set of modern boxing rules that eventually replaced traditional conventions. However, fighting rituals had a wider relevance than one strictly related to sport. Working-class men adopted the highly ceremonial and ritualized form of sporting pugilism in the contexts of street or pub brawling. When fights were brought before the courts (sometimes as the result of an unintended fatality), the discussion between officials and witnesses suggests the specific characteristics that defined "fair," "manly" and "English" fighting. Despite an initially strong degree of cross-class support, courts increasingly felt compelled to punish prizefighting participants as part of an effort to pacify public spaces and to transfer dispute settlement from its customary forms into official processes. As a result, traditional forms of streetfighting became unstable in response to the decline of the sporting model that had sustained it.

Chapter 5 examines nineteenth-century violence from the perspective of social geography. Acts of physical aggression were (and are) constructed and produced within particular "geographies of violence," and I suggest that the nineteenth-century civilization offensive had important spatial components. Customarily, violence was a public event located at the physical and cultural centers of community life. "Legitimate" violence was visible to the community, allowing the public monitoring and community shaping of violence. The nineteenth century saw the emergence of new built spaces (as urbanization increased) and changes in the ways that people imagined the legitimate use of public and private areas. Custom's public structuring of violence was abhorrent to the culture of refinement and contravened the state's commitment to establishing a monopoly on legitimate violence. For example, distinctions between "public" and "private" that were crucial to the "civilizing" project were typically blurred in the working-class dependence upon crowded, shared and multi-use spaces. Furthermore, the increasing class segregation of English life affected the ways that knowledge of violence was shaped.

Chapter 6 combines the theme of mentality with the geographical interests discussed in Chapter 5 to focus on the active appropriation and use of space. The legitimacy and expressive functions of customary violence often relied on particular strategies of employing physical force. The customary language of violence sketched out in Chapter 3 required various stages upon which it could be expressed: different contexts required different strategies. Along with the relationship between "performance" and "legitimacy," this chapter considers the related themes of "exclusion" and "resistance." Working-class communities became excluded as part of nineteenth-century residential trends. Within these communities, however, multiple layers of exclusion coexisted: violence was one means to control or expel certain social groups according to the self-policing imperatives of the customary mentality. Resistance was also an important theme in the contest for dominance over public spaces: the civilized introduction of new forms of order and control (including the police) confronted the customary devotion to maintaining community control over public spaces.

Chapter 7 serves as a general conclusion. It reflects upon the connections between the various aspects of violence noted throughout the book and briefly considers dynamics in violence attitudes at the end of the nineteenth century. In the late nineteenth and early twentieth centuries, new configurations of social otherness – at the same time more limited and more numerous – served to maintain civilizing thought, class identity and state institutions, a dynamic that – with many historical modifications – continues today. Finally, I evaluate some of the conceptual foundations of this study and suggest some of the more generally applicable and relevant conclusions that emerge from this study of violence in the nineteenth century.

1   "Speakable" violence

Mentality and violence, narrative and counternarrative

> When the raw fact of violence is silenced in discussion, what emerges is not theory but worldview. Perhaps in employing this style of analysis people try to make the world a livable place for themselves by controlling what they fear is uncontrollable, speaking what they have been told is unspeakable. Of course, there is no reason to believe that violence is either uncontrollable or unspeakable – for how can we control that which we do not address directly; how can we speak of that which we have banished from our analyses?
>
> Carolyn Nordstrom[1]

> Continuities in history always give the lie to assumed discontinuities. Moreover, people seldom fully absorb the lessons which the social world flings at them. All messages have to compete with collective memories, attitudes, and values bequeathed by past generations, as well as with individuals' compulsions, defenses, and interests in the present.
>
> V. A. C. Gatrell[2]

Although "*un*speakable" is the word commonly paired with "violence," violence has become one of the most discussed aspects of human life in the modern era. Speaking and writing about violence is ubiquitous, and all levels and kinds of violence generate efforts to put its experience into words. Across the spectrum, from individual or small-group interpersonal assault and murder through war and combat to the extremity of mass-slaughter and genocide, violence calls forth a torrent of words that serve a variety of purposes: condemning, justifying, explaining, obscuring or even obliterating its presence.[3] These stories, or narratives, are the main sources for historians interested in violence. Whether in the form of detailed descriptions or abbreviated notations, they have long been compiled and categorized to explain specific incidents, explore police and judicial responses (or the lack thereof) to different kinds of violence, debate crime rates or compare historical levels of violence. All of these approaches have raised important questions and yielded numerous conclusions about the place of physical aggression in the past and in the present. Yet, it is the ambiguity of the phrase "speakable violence" that suggests the two conceptual foundations of my approach. First, it identifies the way that violent acts seem inescapably to generate narratives. Second, it points to the way that violence itself works like a language. People say many things about violence but also communicate with their violence. Violence "speaks": it has various grammars, vocabularies, dialects and meanings, some of which are clear while others are more ambiguous. Individual violent encounters vary as widely as the particularities of countless conversations, yet overall syntaxes of social violence can nonetheless be discerned. I suggest that both aspects of "speakable violence" can help reveal the forces that shape the production and subsequent evaluation of violence, provide glimpses of coherent networks of attitudes toward it, disclose the interactions between the narratives and practices of everyday life and illustrate the social imagination of historical eras.

Collections of narratives about violence – along with the often incomplete and contradictory patterns that they constitute – form the bases of "mentalities" of violence. The ingredients that form mentalities of violence are many and come into contact with other kinds of attitudes regarding diverse forms of social interaction: violence, after all, is not the only component of a person's view of the world. Nonetheless, mentalities of violence contribute to the ways that social life is shaped and maintained. In particular, I call attention to the centrality of conflict within mentalities of violence. They emerge not as pre-packaged cultural configurations – they are not simply *a priori* containers easily taken off the shelf – but develop out of processes of dispute and agreement over the boundaries of legitimate physical force. Moreover, mentalities are continuously re-formed and adapted to new social situations, and they help to define a more general land-scape of cultural confrontation. As there is no single, stable and essentialized structure of attitudes toward violence, various mentalities will coexist in any given society at a particular stage of historical development. This is not to say that all mentalities of violence are equally significant: different configurations of beliefs will, at times, be more prominent than others. Furthermore, in recog-nizing that mentalities differ across cultures and time, I neither suggest that they operate as dictatorial networks of social control that deny choice and agency nor advocate a kind of cultural relativism in which all perspectives are equally good or bad. All people, including the present author, must inevitably take a position on the issue of violence; however, my interest here is in examining the frame-works (and limitations) in which those choices are made. Furthermore, as I will suggest below and at various points in this book, attitudes toward violence are linked to many factors not directly related to violence itself, and violence, along with its mentalities, can serve several purposes.

I have used this approach in examining violence in nineteenth-century England, at a time when self-identified civilizing forces undertook a determined offensive against alternative, customary attitudes toward violence. I do not suggest that these two aspects of a widespread cultural conflict over violence were able to develop comprehensive and unquestionable rulebooks of legitimate behavior, nor do I think that these disputes were neatly contained within precise chronological boundaries. Mentalities, after all, do not work that way. However, I have identified a distinctive configuration in violence mentalities between approximately 1820 and 1870. The lines between them could, in certain contexts, be porous. At times they were like subtly different accents of a common cultural vernacular; in other contexts they were more akin to foreign (and mutually bewildering) tongues. Clearly, when one speaks of violence one is not talking simply about words: there was also fear, pain, injury and blood. But acts of violence are inseparable from the narratives that alternatively shape and analyze them. Narratives have consequences, and their analysis suggests some of the dominant cultural fault lines in the nineteenth century while pointing toward useful approaches to violence more generally. The present chapter introduces and explores the main concepts and theories deployed throughout the remainder of this study.

Violence, narrative and mentality

Although "violence never solved anything" is a modern truism, violence has always settled many things: dominance within social groups, distributions of honor and status and the boundaries between the sexes, to name just a few.[4] However, "violence," in Raymond Williams's understated phrase, is a "difficult word" with a wide variety of meanings.[5] Thus, in analyzing it, some lines have to be drawn, and for this study I have considered "violence" that is physically injurious (rather than purely psychologically damaging) to human beings, small-scale and, in general, not "political" in the formal sense of being related to parties, electoral rituals, terrorism or demonstrations aimed at changing state policies. Of course, as a fluid term subject to many contested meanings, the margins between different sorts of violence are often very difficult to establish. Furthermore, the word "violence" tends to describe more than merely the use of physical force. Generally, a witness or victim also views that force as illegitimate.[6] Physically aggressive acts that are in some way culturally legitimated are often labeled (at least by some groups) as something other than "violence," such as when physical force used by police or military authorities – even when this results in fatalities – is referred to as the "restoration of order." Thus, the term "violence," particularly when used by the victim(s) and his or her (or their) supporters, is normally meant to point to a social transgression, even if one not everyone might recognize as such. All societies are fissured by competing understandings of what is or is not violent, who may use violence and in what circumstances, and the legitimate goals of deploying physical force. Such divisions can be drawn along the well-established categories of class, gender and race, but they might also vary according to geography, age and ideology, and they are built, reinforced and altered through an intermittent process of dispute, evaluation and re-evaluation. Although changeable, attitudes about violence are not free-floating and are instead shaped in reference to particular mentalities, akin to "mental maps," with which we navigate the cultural terrain of violence; the maps, as well as the territories they represent, are subject to change.[7] As a result of this systematizing function played by narrative-driven mentalities, violence as a social phenomenon can be investigated and understood through looking at the way that its narratives are created, maintained and how they interact.

What initially should be apparent is that the flexibility and contingency that characterize the history of attitudes to violence undermines the notion that there is a single "natural" mentality of violence. For instance, despite a distinctly modern view, there is little reason to automatically assume that violence is in fact "unspeakable," indescribable, random or even irrational. In the eighteenth century, as Margaret Hunt notes, "violence was not something repellent, deviant or unspeakable as it came to be later on, and continues to be to this day, even for many of the people who are chronically victimized by it."[8] Even in our own time, a victim of violence will usually find ways of putting that trauma into words, however incomplete they may be in expressing the thoughts and feelings involved, thus contributing to the discourses that develop through the judicial system and in the media. An individual's experience of a violent incident is to some extent unique; nonetheless, particular socially constructed epistemologies organize individualized experiences of violence into recoverable patterns. An episode in Nordstrom's work on civil war in Mozambique describes a conversation with a group of children in a village under attack. She notes,

> The narrative of the attack was not the actual experience of that violence, it was trying to find a meaningful way to deal with it. And this meaning, which changes over time, circumstance and speaker, is a cultural production.[9]

It is here that experiences and mentalities of violence interact: although the actual experience of a violent act is interior and inaccessible, the narratives employed to make sense of it are cultural products available for study.

A large number of the sources in this book are narratives of violence, particularly those contained within pre-trial depositions given to the police. Such witness testimony usually appears to be composed of long, unbroken descriptions of what happened. However, the apparently solid narrative is in most cases actually an accumulation of responses to questions from the police officer or magistrate who was conducting the inquiry. Although we can no longer know the precise contours of the interview, depositions resulted from a two-way dialogue, one that was to some degree filtered through the written hand of the authorities. The vast majority of victims, witnesses and perpetrators were working class, and many of them were illiterate; however, they understood the language of violence and made judgments that allow one to reconstruct its social contexts. In presenting testimony about violent acts, I have tended toward emphasizing the words of those who witnessed them. This does not, of course, give us direct access to the experience of violence, as even primary sources are at least one degree removed that experience itself. However, without naively assuming that the past can speak for itself, sensitivity to the patterns of witness description can, I believe, be very revealing of processes of narrative construction and deserve, when appropriate, to obscure as little as possible. These are, furthermore, sometimes disturbing words; however, in many cases I have deliberately chosen to provide details of violence in the voice of witnesses in order to do justice to the nature of the events they were describing and to avoid the frequent tendency to blanket violence under layers of distancing narrative. It is important to remember that the people who speak in the stories that follow are describing events that had very real impact – terror, injury and often death – and to listen to the ways they viewed and came to terms with such events.

Although Nordstrom's interviews with children in an African village emphasize the way that narratives of violence are formed after an event, narratives also actively shape violence before the fact, affecting the circumstances in which violence is used and the forms it takes. Rather than being inert stores of knowledge, mentalities may have to be called upon to guide action: one might be put into a situation in which he or she must evaluate the likelihood of violence being employed against them and the ways they might defend against it. Even if not directly a participant in, or victim of, a violent act, one may need to judge an event one has seen. There is also a more general social and political discussion of violence that one engages with as a citizen, social observer and voter. Mentalities of violence are the "social imaginaries" through which its experience is organized.[10] Even within the sometimes blurred boundaries of a single mentality, this process of organization can be conflicted, becoming significantly more complex where different mentalities (sometimes with very different fundamental notions about violence) converge and struggle over certain events. The intricacy of these narrative engagements with violent events varied widely, and they are discussed with reference to different themes in the chapters that follow. However, along with recognizing that narratives shape the forms of and reactions to violence, there is yet another link between narrative and violence that highlights the linguistic nature of violence itself. That so many (and such varied) narratives tend to amass around violent events suggests that violence is a phenomenon very open to interpretation. Even where violence has become something generally abhorrent, we still expect it to "say" something, or we at least attempt to interpret the meanings that lay within it. Such interpretative imperatives are, I believe, assisted by the way that violence works in some ways like a language. As a physical act involving the most intense of human emotions and sensations (anger, fear and pain), violence makes an unmistakable entrance into any social encounter. Simply put, it is difficult to ignore. As David Riches notes:

> The expressive function of acts or images of violence capitalizes, firstly, on the visibility of violence, and secondly on the probability that all involved – however different their cultural backgrounds – are likely to draw, at the very least, some basic common understanding from the acts or images concerned. These two properties of violence make it an excellent communicative vehicle.[11]

Along with the "basic common understanding" that may inhere in nearly any act of violence, different societies shape and understand violence according to diverse cultural rules. Violence's language-like structure thus accounts not only for aspects of its universality but also for its cultural specificity. Violence and the reactions it demands are scripted by mentalities that provide a set of guidelines for what form aggression or violence (like any other utterance or social interaction) should take.

However, my suggestion that violence functions in ways analogous to a language is neither an attempt to constrain violence within the bounds of scientific certainty nor an effort to diminish its instabilities, contingencies and physical consequences. Violence, just like language, does not lend itself to being placed within such tidy boxes. In violence, just as in language, the "rules" are not always followed: conventions are broken – people sometimes "go too far" – and, because violence is a physically destructive act, injury and/or death may result. Nevertheless, the fact that violence does not always follow its script does not make it any less linguistic nor does it deny that violence can be seen as a rule-based social activity. The distinction between "rules" and "laws" is an important one:

> There are various types of rules, and these may be distinguished from scientific "laws," in that laws have truth value and are not prescriptive. More importantly, laws cannot be violated, whereas it is a fundamental requirement of a rule that it can be broken.[12]

The "cultural grammar" of any society provides numerous opportunities to breach social rules.[13] So it is with language itself: as Jean-Jacques Lecercle suggests, "the rules of grammar are to be thought of not in terms of the laws of the physical universe, but rather in terms of frontiers."[14] Even when the rules are transgressed, the linguistic structure remains: in a language, "when a rule of syntax is broken, the result is still linguistically coherent, i.e., intelligible...."[15] The rules of violence tend to be constructed similarly: mentalities define and maintain boundaries regarding the legitimacy of particular sorts of violent acts while, as a human activity open to the uncountable contingencies of individual action, such frontiers can be breached. Taking this point further, disruptions of the rule-based system are actually *within* the rules: it is through such transgressions that frontiers are established, fortified or moved in one direction or another.

The specific composition of social forces that observe, organize and shape the cultural arrangement of attitudes toward violence vary historically. In England, the early nineteenth century was an important period in that alignment; at that time a vigorous tension surrounding attitudes to violence – indeed, as I claim in the next chapter, the invention of violence as a social issue – was built upon cultural trends and reformist movements active since the late seventeenth century. Violence's new social position – at the center of a range of cultural, social and institutional developments – connected debates about physical aggression to more general social and cultural trends, in particular the much commented upon growth of a "culture of sensibility."[16] In general, "sensibility" refers to the movement toward a "reformation of manners" and an increasing sensitivity to violence, pain and suffering. As Karen Halttunen has described, "shaped by John Locke's psychology of sensation and by the moral-sense philosophy of his followers, the cult of sensibility took as its hero 'the man of feeling,' whose tender-hearted susceptibility to the torments of others was the mark of his deeply virtuous nature."[17] Sensibility had its greatest impact among the middle classes and contributed to efforts to diminish perceived barbarity, disorder and cruelty. That sustained struggle over standards of behavior was influenced by other factors: increasing social and economic integration (as a result of industrialization and urbanization); growing state power (visible in a more active legislature and judiciary and the emergence of a more highly centralized and effective police force); and a mass culture of social commentary and analysis (based upon published crime statistics, the press and literature) that made behavioral self-control a heated topic of public debate. Establishing the timing and significance of shifting attitudes has proved difficult. The importance of the closing decades of the eighteenth century has been frequently suggested.[18] However, while it is clear that certain elements of the culture of sensibility were active in the eighteenth century, there is much to suggest the importance of continuities lasting long into the nineteenth century (if not the twentieth) that downplay the notion of a sharp break in attitudes to violence.[19]

I believe that the nineteenth century saw the formulation of violence as a social issue and a continuing struggle over what legitimate frontiers should contain it. Since attitudes toward violence raised wide-ranging questions of identity, power, gender, social organization and the role of the state in the context of a society that was undergoing fundamental, if uneven, economic and social transformation, this was an inherently contested process and one that was about more than humanitarianism (which is, in any case, a problematic category) or the emergence of a kindly sympathy on the part of an increasingly sensitive upper class. The invention of violence was built around a conflict between two general mentalities of violence, one "civilized" and one "customary." The "civilized" mentality represented an emergent middle- and upper-class culture of "refinement" that pursued a behavioral ideal of rationality and restraint while "custom" refers to an older cultural figuration – dominant in the seventeenth and eighteenth centuries – that accepted greater expression of certain types of violent behavior, legitimated direct physical confrontation and appealed to less-restrained definitions of propriety. The terms "customary" and "civilized" are, of course, only shorthand definitions that suggest the tendencies of each mentality. Subsequent chapters will detail the ambiguities between and within these generalities, and I believe that the terms are useful in highlighting the axes along which the discussion, understanding and performance of violence took place. It might be protested that these concepts are too dualistic; however, in some cases, attitudes and cultural divisions are made along binary lines. Furthermore, as I will suggest, the relationship between these mentalities was more than simply a two-sided opposition. There were contexts in which relations between these mentalities were rather amicable, and, more importantly, their relationship was fundamentally dialectical: each, to a large extent, gained coherence out of this process of opposition. I would further like to emphasize that my use of the term "civilized" is not intended to suggest that this mentality was superior, nor was the customary mentality an inert, static accumulation of "tradition."[20] I use the terms "civilized" and "civilization" because they had great currency in the social debates of the nineteenth century (though I view some of those uses of the term critically) and because they tie this study into the theory of the "civilizing process" adumbrated by Norbert Elias and subsequently developed by other scholars. I also believe that "custom" is a useful descriptive term for a widespread set of nineteenth-century beliefs and connects my approach to attitudes toward violence to a version of social history rooted in the work of E. P. Thompson. In a general sense, negotiations between advocates of these cultural understandings (closely associated with – though not rigidly determined by – class) occurred in the everyday life of nineteenth-century England.

Civilizing processes and discourses of violence

As I have suggested, the qualitative study of violence requires a broader approach than one solely concerned with the criminal law or even with a narrow approach to what we might think of as "violence" itself. Instead, attitudes toward violence are inextricably connected to issues of identity, class hierarchy, institutional development, codes of behavior, views of recreation, the nature of private and public spaces, and societal arrangements. Taking a historical perspective toward such ways of thinking and attempting to define the dynamics that shape their interactions and changes over time allows one to see how these apparently discrete forces combined to influence mentalities of violence and to consider the nature of the processes underlying historical change and continuity. As I suggested, the historiographies of criminality, sensibility, state formation, social geography and cultural studies have, here and there, already begun to become closely intertwined. At their intersection we may also locate the theories of Norbert Elias. Elias, a German sociologist whose most influential work was originally published in the 1930s, conceptualizes the dynamics that drive both states and individuals to develop increasingly complex structures of self-control. He posits the notion of a "civilizing process" that tends toward more intensive self-control of emotional urges (what he calls "affects") and a more finely regulated system of social interactions.[21] For Elias, the driving forces in increasing "civilization" are greater social interdependence and expanding state power. Interdependence, in productive relationships as well as in daily social life, ties people together in ever-longer chains of mutual reliance. The overall historical trend has been toward an increase in this sort of interdependence and the "differentiation" of specific social roles:

> The more differentiated they become, the larger grows the number of functions and thus of people on whom the individual constantly depends in all his actions, from the simplest and most commonplace to the more complex and uncommon. As more and more people must attune their conduct to that of others, the web of actions must be organized more and more strictly and accurately, if individual action is to fulfill its social function. The indi-

vidual is compelled to regulate his conduct in an increasingly differentiated, more even and more stable manner.[22]

Along with interdependence, the other key social force identified by Elias is the growth of state power. Weber, famously, defined the state by its monopoly on legitimate force.[23] Elias historicizes this definition, explores the interactions between state power and violence and argues that growing state power tends toward limiting legitimate violence – to different degrees in specific historical periods – to the state or its agents. As a result, "pacified social spheres ... normally free from acts of violence" are created in which "the individual is largely protected from sudden attack, the irruption of physical violence into his life" but is also "forced to suppress in himself any passionate impulse urging him to attack another physically."[24] Over time, the external factors of increasing state power and growing social interdependence create a more rigorous, constant and controlling set of internal regulatory mechanisms through shame, guilt and anxiety: behavior becomes more self-controlled and emotional extremes (both joyful and aggressive) are tempered by increasing forethought and rational restraint. The relevance of Elias's theories to violence is obvious: violence (along with sex) might be conceived of as an emotional affect *par excellence*, and it is in the controlling of these subconscious desires toward pleasure that the civilizing process mainly consists.[25]

Elias was also quite radical in the extent to which he asserted the inability to separate the sphere of the "individual" from that of the "social," suggesting that "the structures of personality and of society evolve in an indissoluble interrelationship."[26] Critiquing theories that either opt for a deterministic view of the individual as chained to social rules or a position of absolute independence and free will, Elias suggests the "open personality" who possesses "relative autonomy" but is "fundamentally oriented toward and dependent on other people throughout his life."[27] This is the basis for his conceptualization of what he calls a "figuration," defined as "a structure of mutually oriented and dependent people." I suggest that among the mediating vehicles that connect these "different aspects of the same human being" (i.e., the individual and the social) are the narrative structures of cultural mentalities that emerge out of and in turn shape social interaction.[28] Those social-psychological configurations, although they perform the role of "orienting" the individual toward other people, do not dictate behavior and provide numerous openings for the "relative autonomy" of which Elias speaks. Using his approach, it would seem that, despite the nineteenth-century assumption that violence was "anti-social," no act can truly be "outside" society.[29] Elaborating on this point, it has been noted that "far from being simple antitheses, violence and civilization are characterized by specific forms of interdependence" due to the way that "civilization" is built upon a particular monopoly over violence by the state.[30]

My goal is neither to prove nor disprove Elias's theory. Instead, I accept the general utility of his concepts and broadly apply them to a particular period while maintaining a critical stance toward specific aspects of the civilizing process and suggesting additional factors that should be considered. It is, for instance, immediately apparent that three of the foundations of Elias's civilizing process were active in the nineteenth century. First, the influence of interdependence is apparent in growing urbanization and increasingly socialized labor, whether one considers "industrial" or "manufacturing" processes.[31] Second, the power of the English state grew dramatically across the eighteenth and nineteenth centuries, for example in the development of a professionalized police force. Overall, these trends worked toward inculcating restraint, pacifying public spaces and monopolizing the legitimate uses of force. Third, new social expectations of self-control and a growing reluctance to accept extreme expressions of emotion became significant cultural trends visible in the aforementioned culture of sensibility and, later, in the varieties of Victorian "respectability."[32] Nonetheless, although Elias's theories are highly useful, the bulk of his empirical work was in the medieval and early modern periods. It is not a simple matter to apply his concepts directly to more recent historical epochs, and one needs to take into account various doubts that have been raised regarding his theory. For example, although Elias is at pains to deny that he conceptualizes "automatic" change and a linear, progressive trend of social improvement, he has been criticized on precisely these grounds. In some cases, these complaints are a result of (sometimes understandable) "misconceptions" regarding the nature of the civilizing process.[33] Even at first glance, the phrase "civilizing process" suggests a value judgment and a progressive tendency toward improvement; however, a moral evaluation of "civilization" was never Elias's intention, and he emphasizes that "civilization" (referring to a more thorough, constant and rigorous affect-control structure) can develop "without necessarily implying that it is better or worse, has a positive or negative value."[34] In his usage, civilization merely describes a relative difference between one society and another – or between different historical stages of one society – in terms of their expectations of self-control. In this way, the civilizing process does not abolish violence, it reorganizes it and changes the cultural territory on which it operates. It has, for instance, even been suggested that murder can take a "civilized" form.[35] Although violence does not disappear, it is channeled into different forms and expressions and understood through changing mentalities.[36] Elias was well aware of the problems with any theory of behavior that suggested an easy quantification of behavior, and he directly confronted the question of the problems inherent in conceptualizing "change":

> Our concepts are too coarse; they adhere too much to the image of material substances. In all this we are not concerned merely with gradations, with "more" or "less." Each "increase" in restraints and interdependencies is an expression of the fact that the ties between people, the way they depend on one another, are changing, and changing *qualitatively*. This is what is meant by difference in social structure. And with the dynamic network of dependencies into which a human life is woven, the drives and behaviour of people take on a *different* form. This is what is meant by differences in

personality structure and in social standards of conduct. The fact that such qualitative changes are sometimes, despite all the fluctuations within the movement, changes in one and the same direction over long periods, that is, continuous directed processes rather than a random sequence, permits and indeed causes us to speak in comparative terms when discussing different phases.[37]

Elias also consistently stresses that civilization is a process that emerges dynamically through countless interactions among people rather than being a stable, reified entity. There is no absolute, eternal standard to which he refers and no endpoint at which society is "civilized." Neither does he posit a relentless and irresistible civilizing trend: "de-civilizing" trends can counteract "civilizing" ones.[38] However, even this formulation tends to divide epochs into periods of either de-civilization or civilization rather than recognizing the potential for both tendencies to coexist simultaneously and highlighting the tensions between change and continuity in any given age. This study locates itself within those tensions and focuses on the construction and maintenance of mentalities of violence that were themselves sometimes contradictory.

By this point, the relevance of Michel Foucault's analyses of discourses as well as the relationship between power and narratives of knowledge have likely made themselves clear. For example, Elias's view of the civilizing process's essentially repressive functions regarding violence can be critiqued in much the same way as Foucault attacks the "repressive hypothesis" of Victorian sexuality.[39] Adapting Foucault, I suggest that rather than being repressed, silenced or turned into an unspeakable mystery, violence was subject to a "veritable discursive explosion" during the nineteenth century.[40] Although violence was subject to increasing surveillance, and its "enunciations" (defined as both talking *about* violence and acts of violence themselves) became more "policed" and subject to increasing control (and self-control), in no way was the nineteenth century characterized by an increasing silence on the topic itself.[41] Instead, there was feverish activity in regard to discourses about violence (didactic, categorizing and prohibitive speech that referred to violence) as well as discourses of violence (the mentalities that shaped violent acts themselves). The nineteenth-century "invention of violence" made violence "something to say," something that was "driven out of hiding and constrained to lead a discursive existence."[42] A society that found itself, rather suddenly, confronted with the subject of violence on a wide-ranging social scale responded not by ignoring it, but through a concerted attempt at recognition.[43] Analyses of violence emerged that placed the phenomenon squarely within the social sphere in terms of its causes and effects, forming the basis for new, self-consciously civilized attitudes. Along with sexuality, Foucault also analyzes another relevant discourse, that of criminality, focusing on the late eighteenth and nineteenth centuries. Referring to notions of "sensibility," he observes that during this period there was, perhaps, a change in "attitude," but more certainly and more immediately it was an effort to adjust the mechanisms of power that frame the everyday lives of individuals; an adaptation and a refinement of the machinery that assumes responsibility for and places under surveillance their everyday behavior, their identity, their activity, their apparently unimportant gestures....[44]

Similarly, the necessity to think about violence was inserted into everyday life, and various kinds of machinery (both mental and physical) were erected to understand, contain and control it. Along with new rhetoric about the sources, location and analysis of violence, new disciplines emerged that sought to reform the role of violence in everyday social life. One of the earliest arenas of reform was directly under the control of the emergent civilizing discourse: judicial punishment. While the prison emerged as the preferred institution of punishment, whipping, the pillory and hanging diminished in their centrality to the powers of the state; however, their longevity in England is a reminder of some of the qualifications that must be borne in mind regarding Foucault's supposition of a dramatic shift from a spectacular punishment of the body to one dependent upon modern penal methods.[45] However, the trend toward a more measured, less physically brutal form of judicial punishment is clear, and, as Foucault points out, other disciplinary institutions such as asylums, factories and schools also emerged. The police rank as another of the disciplinary forces in the civilized order. Their history is one of only gradual acceptance; however, their emergence played a vital part in imposing new disciplines upon the populace (increasingly with their consent) and subsumed the violence previously expressed in private vengeance and forms of community self-policing. Moreover, toward the end of the century, increasingly scientific methods were applied to violence, proliferating into the discourses of criminology, sociology, phrenology and psychology. Thus, in both discussion of violence and in the handling of violent acts, new forms of discourse and power developed throughout the nineteenth century.

In some ways, it may appear that the theories of Foucault and Elias are at odds. Foucault's conception of a shift "from a criminality of blood to a criminality of fraud" is similar to the *violence au vol* thesis (in which crime, during a transition to capitalist society, shifts from one marked mainly by violence to one characterized primarily by theft), which has been questioned using Elias's theories.[46] Elias describes increasing layers of repression and self-control, whereas Foucault tends toward focusing on "techniques" and "technologies" of power rather than on prohibition as such.[47] However, I think the theories of these two social philosophers, although they raise points of contention, can be usefully merged, and both will periodically be referred to as helpful assistants in exploring the social meaning of violence. The civilizing offensive was a process reliant upon the creation of a new economy of "affects" as well as new discourses of violence. Furthermore, along with the conceptualizations of Elias and Foucault, I shall be making use of a variety of other theoretical approaches. In its focus on plebeian mentalities and the importance of custom in shaping culture, particularly in Chapter 3, this study clearly owes much to the work of E.

P. Thompson, which emphasizes the recovery of the experiences of hitherto-neglected social groups and highlights the importance of culture in shaping attitudes toward work, leisure and crime. Anthropological studies of violence are useful in explaining the ways that some violence, such as the male fistfighting considered in Chapter 4, was performed; moreover, common anthropological themes – that violence takes specific cultural forms, is shaped by customary understandings, and that those forms and understandings structure the meaning of violent acts – find more general application throughout this work.[48] In addition to specific threads in cultural history and anthropology, I have become convinced of the importance of delineating the ways that violence is acted out within particular material and socially imagined spaces; thus, social-geographical approaches figure prominently in Chapter 5 and Chapter 6. These methodological elements are linked by several themes: elaborating the characteristics of civilized and customary mentalities of violence, tracing their interrelationship, suggesting fruitful ways to qualitatively approach English violence, and applying and critiquing the concept of the civilizing processes.

Civilizing offensives, social control, class and counternarrative

To begin turning this investigation more toward its specific empirical bases, it may be useful to explore a few remaining conceptual themes of importance to nineteenth-century historiography. A legal commentator in 1900, looking back upon the preceding century, concluded that England "witnessed a great change in manners; the substitution of words without blows for blows, with or without words; an approximation in the manners of different classes, a decline in the spirit of lawlessness."[49] Although such *fin-de-siècle* optimism had many causes, it was underpinned by a notable statistical decline in violent crime since the 1860s.[50] The argument that violence actually declined has recently been questioned,[51] however, there seems to have been an increasing perception of social tranquillity, at least relative to the early Victorian era, by the end of the nineteenth century.[52] Although violence remained an important topic of discussion and concern (e.g., the word "hooligan" entered common parlance in the 1890s, and there were prominent arguments about crime and penal theory), the sense that there was a widespread undercurrent of savagery and violence in English society had declined significantly.[53] The calming of social fears suggests that the civilizing offensive of the preceding decades had been a success.[54]

Drives toward social reformation had rippled through English society at many points in its past and that of the nineteenth century did not arise out of thin air. However, although early nineteenth-century social concerns built upon late eighteenth-century sensibilities, there was also something new. V. A. C. Gatrell has suggested that by the 1820s

> [c]rime was becoming a vehicle for articulating mounting anxieties about issues which really had nothing to do with crime at all: social change and the

stability of social hierarchy. These issues invested crime with new meanings, justified vastly accelerated action against it, and have determined attitudes toward it ever since.[55]

So it was with violence. The decades after 1820 had seen a deep concern with "unregulated human power" in the form of "passions" and "savagery," and criminal and penal policy had focused upon "fostering disciplined behavior and a broad ethos of respectability."[56] Concentrated efforts on the part of the state and private reforming organizations sought to alter the perceived brutality of working-class life. The law was expected to inspire new standards of behavior by holding people more responsible for their acts while perspectives on mitigating circumstances narrowed: in many cases, what had previously been acceptable or even a "normal" part of life became increasingly subject to legal sanction.[57] The development of new police forces brought a more active enforcement of the law, increasing its presence in daily life. The police were not only neutral observers of society but actively played the role of "domestic missionaries" enforcing new standards of behavior in working-class communities.[58] By the 1820s, the authorities and respectable classes assumed that violence, particularly homicide, was the almost exclusive preserve of the working class.[59] This was to become a dominant notion: Justice Martin told the Capital Punishment Commission in 1866, "it is a very rare occurrence that any individual of the higher or middle classes is tried for murder."[60] To some extent this was true, and it has been persuasively argued that "criminal violence came to be more socially restricted; although not quite the prerogative of the lower orders by 1800, it was certainly something in which members of the gentry or urban elites were unlikely to be involved."[61] As a result of this social narrowing of propensity for public violence, "increasing alienation came to characterize discussion not only of the criminal but of the lower class in general."[62] That alienation is apparent in the social-problem literature of the early and middle nineteenth century, in which the "savagery" and "brutality" of the working classes frequently threatened the optimistic and assertive middle-class narrative of social progress: violence in this way became a "shadow" of middle-class "refinement."[63] During and following the 1870s, there was an apparent lessening of social fears. The increasing incorporation of the working class into a broadening social consensus changed behavior and attitudes. Violence ceased to be so strongly associated with the working class as a whole. An oppositional culture remained; however, it was increasingly confined to marginal social groups.

This is not to accept the view of many contemporary commentators that the working class was in fact savage and uncontrolled.[64] First, before the gradual growth in civilizing efforts (connected to the Enlightenment and to middle-class evangelicalism) there had been a largely shared mentality of violence. During the civilizing offensive, refined segments of society withdrew from this shared culture and some kinds of previously acceptable behavior were redefined as "savagery." Second, rather than the alternative to civilization being mere anarchy, a customary mentality of violence imposed boundaries on legitimate levels and types of violence. These customary forms distributed, shaped and limited violence in particular ways. Unobserved by the refined rhetoric of mayhem and working-class savagery was a coherent mentality of violence that "made sense," a dynamic similar to the modern relationship between middle-class suburbs and the relatively impoverished urban areas that constitute their cultural "other."[65] While much of that violence might have appeared shocking to a civilized observer (or, indeed, to a modern historian), the goal must be to uncover what the customary understandings were, to examine their origins and, ultimately, to explain the way they shaped the forms and meanings of violence.

As I have suggested, one fruitful way of finding and explaining dynamics within attitudes to violence is to look to structures of violence mentalities. During the nineteenth-century, the English press – a crucial institution for creating and disseminating narratives of violence and for debating and defining the civilized mentality – was expanding both its circulation and cultural impact. The influence of press accounts of crime and the statistical sources on which much of Victorian crime-related writing was based are the focus of Rob Sindall's important work on street violence in the nineteenth century.[66] Sindall begins with an assumption of the "impossibility of understanding the nineteenth-century criminal" due to a lack of sources that tell us anything about the responses of the poor and working class to crime and violence.[67] Since the press was an organ of middle-class sensibility, he argues that it cannot explain anything other than that sensibility itself: as Sindall would have it, the mental world of criminals, the poor and the working classes remains in darkness, enveloped in yet another kind of shadow. As a statement of the limits of our abilities to reconstruct the past, this attitude, though debatable, is relatively unproblematic. However, Sindall goes even further, suggesting that even if sources illuminating lower-class attitudes were available, there would be no point in pursuing them. In his view,

> as it is society that makes a criminal a criminal, there is little justification in research from the bottom up. To attempt to understand crime and its relevance to nineteenth-century society the researcher must approach not from the bottom up, but from the middle down. "Crime" as a cause or a result of social change was not a lower socio-economic group act but a middle-class perception of that act. Therefore, the interest lies not with the motivation of the lower-class act but with the foundations of the middle-class perception.[68]

While the argument that "crime" is a socially constructed category (that "lawmakers create law-breakers") is almost universally accepted, Sindall defines the relevant social interactions solely in middle-class terms. As a result, "if the press does not report an event then in the public mind the event did not take place."[69] There is clearly some truth to this, as well as in his argument that perceptions of violence in the "public mind" were often arbitrary and only tenuously related to "real" crime.

However, the press-fed attitudes of middle classes toward violence were not the only source of social imagination in the nineteenth century. Even if unreported (or misreported) in the press, incidents of crime and violence were parts of the lives of people in poorer communities: even if not in the "public mind" of their social betters, they were a part of what we might call the "popular mind." While it is true that society defines criminality (and violence), society is larger than the "control culture" – the state and middle class – that Sindall examines. V. A. C. Gatrell has similarly highlighted the ways that crime is not only a tool of social control but is also solely defined by those who control the state:

> Over the past couple of centuries, the policeman-state protected and still protects an unequal and fissiparous society; and it did so supported by the convenient and enduring belief that most criminals were likely to be found among poorer people. The history of crime, accordingly, is largely the history of how better-off people discipline their inferiors; of how elites used selected law-breakers to sanction their own authority; or of how in modern times bureaucrats, experts and policemen used them to justify their own expanding functions and influences.[70]

These are guiding principles of much of criminal history, including, to some extent, this book. However, I also begin from the notion that power and authority are products of negotiation as well as imposition. Some work on policing has emphasized the often tentative and incomplete process of installing new policing regimes in the nineteenth century (or even in the twentieth century), which complicates the notion of an all-encompassing engine of social control.[71] Furthermore, even as elements of refined culture gained ground among a wider spectrum of society, there were continuing cultural biases toward more traditional understandings of violence. Some of the historiography of crime, violence and criminal justice has emphasized the resilience of older patterns in policing, punishment and popular culture.[72] Even the judicial establishment, as Carolyn Conley has pointed out, did not act in a cultural vacuum: "their concept of the law had to include community standards and customs," and "despite the new regulations and procedures, older, traditional patterns of judicial discretion and extra-legal community sanctions continued to be practiced with considerable support."[73] Such "community standards and customs" were part of the narratives through which common people organized their lives. Jennifer Davis has emphasized that continuities were as important as contrasts between the eighteenth and nineteenth centuries in terms of law enforcement and the relevance of informal community punishments.[74] Inherited attitudes and practices (and their active reformulations in the face of change) confronted the civilizing offensive on a variety of cultural grounds.

Richard Price has recently considered historical accounts that imagine Victorian England "as a site of battle between the forces of civilized progress represented by the middle class and the uncivilized past represented by section of the plebeians and patricians" and found them wanting due to their relegation of non-civilized cultural forms to the status of mere "survivals."[75] By downgrading the importance of continuities in nineteenth-century English culture, these approaches often echo the point of view of nineteenth-century "enlightened" reformers themselves, who sought to draw a firm line between a previous age of barbarity and a new era of Victorian refinement. It is here that the position of the historian (and his or her readers) becomes very apparent. We live in a "civilized" world in which our attitudes to violence remain highly influenced by patterns that, I argue, emerged early in the nineteenth century. Thus, from our civilized vantage point it is relatively easy to look at a society or era with more violence and assume that the result was a correspondingly diminished quality of life.[76] This approach tends to blind one to the vibrancy and coherence of alternative modes of organizing violence as well as to the contradictions within "civilized" mentalities of violence themselves. In a sense, to paraphrase E. P. Thompson's classic phrase regarding working-class history, there may be some need to rescue violence from the enormous condescension of posterity.[77]

Such a view, I believe, fits well with Elias's notions of historical change. However, he devotes relatively little discussion to resistance against civilizing processes. By suggesting that the crucial issue revolves solely around "affects" (aggression being only one of them), the discussion of alternatives becomes difficult: one is either more or less "regulated" or self-controlled. However resistance to civilizing efforts may not take the form of an inherently *less*-regulated form of behavior but rather one that regulates behavior *differently*, for example according to alternative notions of order and control. As Price suggests: "'survivals' do not necessarily betoken deviation from a progressive norm. They might disclose a counternarrative that also provides an authentic description of the society."[78] That view is highly apposite to the topic of violence: the main tension was not between one cultural mindset that accepted violence and another that did not. Instead, the issue was one of defining the places, situations, forms and agents that could legitimately be linked to the inflicting of physical pain. While Elias shies away from value-laden, progressive judgments about the nature of a given society and emphasizes the relativistic, reversible and contingent nature of the civilizing process, one might see the less-civilized aspects of a society as "survivals." I have already noted that Elias was well aware of the problems related to dealing with historical change and continuity, and the present work intends to delve further in this direction. Rather than denying the relevance of the civilizing process, I want to raise some questions about how it is conceptualized and to suggest some of the complexities inherent within it. There can, of course, be a directional trend in the network of relationships that drive "civilization": particular configurations or mentalities become more widespread or dominant than others at certain times. The second half of the nineteenth century, for instance, saw a decisive shift in power away from individuals and localities to the central government, driven by the increasing uniformity of prosecutorial and judicial procedure, a judicial and elite consensus on "standards of virtue" and the growth in police presence and efficiency.[79] However, I wish to emphasize the contingency and ambiguity that inhered in this process during the nineteenth century and to conceptualize mentalities as part of the "opposing strategies" within various kinds of cultural conflicts.[80] After all, there was ambivalence about the legitimate role of violence even within the most civilized of social thought, and, as J. S. Cockburn has suggested, "the self-righteous Enlightenment model of a newly sensitized society may have concealed cultural continuities and distorted recent historiography."[81]

Another ambiguity is attached to the "civilizing process": its connection with class. Elias himself devoted little sustained attention to the working classes; however, the issue of class is of great relevance to violence history. One study that applies Elias's principles to more modern violence observes:

> In highly stratified societies such as those of Western Europe, not all groups are equally protected by the [state] violence monopoly. This tends to be the case especially for those around the bottom of the social scale because their life-experiences typically lead to the persistent generation of values which tend to be at some variance with those which are dominant within the wider society. In other words, they tend to be less subject to the sorts of civilizing constraints which affect the members of higher classes.[82]

As the authors suggest, the issue is not simply one of lower socio-economic groups being less "restrained" or more "impulsive" in their behavior: rather it is the case that despite the pressure of civilizing processes from above (through policing and social work), the recourse to physical force remains a relatively significant part of their everyday lives. Violence, in the absence of other forms of social power, remains a significant resource for the lower classes, particularly men.[83] Honor expressed through physical prowess had once been a common denominator of masculinity for men of all classes; by the nineteenth century, new measures of sensitized manliness that were not as reliant upon fighting had been elaborated. Among the lower classes, these new measures often made little sense in daily social contexts or were otherwise unattainable, suggesting that legitimate recourse to violence could fit within the networks of social life rather than being merely anti-social deviancy. Nevertheless, the boundary between civilized and customary mentalities was not strictly contiguous with the border between the classes. For example, upper-class men might appreciate observing a customary ritual fight, cross-class shared principles of male privilege shaped attitudes toward domestic violence and retributive notions of justice might color views of punishment among people of all classes. Prior to the civilizing discourses in the eighteenth and nineteenth centuries, violence was not conceived as a sociological problem with a particular class location. The working-class shadow of English refinement allowed violence, along with many other social dysfunctions, to be re-imagined as outside the boundaries of society. The withdrawal of the middle and upper classes from what previously had been a shared culture of violence meant that those who respected traditional attitudes toward violence, adapted them to an urbanizing and industrializing society, and defended them against civilizing hegemony were largely from within the working classes. Class dynamics had changed by the 1870s due to the spread of working-class respectability and an expanding electoral franchise. At the same time, the increasing dominance of forms of sociological and biological criminology cast new shadows that were located either in increasingly marginalized sub-groups or within the human psyche. The civilizing offensive, the rhetoric of savagery and the conflicted nature of new nineteenth-century attitudes to violence are the subjects of the next chapter.

2   A useful savagery
Violence, civilization and middle-class identity

Friendly and courteous behavior seems to increase daily; and gentler manners, arising from the better training and example of the upper and middle classes, which reflects usefully upon the conduct of all.

J. H. Elliott[1]

We do not know ourselves. Neither the Church nor the law tries, or if it tried would be able, to discover the hidden depths of our depravity…. Our civilization, vaunt it as loudly as we will, is full of unclean mysteries; yet we go on boasting of the material and scientific triumphs of our age, as if these were all in all, and never bestow a thought upon the moral shortcomings that render our civilization, however advanced it *may* be, the merest mockery of what it *should* be, if our wealth and virtue kept pace with each other.

Charles Mackay[2]

Violence contributed to the formation – and re-formation – of nineteenth-century ideologies and identities. Reciprocally, changing material realities and cultural patterns influenced the ways that violence was perceived and understood. Nineteenth-century social commentators often wrote as if they were *discovering* violence, and, indeed, the growth in social investigation brought into view much that had been previously ignored. However, they, along with the state and legal profession, were also actively *inventing* violence: developing new views on the nature of physical aggression, debating and redrawing the boundaries of legitimate interpersonal behavior and linking violence to the structures of English social life. I refer to violence's "invention" neither to suggest that there had previously been a corresponding lack of violent acts in England nor to claim that violence had completely failed to generate concern or thought prior to the nineteenth century. There had long been, of course, laws against various sorts of violent acts underpinned by views of violence as a product of sin or a threat to the king's peace and state efforts to restrain and punish those who overstepped the boundaries of legitimate violence. Nevertheless, until the early nineteenth century violence was a remarkably acceptable social activity. The development of a social understanding of violence placed the phenomenon of physical aggression in a profoundly different light. Halttunen notes a developing Anglo-American "revulsion from pain, which, though later regarded as 'instinctive' or 'natural' has in fact proved to be distinctly modern."[3] Similarly, violence was increasingly regarded by a sensitized section of society as repugnant. As a result, violence also needed to be explained, and these explanations were sought not only within the individual, but also in the social factors that formed his or her character. In this chapter, I will outline the salient points of an emergent set of attitudes toward violence in nineteenth-century England, identify some of its key contours and languages, and suggest the influence of violence on identity, particularly in regard to the middle class. As the final section of this chapter notes, there were "limitations" to civilizing thought, and mentalities of violence, like class identities, are typically incomplete and contradictory.

Inventing violence

For centuries, violence had not been perceived as a particularly troublesome social problem in England. J. M. Beattie has found "a high tolerance of violent behavior," noting that "few children in the eighteenth century could have avoided physical punishment at home or at school, in service or as apprentices; and few adults could have failed at least to witness physical violence."[4] Violence was not merely a reluctantly abided "fact of life": rather, the early modern state, community and home were all arenas in which violence was an accepted – indeed, an expected – means of expressing legitimate social power.[5] Margaret Hunt argues that the eighteenth century was not only "a society suffused with personal relationships of dominance and submission, but it was one that saw violence as a necessary, if not always optimal, way of maintaining order in any hierarchical relationship."[6] Acceptance of violence was shared among all social ranks and visible "cruelty" – whether applied to animals, children or adults – was a generally assumed part of daily life.[7] Pieter Spierenburg, writing of early modern Europe more generally, has found "vindictive" and "indifferent" attitudes toward violence evident even at the top of the social scale.[8] The state employed publicly displayed violence in its judicial punishments, which – along with the physically retributive model of justice that underlay them – received widespread popular consent. Although particular whippings, pilloryings and hangings might provoke the (sometimes violent) hostility of crowds, such unrest signaled disagreement over the legitimacy of a specific instance of physical punishment rather than revulsion against pain, retribution or violence per se.[9] The prevalence of violence in English society did not go entirely unquestioned, and, of course, eighteenth-century elites did fear (and fight) crimes against the person along with those against property. Concurrently, reformers, typically from dissenting religious backgrounds, actively opposed popular pastimes, and the "reformation of manners" became a prominent concern. However, violent behavior was generally tolerated as long as it was neither explicitly murderous nor connected to threats to property or the state, and it was rarely a target of early modern Christian reform efforts.[10] Despite the eighteenth century's nascent concern with manners and morals, then, violence remained an inherent part of English culture: there was far more interest among reformers in stamping out various forms of "impurity" and "sin" and attacking earthly pleasures and frivolity among all social ranks than in battling cruelty or violence.[11] Although there were limits on legitimate violent behavior, those frontiers were, by subsequent standards, broad, and violence had yet to become a prominent form of social anxiety.

Beginning in the first decades of the nineteenth century, attitudes toward violence were transformed. Three general tendencies characterized that changing outlook: increasing efforts to define and narrow the limits of legitimate violence, the linking of violence to social causes and effects, and the elaboration of a new "mentality" of violence. In the process, violence was "invented," becoming a key social concern and an increasingly urgent topic for discussion and analysis. The modern approach to violence and our contemporary efforts to engage with its causes and meanings are themselves an end-product of such innovative nineteenth-century narrative efforts to define and differentiate violence as a phenomenon. Proliferating scientific and sociological discourses were among the mechanisms for the differentiation of many kinds of behavior. In applying these discourses to physical aggression – in the process, creating violence as a phenomenon to be understood – neither the state nor social critics achieved a single definition of what it was or how to deal with it. Nevertheless, violence was addressed in new ways, being, so to speak, "put into words" in the nineteenth century.[12]

Law is one of the most obvious contexts in which violence is defined, and, increasingly, when people spoke of "crime" they referred to violent crime. The nineteenth century saw a shifting legal classification of various forms of physical harm: attitudinal changes are visible in legislative and judicial moves toward stricter punishment of violence as well as in the gradual limitation of state-imposed corporal and capital punishment for non-violent offences.[13] In 1803 Lord Ellenborough's Act imposed death sentences for the first time on attempted murder and certain kinds of assault.[14] The 1820s saw the beginning of a decades-long legal effort to define and demarcate violence: penalties for manslaughter were increased in 1822 and an omnibus Offences Against the Person Act was passed in 1828.[15] The latter statute, referred to as Lord Lansdowne's Act, marked a decisive step in legal efforts to bring clarity to the law on violence. It repealed fifty-seven violence-related statutes dating back to the reign of Henry III and was set out, as a contemporary magazine described it, to "make that intelligible which is now obscure" relating to offences against the person; concurrently, it broadened the summary jurisdiction of magistrates over violent offences.[16] Subsequently, the penalties for some kinds of assault were raised in 1837.[17] In 1853, parliament provided the first specific legislative prohibition on violence against women and children.[18] In 1861 another comprehensive Offences Against the Person Act was passed that further redefined crimes and punishments and formed the basis from which the legal distinction between "actual" and "grievous" bodily harm is derived.[19] An in-depth 1875 parliamentary report on "brutal" assaults canvassed opinions among the legal and policing establishment on the state of violence and sought recommendations for defining, distinguishing and punishing various gradations of non-lethal violence.[20] For all these efforts, there remained much that was unclear about the criminal law on violence: a critic noted in the 1880s that "the Act [of 1861] relating to offences against the person throws no light upon it whatsoever," pointing to difficulties with terms such as "homicide," "manslaughter" and "malice aforethought."[21] Thus, the legal categorization of violence was a moving target; nevertheless, there were sustained attempts to define and differentiate it and moves toward stricter and more precise punishment of illegitimate physical force.

Furthermore, violence had a social resonance beyond the law: as the *London Quarterly Review* pointed out in 1866, "murder is not merely a technical word; it has a broad popular meaning," an observation that could be applied equally to lesser forms of violence.[22] Even while many ambiguities remained, concern with violence became a prominent motif of much of the writing aimed at the refined classes. In using a variety of vocabularies and in pursuing different specific aims, nineteenth-century commentators were not always talking about the same thing when they discussed "violence," "brutality" or "savagery." For example, a statistical report on "violent" deaths in Liverpool emphasizes the elasticity of the term: it includes fatalities under the rubrics of "accident," "died from the bite of a mad dog," "exposure to the inclemency of the weather and starvation," "excessive drinking" and "choked while eating."[23] Similarly, "savagery" and "brutality" could be applied to a variety of situations; yet, in most cases, the terms were applied to various kinds of deliberate interpersonal altercations.[24] By the 1820s – concurrent with its more refined legal differentiation – murder could be discussed with detailed attention to its nuances in circumstances and forms.[25] Increasing attention was given to the gradations of violent behavior. For instance, pugilism, a long-accepted – even celebrated – form of sport- and street-fighting, came under new scrutiny in the early nineteenth century. Critics claimed that boxing was "repugnant to the laws and maxims of a civilised state" and argued that accidental fatalities from boxing matches should be classified as manslaughter.[26] Even those who defended traditional forms of prizefighting developed elaborate rules and "systems" and debated the legitimacy of various forms of sporting violence.[27] Later in the century, the parameters of acceptable violence in the home increasingly came under scrutiny.[28]

Although the contexts of these critiques and the authors' arguments varied, such discussions circulated critically (or defensively) around the newly perceived social problem of violence. Physical force as such – rather than only as an accompaniment to other kinds of crime such as robbery or rioting – became a heated topic of public concern. Assault, murder, streetfighting and all varieties of domestic abuse became pressing issues and their causes were located within the network of social and cultural structures. New "humanitarian sensibilities" expressed a heightened sensitivity to visible human suffering and sought explanations for violence not only within the individual's soul, but also within society.[29] Although it is the second half of the nineteenth century that tends to be noted for the birth of sociological epistemologies, strong assertions of the role of environment in shaping behavior are apparent earlier. In letters to the Home Office, investigations into working-class life, or studies of crime, the emphasis upon environment as a cause of violence and brutality, whether within the home or in the wider society, is notable.[30] By the late 1830s it could be argued, in the context of a broad series of articles on the English "moral economy," that "it would be almost just to say, that society prepares the crime, and that the ostensible criminal is only the instrument by which it is executed."[31] Such environmental explanations were central to describing many sorts of violent behavior, notably spousal or family violence.[32] Social analyses of violence in the early nineteenth century always competed with, and often mixed, physical or moral discourses.[33] Throughout the nineteenth century, environmental explanations of crime and violence had their critics, yet the social approach became well established.[34] As investigation developed, there was a tendency toward an even "more finely tuned justice, towards a closer penal mapping of the social body" as new forms of violent "deviancy" were created.[35] Concurrent with such discursive handling of violence came the view that it was eradicable: it could become, as it had not been before, a problem to be solved.[36] Social investigations were not merely a vehicle for a refined and voyeuristic tourism of the dark side of lower-class life but were also underpinned by an expectation that such explorations would open the way for social improvement schemes with the aim of "ameliorating life by making some changes in the conditions of social existence."[37] Social reform was not, of course, only driven by concerns about violence; however, in the efforts of social reformers to map and improve behavior, violence was prominent among their concerns.[38]

Along with putting violence firmly on the map of social criticism, the differentiation and socialization of violence contributed to the elaboration of a new, civilized mentality of violence. "Civilization" was a word with great currency in the nineteenth century and reflected a particular set of attitudes toward behavior and self-restraint that became associated most strongly with middle-class cultural tastes. It was a broad rhetorical umbrella under which attitudes toward pain, crime, punishment, aggression, masculinity, Englishness and public comportment gathered, linking violence with other concerns such as impulsiveness, gender, national identity, imaginations of public space, and so-called immorality and vice. While violence was not the only ingredient in civilizing attitudes, it came to be connected to other aspects of social concern and functioned as a token that could be invoked in numerous contexts of social criticism. Violence took on a new and long-lasting importance in the language of social critique while, reciprocally, attitudes toward violence were influenced by other civilized imperatives.[39] A central issue was applying new narratives to the understanding of violence – defining the places, situations, forms and agents that created a legitimate context for the inflicting of physical pain – while expressing the increasing alienation of a self-conscious culture of "civilization" and "refinement" from the presumed "savagery" of other social groups.

"Civilization" and "savagery"

"Civilization," like "violence" or "brutality," had neither a stable nor uncontested meaning.[40] Nevertheless, repeated, reciprocal connections between "savagery" and "civilization" surfaced in reference to violence and social order. For instance, an 1814 critique of state punishment argued that the pillory excited the passions of "savage life" and aroused "the barbarous spirit of man unsoftened by civilisation."[41] Paralleling legal efforts to define, differentiate and combat violence, civilizing rhetoric would develop further in subsequent decades.[42] In an influential 1836 essay, John Stuart Mill described "Civilisation" as a word with a "double meaning": "it sometimes stands for *human improvement* in general, and sometimes for *certain kinds* of improvement in particular."[43] His main concern was civilization in its "narrow sense: not that in which it is synonymous with improvement, but that in which it is the direct converse or contrary of rudeness or barbarism."[44] In Mill's wide-ranging essay, violence formed one key element in his definition of savagery and the civilized society from which he distinguished it. He made specific references to the necessity of protecting individuals from "injury" inflicted by others, the limitation of visible pain and the replacement of personal or community vengeance by the mechanisms of law.[45] It was civilization's self-conscious differentiation from "savagery" that most importantly implicated violence in new cultural imaginations, not only for Mill, but also for a wide range of social commentators.[46]

Contrasts between advancing "progress," "civilization" and "refinement" and threatening images of "violence," "brutality" and "savagery" were essential elements in the creation of a new mentality of violence. W. C. Taylor claimed "no one can visit the streets in the vicinity of the [Liverpool] docks without feeling that he has seen something very like savage life in close contact with Civilisation."[47] Much like the English explorer examining "savage" societies in Africa and Asia, middle-class observation confirmed that degeneracy and cruelty existed alongside idealized notions of Englishness. In analyzing labor-related violence, one writer in 1849 emphasized the presumed impulsiveness of the lower classes and equated them with supposedly primitive societies:

> a scene ensues calling into operation all the passions of hatred and anger which one might have hoped belonged only to the American Indian or African warrior.[48]

Such comparisons sat uneasily with perceptions of an expanding humanitarianism; however, particularly brutal crimes reinforced the notion that certain groups formed a debased culture unto themselves that was radically disconnected from the civilizing and reforming spirit of the age.[49] For example, violence within lower-class life was claimed to continually recreate patterns of savagery through its influences on workers' children.[50] One correspondent to the Home Office in the late 1820s highlighted the decline of traditional, paternalistic patterns of work training: the erosion of apprenticeship meant that a young man became a "slave to his own passions."[51] At mid century, J. W. Kaye recounted the arguments used by working-class wife beaters to justify their acts, noting "those attendant excuses or palliations, which are not unfairly pleaded on behalf of the poor, uneducated, ignorant man, whose neglected childhood and misguided youth are naturally and necessarily followed by a brutalized manhood."[52] Matthew Davenport-Hill referred to the lack of proper moral education among working-class children, with the result that "they fall into nomadic habits and are a herd of savages in the bosom of civilized society."[53] As one writer argued in the 1890s, "The gangs of juvenile scuttlers, who from time to time run riot through the Manchester streets, have doubtless been reared in homes where mothers are subjected to kicks and blows."[54]

There was another, ethnic element in civilized social analysis: the association of the Irish with violence became "axiomatic."[55] A letter to the Home Office from Doncaster in 1822 attributed an increase in violent robberies and assaults to the engagement of a number of "tramping labourers" who were "principally Irish" at an engineering works there, creating so many threats to the local population that the writer requested that a company of troops be billeted nearby until the project was completed.[56] Thomas Carlyle commented that "in his squalor and unreason, in his falsity and drunken violence [the Irishman is] the ready-made nucleus of degradation and disorder," while for another writer they were "more like beasts than human creatures."[57] More alarming to many contemporaries, Irish savagery was believed to spread like a contagion to English workers. In the early 1830s one writer, referring to Irish immigration, concluded, "the colonisation of savage tribes has ever been attended with effects on Civilisation as fatal as those which have marked the progress of the sand flood over the fertile plains of Egypt."[58] Another wrote of a perceived rise in drunken assaults in factory towns, suggesting that "the inferior order of Irishmen have brought with them all their vices into the manufacturing districts."[59] The Irish were, in general, disproportionately represented in criminal court calendars. It has been suggested that this reflected an importation of different traditions of settling intra- and inter-communal disputes centered on issues of family, region and religion.[60]

The Irish aside, however, there was plenty of homegrown savagery to concern reformers and the state, although there were disagreements about its sources. Some observers suggested that the problem lay in the inability of certain classes or groups to adapt to the demands of an industrializing and urbanizing society. Despite the long-extant idealization of the countryside within English culture, these analyses saw a rural culture unaffected by new disciplines and cultural patterns.[61] A correspondent to the Home Office in 1823, who had had bullets fired through his windows, noted, "the principal inhabitants here are farmers, who have always been considered a very rude and unmanageable set of people."[62] Joseph Fletcher argued in 1849 that the most degraded and violent populations were to be found in rural areas, "furthest removed from every civilising influence, and even from the check of improved police" and put them on a par with "the most neglected of the manufacturing and mining populations."[63]

He continued,

> It is quite possible for a population of small proprietors to be mortgaged
> and sordid barbarians, or, in other words, in much the same condition that
> small tenants generally are; and we have little evidence to a high moral stan-
> dard prevailing among such a people, though it forms the most pleasing
> dream of human existence to associate the simplicity of rural life with the
> refinement which, as yet, has belonged only to a much more elaborate form
> of society or high grade of well-being.[64]

Perhaps the most striking portrayal of the "savage" countryside was the 1851 essay "Cain in the Fields" by Richard Horne and Charles Dickens. Opening with pleasant and bucolic country imagery, its rural idyll is quickly juxtaposed with the recent murder of a woman by her lover, an agricultural laborer, or – as Horne and Dickens describe him – "the selfish and illiterate fiend of the fields."[65] The authors use this case as preface to a more general, and negative, evaluation of rural life, describing "a country hawker … of whose life much has passed in fields and hamlets and villages; can the worst streets of London produce anything to beat this specimen of low cunning and depravity?"[66] Although we are more familiar with the argument that urbanization and industry created violence and disorder, such rural critiques viewed cities and factories as civilizing agents. "But for the renovating influence of its manufactures," wrote Andrew Ure in 1835, "England would have been overrun ere now with the most ignorant and depraved race of men to be met with in any civilised region of the globe."[67] While economic change without a concurrent moral improvement was seen as a recipe for immorality and violence, industry as such was in this view not the main threat.[68] In fact, the worst consequences came from too little mechanization, and some writers sensed a large uncivilized mass prone to ignorance, barbarity and violence existing outside of manufacturing areas. There was, of course, also an alternative tendency toward seeing violence as a symptom of urban and industrial society. Mill, in distinguishing between civilization and savagery, hinted at connections between them: "It is in this sense that we may speak of the vices or the miseries of Civilisation; and that the question has been seriously propounded, whether Civilisation is on the whole a good or an evil?"[69] These analyses often idealized the (sometimes relatively recent) past as a time of more peaceful social relations and viewed rural or agricultural life in rather sanguine terms. One writer in the 1880s pointed to the structures of urban life as sources of new types of cruelty:

> What with our gin-shops and their poisonous and maddening draughts, our
> growing betting mania, our baby burial clubs, our thousands of house-to-
> house child insurance agents, there is *springing up* amongst us a systematic

child injury, torture and murder – has sprung up and has quickly grown to serious proportions – at which pagan Rome might have blushed.[70]

The sense that industrial society was creating its own forms of madness and violence became increasingly common and fed into a sociology of urban life that has tended to see cities as the prime sites of the production of social dysfunction.[71]

Although the sources of savagery could be debated, its social location was generally more agreed upon, and, as earlier, observers in the later nineteenth century continued to see "the existence of this life of savagery, running parallel with the ordinary life of refinement and civilisation … forced under their notice by an act of violence or more than usual daring outrage."[72] A gang rape and murder in Liverpool in 1874 inspired a seething commentary:

> The most brutal, the most cowardly, the most pitiless, the most barbarous deeds done in the world, are being perpetrated by the lower classes of the English people – once held to be by their birth, however lowly, generous, brave, merciful, and civilised. In all the pages of Dr. Livingstone's experience among the Negroes of Africa, there is no single instance approaching this Liverpool story, in savagery of mind and body, in bestiality of heart and act. Nay, we wrong the lower animals by using that last word; the foulest among the beasts which perish is clean, the most ferocious gentle, matched with these Lancashire pitmen, who make sport of the shame and slaying of a woman, and blaspheme nature in their deeds, without even any plea whatever to excuse their cruelty.[73]

Specific incidents built up a generalized discourse of savagery that defined certain groups as inherently impulsive and wild, unconstrained by cultural codes or recognizable boundaries. In the 1880s, Andrew Mearns's wide-ranging analysis of "outcast London" pointed to the contradictions between wealth and poverty, morality and corruption, and religiosity and irreligion, noting "the gulf has been daily widening which separates the lowest classes of the community from our churches and chapels, and from all decency and Civilisation."[74] The depiction of the "lowest classes" by this time tended to be somewhat more differentiated, a trend that had much to do with the development of sociological studies since Mayhew. Concurrently, as I shall consider in the following section, the increasing adoption of civilized values by the working classes also had an impact on the social imagination of violence. Thus, the meaning of "civilization" remained, like that of "violence," very difficult to define precisely: it might, for instance, be labeled a power in its own right, an almost automatic growth of "social progress."[75] However, the general tendency was to see it as something more contingent, a culture of refinement threatened by the "savagery" that surrounded it.

In an apparent paradox, violence was introduced as a social problem by being imagined as "outside" society (detached from the cultural mentality of which it had long been an integral part), a symptom of wild and uncontrolled temperaments and the province of – various and changing – social groups. The relationship between civilization and savagery was succinctly expressed in a mid-nineteenth-century article:

> Growing up in the very midst of this kindliness of spirit, fastidious delicacy, and romantic refinement, there is a tendency to crime more wild, more brutal, more abominable, than the darkest ages of the world ever heard of. …This horrible taint in the national mind occurs in the midst of social, moral, and religious soundness. It is the attendant of our civilisation, the shadow of our refinement.[76]

The image of a "shadow" was perceptive; shadows, after all, cannot exist without something to cast them. The creation of a civilized mentality of violence resulted in the discernment of new and varied threats to refined society as some previously acceptable behavior was redefined as savagery. Violent crimes became the focus of social commentators when they discussed the crime rate or expressed fears of social breakdown.[77] However, the relationship between civilization and savagery was not only one-way: while civilization manufactured the darkness around it, it was, in turn, produced and supported by its shadow. Social observers made use of violence and attempted to give savage elements a social location. Although that location was often unclear, changing or contradictory, the menacing presence of savagery nevertheless brought clarity to the civilized identity.

Violence and identity

The invention of violence interacted with issues of identity in the nineteenth century, particularly those related to class. New standards of personal behavior and attitudes toward violence were influential among those who identified themselves most closely with civilizing trends. The emergence of a civilized mentality of violence was concurrent with a foundational period in middle-class identity. By the mid-nineteenth century, previously "disparate elements" of the middle classes "had been welded together into a powerful unified culture."[78] There were undoubtedly economic gradations and regional variations within "middle-class culture," and its utility as a historiographical concept is complicated by the various ways in which "respectable" standards are applied (or ignored) in different social contexts.[79] However, while middle-class culture was not a monolithic structure, an "imperative moral code" was a touchstone of middle-class identity.[80] Class, like violence, is a term with many meanings, and, as it has been pointed out, "the language of class is always unstable."[81] Rather than a preformed middle-class identity clashing with violence, innovative attitudes toward violence contributed to the formation and maintenance of a fractious and dynamic middle-class self-image. The class associations of the civilized mentality of violence were flexible, particularly as increasing concerns about savagery do not seem to have been related directly to changes in actual violence. Although the statistical measures of violence are notoriously questionable, the period seems to have witnessed either a gradual decline or a relative stagnation in the quantity of violent acts.[82] Moreover, although violence which impacted the middle class directly might fuel one of the moral panics that punctuated Victorian society, violence during this period was markedly intra-class.[83] The violence that preoccupied social commentary was overwhelmingly committed by working-class people upon other working-class people: such intra-class violence – whether in the form of male brawling, domestic abuse or labor-related attacks – provided much of the fuel for nineteenth-century discussions of the topic. Thus, violence was invented as a social problem by that class for which its experience was most remote, at a time when, it appears, statistically measurable violence was not in fact increasing.

Since men committed the vast preponderance of criminally violent acts, changing mentalities of violence involved new definitions of masculinity.[84] While previously dominant masculinities relied on bodily prowess and the ability to deploy violence, respectable male identity came to concentrate on "occupation, on 'rational' public activity, and on one's role as husband and father" rather than on physical vitality.[85] Middle-class culture emphasized restraint in interpersonal behavior, aspiring to at least the appearance of control over "passion," which was often linked to violence.[86] As a result, middle-class identity in regard to violence was elaborated against the class below them. The "civilized" emphasis on self-control and restraint of passion linked sexuality, leisure habits, housing, sports and labor relations as aspects of working-class life in need of reform. These critiques were often directed at the perceived profligacy and spendthrift natures of the poor and working class, contributing to a view of them as impulsive and driven by unthinking emotion. "We cannot expect that they can have much control over their words, feelings or action," wrote one commentator in 1849, "knowing that these must be governed by reflection, and a training of their will to the will of God," and "unlicensed indulgence of the passions" was a "prevailing feature" of working-class life.[87] Two decades later, "undue energy of the passions" continued to be viewed as a prominent source of working-class brutality and misery.[88] As a result, "violence thus acquired a symbolic currency in political discourse, for middle-class men pointed to their own self-control as a justification for their claims to political power while at the same time attacking the working class as too violent to deserve the vote."[89] Though civilized men did not always adhere to their ideals, the exhibition of a restrained, self-controlled demeanor became essential to displaying respectability. Different material circumstances, customary definitions of masculinity and scarcer opportunities to gain civilized signifiers of masculinity gave violence a continuing resonance in working-class masculinity.[90] The civilized mentality of violence not only required that one react internally against violence, but also served as a motivation for the "benevolent and humane" to involve themselves in remedying social causes of violence, producing educational texts, promoting improved housing, reforming law and punishment, and actively intervening in disputes.[91] Customarily popular activities were transformed – both in their rules and social contexts – so that they could take on more refined forms. For example, middle-class men predominated as the heads of the boxing associations that promoted new rules of pugilism and aimed to reform the behavior of working-class men.[92]

As Mill noted in 1836, civilization "stands for that kind of improvement only which distinguishes a wealthy and populous nation from savages or barbarians."[93] Such distinctions were drawn domestically as well as internationally. Although Mill himself did not associate the working classes as such with "savages or barbarians," other writers were less hopeful in their downward glances at the masses around them. In the same year as Mill's essay on civilization, one commentator compared the "refinement" of the middle classes to that of the "inferior classes in the manufacturing towns and districts":

> Judging them by the same rules which have been applied to mark the advancement of man from a savage state, they have made but few steps forward; and though their primitive nature is disguised and modified by the force of external circumstances, they differ but little in inherent qualities from the uncultivated child of nature, and shew [*sic*] their distinction rather in the mode than the reality of their debased condition.[94]

In the opinion of many social observers, such groups remained stubbornly resistant to change: despite the "irresistible power" of the "wheels of Civilisation," they remained "nearly unchanged."[95] As in all industrializing countries, identifying the "dangerous class" was a tenuous and uncertain project. The "vulgar rabble" and "blood-thirsty mob" were contrasted with the more humane middle classes.[96] In 1832, E. G. Wakefield warned of the danger to "householders" from the "populace" – a group organized into sub-classes such as "common thieves," the "rabble" and "desperadoes" – characterized by a "barbarous ignorance" and "degradation" that made them "enemies of all law and order" and the "helots of society."[97] Thomas Arnold, writing in the same year, posed the following question: "Has the world ever seen a population as dangerous … as the manufacturing population of Great Britain?"[98] Artisans, in general, might be pointed to as a prime location of savagery and violence.[99] "It would appear," wrote one author in 1849, "that society requires to be roused from time to time by the protrusion of such enormous facts [i.e., spectacular murders], in order to become unmistakably aware of the fearful amount of ignorance, misery and crime seething in its lower strata."[100] Subsequent social investigators such as Henry Mayhew were often at pains to make finer differentiations and could enthuse about "the virtues of our working men."[101] Yet, other commentators were not so careful in drawing their distinctions, and particular crimes could paint an entire trade, region or class in the colors of savagery, highlighting the ambiguities of class identity and the power of violence as a fearful social imaginary. In the decades from the 1820s to the 1870s, the working classes and poor – no longer merely "the mob" and awaiting the grudging, gradual respectability that admission to the political franchise and adoption of middle-class culture would bring them – tended to represent the social location of violence.

While attitudes toward violence contributed to the construction of middle-class identity, the elaboration of that identity, in return, contributed to the reshaping of attitudes toward violence. An understanding of the nature of violence, its sources and its cultural and social location was created among the classes most involved in nineteenth-century civilizing activities. Although violence was seen as increasingly taboo, it was depicted in ever more vivid terms. There was a widespread growth in "sensation" literature, and murder and violence became pronounced themes in reading material of all classes. Karen Halttunen has analyzed Anglo-American attitudes toward pain in the eighteenth and nineteenth centuries and concluded that as pain became eradicable and a taboo subject, literature became more florid and detailed in its presentation of brutality. This "pornography of pain" made pain more exciting because it was anathema while concurrently inculcating new attitudes to suffering.[102] The "civilized" epistemology of violence functioned similarly. In the literature of social analysis, this was voyeurism with a purpose: beyond titillation, humanitarian narratives showed readers how to react to violence. Violence, particularly working-class violence, was increasingly depicted as something purely impulsive: it was often described as a brutal, unthinking and uncontrolled expression of lower, "savage" impulses.[103] In particular, these descriptions were applied to various forms of behavior associated with (mainly working-class) men. The emphasis upon "rage" and "losing control" constructed masculine behavior norms in ways that have had a long-lasting influence upon criminological and popular understandings of violence and have even functioned as a mitigating factor for male violence.[104] Middle-class men were supposed to overcome this presumed tendency toward uncontrollable anger. Because civilized men had self-consciously abandoned what had previously been a widely accepted customary code of violent behavior, it became more difficult for them to read violence in any terms other than impulsive savagery. As later chapters will show, there were in fact codes that shaped working-class violence; however, those codes were very different from those promulgated by reformers and were based upon a social context increasingly alien to the middle-class mind. The modern "fetishization" of violence emerged from this middle-class imagination of physical aggression.[105] There was similarly the creation of a distinctly modern assumption that violent behavior "is always destructive, 'dysfunctional,' and devoid of meaning."[106] However, it is clear that not all forms of violence were equally important to this process. Elizabeth Stanko has examined a modern "criminological myopia" that she argues originated in the nineteenth century:

> Because of the historical focus on the criminalized actions of working-class and marginalized men, the ideological and practical strength of the image of "real" violence remains firmly fixed on the street.[107]

Civilizing attitudes about the presumed chaos of working-class life and imagined notions of social geography shaped the way that outsiders viewed violence in working-class communities. The focus upon marginalized men as the instigators of violence, and upon their particular modalities and locations of violence (e.g., fistfights in the streets, riots, charivaris, assertions of control over the streets during labor disputes and street robberies) was predicated upon a particular notion of what violence was and – equally important – what it was not.

This process of giving violence a precise social location remained problematic. Confidence in the "otherness" of violence came under question particularly in terms of violence against women (and, to a lesser extent, against children). Although in the 1850s it could be confidently asserted that "men of education and refinement do not strike women; neither do they strike each other" and concern about spousal violence focused more exclusively on the lower classes, the associations of violence and class later became more ambiguous.[108] This was, in part, because the civilizing goal of limiting mainly public violence had been to some extent successful. Attention then turned to forms of violence, such as spousal and child abuse, that previously had been relatively ignored and could not be so easily blamed on a dissolute other.[109] Later in the century, blame for violence could be placed on the legal system (particularly judges) in not punishing such abuse sufficiently.[110] Psychological, or biological, explanations of violence became more popular, locating violence more universally within the human psyche as well as in the specific social conditions of lower-class life.[111] Attention also was drawn to actual violence within respectable home life. "It is a mistake," noted Benjamin Waugh in 1888,

> to suppose that poverty, or large families, or ignorance ... has anything whatever to do with cruelty. The proportion of comparatively well-to-do and well-informed who have fiendish dispositions towards children is found to be greater than those who are very poor.[112]

Moreover, he concluded, "the educated villain is only smarter in his savagery," suggesting an awareness that the civilized mentality had its own contradictions.[113]

The limits of civilization

Despite the influence of civilizing perspectives, the inflicting of physical pain remained a legitimate part of English culture.[114] The continuing tolerance of domestic violence, for example, became an important topic of social criticism in the last few decades of the nineteenth century. Much of this commentary was connected to broader concerns about of the role of women. Noting the precarious position of women in Victorian society, one writer pointed out:

> their so-called protectors daily beat, torture and violently assault them, often with such violence that death results; while the male judges, appointed by a government chosen by an exclusively male electorate, punish the offenders

in a most inadequate manner, holding a woman's life at less value than a purse containing a few shillings.[115]

Comparing the judicial treatment of property crime and spousal abuse became a staple tactic of critics of continuing tolerance for male violence.[116] Such analyses undermined the constructions of a civilized middle class and a savage working class. While accepting that "the men who physically assault women are mostly of the lower and uneducated classes," they drew the axis of attitudes to violence along a line defined by sex rather than class, noting that violence was "acquiesced in by men of all ranks."[117] Parliamentary and judicial inaction thus became signs of male privilege to use violence in the home. The increasing debate about spousal violence at the close of the nineteenth century is one sign that the conflict between civilized and customary mentalities was primarily a disagreement about who could legitimately administer what sorts of violence and in what contexts rather than a broad rejection of violence as such. While some humanitarian narratives highlighted an abhorrence of pain, civilized thought remained ambivalent about violence, and there were limitations to the implementation of refined social policy.

For instance, while civilization tended to be seen as a benefit, some writers suggested there could, indeed, be too much of a good thing. In the second decade of the century, a boxing manual suggested that "the English character might get too *refined*, and the *thorough-bred* bull-dog degenerate into the *whining* puppy."[118] Such a view is perhaps unsurprising from an enthusiast of pugilism; however, similar sentiments emerged in other contexts as well. An 1832 article contained the opinion that people were too willing to accept the repentance of murderers.[119] While Mill argued that violence and pain needed to be kept out of sight, the result endangered social vigor: "There has crept over the refined classes, over the whole class of gentlemen in England, a moral effeminacy, an inaptitude for every kind of struggle."[120] Fears of the "enervating" dangers of too much civilization were expressed in relation to crime and violence.[121] Charles Dickens reacted strongly against a misdirected sympathy toward the perpetrators of crimes.[122] Anxieties about what we might call "over-civilization" also pointed to a perceived decline in the ability of the refined classes to defend themselves. One writer noted,

> People ought to go about armed, as in former times, to resist the ruffian; and they ought, as part of their education, to be trained to defend themselves. … One ruffian disabled on the spot is more exemplary than many punished after the slow and very uncertain process of law.[123]

There was a continuing tension within civilized thought among humanitarianism, the imperatives of social control and fear of the lower classes. The importance of reforming the violent working class while maintaining the possibility of using force against them reflected a concern with public order, since "the mass of people are not of so mild a temper that a laxer doctrine can be safely encouraged among them."[124]

The culture of refinement's expectation of increased self-restraint was balanced by the delegated violence of a police force invested with the power to use "legitimate" force in combating crime and a continuing enthusiasm for physical punishment. Police legitimacy was contested within the middle-class press as well as on the streets, and, particularly in the first half of the century, the authority of the police to employ violence was often a tenuous one.[125] Starting in the 1830s, however, policemen were, in some locations, authorized to carry cutlasses, and the truncheon itself could be used as a formidable weapon. The police were not given *carte blanche* to use force, and although some police began carrying firearms in the 1880s in response to a large number of armed burglaries, these were very rarely drawn or fired.[126] Physical force at the hands of policemen was given generally wide leeway by magistrates, and the middle-class press often suggested that police should be more, rather than less, willing to use force.[127] While the extent of actual police violence is difficult to recover,[128] policing itself is based upon the authorization of a defined group to use physical force underpinned by the authority of the state. Delegation of force in combination with narrowing the boundaries of acceptable violence among the general public brought new patterns to English social life and led to frequent conflicts in working-class communities. While the extent of force allowed to the police was frequently contested, in large measure it escaped the appellation "violence" within civilizing discourses at war with traditional notions of community self-policing. Discussions of punishment also reveal some of the tensions regarding violence within civilized thought. Undoubtedly, state reliance upon public displays of physical punishment declined over the eighteenth and nineteenth centuries as transportation and imprisonment emerged as alternatives. By the 1840s, only murder and treason retained the sanction of the scaffold, and the ceremony of hanging was removed from public display in 1868. However, physically retributive justice remained a crucial part of judicial and social thought, and advocates of physical punishments – particularly hanging and "the lash" – remained vocal critics of humanitarian penal principles.[129] In response to the crime "panics" of the 1850s and 1860s, there was a resurgence of interest in and use of flogging in response to particular kinds of violent assault and street robbery.

A dominant civilizing objection against public physical punishments was that they brutalized the masses and encouraged violence in everyday life. "Brutalization" arguments focused on more than hanging, and a wide variety of social factors were identified as inuring the masses to physical suffering and promoting a savage spirit.[130] Emblematic of a judicial regime driven by impulsive, passionate anger, physical punishments were examples of the sort of culture social reformers sought to eradicate. An early nineteenth-century pamphlet had argued, "The pillory is in direct opposition to the principle upon which all laws are founded, and must serve ... to undermine the foundations of their authority." Laws, it continued, were erected to control the unbridled passions of man, to take from individuals the power of revenge, to render punishments the determinate effect of firm and substantial enactments, instead of fluctuating with the rage and the sympathies of individuals, to prevent parties from being judges of their own injuries, to humanize society by taking from the strongest the power of inflicting arbitrary penalties by which it was reduced to a state of perpetual warfare, and to impress the mind with awe by the weight and solemnity of their decisions.[131]

Half a century later, the abolition of the pillory (which was accomplished in 1837) was recalled as a symbol of social progress:

> It was the abandonment of an ancient principle, the closing of an ancient school. With it died the semi-savage custom by which the mob were called in as instruments of punishment, and were incited to commit assaults in the name of the law.[132]

Private vengeance was "absolutely subversive of the principles on which the order and happiness of society are founded."[133] Echoing this theme later in the century, another writer declared, "I have long ago formed the opinion that the origin of all our errors in punishment, is the tenacity with which we cling to the principle of retribution."[134] In 1895 a critic summed up his views on the resumption of flogging as both a return to brutality and an indictment of the ineffectiveness of the current mode of imprisonment:

> This mode of punishment [i.e., flogging], which had previously been abandoned as both useless and degrading, was reestablished in civil law by Act of Parliament in 1863. …This state of things is to be deplored, not alone as a reversion to the more primitive and brutal customs of the past, but as the most damning evidence which could be produced against our prison system.[135]

Most traditional state punishments had been open to the criticism that they gave too much leeway to the crowd to determine its own reaction to the event.[136] It was also argued that violent punishment promoted a violent populace. Dickens, referring to brutal assaults, "strongly" questioned the revival of flogging as a response, "in consideration for the general tone and feeling, which is very much improved since whipping times," and he claimed that "the whip is a very contagious kind of thing, and difficult to confine within one set of bounds."[137] He argued for longer and harsher prison sentences rather than a more general reintroduction of corporal punishment:

> We shall do much better than by going down into the dark to grope for the whip among the rusty fragments of the rack, and the branding iron, and the

chains and the gibbet from the public roads, and the weights that pressed men to death in the cells of Newgate.[138]

Matthew Davenport-Hill had, like others, been opposed to the reintroduction of flogging in response to the garroting panic of the 1860s because it would run against public opinion as well as being largely ineffective.[139]

"Public opinion," however, was highly flexible and notoriously difficult to identify: judging by its voice in the press, it was as willing to call for the lash as for humanity. The theory that the restraint of violence, abhorrence at the inflicting of pain and the promotion of rational behavior should be the aims of civilized society did not deny a continuing current of retributive anger and harshness.[140] However, in order to fit with the discourse of civility, vengeance had to be clothed in the language of refinement. For example, when flogging made a resurgence, it was repackaged by its proponents as a tool of civilization, particularly in regard to violence against women. Many commentators argued that if civilization were to be maintained, it had to rely upon methods that were an affront to its own sensibilities: the fear of physical punishment could be mobilized for civilized ends.[141] Although J. H. Elliott noted an improvement in manners and a growth in friendliness, kindness and "temperate habits," his suggestions for dealing with the perceived increase in violence contrasted with excessive humanitarianism: he was in favor of hanging, opposed to the rehabilitative emphasis of prisons and forcefully asserted the retributive model of justice:

> It is the instinct – the virtuous instinct – of the whole world to impose retributive pain, for pain inflicted willfully and criminally, just as it is the instinct of the whole world, to slake thirst with drink. …Pain should be the certain punishment for all violent offenses against the person, and either pain or some ignominious instrument, as the pillory, is due to malicious offences against property, especially on living animals.[142]

Similarly, Sindall has noted a willingness to sanction the use of flogging and the "cat," often at the urging of the respectable press.[143]

As traditional patterns of male behavior were critiqued, women were increasingly conceptualized as a victim class – similar to children – to be protected by the intervention of the state.[144] Although relatively little action was taken to actually protect women (and wifely provocation remained a potent justification for spousal violence), the image of the victimized woman justified the resumption of physical punishment and provided an occasion for further debates about working-class viciousness. In order to deter wife beaters, flogging was seen as a useful tool. In 1856, after describing assaults on women as "unmanly," Lewis Dilwyn, MP, introduced a bill to allow flogging as a punishment for domestic violence.[145] Flogging for "brutal assaults" upon women and children was instituted in 1863.[146] A Home Office questionnaire circulated in 1875 revealed that opinion within the policing and judicial hierarchy was divided, but with a strong majority of respondents expressing qualified support for an extension of the penalty.[147] The use of physical punishment to deter violence such as wife abuse was to be legitimated by one writer who argued that

> the elimination by civilization of the tiger element in human nature is still too imperfect to allow without great evil relaxation of the restraint of fear to curb its action. The conscience which deters violence is in the rough the outcome of a dread punishment.[148]

Note the emphasis upon "the rough" rather than upon the working classes as a whole, along with an assertion of the positive example that physical punishment would set.

The most "dread punishment" was hanging. Mill voted to maintain the death penalty in 1868, citing "an enervation, an effeminacy in the general mind of the country" and asserting that hanging was "less cruel" than long-term imprisonment.[149] Commenting upon a century of humanitarian thought, W. S. Lilly wrote "In Praise of Hanging" in 1894, suggesting that "this reaction against the exaggerated severity of former ages [had] been carried too far." Lilly suggested that "the punishment of death alone is commensurate with the crime of willful murder," a precept "true for all time and all stages of political evolution … because it is founded on the nature of things, and is in accordance with the ever-lasting laws of human society and divine justice."[150] Just as with flogging, advocates of capital punishment re-cast their arguments in terms of civilizing discourse itself. Echoing elements of Mill's argument and the nationalist sentiments of some pugilism enthusiasts at the end of the century, Lilly argued that long-term imprisnment was both more brutal and less suited to the English character than hanging:

> A sentence of life imprisonment is merely a more cruel and more cowardly mode of inflicting the death penalty. Hence perhaps the favour it has found with the Italian people, as pandering to their characteristic vices.[151]

Thus, the celebration of the sensitive "man of feeling" was often in tension with fears of cultural emasculation, and these tensions influenced the issue of violence. Perhaps, as violence in the public sphere diminished and larger sections of the working class adopted aspects of respectable behavior, earlier brutalizing concerns faded. Certain forms of violence, then, became imbued with the power to civilize or were seen as essential to encouraging a "masculine" English civilization as Britain faced increasing military and economic competition.

By the later nineteenth century, as we have seen, true "savagery" tended to be identified with marginalized sub-cultures rather than with the working classes as a whole. The effort to "relocate" violence outside of society was a contradictory, ambiguous and imperfect process. That I have adapted nineteenth-century keywords in examining violence does not mean that I accept some commentators' eagerness to draw a line between a civilized present and barbaric past. Quite the contrary, since the invention of violence, after all, built on the previous century's reformative movements, and there were long-term inconsistencies in civilizing thought. Traditional, customary mentalities of violence were no mere licenses for uncontrolled savagery, nor were the middle classes the unquestionably humane force that they sometimes believed. Furthermore, for most English people, violence's place in society did not shift fundamentally until the last decades of the nineteenth century. Alongside difficulties in precisely defining "civilization" or the social "other" of violence came the problem that people of all classes did, to varying degrees, commit violent crimes. Wiener suggests that the nineteenth-century discourse of character feared that "savagery – rooted in human nature, not class – could break out at any social level," and fears of impulsiveness and "passion" were not strictly limited to a particular class.[152] This is true; however, the class associations of violence seem to have been dominant between about 1820 and 1870. To some extent, a variety of explanations for violence coexisted, although the emphases between them changed: while moral, medical and psychological discourses were often the basis for explaining middle-class or aristocratic aggression and violence, working-class violence could be explained as a function of social environment and a "vicious" culture. As wider segments of society accepted civilized standards, and, furthermore, as the working class gained admission to the political state, undifferentiated attacks on working-class culture became less viable.

As the following chapters will describe, there was an alternative mentality of violence. I refer to it as "customary." "Custom" did not articulate itself through the organs of press and sociological essay, yet it had a profound influence upon the daily lives of the majority of English people. Rather than seeing custom and civilization as two sides of a debate about violence, the interrelation was far more complex and dialectical, as each was involved in the process of defining the other and establishing the role violence should play in the family, community and nation. Furthermore, the conflicts between these two mentalities of violence were organized around a variety of topics rather than merely around violence per se. As subsequent chapters explore, attitudes toward legitimacy, justice, autonomy, community, sport, power and the use of space were all part of the struggles (and, in some cases, agreements) between the "civilized" and "customary" mentalities of violence.

3 "Vigorous passions and decided actions"

Custom and the cultural contexts of violence

We have amongst us large masses of a population who have escaped the enervating polish of civilization. To them we may still look occasionally for vigorous passions and decided actions. They have the rude energy, along with the brutal propensities of a more animal existence.

Leslie Stephen[1]

By and large the lower strata, the oppressed and poorer outsider groups at a given stage of development, tend to follow their drives and affects more directly and spontaneously … their conduct is less strictly regulated than that of the respective upper strata.

Norbert Elias[2]

In the 1830s Charles Dickens vividly described his impressions of the Seven Dials area of London:

Now, anybody who passed through the Dials on a hot summer's evening, and saw the different women of the house gossiping on the steps, would be apt to think that all was harmony among them, and that a more primitive set of people than the native Diallers could not be imagined. Alas! The man in the shop ill treats his family; the carpet beater extends his professional pursuits to his wife; the one-pair front has an undying feud with the two-pair front, in consequence of the two-pair front persisting in dancing over his (the one-pair front's) head, when he and his family have retired for the night; the two-pair back *will* interfere with the front kitchen's children; the Irishman comes home drunk every night, and attacks everybody; and the one-pair back screams at everything. Animosities spring up between floor and floor; the very cellar asserts his equality. Mrs. A "smacks" Mrs. B's child for "making faces." Mrs. B forthwith throws cold water on Mrs. A's child for "calling names." The husbands are embroiled – the quarrel becomes general – an assault is the consequence, and a police officer the result.[3]

Clearly, elements of dramatic license, class prejudice and ethnic stereotyping are all present in Dickens's description lower-class life, a humorous, civilized expression of working-class savagery. Nonetheless, it also efficiently encapsulates several actual tendencies of commonplace working-class violence. Violence was a concomitant to everyday life: at work, at home, at school and in the streets. In the domestic sphere, a customary culture sanctioned the beating of children and spousal violence, and family and neighborly rows took place in a largely public arena in which disputes were known generally. However, the patterns of such violence were contoured in ways invisible to the refined imagination. One of the key differences was that, customarily, physical aggression had had a widespread, public legitimacy in community life.[4] That community location is crucial in understanding the customary mentality of violence, and its centrality was cultural as well as spatial. Before discussing some specific forms and contexts of physical force, I shall in this chapter delineate some of the key components of the mentality that underlay much of working-class violence and examine its interaction with the culture of refinement. The customary mentality of violence had three dominant characteristics: it favored physical retribution, valued community autonomy and maintained domestic and public norms through disciplinary force or its implied threat. Particular violent acts often combined these imperatives, but, for the purposes of analysis, they will be considered in turn. As described in the last chapter, for the nineteenth-century middle class, "both the 'language' and the objectives of urban masses were, if intelligible at all, deeply frightening."[5] Violence was part of this unintelligibility; nonetheless, the narratives applied to violence and the expressive nature of violence itself – the two aspects of "speakable" violence – can give some insight into the contours of the customary mentality of violence.

Retribution

While far removed from the Mediterranean culture of the vendetta, English customary culture legitimated the use of violence to settle disputes or to punish deviants, and there was little questioning of the biblical notion of an eye for an eye.[6] Popular belief in vengeance was a powerful motivation for some forms of working-class violence. In 1839 an observer of the industrializing northern towns wrote:

> The notion that justice is only legalized revenge, and that every crime must be atoned for by a certain amount of physical suffering, prevails so universally that it may almost be said to have passed into an article of faith. Never was there a more mischievous delusion.[7]

The retributive notion of justice was, of course, a "delusion" that had been shared – and imparted – by the state. Furthermore, as Chapter 2 suggested, civilized discourses were never entirely successful in purging middle-class thought and state policy of customary elements, suggesting the significance of "resistant mentalities" and highlighting the relevance of customary counternarratives to "progress."[8] Older customs competed with cultural tendencies that preferred to settle disputes in courtrooms rather than in the streets and measured punishment in length of imprisonment rather than in spectacularly displayed physical pain. However, the cultural lessons learned over centuries at the foot of the scaffold and pillory and applied through community self-policing were difficult to shed. Despite England's long history of courts and the common law, legal authority had always coexisted with alternative traditions of social regulation.

Customary retribution was more direct than the state's, representing a "world of 'justice' outside the official courts."[9] Community justice could be activated in response to a variety of transgressions, some of them seemingly mundane. For instance, in 1837, a homicide case came before the Surrey assizes.[10] Three drunken medical students were hurrying from a pub in Woolwich to a carriage to take them back to London and had rapped on windows and doors while running along the streets. One of them, Peter Taylor, broke a window. Although he reimbursed the house's owner, he soon broke another window. This time, he and one of his companions, Isaac Slocomb, continued running until they noticed that the third of their trio, a "Mr. Ledden," was no longer behind them. They traced their route back and found that a group of local men had gathered, accosted Ledden and accused him of breaking windows. A police inspector and a constable arrived on the scene as Taylor remonstrated with the crowd. The inspector deposed that "very high language was being used on both sides as regards the payment of the window."[11] Although Taylor eventually paid for the second broken window, the crowd attacked the three students. Slocomb was seriously bloodied in the affray; nevertheless, with police assistance they escaped the angry crowd and returned to London. Slocomb died from his injuries the following day, and at the resulting trial one of the crowd was convicted of manslaughter.[12] The animosity of the crowd had been driven by the affront given by three outsiders recklessly disturbing the peace. Even though restitution was eventually (and reluctantly) made, the students' cavalier attitude contributed to the crowd's anger, which was unassuaged by the presence of the authorities. The crowd did not seek legal redress (and, in fact, struggled against the police); instead, they drew upon customary forms of direct action.

Local transgressors could face more sustained forms of retribution.[13] Community feeling against "informers" who cooperated with the authorities was particularly strong. Such views had motivated attacks by pillory crowds on people convicted of attempting to prosecute others maliciously (for crimes they had not committed) or those who had given evidence against their criminal cohorts and were pilloried as a form of reduced sentence. As with other crimes that gained popular opprobrium, such as sodomy or child molestation, the reaction of the crowd was often fierce and occasionally fatal.[14] The pillory had been a remarkable instance of the way that extra-legal violence had previously been tolerated (indeed, within some limits, expected) as an instrument of legal punishment. By the mid eighteenth century, some observers were raising qualms about the activities of the pillory crowds and expressing discomfort with the implied legitimacy of injuries to the pilloried.[15] Although the pillory was eventually abolished in 1837 after decades of declining use, informers continued to face community violence. An observer of the London police courts noted, "the feeling excited by the 'copper's mark,' as he is called – the traitor who has betrayed his companion in crime, who has given information to the police – is far different [than the respect generally afforded to the police]; and [he is] not infrequently the victim of the most savage vengeance."[16]

Even toward the end of the nineteenth century, the customary legitimacy of violent and ritualized punishment as well as the animosity toward informers remained. In February 1882, Arthur Blatch, a driver for a London cartage firm, arrived at work at eight o'clock on a Saturday morning.[17] He made his breakfast and was eating it in the mess room when some of his co-workers entered. One said to him, "This is the last meal you are to have." "Have you any dying speech to make?" another menaced, "You had better say your prayers." There were further threats as more employees entered the room until, Blatch estimated, there were about twenty present. One of them made a speech (the details of which are not revealed) that was cheered by the assembled men who then set upon Blatch:

> I was then thrown down on the floor and all the prisoners seized hold of me. A rope was thrown over my neck. I got rid of that. A rope was then thrown round my body and another round my legs. I was dragged across the room to the door and was cast down the steps headfirst. I lost consciousness and when I came round I found myself in the stables. Those steps are 10 or 15 feet deep. …When I came to, pails of water and fluid from the urinal were thrown over me and a quantity of filth was put over my face and mouth.

After the attack, Blatch was taken upstairs and given hot tea, remaining in the mess room until 11:30 or noon. He went out to work, but deposed, "While out with the cart I fell off the cart, in consequence of the state I was in," and he was later confined to bed under a doctor's orders because of his injuries. According to an apothecary's testimony, Blatch had wounds consistent with the attack as he described it. Seven men were charged with conspiracy and assault as a result of the incident.

The motives for the attack on Blatch by his co-workers' were in some dispute. As Blatch testified:

> I went to the Mansion House [i.e., a magistrate's court] in consequence of some service I had rendered to the police in apprehending some boys who had committed a robbery at Gracechurch St[reet] on Thursday. It was on Friday that I went to the Mansion House to give evidence.

Friday was the day before his co-workers attacked him. However, the evidence given by witnesses – other employees of the firm who were not charged in the assault – suggested that the motive for the ducking was not Blatch's testimony against the juvenile robbers, but was instead a response to his consistently arriving late to work. John Foster, a driver who had not been present at the assault, testified,

It was threatened to duck Blatch because he was late in the mornings and shirked his work. I have done Blatch's first journey in the morning sometimes because he was late.

Foster admitted that he had "heard someone talk about Blatch giving evidence at the Mansion House," but claimed that he had not heard conversation among the prisoners about his being an informer. Another driver, Henry Gosling, testified that on the Saturday prior to the assault, "we were talking about his being late in the mornings and long on his journeys. At last it was said he would have to go in the tank." Going "in the tank" was a reference to the two water troughs in the stable yard. Blatch claimed that he had "never been threatened with being put in the tank before" and that during the threats made before the assault he was asked "Are you ready for the tank?" These comments suggest that it was a regular form of punishment. Gosling stated, "I have been threatened myself with being put in the tank and have been carried as far but not put in." After being recalled to testify further, Blatch deposed, "I heard them say that I was not the first who had gone in the tank and [I] had better go in quietly or it would only be worse for me."

Despite his co-workers' claims, Blatch was insistent that he had been assaulted due to his participation in the legal proceedings against the boys:

> It was not because I was late that this was done to me. I had not been late for 6 weeks. It was on account of the part I took at the Mansion House court.

During the pre-assault conversation with his co-workers, in response to their question about whether he was ready for a ducking, Blatch replied "that if the fines imposed on the boys at the Mansion House caused any disturbance I would pay the parents. They said that would not do." The reply suggests that Blatch's informing contributed to the attack, though it was clearly in the interests of the defendants to downplay any suggestion that they had engaged in witness intimidation. It is possible that the motives were mixed: there may have been some background animosity toward Blatch due to his lack of punctuality and poor work habits that increased demands on his co-workers. However, the timing of the attack and the refusal of Blatch's offer of restitution in the Mansion House case suggest that at least part of the motive for the assault was that Blatch was an informer. Whatever the balance of motivations, the depositions show that group assault and ducking were common occurrences at this firm: going "in the tank" was an implicit threat to those who broke with the various expectations of their fellow workers. In taking revenge upon an informer and perceived malingerer, they relied upon long-standing traditions of folk-violence and shaming rituals that legitimated physical force.[18] For instance, ducking was a customary punishment with a long history for those who violated community norms. Those accused of witchcraft, famously, had been ducked, but it was a feature of other dispute contexts.[19] In Blatch's case, it was a limited attack, and, afterward, he was given tea and allowed time to rest and, perhaps, to reflect upon what he had done to provoke them. Blatch was reintegrated with the group after a measured form of retributive violence had been applied. While Blatch's co-workers shaped their violence along customary lines, one of his tormentor's references to "last dying speeches" (a staple of scaffold culture) points to the influence of official violence on customary attitudes. There are suggestions from contexts such as work or prison that elements of official legal rituals – for example, mock "trials" – were at times mixed with popular justice.[20]

Outside these more structured situations, social transgressors remained in danger of community retribution, a pattern suggested by a case from 1828. Philip Taber was in a public house in Waltham Abbey, Essex, when Robert Franks entered.[21] Taber testified that Franks "immediately began abusing me, calling me an informer and said if I went out of doors he would serve me out." Franks's threats frightened Taber, and he waited to leave the pub until he heard the watchman nearby. Taber testified:

> Immediately [after] I got out, Robert Franks ... followed me. When I got near the Greyhound public house there were several people out there, drawn together, I imagine, by the noise Franks made in hooting and calling me names. He ran over to them and said to them, "Damn you, come along." The people then followed him and they all came after me. As I was going on, I met coming up the street William Blenkins .... Franks called out to him "here he is," and Blenkins then said "Damn him, kill the bugger." Blenkins then joined the mob and followed me till I got near my own house.

The watchman, William Randall, was quickly on the scene. He deposed:

> I heard a great noise of hollowing, I went to see what it was when I saw a great many people, about a score, following Philip Taber ... calling him an informer. I went up and Taber gave Robert Franks in charge.

He attempted to apprehend Franks, but some of the mob – led by Blenkins – began assaulting Taber. The watchman then tried to protect Taber, but in the process he was struck several times. Taber's father, who lived nearby and heard the disturbance, arrived and assisted the watchman in helping Taber escape the crowd.[22] Watchmen and constables were often hard pressed to restrain such angry crowds. As reported in *The Times* in 1828, a group of bookbinders were brought before the Guildhall police court accused of "having beaten and kicked sundry watchmen."[23] Charles Jones, one of the bookbinders, had accosted a woman by the name of Sarah Sharp. She had screamed and a watchman came to her assistance.

> Davis, a watchman, ran up to them, and received charge of Jones, who said, upon being collared, that he would "floor" the watchman "like a cock," and

showed an intention to resist; whereupon Davis tripped up his heels, and threw him upon the pavement.

The watchman's actions brought immediate intervention from Jones's fellow workers.

> [Jones] had hardly reached the ground, however, when a body of from 20 to 30 bookbinders set upon the watchman, and knocked him down, and beat and kicked him. …Some watchmen came up, and each was successively beset by half a dozen of the fellows, who beat and threw him down. The cries of the vanquished, and the shouts of the victors, spread dismay throughout the neighbourhood, and the noise was so astounding, that nearly all the watchmen in the three parishes flocked to the spot.

The bookbinders who fought on Jones's behalf denied knowing him and said they were "casually passing through the lane, when Davis threw the prisoner down."

Constables themselves could be targets. In 1833 a constable named Mason testified at a Cambridgeshire petty sessions and became the object of a mob's anger.[24] Lord Godolphin, one of the presiding magistrates, testified that he found a large crowd gathered outside the inn at which the sessions were being held; they were there because of a case being decided between some poor inhabitants of the parish and a local landowner. The case was decided against the inhabitants, "they having destroyed and carried away a considerable quantity of wood to which they thought they had a right," as Godolphin deposed. The magistrates moved on to other business, including Mason's claim that the landlord of the Crown Inn had assaulted him. The magistrates decided that the case against the innkeeper was "not made out" and they prepared to leave. However, the chief constable informed Godolphin and the other magistrates that "the house was surrounded by a number of persons who expressed their determination to assault the said Mason again, who himself stated he could not leave the house in safety." The magistrates went to the door and "remonstrated" with the crowd to no effect. As Godolphin testified, "they said they did not wish to hurt the magistrates, but they were determined to have the informer." The magistrates attempted to smuggle Mason out the back door but failed, and, determined to get him home safely, they "proceeded to swear in special constables under the act lately passed for that purpose." The constables and magistrates surrounded Mason as they set off from the inn. The crowd threw stones and pressed closely upon the little group; there were several brawls between men in the crowd and the special constables and magistrates by the time Mason safely reached his home.

Violence was customarily legitimate in a number of contexts when it was restrained. However, violence that arose from customary motivations could exceed the boundaries that had evolved to constrain it. In the summer of 1863, Richard Steed was found dead.[25] He had been beaten so severely that his features were unrecognizable; his daughter identified him by his clothing and his hands. Suspicion fell upon Alfred Eldridge, one of a group of men who were constructing a railway in Kent. Steed's widow, Hannah, deposed:

> I know the prisoner. There have been differences between my husband and him. He owed my husband a little money about three months back, a few shillings, and my husband asked him for it and said if he did not pay it, he would summon him. The prisoner said he would never get it. My husband summoned him for the money in the county court, and the day after the summons came out [the] prisoner came to the bakehouse door. My husband was at supper and the prisoner went into the room and offered him a shilling and my husband said he could not take it as the summons was out. They jangled for some minutes about it and my husband asked him to walk out. As he did not go, my husband got up and pushed him out and as [the] prisoner was going out the door he said to my husband, "Oh you bugger, I'll do it up for you before many weeks."

The day of the murder, witnesses saw the two men walking together, shortly before Steed's body was found. Eldridge denied the murder but blood and gray and black hair found on his boot heels provided damning evidence.[26] Eldridge was found guilty of murder and sentenced to death.[27] Although a secretive murder was extreme and not customarily sanctioned, homicide was part of a wide spectrum of violence, and murders often arose from a customary context that legitimated attacks on informers or people who commenced legal actions.

As Arthur Blatch's ducking suggests, work was another arena of retributive customary violence, with labor disputes often taking the form of riots against an employer.[28] However, such wrath was also directed against workers who cooperated with employers or who were in other ways seen as undermining the unity of the trade.[29] During an agricultural dispute in Norfolk in 1835, a group of men attacked two laborers who had taken employment with a farmer whose men had stopped work due to a dispute.[30] John Hunter, a farmer, deposed,

> On Saturday the 27th day of June last he was requested by Thomas Hebgin of Great Bircham, farmer, to furnish him with some labourers as his own men had struck work for the last week. …On the following Monday … he went to Bircham with two men by the names of Collinson and Simmonds to Mr. Hebgin's house…. Collinson and Simmonds had mounted two of Mr. Hebgin's horses to go to work, and were proceeding to the field to plough, [when] they were attacked by several persons, to the number of 20 at least, and violently and forcibly pulled off their horses.

Although the mob also attacked Hunter and attempted to pull him off his horse while threatening to murder him, he was able to ride away along with Hebgin, who testified to the same events.[31] In Bristol in 1827, James Bevan, a journeyman shipwright, was convicted of riot and assault against James Tuckfield aimed at preventing him from "working under wages."[32] Bevan had participated in a "ride," a customary, ritual humiliation in which the victim was carried on a pole and subjected to public abuse.[33] The master shipwrights of Bristol had lowered wages, and the workers had "agreed to stand out for the wages then given." Tuckfield had agreed to work for the lower wages, and "the shipwrights had, at a meeting held the evening before, agreed to give him what they termed a ride." The next morning, "they met him at a quarter before six o'clock and proceeded through various streets of the city carrying him on a pole and at the same time most disgracefully ill-using and abusing his person." Bevan argued that he had only participated in the ride "under severe threatenings … and that he continued under such threatenings to accompany the mob without attempting to join in the outrage through the fear of receiving some serious bodily injury."[34]

Such rituals were common throughout England: "stang riding" was a form of popular violence that "had been used around Newcastle against blacklegs in labour disputes, and in Sunderland against those who informed on striking keelmen and those who were instrumental in the kidnapping and impressment of sailors."[35] Two men convicted of a similar type of assault at the Norwich quarter sessions in 1836 argued that they had been compelled to participate.[36] In another case, a strike by sailors for an advance of wages in Durham in 1835 led to a breach of the peace after which five sailors were imprisoned for three months. A petition sent to the Home Office by the men's wives and mothers stated that during the dispute most of the seamen left their ships and came on shore. A few remained on board,

> for the purpose of proceeding to sea without the advance of wages; consequently those seamen who had quitted their ships went on board and brought them on shore. And while in the act of bringing those seamen along the streets a trifling altercation took place between some of the seamen and a Mr. Kidson, the solicitor to the shipowners.[37]

Folk-violence had been employed against blacklegs since at least the seventeenth century.[38] Workers had long used violence of some kind (typically limited) to enforce group discipline in the face of labor disputes and to punish laggards. Informers, blacklegs and others who undermined or threatened the customary control of work or neighborhood values could receive a ducking, riding or bludgeoning. The degree of violence varied according to circumstances. In some cases, customary rules might limit violence, and, at the conclusion of punishment, reconciliation and re-acceptance became possible. If the perceived threat came from outsiders, the response could be more violent, involving weapons and more serious injuries. Underlying these acts were customary attitudes that saw direct, physical retribution administered by the community (however defined in different contexts) as legitimate.

Autonomy

Some of the preceding cases have suggested another important element in the customary mentality of violence: the settling of disputes outside of legal processes that were becoming more common among the middle and upper classes. The use of retributive violence to settle disagreements among themselves had originated in a society with relatively weak state policing institutions in which behavior was often regulated within a community context. Traditions of such "self-policing" were deeply ingrained in working-class culture and connected to challenges to honor, respectability or the stability and cohesion of community life.[39] The law's reliance on private prosecution encouraged the legitimacy of personal violence: crime victims typically had to apprehend accused criminals themselves, frequently without the assistance of a constable.[40] As the state increasingly intervened in the public sphere, there was a growing effort to bring the settlement of disputes within the purview of the courts.[41] This process involved making legal proceedings more accessible as well as using the police to ensure that more violent incidents came before the courts. Over time, there was an increasing acceptance of using courts for the settlement of disputes; however, even at the end of the nineteenth century this acceptance was highly ambivalent.

The legitimacy of defending honor or settling disputes through the immediate use of force was an important part of customary culture as the following two cases suggest. On a summer evening in 1828 in Kent, Philip Holloway was out walking with his mother and his sister.[42] They went to a public house, where Philip spoke to his brother.

> During the time we were standing in the street talking together, three men dressed in the clothes of the Sappers and Miners Corps came up to us. One of the three struck my mother on the breast saying at the same time "You damned old whore, take that." No sort of provocation was given to either of them. My mother screamed out. My brother ran over to the door of the Prince of Wales and called out for assistance.

Three men from the pub immediately came out and joined the Holloways.

> Before they were quite along side of us I said to the sappers, "you ought to be ashamed of yourselves to ill-use my poor old mother so." Wallace and the other two who came with him also asked the sappers their reason for it. Further words then passed between us. They were certainly uttered in a great passion, one with another, then Wallace, Williams and Peake got to blows with the three sappers. They at first used only their fists. Then one of the sappers drew his bayonet and stabbed Wallace in the back.

After the stabbing, the sappers walked away, and Wallace soon died. The fatality of the incident was unusual; however, it highlights the ready availability of assistance to defend the respectability of a local woman. Such clashes between soldiers and locals were commonplace, driven by locals' perceptions of soldiers as invaders from outside their community.[43] However, such responses could also be mobilized against local transgressors, as occurred when William Hall attempted to enter Martha Asplin's house, noisily beating and kicking her door until after midnight. Hall later died of injuries sustained after a beating by two men.[44] The witnesses, Asplin and the neighboring Lewis family, had discussed keeping the incident quiet. While some reticence was in each side's interest, there was a more general lack of cooperation with the authorities. For instance, the testimony of Ellen Lewis characterized her brother's participation in that night's events in a rather positive light; nevertheless, he had urged her to keep quiet. Thus, the residents of "Poor Folks Lane" had attempted to solve an unruly disturbance on their own, since – for all their threats of calling for a constable – nobody had sent for a policeman until after Hall had died.[45]

Traditions of self-policing remained vibrant well into the nineteenth century. Simmons Stammers was employed at a burial ground in Southwark and resided in a lodge belonging to the premises.[46] Stammers frequently used force to prevent assemblages of "rude and mischievous boys" and to "preserve the premises in his care from injury." On one occasion Stammers got into an "affray" with one of the boys, who later died. Stammers was convicted of manslaughter and jailed in Brixton for six months. His wife, in her petition for mercy, pleaded that "he had no evil intentions regarding the said deceased boy, but considered himself in the discharge of his duty and [was] reasonably checking very rude and provoking behavior…". Respecting such "duty" could be the basis of a claim that violent behavior was justifiable, as it was for a toll-gate keeper sentenced to two years' imprisonment for shooting at a man attempting to cross his bridge without paying.[47] Thieves were also legitimate targets. A second-hand boot seller in mid-century London reported that when he caught young thieves pilfering from his stock he took the matter into his own hands: "I've been robbed before, and I've caught young rips in the act. If it's boots or shoes they've tried to prig, I gives them a stirruping with whichever it is, and a kick, and lets them go."[48] Similarly, the community dealt with thieves at a large clothing exchange summarily:

> Sometimes when these boys are caught pilfering, they are severely beaten, especially by the women, who are aided by the men, if the thief offers any formidable resistance, or struggles to return the blows.[49]

Such vigilante-style acts were common and accepted by the general community, including some thieves themselves. In Shropshire, the occupier of a home caught a burglar in the act in 1836. A constable was not immediately available. People gathered around, and "someone said: 'Give him a good thrashing and let him go.' [The burglar] asked Reeves [the occupier] if he would be satisfied with that, but Reeves said no."[50] In that instance, the occupier chose not to seek personal vengeance. However, if he had, his neighbors – and the thief – would have seen such a settlement as fair. Such self-help could lose legitimacy if excessive force were employed; however, there was a tendency to accept the use of violence to defend property, including property belonging to the working classes.[51]

Self-policing and self-defense were acceptable arguments for the use of violence; at times, the police agreed. In 1846, Richard Crump, a police constable in Margate, Kent, was informed of an incident between two men along a footpath near his beat.[52] He followed the footpath until he came across John Price standing over the inert form of John Sutton, who lay on his back, insensible:

> Price said to me, "I have been stopped in the high road by this man and I will give him in charge." I asked him what was said to him, to which he replied, "He asked me, 'Have you a watch?' I said, 'Yes, I have.' He then asked, 'Have you any money?' I answered, 'I have.'" He [Price] then added, "I up fast and knocked him down, that I then had a very severe struggle with him and was twice under him. That I had been with him near three-quarters of an hour struggling and calling out for help...."

The policeman's response to this story was immediate, "If this man stopped you on the road he had met with his just reward." The officer got some assistance and carried Sutton to the police station, where he was charged with attempted robbery. However, Sutton died of his injuries, and Price was charged with murder. Constable Crump noticed that Price was "not quite sober" when he saw him near the body and that his "dress was not disordered." He mentioned this lack of dishevelment to Price.

> I said to Price, "You have not got much of it at all events," to which he answered, "No, but I had as much as I could do to master him." He said further, "You may depend on it, I have given it to him as much as I could."

There were no witnesses to the attempted robbery though there was evidence of a struggle and footprints leading from a hedge by the side of the road to where the struggle began. Price publicly demonstrated how he had thrust Sutton's head against the ground and proudly declared that he had given his would-be robber "a Scotch prize." Sutton had been unarmed; however, Price was acquitted of all charges.[53] A case ten years earlier, however, suggests that self-defense was not an unproblematic defense.[54] Alexander Milligan, a "tea hawker," had stopped by the side of the road to sleep. A passer-by, John Rowlat, woke Milligan, who, being startled and having drunk quite a lot of ale, thought he was being robbed. He "drew a sword from a stick that he carried with him for protection of himself and property" and stabbed Rowlat to death. Milligan was convicted of manslaughter and sentenced to transportation, but his sentence was reduced to three years' imprisonment.

Thus, violence might arise very suddenly; however, once passions had cooled, there was frequently a desire not to further prosecute the matter, and reconciliation, customarily, was often swift. The expansion of police forces, their increasing role in taking matters before magistrates and magistrates' determination to bind over witnesses, prosecutors and defendants meant that official law more consistently drew offences against the person into legal proceedings.[55] For example, William Bridges and George Mead fought in a London street in 1834.[56] Mead had been driving a cart laden with macaroni when he came upon an omnibus driven by Bridges; concerned that his cargo would be damaged by approaching rain, he was in a great rush. He wanted to pass Mead's omnibus, but could not,

> which so enraged him that he flew in a passion and took hold of the heads of the horses then being driven by your petitioner with one hand. His whip being in the other hand, the lash of it struck your petitioner [Bridges] which provoked him so much that he struck the said George Mead several times, who defended himself by striking again at your petitioner and a fight ensued which was of only two or three minutes duration.

They were quickly taken to a magistrate's office and Bridges was sentenced to nine months' imprisonment for assault. Mead, the prosecutor, was the first signatory to Bridges's petition for mercy, and the petition notes that "the prosecutor considers the assault by no means of a serious character and he has written to your petitioner and also called on him in the prison and declared he will willingly lose a day or two's work or do anything in his power to get your petitioner's imprisonment shortened and has signed the petition for that purpose." Among two men of humble means, the fight was a trifling matter, and had they not been hustled before a magistrate the case would likely never have gone to trial. The prosecutor appears to not have seen himself as a victim and perhaps viewed the altercation as a "fair fight" of the sort to be discussed in Chapter 4.

A similar pattern marked an assault in 1835. Three men were sentenced to six months' imprisonment for an assault that arose out of the assistance they rendered to a police constable in arresting a man in Cheltenham, Gloucestershire.[57] Friends of the man challenged their right to interfere and started a fight. Afterwards, the three men who assisted the constable found themselves charged with assault: the prosecutors were the men they had helped to arrest. After the charges had been made, the prosecutors,

> on mature reflection, considered your petitioners had not acted on the night in question with a view to make a riot or commit any assault and therefore felt very anxious to compromise the matter which your petitioners consented to and a friendly meeting took place between all the parties when it was agreed that the matter should drop and your petitioners did not expect again to hear any more about it.

Unfortunately a magistrate refused to let the matter lie, and the prosecutors were compelled to testify. The constable included a letter verifying the men's assistance to him, and a release was granted halfway through their six-month sentence.[58] Magistrates were not entirely averse to private arrangements between the people who came into their courts, at least early in the century. George White had been sentenced at the Old Bailey in September 1835 to three months' imprisonment for an assault committed on the high seas against a fellow sailor. In response to White's petition for mercy, the presiding magistrate wrote to the Home Office regarding White's sentence:

> I sentenced him to an imprisonment of three months. Being very desirous that the poor sailor should receive some compensation for the injury which he had received, I intimated privately to the clerk of assizes that if the defendant made him [the victim] a compensation the punishment should be reduced. I find that the defendant has made up the sum of £5 and that the prosecutor is willing to receive it. I consider this a very inadequate compensation and intended that the defendant should have paid much more – but if he be unable to pay nine, and the prosecutor be willing to receive it, I submit to your Lordship that it may be proper to remit the remainder of his imprisonment.[59]

White's recommendation for release was prepared on 27 October. However, increasing regularization of police and legal procedure would limit the role of such informal arrangements.

Although community self-policing and extra-legal violence were often criticized in civilized discourse and punished by the authorities, there were dissenting voices who suggested that the propensity to violence of the lower classes was evidence of a vigorous and manly outlook that refined men lacked. As noted in Chapter 2, especially during crime panics, civilized approaches could become inflected with echoes of the customary mentality: in response to a series of garroting incidents, the *Daily News* warned in December 1862 that if such robberies continued, vigilante committees would hang offenders from lampposts.[60] Recognizing the innovation and fragility of the civilized shift away from customary, autonomous retribution, J. F. Stephen wrote,

> I suppose that in ages when violence was extremely common people were left in this matter to defend and to revenge themselves. The effect of this was that till quite modern times the most violent attempts to murder were only misdemeanours.[61]

The ambivalence of Stephen and others toward the civilizing order did not prevent a determined effort on the part of the state to transfer responsibility for self-defense and revenge away from the citizen to the state and to gradually limit extra-legal violence. Furthermore, the distinction of "extra-legal" acquired new force as the state pushed toward the monopolization of legitimate force and the early modern "margin of tolerated illegalities" narrowed.[62] Gradually, this began to influence working-class life. Shani D'Cruze has noted the increasing willingness to use courts as "an arena for the arbitration and management of violent marriages" among the working class.[63] Nonetheless, while workers increasingly made use of legal options or appealed to the police to settle disputes, the emphasis upon community autonomy remained. The customary mentality of violent "self-help" contributed to a complicated relationship between working-class people and authority figures such as the police: official and popular versions of justice were mixed. As Jennifer Davis has noted, in the context of a study of nineteenth-century police courts,

> the business of the courts demonstrates, in particular, that historians have underestimated the extent to which informal sanctions against wrongdoers applied within the community survived alongside official law enforcement as applied by the police and the courts at least until the end of the nineteenth century; while historians have similarly overestimated the extent to which the nineteenth-century state was either able or willing to intervene in the everyday affairs of its subjects through the agency of the newly organized police and police courts in order to systematically suppress lawbreaking.[64]

Both because of the inability of the police to fully dominate and control working-class areas and the ambivalent attitude of those classes toward official justice, autonomous settlement of differences and the imposition of community sanctions through violence continued to possess widespread legitimacy.

Discipline

As we have seen, violence or its implied threat patrolled the boundaries of acceptable social conventions and behavior in streets and workplaces, forming a resource that could be quickly, decisively and autonomously mobilized to enforce conformity to community standards. Similar dynamics structured violence in the domestic sphere, particularly regarding the issue of discipline. Domestic violence between spouses or against children, while it can be differentiated from other forms of violence, also fit within a wider set of customary cultural norms.[65] Domestic violence was, of course, in some ways a distinctive form of violence shaped by particular attitudes toward marriage and child rearing; for instance, it was undoubtedly an ingredient in maintaining male dominance and privilege across classes.[66] Men were given relatively free license to use violence in the home to "discipline" their wives and children, and judicial and police authorities were frequently reticent in responding to domestic strife.[67] However, doctrines of male superiority and female powerlessness must be considered part of a wider customary economy of violence that legitimated the use of force to maintain order and hierarchy within as well as outside the home. The disciplinary power of husbands did not exist in isolation, and discipline was not merely a male prerogative. Women used disciplinary violence within the home against servants and children, and working-class women freely used physical force against husbands, neighbors or strangers if provoked.[68] Overall, while both customary and civilized mentalities subordinated women, it seems that custom accepted some greater legitimacy of violent action: women could expect more violence but were relatively free to use it themselves in public or in private.[69]

To be legitimate, husbands' violence against their wives must have been seen to respond to particular kinds of provocation in commensurate ways. If physical force remained within these boundaries, it was "discipline" rather than "violence."[70] That distinction reached across classes, and magistrates were often lenient in handling abusive husbands. Later in the century, domestic abuse was to become seen as an important social problem as the working classes came under increasing scrutiny and incremental steps were taken to provide some relief for the most seriously abused wives. In 1853 parliament passed "An Act for the Better Prevention and Punishment of Aggravated Assaults upon Women and Children," which increased magistrates' powers to inflict summary penalties for certain assaults.[71] An act in the next decade gave magistrates discretion to use flogging in response to "brutal" assaults upon women and children.[72] The Matrimonial Causes Act of 1878 gave magistrates the ability to grant separation and maintenance orders for assaulted wives.[73] In 1891, the case *R. v. Jackson* ended the legal right of a husband to beat or confine his wife.[74] Although discussed in ways similar to other types of working-class violence – it was impulsive, driven by passionate feelings and maintained by a brutalized environment – violence within the home was increasingly regarded as a distinctive sphere of violent activity and its depiction reinforced negative views of working-class men. As a quarter sessions chairman, in discussing the possibility of extending the punishment of flogging to wife beaters, explained:

> In the class of assaults upon wives and children, the offence is seldom premeditated, and in almost all other cases it is committed by persons of brutal passions when inflamed and excited by drink and by habits of drinking. At such moments, when reason and reflection are blinded, and all feelings but those of the brute are blunted, it is unlikely that the punishment of flogging, if imposed, would be present to the mind, or, if present would have a deterring effect. And, therefore, I doubt much whether such a punishment would repress the offence, or have any other effect than that of brutalizing, when sober, the feelings of a man who had proved himself a brute when drunk.[75]

Environmental causes figured prominently in mid-century opinions on wife beating.[76] Although one essay expressed outrage about its prevalence, the author blamed violence by husbands less on inherent viciousness than on the structure of working-class lives.

> Men beat their wives, not because they delight in giving pain – not because they are abstractly tyrannous and cruel, but because their whole lives are lives of such excessive aggravation – because they are so wrought upon by a

continual succession of irritating circumstances that their tempers are not proof against individual annoyances as they arrive.[77]

As in other discussions about social conditions, the lower classes were often viewed as impulsive, passionate and largely incapable of rationally considered actions in the context of a generally brutalizing environment.

The argument that domestic violence was caused merely by unrestrained impulse becomes more problematic when one considers the cultural legitimacy of violence in the home. The justifications offered by wife beaters typically cited the disciplining of errant female behavior, excuses that echoed long-extant legal doctrines legitimating wifely submission and physical discipline.[78] In legal manuals, the legal right of husbands to beat wives was noted as early as 1516. Similar to the disciplinary rights of masters over servants, schoolmasters over pupils, jailers over prisoners and lords over vassals, husbands were granted a civil power to punish misbehavior.[79] This disciplinary power was not unfettered: punishment had to be "reasonable." Nonetheless, what might constitute excessive force remained unclear. A legal manual published in 1736, included the following passage:

> The husband hath, by law, power and dominion over his wife, and may keep her by force within the bounds of duty, and may beat her, but not in a violent or cruel manner; for, in such case, or if he but threaten to beat her outrageously, or use her barbarously, she may bind him to the peace by suing a writ of *supplicavit* out of chancery.[80]

This manual went through seven editions, the last in 1832, and these words remained unchanged.[81] Legal practice often varied in determining whether or not punishment had been excessive; however, there was little doubt that "reasonable chastisement" was a fundamental right of married men.

As a result of this traditional alliance between popular custom and legal practice, husbands were long accustomed to the right to use force. When brought before the courts, they justified their acts in ways that spoke to this long history.[82] One chief constable wrote to the Home Office, "In many of the cases of brutal assaults by husbands on their wives the defendants alleged that on returning from work they found their wives drunk, their homes and families neglected, and that quarreling and passion followed, which ended in the crimes of violence complained of."[83] William Carpenter was convicted of assaulting his wife in 1827, and his petition for mercy claimed "that your petitioner's wife and prosecutor, Alice Carpenter, is a woman of bad character who has for some time past formed a connection with some of the worst and most profligate of her sex – getting intoxicated continually and destroying during those times your petitioner's property."[84] Domestic disputes were often about a more general "aggravation" or unruliness than specific household failings.[85] On a Saturday evening in 1830, James Franklin beat to death his wife Mary – with whom he ran a public house and quarreled frequently – during a fight in which he "stamped" on her stomach, causing severe internal injuries.[86] He had said to witnesses that "he could not live with his wife" and that "his wife had been aggravating him."[87] When Mary McCarthy was beaten to death by her cohabitant, John Cockering, in a rooming house in Kent in 1844, witnesses to the struggle – both men and women – emphasized that McCarthy was in a great "passion" and verbally abused and struck at Cockering many times. Even witnesses who had been sympathetic to McCarthy's plight emphasized her quarrelsomeness and intoxication. The grand jury reduced the murder charge to one of manslaughter, and, in the end, Cockering was sentenced to four months' imprisonment for assault only.[88] By contrast, in 1853 a woman who stabbed her husband after an argument about her drinking was convicted of manslaughter and transported for ten years. A widow who lived next door said of the wife: "Sarah Smith has always been a passionate woman, particularly after she has been drinking."[89] Impulsive violence in the disciplining of wives was expected, particularly against women who were "passionate" or sharp-tongued. The wife of a "respectable tradesman" had complained to the police of her husband's abuse. At the police court, the magistrate asked her if she had attempted to "sooth her husband's displeasure" at her attendance of a friend's Christmas party. She replied, "Oh dear no, Sir. I thought it proper to show a little resentment." The husband retorted, "Which is constantly your practice. You're the very spirit of contradiction, and your tongue's enough to provoke a saint," while calling attention to what the court reported described as his "well-scratched face." The man considered that he "had a right to govern in his own house," to which the magistrate assented although he criticized the extent of the violence used.[90]

Jealousy was a frequent contributor to domestic assault and murder and fit into a more general context that accepted disciplinary violence against wives. At times, men described their violence in sexually charged language, and sexual jealousy was commonly a provoking factor.[91] Legal interpreters had legitimated the notion of impulsive, jealous violence: "Under a blow, or in the sudden discovery of his wife's infidelity, a man may well strike and not be construed in the same degree criminal as a deliberate murderer ... not that the injury is deserved, but that the injurer's blood is hot, and reasonably so."[92] Legal tolerance for "hot-blooded" crimes waned somewhat by the end of the nineteenth century; however, "there was a persistent belief, at all levels of male society, that wifely delinquency was the most potent of threats to masculine self-control."[93] In working-class culture, this threat was often responded to with the tools of customary disapproval: violence and shaming rituals. Cuckolds were particular targets of public shaming because of their loss of control over their wives. Thus, while explicit "civilized" and state tolerance for wife beating diminished, the practice of the courts and the Home Office was, in fact, to remain quite sympathetic to some motivations for violent acts, tacitly agreeing with customary attitudes.[94] If, as some historians have suggested, domestic life in working-class England was an openly declared war, women may have won some of the battles; however, they were generally physically weaker (although that discrepancy was perhaps less marked when manual labor was the norm for working-class women as well as men) and restrained by customary as well as civilized notions that they were to remain submissive. Abused husbands undoubtedly existed; yet such cases rarely came to court and it is extremely difficult to measure the precise rate of women's violence in the domestic sphere. Although the actual comparative rate of domestic violence (and its overall prevalence) is murky, the cultural meanings of "abuse" and "violence" were sharply gendered for both customary and civilized mentalities. Violence within the family was taken for granted, a key factor in its social meaning.[95]

Cultural expectations also legitimated violence against children. Indeed, child abuse has been described as the "last refuge of cruelty," and it was not until the 1880s that "a child's right to reasonable treatment within the family" became a major issue of public concern.[96] Working-class children grew up amidst a culture of violence that accepted frequent and explosive outbursts of physical aggression at home, in school and at work. Conley has noted that 43 percent of homicide victims in Victorian Kent were children under the age of twelve, compared to only 4 percent in 1974.[97] In the assize depositions, if one finds a woman charged with murder, the victim was typically one of her children. In the working-class home, mothers assumed the lion's share of responsibility for raising children, and the added pressures of time, labor (both the added labor of unassisted domestic chores and, frequently, the necessity of working outside the home) and money added to the frustrations inherent in parenting. Even if spouses frequently warred against each other, they often joined forces – or at least agreed in principle – on the physical disciplining of children. On this point, the state also tended to agree: the parameters of reasonable parental discipline were vague, and there was profound reluctance to interfere with the "liberties" of parents to treat their children as they saw fit.[98] Not all parents, of course, were physically abusive, and there is evidence from later in the century that women often assisted each other in protecting children from violent husbands.[99] Moreover, violence against children, like domestic violence more generally, was not merely a working-class phenomenon: prosperous parents also beat their children, and harsh discipline was often meted out in schools, regardless of which classes they served.

However, Enlightenment and evangelical ideals had begun to influence middle-class parenting as early as the first half of the nineteenth century. If violence were used in a middle-class household, for instance, it appears, overall, to have been less frequent, severe and visible. Ideals of more consistent and less physical disciplinary methods gained wide purchase among the middle classes: to raise a more emotionally controlled and sensitive individual, less violent (though possibly more relentless) methods were called upon. Importantly, middle-class parents were under social pressure to restrain themselves from the more flagrant abuse of their children, a social pressure absent from most working-class communities before the 1870s. Increasingly, a resort to physical violence that was a commonplace in working-class life would have signified a failure on the part of a middle-class parent to control his or her children through other means. Because of the vast unknown figures of actual violence in domestic life (particularly in the more private sphere of the middle-class home), many of the discrepancies between the classes and their actual child-rearing practices are lost to the historian. However, in terms of cultural mentalities, the different meanings of violence are more visible. Discipline and self-control were paramount middle-class virtues that signaled civility, and though Victorian middle-class fathers might be "imperious" or "remote," they were rarely "harsh" or "tyrannical."[100] A doctor writing at mid century on the "healthy discipline of the home" highlighted the deleterious effect of uncontrolled passions:

> The passions, when controlled and guided by reason, are the charm of life; they are the source of all that is great and good in man's nature; they are the grateful stimulants of the mind in the same degree that generous and nourishing food and drinks are stimulants to the body … but when used to excess, they disturb the healthy balance of the system.[101]

If such ideals were not always adhered to, the expectations themselves influenced perception. Civilizers viewed many forms of violence as a throwback to an unenlightened past and an affront to humanitarian interpretations of Christian morality. Sensitized reformers worked to publicize and inculcate civilized values to restrain the widespread physicality of domestic discipline, and, again, to control "passion":

> The cultivation of a peaceful and quiet temper is not only necessary to happiness in the present world, but is an important part of our preparation for a better. In no respect have parents a greater power committed to them than in this. If they are quick in resenting every trifling injury, quick in dealing blows, or in raising the tone of anger and reproach – the children may be expected to have the same sort of disposition.[102]

Civilization, like charity and beating, would begin at home.[103] The social and domestic parallels are striking: the same logic that reformers applied to public judicial brutality was applied later to the home, emphasizing the point that domestic violence was part of a more general pattern of violent behavior.[104]

For much of the working class, even those who aspired to respectability, the pull of customary understandings of violence remained strong. While it was not an unlimited license to abuse, the customary boundaries of violence against children (as with violence in the home more generally) were relatively wide. Within customary understandings, immediate and physical chastisement was the preferred punishment for adults as well as children: the same rules applied to unruly children as well as to neighbors or co-workers who transgressed customary boundaries of expected behavior. Outside the household, in both schools and the working world, adults regularly beat children. There were some signs that institutional violence, such as in schools and workhouses, was waning, at least relative to what had previously been allowed. In schools, "people are beginning to suspect that the rod in most, if not in all cases, was merely a barbarous expedient to hide the incapacity of the teacher."[105] This observation from 1839 was most likely directed at schools for the middle classes, since universal education awaited the end of the century. However, it signifies a growing discomfort in middle-class opinion about some aspects of what had been a shared culture of violent discipline. In a lecture to the Elementary Teachers' Association in 1859, Alfred Jones tied educational reform to a general cultural shift and emphasized internal self-restraint.[106] Jones saw education as the main vehicle of increasing "civilization," which meant the reduction, if not the elimination, of violence from daily life. The civilizing mission was incomplete:

> There is a skeleton in the house of the schoolmaster, a grim phantom, waiting on him ever, which he would gladly exorcise and knows not how. He speaks of it in an undertone. To the intellectual, gentle-natured, it is the one dark shadow in the sun of his life.[107]

Refinement's "shadow" in this case was the continuing, if diminished, use of corporal punishment in schools. Nonetheless, schools reflected the "spirit of the age":

> The reign of terror is over. Dr. Busby, Dr. Johnson, would not have public sympathy, would not have teachers' sympathy, were they now here, with their first, last argument – the rod.[108]

Physical "coercion" in schools, however, lasted throughout the nineteenth century and into the twentieth. As primary education became universal in the latter half of the Victorian era, many students continued to be subject to the "reign of terror" Jones dismissed as the relic of a barbarous past.

If school was an arena of childhood discipline, work was, if anything, even worse. Apprentices had long been subject to physical abuse in the pre-industrial period of handwork and manufacture. With the expansion of production and the increased division of labor as England industrialized, children entered workplaces and factories in larger numbers. Physical dangers were manifold in the industrialized workplace, and children were frequently maimed through accidents. However, they faced dangers not only from machinery but also from their adult supervisors. Such threats were manifest not only in the modern and increasingly industrialized trades such as spinning, weaving and mining (where a growing government inspectorate gradually publicized and sought to ameliorate their sufferings), but also in the smaller-scale and more traditional forms of labor. Practice varied among different workshops; however, disciplinary beating or flogging was commonly employed against apprentices and child workers. Moreover, magistrates often accepted the flogging of child workers by their masters. A London workman interviewed by Henry Mayhew testified to the discipline he received from one of his old masters:

> He was pretty severe in the way of flogging. …When I first ran away I complained to Mr. ——, the magistrate, and he was going to give me six weeks [imprisonment]. He said it would do me good; but Mr. —— interfered, and I was let go. I don't know what he was going to give me six weeks for, unless it was for having a black eye that my master had given me with the stirrup.[109]

The extent of harsh discipline appears to have varied by trade as well as individual workshop: some trades, such as chimney sweeping, were notorious for the harsh treatment of their young labor-force:

> It was also stated that the journeymen used the boys with greater cruelty than did the masters – indeed a delegated cruelty is often the worst – that for very little faults they kicked and slapped the children, and sometimes flogged them with a cat made of rope, hard at each end, and as thick as your thumb.[110]

There was a generally understood set of criteria to determine when physical force went beyond the pale, and, at such times, violence could form part of the response. Community violence could be used to show disapproval of wife and child abusers, and the occurrence of such events appears to have increased. Robert Storch has found that in Devon after 1850, Fifth of November celebrations increasingly incorporated community violence against child abusers or other social deviants.[111] Thompson has found that the focus for rough music shifted to some extent from adulterous wives to abusive husbands.[112] One man recalled a mid-century example of community ire being vented on two child abusers:

> Another year the effigies of a man and his wife named Fawn, who lived in the Bishopric, were hanged up on the signpost at the "Green Dragon." Together they had cruelly ill-used a boy, son of the man and stepson of the woman; they had also whipped him with sting-nettles. There they hung, each with a bunch of sting nettles in the hand until November 5th, when a hostile crowd collected, some of whom went down to Fawn's house, assaulted him and smashed his hand-cart. For this, [the members of the crowd] were summoned and fined £2 each, an amount quickly covered by public subscriptions.[113]

In this and other cases, violence could be called upon to fight violence, driven by the customary legitimacy of direct retribution but hinting at the growing infiltration of refined thought into customary settings. In this movement, civilized ideas mixed with customary self-policing. Just as civilizing thought continued to be inflected with older notions, we see here that blending was possible between the two mentalities in a variety of contexts.

In conclusion, violent acts can be categorized in a variety of ways: by the type of victim (for example, adult, child, male or female), by the relationship between victim and perpetrator (husband/wife or worker/boss), by severity (assault, aggravated assault or murder), by method (bludgeoning, stabbing or shooting) or by social context (home, work or public spaces). These differences are highly significant; however, focusing on them has the potential to conceal the outlines of a comprehensive and more or less coherent mentality of violence, a distortion also enhanced by the middle-class view of violence as purely a product of rage and unrestrained impulse. The civilizing offensive sought to undermine the "savage," "wild" and "uncontrolled" aspects of customary culture across a broad cultural front: violence, of course, was only one of its targets.[114] However, while a civilized mentality of violence organized attitudes toward violence among the sensitized middle and upper classes, an alternative mentality remained significant to a large part of England's population in shaping attitudes toward violence (and structuring violence itself). Custom did not proclaim itself in the manner of the culture of refinement: there was no literate, public debate about the nature of the customary mentality. Nonetheless, its outline can be glimpsed in the records of crime and the descriptions of violent incidents among the working class. Like civilization, custom was a flexible construction which maintained its relevance as it faced a changing set of social circumstances. It was rooted in imperatives of retributive justice, autonomy and social discipline and managed to script violence in particular ways, according to community standards. Although there were undoubtedly regional variations and particular local customs, the general cultural milieu out of which custom emerged prevailed throughout England and was adapted to urban and industrial contexts. Violence was generally legitimate among the lower classes as long as it was constrained within certain bounds of form and proportionality, but these boundaries might be ignored as a result of great emotion or against a variety of "outsider" groups.[115] The following chapters take a closer look at the structures and strategies of the customary mentality and trace some of its interactions with the culture of refinement.

4 "The brave old English custom"

Dispute, recreation and ritual violence among working-class men

Scorning all treach'rous feud and deadly strife, The dark stiletto and the murderous knife, We boast a science sprung from manly pride Linked with true courage, and to health allied; A noble pastime, void of vain pretence The good old English Art of self-defence.

Poem quoted by Owen Swift[1]

You always settled your arguments with a fight. You see it was the only expression you had.

William Luby[2]

In October 1827, a story by Sir Walter Scott entitled "The Two Drovers" appeared in the *London Weekly Review*.[3] The title refers to two men employed in driving cattle from a town on the Scottish border into England. One, Robin Oig M'Combich, is a Scottish highlander; the other, Harry Wakefield, is an Englishman. Scott describes Harry as "the model of Old England's merry yeoman" who, although possessing a "sanguine temper,"

> was not without his defects. He was irascible, sometimes to the verge of being quarrelsome; and perhaps not the less inclined to bring his disputes to a pugilistic decision, because he found few antagonists able to stand up to him in the boxing-ring. (pp. 8–9)

Robin and Harry are close friends; however, during their journey a complicated misunderstanding over the use of a particular field arises. Tensions mount, but Harry finds other accommodation for his cattle and retires to an alehouse where his wounded honor and conviction that Robin has cheated him is stoked by drinking with a few English guests. Robin soon arrives, intending to soothe his friend's temper. Harry takes Robin's offered hand; however, the reconciliation will not be as simple as the Scotsman thinks:

"Robin," he said, "thou hast used me ill enough this day; but if you mean, like a frank fellow, to shake hands, and take a tussle for love on the sod, why, I'll forgie thee, man, and we shall be better friends than ever." (p. 15)

Robin rejects the offer of a reconciliatory fight; Harry suggests that he is a coward. Robin denies this, his own honor now in question.

"But," continued Robin, "if I am to fight, I have no skill to fight like a jack-anapes, with hands and nails."

"How would you fight, then?" said his antagonist; "Though I am thinking it would be hard to bring you to the scratch anyhow."

"I would fight with proadswords, and sink point on the first plood drawn – like a gentleman." (p. 16)

Robin's offer brings laughter from the assembled Englishmen, and, after further talk and rising tempers, Harry beats Robin severely with his fists. The Scotsman retrieves his dirk, the customary knife carried by Scottish men, and returns to the pub. Here, ignoring Harry's comment that "not having the luck to be an Englishman, thou canst not fight more than a school girl," he stabs the Englishman to death.

Robin is brought before the assizes at Carlisle on a charge of murder. The judge's charge to the jury takes up a significant part of the story and highlights the causes that led to Harry Wakefield's death. The judge states:

Gentlemen of the Jury, it was with some impatience that I heard my learned brother, who opened the case for the crown, give an unfavourable turn to the prisoner's conduct on this occasion. He said the prisoner was afraid to encounter his antagonist in fair fight, or to submit to the laws of the ring; and that therefore, like a cowardly Italian, he had recourse to his fatal stiletto, to murder the man whom he dared not meet in manly encounter. (p. 23)

The judge rebuts these statements: Robin's crime lay not in cowardly murder but, in essence, in being educated in a different code of violence, a highland code of vengeance comparable to that of "North American Indians."

Those laws of the ring, as my brother terms them, were unknown to the race of warlike mountaineers; that decision of quarrels by no other weapons than those which nature has given every man must to them have seemed as vulgar and as preposterous as to the noblesse of France. (p. 25)

Despite an awareness of the different traditions of dispute settlement in England and Scotland and a tearful statement that Robin "ought personally to be the object rather of our pity than our abhorrence,"

> His crime is not the less that of murder, gentlemen, and, in your high and important office, it is your duty so to find. Englishmen have their angry passions as well as Scots; and should this man's action remain unpunished, you may unsheath, under various pretences, a thousand daggers betwixt the Land's-end and the Orkneys. (p. 25)

Robin is found guilty and sentenced to death.

Scott was experienced in the law, and he wrote "The Two Drovers" at a time when attitudes toward violence were already in flux. Even fistfighting, one of the most prominent and widespread forms of public violence in England, was becoming controversial and a target of the civilizing offensive. However, the history of fighting in this period is also marked by its cross-class appeal and association with national identity and masculinity. "Two Drovers" rests upon the tendency of English working-class men to assert themselves through a widely understood ritual in which fights took place according to rules and were bracketed by pre- and post-fight ceremonies of challenge and reconciliation. The ritual form did not necessarily determine the conduct of every altercation; however, it was a common convention that channeled aggression into a limited and predictable form. The centrality and visibility of fistfighting, its well-defined structure and its popularity as a sport make it a useful topic for exploring the tensions and agreements between civilized and customary mentalities of violence.

Sport fighting and streetfighting

In the late seventeenth century, prizefighting, one of a number of popular rough sports, emerged as the dominant form of sporting violence, largely replacing fencing or fighting with sticks. As early as the mid eighteenth century, a boxing champion had enumerated "Broughton's Rules." Although rudimentary (the guidelines on acceptable blows consists of two sentences), they were later elaborated upon, and by 1840, when Owen Swift published his *Handbook of Boxing*, the rules on fair fighting had developed significantly.[4] Such handbooks did more than define acceptable technique: they were also concerned with the ceremonial and business aspects of fighting. Although it is unlikely that these books were on the shelves of workers – Swift's title page notes that his book was "elegantly illustrated in steel and wood" and frequently addresses itself to "gentlemen" – they were important in shaping the way that sport fighting developed. The rules remained fundamentally stable and were dominant until replaced by the Queensberry Rules, which originated in 1867 and became ascendant in the 1880s and 1890s.[5] Pre-Queensberry, there was a striking parallel between sport fighting and working-class dispute settlement: the rituals of prizefighters in boxing rings were virtually identical to those of laborers in streets and fields.

Foreign visitors had long noted that Englishmen were exceptionally willing to fight one another, and, by the middle of the eighteenth century, boxing had even become associated with English national identity. "The dexterous use of the fist," wrote the editor of the *Connoisseur*, "is a truly British exercise" through which Englishmen showed their superiority over their Continental rivals:

> [T]he sturdy English have been as much renowned for their boxing as for their beef; both of which are by no means suited to the watery stomachs and weak sinews of their enemies the French. To this nutriment and this art is owing that long established maxim, that one Englishman can beat three Frenchmen.[6]

An eighteenth-century French visitor observed,

> When two men of the lower class have an argument which cannot be taken care of in a friendly manner, they go to a remote and fitting place where they undress completely from the waist up. All that watched them prepare for a fight follow them quickly, not to separate them but to see them hit each other ... to judge the hits and to prevent one of the fighters from acting against certain rules which seem to exist between them.[7]

Such traditions of working-class fighting may seem to have derived from aristocratic dueling, which, although falling out of favor, remained a feature of early nineteenth-century life.[8] However, it was sport fighting rather than dueling that shaped working-class dispute settlements. Fighting was an important part of working-class life and the ritual form was inculcated early; the "habit of fighting from boyhood" was deeply ingrained in English culture.[9] In 1803 William Fairbairn, living in North Shields, discovered at the age of 14 that

> among the "pit lads", boxing was considered a manly exercise and a favourite amusement, and I believed I counted up no less than seventeen battles which I reluctantly had to fight before I was able to attain a position calculated to ensure respect.[10]

The writer of one boxing manual argued that "it is curious and interesting to see the beneficent rules of boxing affecting all the contests even of children." He continued:

> In passing a field at Paddington, I one day observed a juvenile fight. It was a serious affair: for there they were – the four alone, and no spectator, but I myself, who came upon them accidentally. ... Each little antagonist had his little second, who, after a round, fell on one knee, and presented the other in the rectangular form adapted for a seat, to which, at the close of each round he perseveringly pulled his principal, who sat there, puffing and blowing as if he had been engaged in mortal combat.[11]

The value of fighting to grant status or respect to males continued into adulthood. Through watching boxers and streetfighters, males were educated from a young age in the proper ways to use their fists.[12]

Because ritualized fistfighting was highly visible and embodied the retributive, autonomous and disciplinary tendencies common to the "customary" mentality, it became an emblematic form of "working-class" violence. However, there was continuing enthusiasm for fistfighting among men of all classes. As a result, fighting as a sport survived (although in a "civilized" form), and the customary ritual form of working-class male dispute settlement lasted long into the nineteenth century.[13] This longevity highlights the fact that, although law is one arena in which the boundary between "legitimate" and "illegitimate" violence is drawn, violence's social meaning cannot be solely encompassed by the notion of "crime." Traditional prizefighting was one stage in regulating aggressive affects as well as a popular spectacle of combat.[14] While the middle-classes feared the lack of civilization among the lower classes, sport fighting remained part of a shared culture. Prizefighters themselves were working class, but the model of a "fair fight" was understood not only by the frequently illiterate defendants and witnesses who left their depositions in court marked with an "X" rather than a signature but also by the police and court officials. Fighting to settle a dispute or to prove one's manliness was nearly always a public act and was therefore open to the scrutiny and interpretation of the combatants' peers. For instance, four witnesses to a prizefight in 1851, a laborer, a farmer, a surgeon and a watchmaker, all described the fight as "fair."[15] Fighting schools were widespread in England, and published fighting manuals were popular.[16] It was widely believed that fighting developed personal vigor and contributed to the health and vitality of the nation, and the respectable classes helped make up the crowds that flocked to prizefights.

Nonetheless, sport fighting came under increased scrutiny and condemnation due to the increasing social and cultural distance between the classes. As Elias notes, "the boxing match … represents a strongly tempered form of the impulses of aggressiveness and cruelty" compared to the violent sports of earlier times.[17] However, the "boxing match" was itself an evolving concept: as the cultural legitimacy of violence is eroded and narrowed,

> the greater becomes the sensitivity to shades and nuances of conduct, the more finely attuned people grow to minute gestures and forms, and the more complex becomes their experience of themselves and their world at levels which were previously hidden from consciousness through the veil of strong affects.[18]

Increased awareness of the "nuances" of violence contributed to the continuing refinement of sport fighting. The civilizing of boxing was concurrent with the reorganization of sports and their demarcation from everyday life: other sports – from football to track-and-field – took on their modern forms, replacing the village-oriented games that had previously dominated. The resulting form of modern boxing, though related to its traditional precursor, had different rules, equipment and rituals. Because it was legal, it could also be mass-marketed in ways that customary prizefighting could not. This shift affected more than sports: without a legitimate sporting form to maintain it, the streetfighting ritual also declined. As a result, the centrality of public fighting to working-class masculinity changed. As the syntax of ritual fighting lost its resonance, its performative and expressive functions withered, and the link between sport and streetfighting was severed. Although fistfighting has not disappeared from English culture (either in the arena or the street) the forms and understandings that structure it have changed dramatically, raising questions about class, violence, custom and the civilizing process.

Most of the cases in this chapter refer to incidents in which one of the combatants died during a fight or soon after participating in one. The surviving fighter was then usually brought before the court on a homicide charge. The vast majority of fights did not end in a fatality and are likely never to have come to the attention of the police or the courts. As a result, fatal fights, which attracted more detailed investigation, are very valuable for the historian and some well-documented cases will be referred to in different contexts. Furthermore, although the link between lesser forms of violence and homicide is problematic, there is no reason to believe that fatal brawls generally differed from non-fatal ones either in terms of motivation or form. Homicides, in a sense, have been described as "casualties" of lesser forms of violence that are often acceptable to society in general.[19] Finally, participants in the cases considered in this chapter were overwhelmingly working class and male. This is not to say that women did not use violence: working-class women were generally willing and able to use violent means to settle differences or grievances.[20] Courts did not find this particularly shocking, despite the Victorian idealization of female meekness, and the tradition of women challenging each other to fight in order to settle disputes reached back at least to the eighteenth century.[21] However, that tradition was separate from the one that shaped masculine ritual fighting.

Locations and motives

The drop in European violent crime over the past five centuries has been associated with a civilizing process that established the courts rather than taverns and street corners as arenas for dispute settlement.[22] However, this process was not completed by the early nineteenth century. Pubs were central institutions of working-class life and were a popular venue for settling scores. There was a pattern to the insults, quarrels and challenges that led to fights, including the implicit expectation of having to "step outside." With some exceptions, while the initial escalation occurred inside pubs, ritual fighting usually commenced outdoors.[23] Pubs were also a source of alcohol, a frequent concomitant to violence, ritual or otherwise.[24] Although a participant in one brawl suggested postponing it so that he and his adversary would both be "solid and sober together," his opponent was determined to continue because he was "in the humour."[25] A published defense of pugilism contended that "men ought not to be encouraged to fight while their blood is up; because when their blood is up their reason is down, and that state of irritation mostly happens when they are in drink. ... It is, therefore, the office of true humanity to dissuade men from fighting when their blood is up, and to persuade them to wait until the next day, or some after period, when it has become cool."[26]

Authorities, however, were convinced that pubs were cradles of vice and that drunkenness was a major cause of violence. A correspondent to the Secretary of State, referring to an assault on a Leamington constable, complained that "these assaults are continuously taking place of a *Sunday* in public houses."[27] In 1868, the Chief Constable of Leeds wrote, "I am sure that so long as the working classes imbibe the decoctions of bar sellers there will not only be drunkenness and poverty but crimes of open violence among us."[28] Such complaints were prominent in a government report in 1875, in which violence – particularly that of a worryingly "brutal" nature – was blamed on increased leisure and higher wages.[29] There was, at the same time, a gradual lessening of official tolerance of the drink defense.[30] While the actual relationship between alcohol and violence is difficult to measure, "drunken brawls" were culturally significant. However, alcohol did not accompany all acts of violence and not all drinking occasions turned violent. Furthermore, it is more likely that the cultural expectations of what drinking entails (e.g., what one may "legitimately" do in a pub) is more important than simply the presence or absence of alcohol.[31] Even when drunk, workingmen tended to observe the constraints of the fighting ritual. Like pubs, rural fairs, common in the nineteenth century, were also typical locations for ritual fighting; as in other countries, the presence of relative strangers combined with drunkenness contributed to quarrels and disputes.[32] Many fighters were more interested in displaying their prowess than in settling an actual quarrel: fighting was a popular entertainment at fairs and always drew enthusiastic crowds. There were often multiple fights going on throughout the day, some involving the same fighters.[33]

On-the-job interpersonal violence was limited by the greater disciplinary constraints of workplaces. Nevertheless, workers did sometimes fight at work. John Weeks, a plasterer at Wroth, Sussex, died after a long fight with Frederick Andrews, a carpenter, at a site where several workers were building a new house. Although previously "on good terms," a dispute about work duties led them to fight for approximately an hour and a half.[34] A dispute between two cherry pickers at Beaconsfield, Buckinghamshire, led to a gradual escalation of violence and a ritual fight.[35] Seamen sometimes fought aboard their ships.[36] If the workplace itself was not the location of a fight, it could easily be the source of disputes or rivalries that led to fighting. One such instance in 1843 led to the death of a 21-year-old laborer, George Grey. Grey's opponent, Henry Ball, deposed that Grey had been taunting him continuously: "when I was in my work, he was always at me to fight. He would never leave me alone."[37] In Cambridgeshire in 1833 a crowd followed two men from their workplace to a patch of land where they commenced a fight that was the result of an ongoing quarrel.[38]

Although the specific motives of particular fights are often difficult to recover and lost in vague descriptions of "a quarrel" at a pub, there were two dominant motivations for ritual fighting: dispute settlement or "amicable contests." Sometimes these motives were mixed. Violence serves expressive as well as instrumental purposes: it might allow someone to take something from another or to win a contest, but it also symbolically articulates a variety of social meanings.[39] It also served a variety of strategic purposes, allowing one to "impose one's beliefs or perceptions on another, to claim authority, power or rights that would not otherwise be accorded one."[40] Although the point being made by these fighters may seem trivial – or the "power" or "authority" inconsequential – a disagreement over a perceived slight or an accusation of cheating in a card game was important enough to compel them to face serious (sometimes fatal) injury through ritual fighting.

Fights might be the final culmination of a long history of animosity. In an Essex public house in 1825, Benjamin Goodday and John Payne were drinking separately. Goodday twice offered to fight Payne, but Payne refused, saying that he had previously had "nine months of it [i.e., he had been incarcerated] for a frolic of this kind and I'll have no more of it." Half an hour later Payne changed his mind and said to his challenger, "You have been very aggravating to me for a long time, now we will have a turn if you like."[41] There is also evidence of a long-term quarrel that led to the death of John Love in Cambridgeshire in 1833.[42] A fighting case tried at the Central Criminal Court "arose out of a previous quarrel between the prosecutor and a man named Pearce who has never been apprehended."[43] Thomas Own fought John Walding at Croxley Green Fair in Hertfordshire due to a "quarrel they had had in the winter."[44] Another fatal brawl, between two men at a public house in Woolwich, began when John Rice questioned Thomas Stevens about statements Stevens had made a week before. According to one witness,

> Rice said to Stevens who was acting as a waiter, "I understand that last Saturday night you degraded my character," and Stevens said he would be damned if he had ever said a word against his character, and other words passed between them, and Rice said to Stevens he (Rice) was a man, and Stevens said the same to Rice, and Rice struck Stevens with his fist on the mouth which knocked Stevens down on his breech.[45]

Sometimes, the dispute was more sudden, as when two men attacked a pair of constables who intervened in a dispute at an inn over the measure of a quart of beer.[46] In Sudbury in 1867, a police constable on his rounds was informed that trouble was brewing at a nearby beer shop. The proprietor informed him that John Burbridge had been "trying to kick up a row" and asked the officer to help him clear the house. After assisting the owner, the constable resumed his rounds. Later, at the Rose Inn, he came upon Burbridge, who said he had not been the one to raise the earlier dispute: "Those buggers mean getting on to me tonight," he said, referring to the brothers William and "Topper" Martin who had harassed him. This dispute led to a fight later in the evening, long after Burbridge had ignored the officer's advice to go home.[47] Gambling and contests could easily provoke disputes over winning and losing, rules and honesty. On 12 May 1834, Robert Waller died after a fight with William Seaman. Seaman was "master of the beer shop," and several men appear to have been playing a game of "three corner pins." They also appear to have engaged in some sort of test of strength or agility: "they did go the slap of the face, but I do not know which was the best man." It is perhaps unsurprising that a game involving "the slap of the face" might lead to tension – particularly among men who were drinking – and in the subsequent dispute Seaman attacked Waller, beating him severely.[48] Drunken disputes over a card game in Sussex in 1830 and another over pitching pennies at a chalk line on the bar top in Essex in 1831 led to fatal brawls.[49] Before fighting in 1871, James Sellen and Peter Smith were in a dispute regarding, in part, a skittle game. "The prisoner and Smith," deposed an under-bailiff who was present in the taproom of the public house, "were talking together and chaffing each other about skittle playing."[50]

Whatever the long or short-term causes of grudge fights, typically they began with an exchange of insults or challenges that often questioned the character of the other man.[51] "Damn you," said John Payne to Benjamin Goodday, "if you aggravate me too much I will damnably shake you." Goodday's reply, "I don't know that you can," was a typical sort of degrading response.[52] Outside the Queen's Head Inn in Horsham, Sussex, the local headborough had stopped a fight and convinced the two men to shake hands. One of the men's seconds, Henry Hewitt, told the other combatant he was "a bloody coward" for ending the fight. A bystander said to Hewitt, "Who do you call a bloody coward, and do you want anything?" and challenged him to fight if he was "a man."[53] On board the docked ship *Violet*, Joseph Wright, a stoker, called fellow seaman Richard Sharpe "a damned drunken swab." Sharpe responded "Don't call me that again or I will strike you," to which Wright replied "That would take a man, not a thing like you."[54] In a pub in Great Yarmouth in 1870, a fight began after John Godfrey was "aggravating" William Neave by calling him "lazy" and "lousy."[55] The escalation from verbal to physical confrontation often involved an explicit challenge, such as "I will fight you" accompanied by an oath or insult.[56] At times, however, words were not necessary: a shove could also lead to fighting, as it did at a fair in Essex in 1825, where William Speller pushed Richard Webb while they were both watching another fight.[57] The removal of clothing, either stripping to the waist or taking off a work smock, could also suffice.[58] "Stripping" was a challenge that would convince even a reluctant combatant to participate. For example, in 1848 Samuel Porter verbally challenged William Pinnion – and had even knocked him down – without successfully goading him into a fight. However, when Porter "stripped himself" for fighting, Pinnion relented, saying, "Then I suppose I must fight."[59]

There was another traditional motivation for working-class fighting – the "amicable contest," unmotivated by animosity or dispute.[60] Such amicable contests were more informal versions of prizefighting and fully accepted in working-class culture. Although such fights were often "instrumental" or goal-oriented (e.g., determining who would buy whom a beer or some similar prize), they were about more than immediate rewards and were related to gaining or maintaining masculine honor. Indeed, there was often a remarkable amount of sociability between the participants before (and sometimes after) fights, and friendly fighting was a common occurrence. A petition for mercy sent to the Secretary of State in March 1836 described an amicable contest that ended fatally. A letter on behalf of the victor stated that "a number of agricultural laborers had been drinking in a neighbouring parish, and (as is too often the case) two men, John Langley and William Thorp, both intoxicated, agreed to fight two rounds without any quarrel whatever." Thorp died after only a few blows, and Langley was subsequently sentenced to six months' imprisonment for manslaughter. The letter, in addition to other arguments, maintains that Langley should have his sentence mitigated since "the parties were old friends" and there was an absence of malice.[61] Fighting could be seen as a normal, even playful part of young men's lives, as when a carpenter noticed two young men fighting at his work site: "they were scuffling with one another and I thought at play."[62] Fights often arose out of situations in which men had been drinking and talking together, and some resumed their sociability after fighting, ale being a traditional component in "rituals of reconciliation" implying friendship.[63] Amicable contests were understood, even accepted, by the courts. The legal writer J. F. Stephen noted that in cases where two people fought upon equal terms, they gave provocation to each other, thereby offering an argument for mitigation of their sentences.[64] Guides to the law noted the acceptability of violence in cases of amicable contest.[65]

Sometimes, motives are difficult to reconstruct. After an evening of dancing at a fair held on Box Hill in Surrey, Francis Taylor searched for the man whom he claimed had challenged him to fight; the man had shoved something "glistening" into the face of at least one other person and brandished a knife saying "damn your eyes, draw your knives that's got any."[66] The evening ended in a fatal stabbing.[67] Seemingly innocuous roughhousing could turn more serious if it exceeded someone's tolerance. Six workers were employed in picking cherries at an orchard in Buckinghamshire in July 1864. One of the farm's plowmen described the scene:

> Dale and Price and the other men were having some beer together. Several of the men including Dale and Price were smearing each other's faces with cherries. Dale ran after Price and overtook him and smeared his face with cherries. Then they began grumbling. Dale went to hit Price with his hand and knocked him down. Price then got up ran his head between Dale's legs and tried to throw him up. Dale said to Price "What do you mean [by] that you B——?"[68]

The fight ended with Dale's death from a blow from a "cherry cudgel." The two were previously on good terms: they had attended a "cherry feast" together on the night before, and Price expressed great remorse for Dale's death. Men who fought – concerned with their own position in the social hierarchy of their peers

– were doing something they believed legitimate and justified. In 1843 in Kent, a group of men "belonging to the Coast Guard" went to two public houses in Folkestone. At the second pub, one of them, George Watts, picked up a musket belonging to his companion, George Spencer, and fired it out of the window.

> Spencer found fault with Watts for firing the musket and said he had a good mind to strike him. Watts afterwards said to Spencer that he would fight him for a pot [of beer] if he liked, and Watts took off his coat and began to fight with Spencer in the room.

Although ejected from the pub, Watts continued his provoking behavior and "made game of those within," until someone "then struck him in the face through the window, which was open." After this point, they took their dispute outside and gathered in a nearby field to fight. Whether or not the pot of beer was still on offer is unclear.[69]

The fighting ritual

Once fights had begun, they tended to follow a common pattern. One representative example, in which John King died after fighting with a man referred to as Griffiths or "Griffin," occurred in Hertfordshire at a summer fair in 1830.[70] James Hosler, a laborer, stated the following:

> Leverstock Green fair was on Monday last the 31st of May. I was there. I came about seven o'clock in the evening. I saw the deceased there. He was in the Leather Bottle public house drinking. I saw a man of the name of Griffin there too. Between eight and nine o'clock there was a dispute about a whip which had been run for. A crowd of people were assembled and among them the deceased and Griffin. In all there were about twenty or thirty. It was getting dusk.

Another deposition from William Wright, a farmer, clarified the origin of the fight:

> I saw the deceased and Griffiths, who is my ploughman, there. There was a dispute about a whip which had been run for, which a man of the name of Kitchener had won, and which Griffiths said he should not have as he had not won it fairly, and Griffiths and John Jennings took it away from him. The deceased then interfered and struck Griffiths. Griffiths did not strike deceased again but went away.

James Hosler's deposition continued:

> The deceased complained of some person having struck him on the head and said he should like to know who it was. They fixed upon Griffin as the

man who had struck the deceased, and he and Griffin then stripped and began fighting. They were neither of them quite sober. A ring was formed. Each put himself in a fighting attitude. I don't know which struck the first blow. In the first round, the deceased knocked Griffin down. William Deacon seconded the deceased, and a man whose name I think was Jennings seconded Griffin. Mr. W[illia]m White and W[illia]m Jennings kept time. They fought for an hour and ten minutes.

Another witness, William Burr, had urged that the men be separated. White described the exchange:

I heard W[illia]m Burr say it was a shame they should be allowed to fight, but I said "They've fallen out, let them fight." There was nothing unfair. In the last but three [rounds] Griffiths's second wished the deceased to give out. Deceased said "No, I'll either beat him or else he shall kill me."

King was approaching the latter result as James Hosler witnessed the conclusion of the fight.

At the end of which time Griffin hit the deceased on the left side of his neck, upon which he immediately fell down senseless. We removed him into a stable belonging to the Leather Bottle. I remained with him until he died. He was insensible the whole time and speechless. He died at six o'clock yesterday morning. As soon as the deceased was hurt we sent for Mr. Berlin, a surgeon who did not attend, and then we sent for Mr. Cherrington who attended immediately. But this was about four hours after the deceased was knocked down.

When the case came to trial, Griffiths was convicted of manslaughter and sentenced to one calendar month in jail without hard labor.[71] Although every fight had its own particularities, the case of *R.* v. *Griffiths* presents the typical pattern of the ritual fight.

For instance, before fighting workers typically "stripped" themselves, removing shirts or work clothing such as "smocks."[72] Stripping to the waist was the most common prelude to fighting and would clearly serve several practical purposes: freeing the fighters from restrictive clothing and ensuring that clothes did not become damaged or bloodied. As noted above, it could also serve as a challenge to fight. At other times, stripping came after a challenge had been issued and accepted. After one such challenge, "They then went outside, stripped off their shirts and started fighting."[73] Recounting a fight in Sussex, one witness said, "Woodman stripped but Mitchell pulled off only a round frock," and another emphasized that "Woodman was stripped but Mitchell was not." Similarly, from the same case, "The deceased had his frock off but the two Hewitts had their clothes on."[74] William Dale was "taking his slop and cap off" in preparation for fighting Thomas Price when he was fatally struck in the head by a "cherry cudgel" that Price threw at him.[75] Testimony regarding stripping and verbal challenges informed the authorities about who started a fight, helped establish its motives and suggested relevant provocations.

Witnesses also commented on the relative fighting ability and size of combatants, suggesting that a fight could not be entirely "fair" if the men were poorly matched. A witness in one case deposed that the deceased fighter in a Hertfordshire case was "a bigger man" than his victorious opponent.[76] The criteria for determining how much of a difference was enough to make a fight "unfair" are uncertain, and some difference in size and ability was frequently unavoidable. Discussion of the relative ability of fighters was accompanied by comments as to who had the "best" of the fight. A witness in the Griffiths case noted, "Griffin is a much more powerful man than the deceased"; however, this was perhaps mitigated by other witnesses' comments that he had been "more knocked about at the end of the fight than the deceased" and that "the deceased had the best of the fight during the first two rounds."[77] "I believe it was a very fair fight," one witness in another case deposed, "they were pretty equally matched but I think Seager was rather the best man."[78] Witnesses to longer fights frequently referred to both fighters doing well at some point. Whether or not that was an effort to make the fight look fairer is impossible to know, but it is clear that the issue of "unfair advantage" was of significance to the court and witnesses.

Prizefights and streetfights both took place within "rings." In 1840, Swift's *Handbook of Boxing* described a standard ring for a formal prizefight, stating

> that the ring shall be made on turf, and shall be four-and-twenty feet square formed of eight stakes and ropes, the latter extending in double lines, the upper-most line being four feet from the ground, the lower two feet from the ground. That in the centre of the ring a mark be formed, to be termed "a scratch"; and that at two opposite corners, as may be selected, spaces be enclosed by other marks sufficiently large for the reception of the seconds and the bottle-holders, to be entitled "*the corners.*"[79]

A model prizefighting ring was not always constructed, and a witness to a fight in 1844 deposed that "a ring was formed by persons standing round, not with ropes or stakes."[80] Whatever the particular form, rings were a clearly demarcated space. The "scratch" and the "corners" were important places in the ring and were used in everyday fighting rituals where "persons standing round" typically formed the space for fighting. A crowd followed two fighters from their place of work and formed a ring, later re-forming it nearby when a constable intervened.[81] At a fair in 1830 "a ring was formed on the green" for the fight between John Walding and Thomas Owen.[82] The ring sometimes required supervision. One witness to a fight at a fair commented, "I was keeping the ring."[83] Rings were not always orderly: "In the last round but one the deceased complained that the people round crowded upon him and prevented his falling."[84] A poorly kept ring posed potential problems for fighters since a fall marked the end of a round, and complaints were voiced even at large-scale formalized prizefights: "the ring was badly kept as the people pressed close upon them."[85]

The men who assisted prizefighters, the "seconds," were crucial figures. Although seconds had more active and formal roles in sport fights, any ritual fight included the presence of one or two seconds per fighter.[86] In formal prize-fighting, seconds were the foundation of the officiating hierarchy, and they performed some of the essential ceremonial acts that preceded the commencement of fighting:

> The first duty of seconds is to choose and agree upon the appointment of two umpires and the referee; then to tie to colours of both men to the centre stake; then to toss for shade of the sun.... These matters arranged, the seconds, that is the active second and "the bottle holder," take their men to "the scratch," and then retire into their separate corners.[87]

At times, seconds, like the fighters themselves, also shook hands before the fight.[88] Streetfights did not feature the elaborate opening rituals sketched by Swift in his description of prizefighting, and there also tended to be only one second per fighter. Streetfights at pubs did not have umpires and referees either; however, some fights were officiated in equivalent ways. When the initial ceremonies had concluded, the fight began, at which point the "duty of the second becomes more responsible and onerous":

> The "second" then is competent to instruct his man as to his mode of fighting; to point out to him *"opportunities"* and *"openings,"* when he should and when he should not "make play"; when it is necessary that he should be on his *guard*, and *awake* to the maneuvers of his adversary; when he should *stop*, and when he should *hit*, when he should struggle for the fall, or when he should *slip down* to avoid punishment.[89]

The "active second" was to encourage his fighter and give advice as to tactics and opportunities. This role translated to everyday settings, as is clear from the Griffiths case, in which "the seconds encouraged them throughout the fight."[90] Although essential, his participation was also limited. A second had to actively support his man but not confuse or demoralize the opponent. "Broughton's Rules" included the admonition that "no second is to be allowed to ask his man's adversary any questions, or advise him to give out."[91] This rule remained in force, and a century later Swift was adamant that "the seconds and bottle holders shall not interfere with, advise or direct the adversary of their principal, and shall refrain from all offensive or irritating expressions."[92] This advice was, clearly, not always heeded, and Swift was highly critical of what he called the "system of *chaff*" in which seconds systematically tried to demoralize, denigrate and distract their fighter's opponent.[93] In streetfights, the active support offered by seconds varied, which is unsurprising considering the haphazard way in which seconds were chosen. In some cases, brothers or close friends seconded each other; in others, this role was taken by men who happened to be standing around.

One of the seconds' most significant practical tasks was assisting fighters when they fell. "When the man falls," Swift advised, "it is the duty of the seconds to advance from their *corners* and pick him up, carry him to their corner, place him on the bottle holder's knee, and to comfort and relieve him to the best of their judgement."[94] Seconds played a similar role in streetfights.[95] A fall marked the end of a round: only later, under the Queensberry rules, were rounds timed and of uniform duration. The seconds had a limited amount of time to revive and encourage their fighters to resume fighting. Thirty seconds after a fall, "time" was called; if a fighter was unable to stand without assistance at the scratch within eight seconds from time being called, he lost the fight.[96] Correct timekeeping was considered important: a witness to one prizefight noted, "there was no complaint about the time being kept incorrectly."[97] In streetfights, time was also kept assiduously. Some fights had designated time-keepers, but in other cases seconds,[98] bystanders[99] or the fighters themselves[100] kept time. Besides rest, a variety of means were used to revive fighters. Swift advised, "If the man feels sick, the second, if he understands his business, will invariably give him a little drop of brandy, or brandy and water; on no account should water be drank *alone*."[101] Such encouragement was also common in streetfights.[102] At the end of a fight, one fighter was frequently unconscious, and seconds led the effort at reviving and dressing him and seeking medical assistance. When one prizefighter was knocked unconscious, "his seconds gave him some brandy."[103] After his defeat, one fighter was unable to walk and his second and others carried him to an "arbor" and sent for a surgeon.[104]

The distinction between the "active second" and the "bottle holder" was elided or erased altogether in streetfights; nevertheless, seconds were clearly present, and courts were keen to identify them: "Each of them had a second. Thomas Weeks, the brother of the deceased, was his second and a man named Charles Luckins was the second of Andrews."[105] Seconds had a motive to play down their roles, since they could be prosecuted also. "I am not sure whether I had him on my knee more than once or twice," testified one, "I assisted him in the course of the fight, but I don't consider that I acted as second."[106] In *R.* v. *Hewitt* a witness named Smithers claimed that he saw "none acting as seconds." Another witness to the same fight avoided the word "second" but said he did see men keeping each fighter "on his knee": one of them was Smithers, who was clearly reluctant to admit his participation.[107] Courts sometimes gave seconds sentences identical to those of surviving fighters: Thomas Andrews received one day in the house of correction for manslaughter resulting from a fight, and his second, having been charged with the same crime, received the same. The other second had not joined in until the fight was already underway and was found not guilty.[108] In another case, a fatal prizefight led to a month's imprisonment for the surviving fighter and all three of the known seconds.[109] At other times, seconds received lower sentences. In 1830 one second received the same sentence as the victor – one month's imprisonment – while the other, who had been seconding the deceased fighter, was fined a shilling and released.[110]

One of the features that made the rules of prizefighting so easily transferable to everyday life was their decisive result. Winning on "points" or by "decision" is a feature only of post-Queensberry boxing.[111] As Swift noted, "a fight is only ended by one party 'giving in' himself, or by his seconds giving in for him; by his being knocked out of time, or by a foul blow being struck."[112] Being "knocked out of time" referred to a fighter not being able to be at the scratch within the time limit. As one fight ended, "Grey fell from a blow and was unable to come again to the scratch when time was called."[113] In general, there was great reluctance to forfeit a fight. Fighters would often reach the point of near-unconsciousness or serious injury before admitting defeat, one of the things that so disturbed civilized critics of traditional fighting. Even fighters who were clearly getting the worst of a fight were often loath to give up.[114] Courts frequently queried witnesses on whether or not both parties in a fight were willing to continue and if the men had been given the chance to yield. Witnesses often gave statements that the fighters were both "equally willing" to fight, that they "did not hear either of them express a wish to give up" or that "each appeared equally anxious to fight."[115]

Fights sometimes stopped for reasons other than a fighter's admission of defeat or inability to continue. In rare instances, seconds intervened if it became clear that one man was not going to win or was seriously injured. Swift asserted that seconds had the right, if not an obligation, to intervene to end a fight if there were good cause:

> The discretion as to giving or prolonging a fight, which is wisely given the seconds, is perhaps one of the most salutary of all the regulations of the prize ring, because, when a second sees that his man is fairly beaten, or that he does not stand a chance of winning, he can very properly take him away, and "give in" for him. This rule is a kind of protection to the second; for his own discretion, wisely exercised, often saves the life of his man, and prevent[s] the possibility of himself being tried for manslaughter.[116]

Such intervention appears to have been rarely exercised, particularly in street-fights, since there was a great reluctance to end a fight before a decisive conclusion. The failure of seconds to stop a prizefight in 1830 led to protesting letters to the government. One writer noted "the outrage which led to the death of Mackay [has] called forth a general expression of disgust at the conduct of the seconds and backers of the combatants for permitting the deceased to continue fighting after every chance of success was extinct, and when he had lost all power to defend himself."[117] It is unclear how general this disgust was; however, the principles of "fair play" prohibited attacking those who were defenseless. Fights occasionally ended upon such a "foul blow" being struck. However, the structure of customary fighting combined with a hesitation to interfere meant that fights were frequently very lengthy. Appended to Swift's

Handbook is a chronology of prizefights from 1740 to 1840. There were fights of all durations, but it was not uncommon for fights to last more than one or two hours.[118] This was also common outside the prize ring. "I looked on for about half an hour," recalled a witness to a work-site brawl in 1863, "during which time they tried to hit each other but were too weak to do so." Other testimony suggests that the men fought for a total of an hour and a half.[119] The Griffiths fight detailed at the beginning of this section lasted over an hour. Of course, many fights were much shorter, possibly as short as a few blows.[120]

Foul blows, brutal assaults and violence

In their quotidian brawls, workers emulated the ceremonies and rules of the professional prizefight; thus, sport rituals shaped streetfights. Rings were no less significant for their informal transience. A scratch was marked and time was kept. Seconding was a central part of the ritual fight. A "fair" fight was furthermore distinguished by the absence of "foul blows," especially in regard to sport fighting since the rules were written down and published. "Broughton's Rules" had declared that "no person is to hit his adversary when he is down or seize him by the ham, the breeches, or any part below the waist," and that a man on his knees was to be considered "down."[121] About a century later, Owen Swift describes foul blows at several points in his *Handbook*, and the section marked "Foul Play" states the following:

> It is foul to lay hold of the waistband of your antagonist, or to strike him or to take hold of him anywhere below the waistband, or to strike him when down on both knees, or one knee and both hands, or when sitting on his second's knee; or, as a matter of course, when lying on the ground, even though both be down.[122]

Furthermore, Swift specifically identifies head-butting, gouging, "tearing the flesh," biting, kicking and deliberately falling on a man knees-first as "foul."[123] In streetfights, witnesses frequently asserted the absence of "foul blows." In that context, definitions are murkier; however, the term seems to have been understood generally.

The dominant method of attack was striking an opponent with fists. A fair blow was above the waist, with most strikes landing on an opponent's torso or head. Other techniques were also considered fair. "If you get into close quarters," Swift advises, "and your adversary holds you round the neck with his left hand, and hits you with this right hand, the practice has always been to seize him in the same way, and hit with the loose hand." This move, referred to as getting someone "in Chancery," was common. Takedowns and wrestling tactics were also common in streetfighting: as one witness deposed, "In the third round, deceased threw Owen down by throwing his arms round him and they both fell together."[124] In a fight in 1848, "Both parties fell together after every round except one, when Porter knocked Pinnion backward."[125] Taking an opponent down in a fall was permissible, a move referred to as "cross-buttocking."[126] A witness to another fight testified that he "saw no blows struck, only wrestling together and they fell together on the ground."[127] In falling, the goal was often to use the force of the fall to injure one's opponent, particularly if a fighter could manage to land on top. Testimony of witnesses often dwelt on whether or not there were falls, who landed "undermost" and the hardness of the ground on which they fell. Fighters who wrestled and "rolled about" were not considered to be acting unfairly.[128] Kicking, scratching, biting, attacking a man when he was down, multiple attackers fighting a single opponent and the use of weapons, however, were clearly unacceptable. Kicking was associated in particular with northern men and their presumed predilection for "clogging." For the most part, this problem was seen as most troublesome when husbands kicked their wives, but northern kicking had great resonance with reference to other forms of "cowardly" attack.[129] A lack of boxing knowledge was sometimes seen as an ingredient in northern brutality.[130] Regional variations were clearly important; however, even in "brutal" Lancashire, there is evidence of the ritualized fistfight, though it faced competition from other forms of confrontation.[131] A "fair fight," then, featured two men, evenly matched, using a clearly delimited variety of fighting techniques. Multiple attackers were never a part of a formal, ritualized streetfight. Of course, some brawls involved many sorts of elements seen as unfair or brutal. For example, an attack by several men upon a police constable and other men after an evening's drinking was described by a witness as "cowardly," since the men had attacked individuals as a group and had kicked and used weapons during the fight.[132]

There are signs of subtle shifts in the nature of fighting, and cases from the 1860s and early 1870s, along with other evidence, suggest a weakening in the old ritual form. Fights became less predictable and formalized. Witnesses begin to describe "violent" blows and more unrestrained combats without strict adherence to a clear set of rules and there was increasing concern about "brutal assaults." While it is difficult to reach firm conclusions, I suggest that the decline in traditional prizefighting as a sport had an impact on streetfighting. Police action was successful in eventually driving prizefighting bouts underground, but they were unable to eradicate it entirely. Nevertheless, police pressure made it more difficult for fights to be arranged, and changing social fashions and market forces seem to have put the customary prizefight under considerable pressure by the 1860s.[133] An incident in Naseby, Northamptonshire in 1865 suggests the ways that custom was weakening, particularly when compared to the 1830 Griffiths case described earlier. On the evening of 13 September, William Manning, an engine driver, went to the Royal Oak public house.[134] While there, he saw a ritual fistfight between James Jarman and John Vialls. However, "Jarman struck Vialls a foul blow when he was down." As a result, another bystander, William Burt, intervened and "immediately went and struck Jarman." After Burt struck Jarman, William Cross "struck Burt over the face."

Then they two, William Cross and Burt had a rough round together and both fell. Then Burt got up and Jarman and Burt had a round together. They rolled about and by some means got down the steps into the farmyard. Burt got up from the ground. He immediately got up on the Muck Hill and challenged to fight Jarman again.

At this point, the situation, though fluid, was still being largely conducted according to traditional rules. Challenges were being issued, and the fighting was still seen in the context of rounds. However, events began to escalate beyond the familiar pattern of a ritual fight, at which point William Tye, a police officer, arrived. As William Manning described it,

And directly after [Tye's arrival] Burt and William Cross and Vialls and Frederick Cross [the son of William Cross] all began to fight and scuffle together up and down together in such a way as I never saw before. I said I could not stand that and I came into the house and left the yard.

Inspector Tye described what followed:

Vialls and Cross were apparently fighting against Burt, who was at that moment pushing to prevent himself falling down the steps. William Cross was then 4 or 5 yards away; he was urging his son on, saying, "Go into him." I did not know his son at that time, but I could tell whom he spoke to from the effects produced. The young man appeared more eager. I pulled Vialls away and at [the] same time told young Cross to be quiet, no more fighting. That stopped the fighting for a second or two. Then Old Cross came running up flourishing his arms and saying, "Go at him." I took hold of him and put him down on the muck hill. I then turned to Vialls and young Cross to separate them, they two had then got fighting together again, and Burt then slipped by me and kicked Old William Cross whilst he was lying on the muck hill, on the thigh half way up from the knee. That was the fist kick I saw.

Burt's kick appears to have inspired further attacks, and matters deteriorated once the boundary of fairness had been breached:

I then turned to prevent Burt kicking Old Cross, Burt again passed, and the three began fighting again, my back being turned at that time. Old Cross said, "Boy, he has kicked me, go into him." I then turned my head and saw Burt falling down, a sort of sliding fall down to the side of the wall, falling with his head downhill. He rose himself on his right elbow, 12 or 13 inches high, Young Cross came up to him and kicked him apparently on the left side and Vialls standing on the left side gave him a kick about the knee. Burt fell back on his back and did not stir again after giving two deep sighs.

Burt was plied with brandy but could not be revived. Vialls, Cross and his son were taken into custody. Many of the witnesses described the fighting that ensued after Burt's intervention as "violent": Manning, for example, stated that "Burt appeared to me to be more eager and violent than any of them," and Jacob Burdett described Frederick Cross's kick against Burt as "apparently a violent one." Tye stated, "The kicks given by Burt to W. Cross and Vialls to the deceased appeared to be less violent than that given by F. Cross to the deceased which was a violent one." The word "violent" was never used in descriptions of ritual fights, no matter how long or hard the men fought, so long as none of the blows were seen as unfair.

Fully ritual fights are not visible in late 1860s and early 1870s assize depositions from the Southeastern Circuit, and there appears to be more volatility surrounding disputes, which sometimes led to the use of knives. In 1867, two men involved in a dispute began "rushing" at each other without any preliminary ceremonies and without seconds; the result was a stabbing death after a series of "scuffles."[135] In Leicestershire, William Gilley came upon William Jones, a framework knitter, walking with a female companion with whom he was "keeping company." Intoxicated, Gilley began taunting them and using "foul language," whereupon Jones struck Gilley with his fist. Gilley swore, stabbed Jones in the stomach and said, "I will learn you how to strike me."[136] In Great Yarmouth, Norfolk in 1870, John Godfrey and William Neave came to blows after Godfrey had "aggravated" Neave by insulting him. Without observing customary preliminaries or stepping out of the pub, they commenced shoving, wrestling and striking one another. Neave hit Godfrey while he was on the ground and a bystander struck Neave and called him a "coward."[137] In the following year, James Sellen stabbed Peter Smith, a hop-picker, in Turnham, Kent. They had been arguing throughout the evening, and after leaving the pub, Smith slapped Sellen provocatively. Charles Gulvin, an under-bailiff, deposed:

> It was a slap of the face, not particularly hard. Smith then told [Sellen] that he could return it if he liked. [Sellen] said that he was not fit for fighting tonight.

They appeared to reconcile and shook hands. Sellen turned to head home, but then he stopped and issued a challenge. Smith approached and was stabbed by Sellen.[138] In 1871 in King's Cliffe, Northamptonshire, Alfred Reedman scuffled with a barman who refused to serve him, and he then drew a knife, wounding another patron in the struggle.[139] In these cases, there is often a hint of ritual, such as the removal of a jacket; however, they suggest certain instabilities in the expectations of how a fight would be conducted. A prizefight in Liverpool in 1878 which was described as "customary" had involved gloves and, apparently, biting. An attorney argued that the men had fought "according to well-known rules" and that the fight was not "an offence in law"; however, the case was determined against the defendants.[140]

Along with a certain amount of ambiguity in popular notions of fighting came a concurrent increase in the state's attention to assault cases. In order to establish whether or not the state should take more action "for the more effectual repression of the crimes of violence, now unhappily so common among certain classes of the population," the Home Office circulated a letter in the mid 1870s to canvass judicial and policing opinions on the state of "brutal assaults." Although divided upon the issue of whether brutality was increasing as well as whether or not flogging should be reintroduced for aggravated assaults, many of the respondents called for heightened severity in certain classes of assaults. Attacks on men who were on the ground or by multiple men on a single victim were compared to assaults on women and children since the man had been rendered equally "helpless," and there were frequent references to increasing the severity of the law to deal with kicking, biting and the use of weapons.[141] The report's comments upon increasing "cowardly" or "brutal" attacks by men on other men may be evidence of a relaxation of the old restraints.

Fighting remained a part of working-class culture; however, several factors may have changed its role. "Respectable" workers increasingly sought to distinguish themselves from the "rough," and the adoption of respectable behavior by increasing segments of the working class made street violence less acceptable.[142] Engaging in a fight became more likely to cause trouble with the law and to damage one's respectability. Among the "rough," however, fighting remained important, indeed perhaps central, to definitions of manliness and power. Streetfighting, once a point of English pride, was increasingly becoming the province of less respectable subcultures. In his 1899 book *Hooligan Nights*, Clarence Rook recounted the story of "Alf," a lower-class youth. In describing an average "hooligan," Rook notes,

> He has usually done a bit of fighting with the gloves, for in Lambeth boxing is one of the most popular forms of sport. But he is better with the raws, and is very bad to tackle in a street row, where there are no rules to observe. …The Hooligan is by no means deficient in courage. He is always ready to fight, though he does not fight fair.[143]

Although he did not always fight "fair," this was no longer defined as cowardice or, necessarily, un-English. Rook described that Alf might at times fight under the Queensberry rules. What this meant in practice, however, remains unclear since the altercations he describes were not, for instance, fought using gloves. Applied to the streets it perhaps referred simply to a more restrained brand of fighting. As Rook notes:

> Young Alf is not, as you will have gathered, a man of peace. He has fought his fellows again and again, with varying success. But there is more than one kind of fighting. You may fight under Queensberry rules, and I have seen

young Alf so trammeled.... You may, on the other hand, fight without any rules at all, with the sole object of rendering your opponent incapable of any further action in the immediate future. I have seen young Alf fighting in that way too, and shall not speedily forget it.[144]

Fighting, Englishness and working-class life

In an interview, William Luby, a former sweet-boiler, described the common procedure for settling disputes in Manchester around the turn of the century:

> You always settled your arguments with a fight. You see it was the only expression you had. They wouldn't listen to you arguing, you know what I mean. He'd be looking while he's arguing with you … he'd be looking for an opening to let you have one. You see … it was very common. In fact, in the workshops, the public houses at the time of Sullivan or Corbett, the men were always fighting. In fact, behind my grandfather's house there was a canal and a croft. Any quarrels which my grandfather and any of his sons had with anybody would be settled by one son on the Sunday morning on this croft.[145]

Luby's mention of fights being settled by "one son" raised further questions:

Question: How do you mean … how do you mean by one son?
Answer: Because one son was kept for that purpose, fighting.
Question: He was a fighter for the family?
Answer: He was a fighter for the family. Bare fists … and very often his opponent was knocked out. They'd throw him in the canal and then bring
him out when he'd recovered. 'Course, often as not, a ducking would
be enough.[146]

Besides emphasizing the ubiquity of fighting to settle disputes, Luby's comments about "ducking," a customary method of ritual humiliation, highlight the continuing survival of traditions in working-class violence. The state's efforts to replace community violence with more civilized processes had begun to mean that "violence in its visible form could increasingly be described as the preserve of the poor, while the prosperous used other kinds of power to enact their will and could hide their overt violence behind closed doors, protected by the privacy of family life."[147] The development of non-violent means of dispute settlement was tied to new forms of legal, economic and political power to which some classes had increasing access. However, a text defending pugilism suggested that the notion "that labouring men,"

> like their betters, should always appeal to the laws when they quarrel, is rank hypocrisy and an insult to common sense. They have neither time nor money to offer in sacrifices for the protection of our Courts of Law and

> Equity, such as they are: they must settle the quarrels amongst themselves as well as they can; and out of this necessity have sprung up *boxing and the laws of the ring.*"[148]

Violence built on customary traditions of self-help in the settling of disputes and, in the absence of economic and legal power, it formed a resource over which working people had direct control.[149] The long-lasting cultural legitimacy of fighting suggests that the "civilizing process" cannot be understood as an undifferentiated attack on violence per se; cultural tensions concerned the shifting boundaries between legitimate and illegitimate violence. "Fair" fighting remained reasonably legitimate even though (or precisely because) the meaning of fairness was evolving. While not everyone appreciated the "science" of pugilism, English men of all classes had for nearly two centuries understood the customary language of the "fair fight." The use of physical force to inflict pain on another person was not, in itself, a problem for such men as long as aggression and force were channeled through certain ritual forms and limited to certain techniques.

"Fair" violence was not only tolerated, but among some observers it even had many positive associations: it developed character, displayed a manly physical vigor and symbolized nationalist pride. As "The Two Drovers" suggested, "English" violence was seen as a component of a particular kind of Englishness. In 1818, Pierce Egan argued that pugilism added courage to the "national character" and spoke glowingly of "a country where the stiletto is not known – where trifling quarrels do not produce assassination, and where revenge is not finished by murder."[150] He continued,

> Prejudice does much in favour of our native soil; but, upon a dispassionate review of those countries where Pugilism is unknown, we find, that, upon the most trifling misunderstanding, the life of the individual is in danger. In Holland the long knife decides too frequently; scarcely any person in Italy is without the stiletto; and France and Germany are not particular in using stones, sticks, &c. to gratify revenge; but, in England, the FIST only is used.[151]

The use of knives was fundamentally "un-English."[152] In 1840 another author described continental European wrestling practices as "unseemly and disgusting" and noted the "barbarous contests" prevalent in some parts of the United States: "kicking, biting, and even gouging, disgrace their inhuman fights."[153] An English rubbish carter spoke to Henry Mayhew about local fights in his neighborhood, claiming that the Irish fought in ways that were neither civilized nor manly:

> "Fair fights! sir," he said, "why, the Irishes [*sic*] don't stand up to you like men. They don't fight like Christians, sir; not a bit of it. They kick and

scratch, and bite and tear, like devils, or cats or women. They're soon settled if you can get an honest knock at them, but it isn't easy."[154]

Even nuances between certain types of styles apparently prevalent within England could mark distinctions between "savage" and "civilized" behavior.[155]

Traditional prizefighting had still been respectable in the 1820s, when William Hazlitt wrote the following paean to fighting:

> To see two men smashed to the ground, smeared with gore, stunned, sense-less, the breath beaten out of their bodies; and then, before you recover from the shock, to see them rise up with new strength and courage, stand ready to inflict or receive mortal offence, and rush upon each other "like two clouds over the Caspian" – this is the most astonishing thing of all: this is the high and heroic state of man![156]

However, by the middle of the nineteenth century, there was increasing discom-fort about prizefighting. "Brutality" was not only to be attacked as uncivilized but increasingly redefined as unmanly, un-English and unacceptable. As with other violent sports, customary prizefighting stood out as a sign of a brutal past that respectable society sought to suppress. While the wholesale policing of morals was a failure, it was one of the factors that put pressure on the customs of sport fighting. When the modern form of amateur boxing, initially a middle-class pursuit, was transformed into a popular working-class sport in the 1880s and 1890s, the traditional form could not compete.[157] Modern boxing was legal, with an institutional base in its clubs and a press that covered it enthusiastically. Since injury was limited through equipment and scoring methods, it again became respectable for middle-class men to show interest in the "art" of fighting, even if some found the "glove-business" unsatisfying.[158] Middle-class men predominated as the heads of the boxing associations that spread the new rules of modern boxing and which aimed not only to promote a sporting interest in boxing but also to civilize the behavior of working-class men.[159] As violence in society became less widely prevalent and larger groups ceased to participate in it, more finely graded distinctions were made: what was previously laudable became deplorable. The old "fair fight" was attacked as too violent, since it emphasized brute force and endurance over the niceties of technique and the accumulation of points for well-struck blows.[160]

Nevertheless, the effort to reform the working class's fighting culture through changes in the structure of sporting violence may have had contradictory effects. Workers became enthusiasts of civilized forms of boxing and the fair fight lived on. However, as a result of its simplicity of form and clearly defined conclusion, customary sport fighting had been translated to everyday life in a way that modern boxing, with its timed rounds and complicated scoring, could not be. The prizefighting ritual had also matched a customary form of masculinity based upon strength, endurance and honor. With the connection between sport and everyday fighting disrupted, the customary rules of seconds, rounds and "foul blows" faded away and streetfighting lost its ritual form by the end of the nineteenth century. Whether or not the decline of the fair-fighting ritual resulted in greater or lesser "violence" is a difficult question. Ideas of "fair" or "unfair" did not necessarily die with the ritual form that had maintained them. However, in the absence of a well-defined structure to shape fighting and maintain "fairness," I would suggest that there was a weakening in the limits of what was acceptable when two men came to blows.

5 "The wrongdoing of the poor man is as open as day"
Built space, imagined space, knowledge and violence

In a dark, dirty, crowded, ill-ventilated court or back street, common sense perceives, what is confirmed by the largest experience, that it is as difficult for health or virtue to exist, as for the vegetation of the tropics to thrive amid the snows of Iceland. The improvement of the material circumstances of the working classes is the condition precedent to all other efforts for raising their moral character.

James Hole[1]

Both space and society are implicated in the construction of the boundaries of the self, but ... the self is also projected onto society and onto space. Self and other, and the spaces they create and are alienated from, are defined through projection and introjection. Thus, the built environment assumes symbolic importance, reinforcing a desire for order and conformity if the environment itself is ordered and purified; in this way, space is implicated in the construction of deviancy. Pure spaces expose difference and facilitate the policing of boundaries.

David Sibley[2]

On the morning of Saturday, 14 April 1866, a cry of "Murder!" went out from a house in Tunbridge Wells, Kent.[3] Ann Lawrence and Walter Highams, unmarried though "living as man and wife," and two children (a four-year-old and an infant child) occupied Number Two Ebury Cottages.[4] Maria Taylor, of the adjacent Three Ebury Cottages, deposed that she awoke to "a great noise of tussling." She and her husband, a bricklayer's laborer, were separated from their neighbors by only a "slight brick partition" and soon heard a scream of "Murder!" from next door. She then heard Highams call out "Missus, Missus, come in and assist me and go for a doctor or I shall die."

I then got up and went downstairs and into the backyard, and there I saw [Highams] in Mrs. Mowcumber's house. He had only his shirt on, and he was covered with blood. I went to the front of the house. [Lawrence] was running up her front yard towards her own house. She was dressed in a black stuff dress and a colored apron. The dress was fastened and the sleeves were stripped up. Her arms and face, dress and apron were covered

> with blood. I heard [her] say "You dirty bugger, see what it's brought you to.
> I told you I would do it for you. Live like this I won't."

Mrs. Taylor was only one of the witnesses to the events that morning: Eliza Mowcumber resided on the opposite side of Lawrence's house, in One Ebury Cottages. She had awoken at four o'clock that morning when her husband went off to work. While lying in bed she heard someone in Lawrence's house go out to the water pump, draw water, return to the house and stir the fire. Then,

> about twenty minutes to six, I heard cries of "Murder!" They came from
> Walter Highams. I got out of bed and called my son to get up. I then went
> back to my room on the first floor and heard some scuffling. The sound
> came from the adjoining house … from the front bedroom. I again heard
> the cry of murder and heard Highams say, "Do leave off." He also said, "Do
> come somebody" several times. I then heard the screams of a child for a few
> seconds. Those screams came from the little boy, [Jeremiah] Lawrence, and
> not from the baby which is only nine months old.

Shortly afterwards Highams, covered with blood and wearing only his shirt, appeared at the door of the Mowcumbers' house. Eliza's son Edwin let him into the house and took him to their back room. Edwin Mowcumber had also heard the commotion that morning:

> I heard Walter Highams screaming "Murder!" He called out "Do leave off
> Annie, do leave off, dear." I could hear her say "I'll give it to you, you
> bugger." I went downstairs. When I got out of the front door I saw
> [Lawrence] at the pump. …Her arms and hands were covered with blood.
> She pumped some water into her hands and threw it up into her face. I went
> up to her at the pump. She turned to me and said "One is dead, and I hope
> the other bugger will be soon."

Thus, on both sides of the crime scene people were privy to the sounds and sights of a violent crime. But it was not only their immediate neighbors who became involved.

John Allen, a laborer, lived on an adjacent street and was walking to work when he heard shouts of "Murder!" and saw Lawrence emerge from her house covered with blood. She said to him "Go for the police. I'll give myself up to them." Immediately afterward, Allen met Edmund Cavil, a brickmaker, also on his way to work. Allen told Cavil what he had seen. Cavil went to Lawrence's and Highams's house and looked in the window:

> [I] saw her holding his hair with both hands and pushing his head back-
> wards and forwards against the wall, just where some sack of something

stood on the floor. As soon as they saw me the man called out "Murder, run for a policeman!"

Cavil left, but he quickly returned with two men he met at the top of the court. The door had been locked, and they looked through the window:

> It appeared to me that the man had not the strength to resist her. They were both covered with blood. The men who were with me rushed to the door at the same time as I did. I opened the door and Lawrence came out between the three of us. She said "Go for the police for there's murder in the house." The woman stayed outside in the front court with us ten minutes. The man walked out after her in his shirt and walked up and down, I should say five minutes, before he was let into the next house. She kept continually calling him a rogue and a villain and said he had murdered the child. The man made no answer. He appeared to be suffering great agony and asked me several times to wash him.

Police Constable May soon arrived. He walked upstairs to the front bedroom where he found four-year-old Jeremiah Lawrence lying on a bed with his throat slit and the razor still resting in the wound. PC May returned to the ground floor and informed the newly arrived PC Henley of the dead child. Lawrence stated that "the little one" was not dead. May had not realized there were two children in the house, and he returned upstairs to find the blood-spattered – but unharmed – infant lying on the same bed as the body of Jeremiah Lawrence. He brought the infant downstairs and gave him to Lawrence who immediately began to breastfeed him. Other constables arrived, and someone sent for a doctor. PC Henley spoke to Lawrence:

> I said to her, "Is the child upstairs yours?" She said, "It's mine, but not his, and he has killed it and he meant to do for me, but I was too quick for him." I said "Who do you mean by he?" She said "Walter." I then asked her if she wounded the man Walter. She said "Yes, I did, and I meant to do for him, and I'm sorry if I haven't."

The police examined the house and questioned Lawrence, Highams and the witnesses. Highams and Lawrence disputed the circumstances of the child's death and Highams's injuries. Lawrence claimed she had awakened to find that Highams had killed one of the children and fought him off in self-defense. Highams claimed Lawrence had attacked him with a razor, killed the child while he was incapacitated and then resumed assaulting him. In the end, a jury determined that Ann Lawrence had killed her child and attempted to kill Highams.[5] Her apparent motive was jealousy: Highams had been carrying on a relationship with another woman.[6]

The events at Number Two Ebury Cottages could be characterized as a "domestic" crime, with all that implies of privacy and intimate relationships.

However, in many communities the private was often very public. A "slight brick partition" was all that separated the house that Lawrence and Highams shared from their neighbors, and the sights and sounds of her violence spilled into the yard and street, drawing in the lives of those around them. Furthermore, her neighbors were aware of their history of domestic strife, a knowledge that colored their interpretations of the crime. Lawrence's apparent attempt to use a public forum for her own ends was undermined by a built environment that opened domestic life to the scrutiny of the community and, in this case, contributed to the evidentiary tools of English justice. Previous chapters have suggested various aspects of the relationship between space, violence and meaning. Chapter 2 described the evolution of new attitudes toward violence formed among social groups increasingly distanced from the working class and violence itself. Chapter 3 delineated the structure of customary attitudes to violence that had originated in a pre-industrial and largely pre-urban plebeian experience. The ritual fights of Chapter 4 depended on the deliberate use of public spaces. These points have already hinted at "geographies of violence," the spatial contexts in which violence is both produced (i.e., shaped into particular forms) and constructed (i.e., interpreted in relation to an underlying mentality).[7] In the nineteenth century, the production and construction of violence were mutually influencing and located within a particular set of spatial contexts relating to "built" space, "imagined" space and the ways that knowledge about violence was formed.

Built spaces

Growing class separation was apparent by the closing decades of the eighteenth century. In London, for instance, a period of increasing geographical and political alienation was inaugurated that lasted through the middle of the nineteenth century.[8] As new industrial towns developed, workers flooded into neighborhoods established to provide housing for factory labor. By the 1870s, if not earlier, "workers lived in neighborhoods from which the middle classes had largely fled."[9] Friedrich Engels, writing generally of urban poverty throughout Britain, described the connection between class and segregated housing:

> Every great city has one or more slums, where the working-class is crowded together. True, poverty often dwells in hidden alleys close to the palaces of the rich; but, in general, a separate territory has been assigned to it, where, removed from the sight of the happier classes, it may struggle along as it can.[10]

Such "separate territories" were not merely a physical division, and the creation of "working-class" neighborhoods – along with the resulting class-based cultural estrangement – was a project of both material and imagined geographies.[11] At mid century, the impoverished inhabitants of urban "rookeries" could be described as "pariahs" and "a distinct caste."[12] The dramatic extent of this process was strikingly apparent by the 1880s:

> Less than half-a-century ago this class [i.e., the poor] was distributed all over London. [...] What have we now? In certain directions you may walk for miles, and never see any sign of distress, any evidence of the existence of the poor! ...They are not in "our part" of London; and, with some of us, that, doubtless, is a sufficient cause for thankfulness.[13]

Spatial alienation helped to make cultural differences more apparent while also making them more difficult to interpret, understand and accept: the working classes and poor were delimited by geographic boundaries, and their culture was pushed to the borders of "civilization."[14] In dealing with such social "insulation" and the "terra incognita" of working-class areas, the middle classes "had a rudimentary interpretive scheme of the territory, peopled with stereotypes that represented imaginary projections of the role-specific behaviour met with in the intermittent social exchanges of real life."[15] The seemingly disordered and violent spaces of the poor and working classes were alien and disgusting; however, they were also as exotic and exciting as any "savage" foreign land.[16]

In 1854 Charles Dickens wrote an article for *Household Words* about his visit to "Wild Court," a London housing court, in the company of several members of the Society for Improving the Condition of the Labouring Classes and other reformers. Its opening points to the widening gulf between the classes:

> The room was full of amateur inspectors, and Wild Court down below was full of pale and ragged men, women, and children. There they were all standing in a crowd, to talk about and stare at the twelve or fourteen monsters of civilisation in broadcloth – the said amateurs – whenever for the purpose of passing from house to house, or holding colloquy together in the gutter, they came out into what is called by the people of that district the open air.[17]

The "monsters of civilisation" were inspecting of the property. They were, after all, its new owners: their society had purchased 13 of its 14 houses in order to "revise and amend" them and create "decent and wholesome dwellings." The typical problems of working-class housing were rife: lack of clean air, crowding, poor sanitation and disease. The reformers proposed to remedy these material ills, "offering every accommodation that good health can need." However, the most important aim was moral rather than physical regeneration. As Dickens wrote approvingly, "The conversion to Christianity of heathen dwellings in our courts and alleys is, we are glad to say, now made a main object of consideration with the society over which Lord Shaftesbury presides."[18] Reprising the common theme of "savagery," one observer of poor housing described its inhabitants' moral nature in stark terms, emphasizing their attachment to varieties of impulsive behavior:

> The habits of their tenants are gross – they are ill-fed, ill-clothed, and uneconomical – at once spendthrifts and destitute – denying themselves the comforts of life, in order that they may wallow in the unrestrained license of animal appetite.[19]

The spaces of the poor and working classes were seen, at times, as a carnival of immoral, unrestrained and carnal impulses, as one writer explained in 1858:

> The squalor and filth to be met with in the street and neighborhood are a commentary on our boasted sanitary progress and improved dwellings for the working classes. Beershops and brothels, gin palaces and gin drinkers, wretched women, giddy girls, bloated bullies and blackguard boys, semi-nude outcasts, and mud-loving, mischief-making manikins here abound.[20]

Eight years later, James Hole, in contemplating "the hordes who dwell in the wretched homes and streets of our large towns," concluded that "it is the home of the working man which, more than any other circumstance, affects his condition, his health, his morals; and its goodness may almost be taken as a measure of his civilization."[21] "Wretched accommodation in dwellings," as another writer put it, was thus a cause of many "social evils," violence among them.[22] Comparisons were explicitly made between the "immoral" English poor and two other groups who were frequently referred to as carriers of "impure" cultural contagion:

> The wretchedness of the dwellings re-acts on the habits of the occupier, and produces a recklessness as to filth and untidiness which probably ends in the formation of a character partaking of the Irish cottier and the English gipsey.[23]

From a civilized perspective, the prevalence of "unrespectable" behavior, the elision of the boundary between public and private spheres and the unconstrained mingling of the sexes were seen to contribute to the social problems of the lower classes. For civilized observers, these were the spaces in which the problems of dirt, disorder and brutality came together.

Although nearly all reformers believed that material reconstruction was necessary to promote a thrifty, moral and civilized working-class culture, there was an ongoing debate about the precise relationship between environment and morality. Referring to Liverpool in 1840, W. C. Taylor wrote that "much, if not most, of the vice and misery usually attributed ... to the pravity of human nature ... may be traced to circumstances in the physical condition of the working classes...."[24] Echoing these sentiments in 1866, Henry Roberts wrote, "After studying with religious anxiety the domestic life of a large number of work people, I am bold to affirm that the unhealthy and wretched condition of their dwellings is the primary cause of the misery, the vice and the calamities of their social existence."[25] Writing in the same year, James Hole used an agricultural metaphor to describe working-class brutality: "No wonder," he wrote, "that crime should be so rife, that not a week passes without some act of cold brutality, enough to make us cringe with horror – crimes which are not detached and exceptional facts of social existence," but rather the predictable "outgrowth of a soil well-fitted to encourage them."[26] Others were more ambivalent about the precise relationship between environment and morality. In the 1880s, Octavia Hill argued that

> the people's houses are bad, partly because they are badly built and arranged; they are ten-fold worse because the tenants' habits and lives are what they are. Transport them tomorrow to healthy and commodious homes, and they would pollute and destroy them.[27]

Nevertheless, she emphasized the importance of "fair and quiet spaces" – which she believed to be absent in London – "and I feel as if that quiet, that beauty, that space, would be more powerful to calm the wild excesses about me than all my frantic striving with it...."[28] This was a prominent view, and the reform of space was seen as having a potentially beneficial effect on all classes. Spaces were to be both "purified" and "pacified": cleansed physically and morally while being increasingly patrolled by the police.

Not only was space in itself important but also the ways in which it was used. The middle and upper classes were reforming and reshaping their spatial world: demarcating specialist spaces appropriate for particular activities.[29] Whereas the middle-class environment was becoming increasingly differentiated, working-class space remained crowded, mixed and "promiscuous," using a given space for a variety of purposes.[30] The working class's apparent disregard for privacy, particularly in relation to the mixing of the sexes, was profoundly distressing to middle-class writers.[31] While this distinction was relevant to many cultural contexts (e.g., attitudes to sex, cleanliness and sociability), it is also important to understanding divergent attitudes toward violence. Had working-class violence been more private, this would have posed less of a problem, for until the last decades of the nineteenth century the civilizing offensive concentrated largely on the public sphere. Knowledge of how to interpret working-class culture was increasingly elusive: when middle-class people entered working-class areas, their descriptions strike a note of confused sensory overload and disgust. Violent metaphors were even, for example, applied to the hustle and bustle of an open-air clothes market:

> To the uninitiated it would seem that pugilistic encounters were going on in twenty different spots at one and the same time; for there may be seen able bodied men and strapping lads stripping themselves of their outer garments, and that with an earnestness of purpose that can apparently only indicate impending fisticuffs, especially as in each cases there is something of a "ring" formed, and the individual reduced to his shirt and trousers is sedulously "attended to" by a friend who holds his jacket and waistcoat. But

> there is no battle, nor is one intended, and all this stripping portends
> nothing more alarming than the trying on of some garment offered for
> sale.[32]

"Civilizers" were thus confronted with a highly public – yet often inscrutable –
set of violent events.

The crowding characteristic of impoverished areas was widely commented
upon by social investigators, forming the essential background for complaints
about the nature of working-class life.[33] Writing of Spitalfields in London, James
Greenwood observed, "There are houses behind houses, with no rearward yard
or space for privacy or decency, and one and all are in a dilapidated state from
cellar to roof and quite unfit to live in."[34] Houses were built with very narrow
spaces between them:

> Many ranges of houses are built back to back, fronting one way into a
> narrow court, across which the inmates of the opposite houses may shake
> hands without stepping out of their own doors; and the other way, into a
> back street, unpaved and unsewered.[35]

Engels's extensive tour through the larger towns and cities of the north and
south of England is well known and is consistent with government reports.[36]
Crowding was combined with the typically poor state of accommodations. One
observer described the apartments in a tenement in the Collier's Rents area of
London in terms reminiscent of the "slight brick partition" referred to in the
Anne Lawrence case at the beginning of this chapter:

> Ascending as best you can, you gain admission to one of the rooms. You
> find that although the front and back of the house are of brick, the rooms
> are separated only by partitions of boards, some of which are an inch apart.
> There are no locks on the doors, and it would seem that they can only be
> fastened on the outside by padlock.[37]

Even when a family had a relatively "private" abode, they remained tied to their
neighbors through the use of common spaces, and the dense interconnections of
working-class life and the frequent comings and goings of neighbors are
apparent in the records of the criminal courts.[38]

Public spaces were thus important to working-class life. Streets and courtyards
were more than areas to travel through and were sites of a variety of activities,
thereby ensuring that life remained open to scrutiny. Pubs were particularly
important to sociability, and commentators were struck by the contrasts between
pubs and the squalor of working-class housing:

> Look into one of those glittering saloons, with its motley, miserable crowd,
> and you may be horrified as you think of the evil that is nightly wrought
> there; but contrast it with any of the abodes which you find in the fetid

courts behind them, and you will wonder no longer that it is crowded. With its brightness, its excitement, and its temporary forgetfulness of misery, it is a comparative haven to tens of thousands.[39]

The fact that many pubs were often shabby anterooms in a publican's house questions such depictions of an "Elysian field of the tired toiler."[40] Nevertheless, pubs and streets were the predominant spaces for working-class sociability because workers and their families often lacked agreeable domestic spaces. They were also closely associated with workplaces, and in pubs "the unwritten lore of the shop could be reflected and reinforced outside of the workplace."[41] Various sorts of social life also took place at work, and despite the increased demands of discipline, tensions, disputes and violence were part of working life.[42] Furthermore, the continuing relevance of customary work culture continued to influence efforts by unions to control work; unions frequently used violence and spatial exclusion during labor disputes, as described in Chapter 6.

The built environment of working-class life had important implications for both the production and construction of violence. First, the particular nature of working-class material spaces created numerous opportunities for disagreements over common resources, boundaries, privacy, borrowing and noise; such disputes often arose on a daily basis.[43] Octavia Hill described the public nature of working-class life and suggested that its acrimonious tone was partly a result of crowding and the nature of the physical surroundings:

> I go sometimes on a hot summer evening into a narrow paved court, with houses on each side. The sun has heated them all day, till it has driven nearly every inmate out of doors. Those who are not at the public-house are standing or sitting on their door-steps, quarrelsome, hot, dirty; the children are crawling or sitting on the hard hot stones till every corner of the place looks alive, and it seems as if I must step on them, do what I would, if I am to walk up the court at all. Everyone looks in everyone else's way, the place echoes with words not of the gentlest. In fact it is on such evenings that the drinking is wildest, the fighting fiercest, and the language most violent.[44]

Shared possessions and living spaces were an essential part of the sociability and support networks that extended beyond the private sphere of the family.[45] Nevertheless, there were frequent disputes related to them.[46] An 1852 essay considered the prevalence of such neighborly fights. "In cases of assault, particularly among women," it noted, "two of them having quarreled over the not returning of a smoothing iron, or one having cuffed the other's child for throwing mud on her washed clothes, they join issue on the matter."[47] Hill described the "deadly quarrels [that] spring up and deepen and widen between families compelled to live very near one another, to use many things in common...."[48] Two of her female tenants often quarreled and fought:

> The women occupied adjoining rooms, they met in the passages, they used the same yard and wash-house, endless were the opportunities of collision while they were engaged with each other.[49]

Traditions of sharing, though important for survival, were a further inflammatory factor in working-class violence.[50] There was a way in which these networks were gendered, as "goods, services, friendship, and certain spaces – in shops, pubs, doorways, streets – were shared with members of the same sex, and not with spouses."[51] Support networks extending outside of the family among other women – sometimes including "outcasts," such as prostitutes[52] – were part of the fissures that characterized working-class marriages. Thus, the dense networks of working-class home life were implicated in the production of violence and shaped the subsequent construction of violent events. Violence was a "daily concern" and a strategy for controlling boundaries and social arrangements in a context of scarce resources, and the "closeness" of violence was a constant feature of working-class life.[53]

Domestic disputes and neighborly disagreements were, of course, not unique to the working class. However, the spatial arrangement of their neighborhoods provided motivations for disputes and meant that violence, when it occurred, was common knowledge. An 1856 article on spousal violence graphically pointed out the particular spatial contexts of violence among the working class and poor:

> The wrongdoing of the poor man is as open as day. The screams of his wife or paramour cannot be stifled in the close alley or teeming courtyard wherein he dwells. His home is perhaps a single room in a house where half a dozen families are herded together. Every sound is heard through the thin, dilapidated partition-walls. A score of witnesses are ever ready, if need be, to divulge his offence.[54]

Whereas for the wealthy man "everything is as secret as death."[55] The distinction between the absolute openness of poverty and the privacy that wealth could buy is, of course, a generalization. There were working-class crimes that remained secret, and the crimes of wealthy men and women were often discovered and much publicized; however, the production and construction of typical types of violence were affected by such class and spatial contexts. For example, "open air fighting" was a normal phenomenon in working-class neighborhoods. Civilized observers critically noted the prevalence and popularity of fighting in public spaces, tying fighting to other forms of rough, customary entertainments:

> But let the yell of a couple of bull dogs be heard in the vicinity, or the cry of "A fight! A fight!" be raised, and it will be the tocsin of mirth to a quickly

assembled crowd, who will drink in savage delight, and hail the sport with shouts of blackguard exultation.[56]

William Reynolds was witness to a fight in 1830. His testimony shows the typical way observers were drawn to public fighting:

> On Saturday last I had been kept late at work at my master's shop and did not get to my lodgings until about a quarter before eleven. Whilst undressing in my bedroom, I heard a fight in the streets. I went downstairs and went out to it.[57]

Even "private" disputes took on a public character. Henry Mayhew found the "usual disturbance" while visiting a rat-catcher; entering a housing court, he discovered "one end or branch of it filled with a mob of eager listeners, principally women, all attracted to a particular house by the sounds of quarrelling."[58] A district nurse who visited working-class homes commented upon the public spousal violence she witnessed and particularly noted the prevalence of violence on weekends, when wages were distributed. From Saturday until Monday "the court was often a field of battle and bloodshed, and Sunday was a pitiful day," and she described "men kicking their wives round the court like footballs, and women fighting like wild tigers!"[59] Thus, due to the nature of the built environment, violence – when it occurred – was typically either within the sight or hearing of others in the neighborhood.[60]

Imagined spaces

Although built spaces shape the contexts of everyday life and constitute some of the more stable aspects of social experience, the physical environment is not merely an inert setting for social interaction. Physical environments interact with culture to create "imagined" spaces: notions of what being in particular spaces means, the actions that are appropriate within them and the ways that people make use of built space. For example, there is a material street and also a sense of what "the street" or "being in the street" signifies and means. Similarly, "home" is both a material space and a set of ideas about gender roles, power and discipline. Such "imaginations" of space are therefore integral to the constitution and maintenance of meaning.[61] The interaction between physical and imagined space is complex. For instance, Michel de Certeau describes the relationship between the built spaces of modern cities and the "pedestrian speech acts" that, through a "spatial acting-out of the place," create new and unexpected uses of those spaces.[62] Violence is also an "acting-out": certain types of violence become associated with particular types of spaces, are related to certain uses of space or are deeply embedded in certain kinds of imagined spaces. In some cases, imagined geographies of violence and the built spaces within which violence occurs coincide; in others, built spaces and the imagined meanings of the violence within them seem contradictory. For instance, though the concentration and crowding of urban life created a new spatial context for working-class life, urban workers maintained aspects of a pre-industrial sense of space. The self-regulation of community life – through neighborly surveillance, gossip networks, and the implicit threat and explicit use of violence – continued within, and may have been enhanced by, new urban environments. Working-class life remained structured by "high-density social networks" in which "most links [between people] are strong and one is likely to know and have direct ties to most people affected by the misbehavior of a member of one's network."[63] Thus, the community closely regulated the behavior of individuals within it. Nineteenth-century working-class communities comprised such closely-knit, high-density social networks and were also characterized by a shared set of principles and attitudes regarding behavior. On the one hand, the different spatial constitution of working- and middle-class life fed divergent class interpretations of the meaning of violence and impacted diagnoses of social problems and reform activities. Alternatively, a degree of agreement between civilized and customary views on other aspects of imagined spaces may have reinforced the legitimacy of some kinds of violence. The concepts of "the street" and "the home" are particularly relevant.

"The street" refers not only to streets per se, but also to the variety of alleyways, housing courtyards, small crofts and squares that constituted the built spaces of working-class life. The street was a place for a variety of activities – work, play, socializing, travel and arguing – which contributed to the openness of private life.[64] Working-class people also viewed streets as legitimate arenas for certain kinds of violence, in sharp distinction to emerging civilized attitudes. Imagined geographies of violence that had originated in a village-centered life that accepted violence as a social act (as long as it remained within customary boundaries) and expected community surveillance of physical aggression were maintained. "The street" became the equivalent urban site for the legitimate settling of community grievances. Thus, the creation of urbanized sites of working-class experience did not, in itself, fully undermine customary notions. As the century progressed, however, the state and civilizing forces sought to create a new model of "the street" and to refine working-class uses of space. Increasingly, the middle class erected boundaries between public and private. Their reinforcement of private life was in large measure based on their ability to afford more capacious living spaces, but "imagined" privacy preceded the material practices that constructed middle-class identity.[65] In both civilized and customary thinking, attitudes toward the street were gendered. For instance, while there were instances of women fighting in public (sometimes as a result of disputes emerging out of the shared uses of "domestic" spaces), women – with only rare exceptions – did not participate in the male ritual fight, which was inseparably connected to the street. The growing public/private distinction was a predominantly middle-class version of gendered propriety. Because of the imperatives of work and social life, working-class women used public spaces in ways that contravened middle-class notions of propriety, and customary notions of space and gender granted them a relative freedom to use violence in the public sphere.[66]

However, as nineteenth-century towns and cities developed, public spaces were increasingly defined in terms of gendered notions of fear, danger and respectability. A discourse of street danger contributed to a gendered delineation of space: increasingly, public spaces were defined as a source of danger to women, even though they were more likely to face violence in the private sphere.[67]

Just as streets were both a material structure and a social state of mind, the nineteenth-century "home" had both built and imagined spatial contexts.[68] The imagined space of "the home" took on a powerful set of cultural meanings in the nineteenth century: an emerging discourse emphasized it as a site of private family activity protected from the public sphere. The nineteenth-century "home" was predominantly a middle-class ideal, even if attitudes toward domesticity were always contested.[69] Although the legal basis of women's submission was under challenge in the early nineteenth century, male dominance was reinforced by dominant trends in Victorian culture. These "new repressive ideas" had a religious origin and emphasized a "commitment to home and family life."[70] The "encapsulation" of family life was a building block of the civilized use of space, and the home became one of the institutional forms within which new "disciplines" could be articulated and structured.[71] Idealized, hegemonic views of separately gendered spheres sought to make women responsible for the management of home life, accorded them a subordinate role in the hierarchy of family power, and restricted them spatially. The production of violence in the home took place in markedly different spatial and cultural circumstances than, for example, ritualized male fighting. Although spousal violence was structured by a notion of privacy, neighborly surveillance and the openness of everyday life ensured that private violence was also public. At other times, as Chapter 6 discusses, working-class domestic violence was deliberately public. Thus, the spaces (both built and imagined) of working-class domesticity were in conflict with the "separate spheres" ideology of the eighteenth and nineteenth centuries.

The class associations of wife abuse were common, initially allowing the issue of violence to be displaced onto the working class. Although the view of working-class marriage as a constant battleground contained elements of stereotype and class contempt, there does seem to have been a tendency for laboring men to rule their households through physical force. While the working-class "home" was, like its middle-class counterpart, shaped by the ideal of male dominance, it was also built around tensions involving that dominance, the management of family resources and the power relationships implied in marriage. As Ross has noted, "unchallenged male power [was] rare in large parts of working-class London," and the home was "fissured" along sex lines: husbands and wives often did not fully share the resources of the home and often fought over their distribution.[72] Further, while domestic violence was a potential feature of all families, regardless of class, middle-class life was generally (in relative terms) increasingly restrained by new ideals of civility and companionate marriage that touched working-class communities only lightly, if at all.

Domestic violence was legitimated by a defense of "the home" and its power relationships. During a street dispute in Lancashire in 1874, a husband kicked his wife in the ribs. A policeman intervened, but merely urged them to "return home to settle their quarrel."[73] In 1835, John Woods brought home a cod for his wife Harriet to cook. When she refused, he beat her severely, causing wounds from which she later died. All the while, her brother was present in the kitchen and watched the unfolding violence but did not interfere.[74] His inaction was not an uncommon response, even by a family member, to domestic violence between husbands and wives in the home. In the last decade of the nineteenth century, an article on domestic abuse described a "labouring man" in Wigan who "stood calmly by whilst a collier kicked his wife to death [and] said at the trial he did not interfere as it was not for him 'to step in between man and wife.'"[75] The legitimacy of inter-sexual violence was closely linked to marriage. As Richard Horne and Charles Dickens noted, "The fact of a woman being the lawful wife of a man, appears to impress certain preposterous juries with some notion of a kind of right in the man to maltreat her brutally, even when this causes her death; but if she be not yet married, the case assumes a different aspect in their minds – a man then has no right to murder a woman – and a verdict of murder is found accordingly."[76] Men could "legitimately" abuse wives in a way they could not abuse women with whom they lacked domestic bonds. James Coghlan, a "floorcloth worker," beat his wife in a London street after she had "made him look small" in front of his friends by pleading with him not to go drinking. A constable was attracted to the site of the incident by her screams and took him into custody, but only at the "insistence of the woman."[77] Outside of marriage, other people intervened – sometimes violently – to protect women.[78] Edward Tupman assaulted a man who had been "violently forcing along the streets in Hull two females." The women were "riotous and disorderly" prostitutes arrested by a constable named Bentley who had not made it clear that he was a police officer or that the women were under arrest.[79]

In order to defend the idealized space of "the home," husbands could legitimately use violence against wives who undermined their authority, failed to maintain their gendered duties or strayed sexually.[80] In petitioning for a reduction of his assault conviction, William Carpenter argued that his wife was a woman "of bad character," who had "for some time past formed a connection with some of the worst and most profligate of her sex – getting intoxicated continually and destroying at those times your petitioner's property."[81] In court, a wife's drunkenness or "provoking" behavior could even serve as a mitigating factor for wife abuse.[82] Women who failed to meet their husbands' expectations regarding their management of the home could find themselves at the receiving end of physical "chastisement," and magistrates often ignored or even supported the husband's actions.[83] Frequently, it is difficult to separate "disciplinary" from homicidal or potentially fatal violence, and courts were clearly more willing to grant men the benefit of the doubt.

While marriage was the defining relationship of middle-class domestic life, working-class relationships that defined the male power to use violence against women were more flexible. Unmarried cohabitation, sometimes referred to as "living as man and wife," was common in working-class communities. Combined with a looser notion of marital and sexual propriety, working-class definitions of "home" were more varied and included the transient and shared living accommodations of, for example, rooming houses. In Victorian Kent, 83 percent of all adult female homicide victims were killed by a spouse, cohabitant or would-be lover.[84] In 1835, John Cassell struck Mary Brown, with whom he had been cohabiting, after they quarreled over the possession of some shirts and Brown "flew at" Cassell.[85] In another case, James Palmer beat his cohabitant to death after she told him she planned on earning her living in a taproom. The judge in the case, in justifying a three-month prison sentence, noted,

> It was the minor offense of manslaughter. The blows were a mere chastisement. She was not his wife, or sister, or legitimately a member of his household, but human nature is human nature and he was provoked because she was drunk.[86]

The social and spatial flexibility of "domestic" life, as well as its often public nature, is emphasized by the case of Mary McCarthy and John Cockering.[87] They were unmarried but sharing a room at the "Horse and Jockey" lodging house in Dover and argued almost constantly about money from the moment they arrived. Cockering beat McCarthy frequently, leading to her death. The insults and violence occurred within plain view of some of the other residents in the shared space of the kitchen; however, none of them took any action until it seemed that Cockering might beat McCarthy to death. At that point, one of the witnesses, Elizabeth Jackson, the wife of a laborer, fetched the barman. By the time he arrived, the pair had quieted and they appeared to reconcile. However, the next day, McCarthy seemed unwell. Ann Goodwin shared a room with the couple, as was not uncommon in rooming houses.

> Nothing passed during the night, but on Tuesday morning about seven o'clock, he was scolding her, but did not strike her. He got up, leaving her in bed as she had complained to him several times she was unable to get up. I shortly after dressed and went downstairs and on going up to the room again about ten o'clock on that morning I saw her in bed.

While making breakfast, Goodwin saw McCarthy fall out of bed, briefly unconscious, although she later revived. Cockering returned, and, in front of Goodwin, beat McCarthy with a stick while she lay in bed. Goodwin went out to go about her business but later returned, found McCarthy unwell and sat with her until she died.

Thus, notions of male dominance, flexible views on committed relationships and relatively elastic contexts of domesticity structured attitudes toward violence in the working-class home. Both customary and civilized mentalities of violence legitimated male dominance of the home; however, the middle and upper classes were, in relative terms, restrained by new constructions of family life. It is possible that custom granted a slightly higher degree of freedom to women in their use of violence and accepted – possibly even expected – aggressive feminine attributes. Nevertheless, women were overwhelmingly the victims of domestic spousal violence rather than its perpetrators.

Gender relations are, of course, neither stable nor immutable. Attention to wife abuse heightened (slowly), and legislation marginally increased the state's proscriptions on male domestic power.[88] The 1880s saw a shift toward the state becoming willing to interfere in private matters, from domestic violence to compulsory school attendance. Since much of the public sphere had, by that point, been successfully pacified, attention to violence shifted somewhat toward the private sphere of the home, particularly in the context of an expanding electorate.[89] As the next section will suggest, the physical environment of working-class life certainly left few illusions as to the nature of what was expected in marriage, since private disputes and violence became widespread public knowledge. Nevertheless, despite the various tensions in working-class domesticity, the imagined privacy of the home – measured by the motivations for violence, the license granted to men to use violence in particular "domestic" contexts, and the general unwillingness of witnesses to intervene – was a durable, flexible and mobile construction. The home's imagined boundaries were generally respected even if various sorts of neighborly surveillance and commentary penetrated its physical foundations. Domestic power relationships and constructions of masculine dominance were adaptable, even to the formidable openness of working-class life.

Knowledge of violence

Violence is influenced by the ways that knowledge about it is gained. Knowledge of violence is shaped by space and forms, in a sense, a mental "space" of its own. Violent acts take particular forms, and participants and observers shape the meanings of those acts in relation to what they know about previous violence. The ways that people are educated in violence are thus significant in understanding its nature and meaning. In working-class communities, built spaces ensured that the sounds and sights of violence were widely dispersed: people often watched and listened to their neighbors' arguments and fights.[90] Mayhew's visit to a housing court highlights the ways that built space contributed to the visibility of violence:

> At the time of my visit, which was in the evening, after the inmates had returned from their various employments, some quarrel had arisen among them. The court was so thronged with the friends of the contending individuals and spectators of the fight that I was obliged to stand at the entrance, unable to force my way through the dense multitude, while labourers and street-folk with shaggy heads, and women with dirty caps and fuzzy hair, thronged every window above, and peered down anxiously at the affray.

There must have been some hundreds of people collected there, and yet all were inhabitants of this very court, for the noise of the quarrel had not yet reached the street.[91]

Visiting Drury Lane, Mayhew found a familiar scene:

As I entered the court, a "row" was going on…. This "row" had the effect of drawing all the lodgers to the windows – their heads popping out as suddenly as dogs from their kennels in a fancier's yard.[92]

Violent disputes could thus form a sort of spectator event, and it is in cases of domestic violence that such visibility is most striking. As we have seen, imagined spaces helped constitute attitudes toward what was appropriate behavior in different environments. Awareness of violence – at home, at work and in the streets – was widespread and each incident interacted with previous experiences.

Disputes and tensions in the domestic sphere were widely known, and neighbors, in one way or another, often became involved.[93] Mary and James Franklin ran a public house, and they frequently – and publicly – quarreled, a history that ended with Mary's death in 1830.[94] A neighbor, Thomas Quilter, deposed,

I live very near the prisoner's house, and on Saturday evening about six o'clock, I heard screams in the street.

More than one witness heard the actual fight that night. One recalled,

I heard a scuffle between the prisoner and his wife in the bar and I saw the deceased getting up off the floor in the passage leading into the street, and she ran into the street accompanied by two of her daughters who were screaming and they all went to Mrs. Quilter's.

Charles Bull, a bricklayer, deposed: "I heard him and his wife quarrelling in the passage by the side of the tap leading to the street, and I heard words and blows and children screaming." Elizabeth Quilter, Thomas's wife, also "heard screams in the street," and went out to the Franklin house.

In another case, from 1871, after a long history of public quarreling, Richard Addington stabbed his wife to death.[95] One of their neighbors, Elizabeth Warren, lived across the street and saw the last of their disputes:

He went into his house and said, "Mary, come in." She said, "I told you I would not come in." He came out of the house and caught hold of her and carried her into the house and shut the door. I heard her scream out such a scream I had never heard in my life before.

Although Warren deposed that she "thought they were very comfortable that morning until she said she would not go in," all had not been quiet in the previous night:

The night before I had got up twice, hearing some noise in the yard and I twice saw him carry her into the house. She was then standing outside and saying she would not go in. When he carried her in the second time it might be about twelve o'clock. I heard her screaming in the house.

Elizabeth Harris and her husband shared a yard with the Addingtons. She had seen part of their dispute on the morning of the stabbing, but had gone about her daily tasks until she heard a scream.

I was in my bedroom and heard a scream. I ran downstairs into the yard, I saw Richard Addington coming from his own door. I said to him, "What is the matter?" He said, "Betsy, I have cut her throat; you may go and look at her if you like." I said, "Oh, you have never done such a cruel thing as that." He said, "I have, [and] she is a dead woman. You can take me." I saw his hands were bloody. I went and told the constable.

Before she died, Mary Addington had made it across the street, to Elizabeth Warren's house. She was badly wounded, but managed to speak to Warren.

She said, "Oh, Mrs. Warren, look here," pointing at her neck, "he has killed me." Blood was running from her neck. She sat down. In about a minute or two afterwards, her husband came in. She said to him, "My dear husband, I am a dying woman." He said, "Yes, I know my dear, you will be dead in a few minutes." She put a finger up to her throat. He said, "That is not the worst." He stroked down her bowels with his hand and said, "that is the worst place." He asked her to forgive him.

Similarly, Sarah Marshall's screams were audible to many of her neighbors on the night she was stabbed to death by William Bull in December 1870.[96] Marshall lived alone. One of her neighbors, Mary Hawkins, deposed:

I live near the cottage in which the deceased lived on the opposite side of the road. In the night … I heard a rapping which seemed to me to be at Sarah Marshall's door. I then heard a squeal.

At least three neighbors heard Marshall squeal or scream, but all of them deposed that they did not get up because "it was a common thing to hear such a noise from her house." A surgeon deposed that she "was a person of childish and weak intellect from her birth…. She was easily excited and used very strong language." Marshall had been much talked about, and her reputation as an excitable woman meant that the sounds of Bull's attack were ignored.

The middle classes, generally, gained their knowledge of working-class violence from the press. In this way they became increasingly subject to the "crime stories" being circulated by new civilizing discourses.[97] These sources were built upon (and contributed to) stereotyped views of the working class and violence. Workers also read papers (or listened to others reading them aloud), and a sensationalist popular press was increasingly relevant to working-class culture during the nineteenth century. However, within the working class, knowledge of violence in their neighborhoods was also mediated through other means. "Stories" were the vehicle for shaping each mentality of violence, yet, within working-class communities such stories were created in relation to distinct knowledge of (and attitudes toward) violence. Violence was debated: sides might be taken and legitimacy might be contested.[98] For example, prizefights were discussed repeatedly and became a part of pub conversations. Before a fight and as word spread, the backers of each fighter would debate the merits of the men involved, compare them to other boxers and tell tales of past bouts. In the more informal world of the streetfight, such stories were also prevalent. Men who fought unfairly might find their reputations damaged, while men who fought well could enhance their reputations. Domestic and family disputes were also subject to widespread public discussion. Thus, the "visibility" of violence did not end with those who had witnessed directly a fight between spouses. Middle-class observers noted the vibrancy of working-class gossip networks and found a potential factor for encouraging violence in the narrative breaching of the domestic threshold:

> these disturbances in the families are not kept silent as among the middle classes of society, for during the day the wife is to be found for the most of her time either gossiping with her neighbours, and holding a colloquy about some trifling matter (which mortals unaccustomed to such things are barely able to describe), or unbosoming her cares to her female friends, who each have something to say upon the matter; by which the family peace is soon destroyed; and as a natural consequence all respect for herself as the mother of a family is entirely lost.[99]

As Anna Davin notes, "Women also colluded to avoid trouble from husbands, hiding children or each other when violence threatened."[100] The power of social networks that stretched across the threshold of the home has been noted, and information about violence and domestic troubles traveled easily along them.

Glimpses of such storytelling are apparent in the depositions gathered by the police and magistracy in preparation for a criminal trial, particularly for murder trials at the assizes. The story of a violent crime brought with it a great deal of information about its motives and circumstances. After Sarah Bacon's murder in 1867, a close neighbor, Emma Price, recounted the recent history of strife within the Bacon household.

> On Monday … she told me it [i.e., a previous violent incident] was because she had run him into debt. On Sunday aft[ernoon], she said she thought he would kill her. About half past two, I heard her hallow. I asked her what was the matter. She said he ran after her with a chopper.[101]

Similarly, long before Mary Addington's husband killed her, the community had been well aware of their marriage problems and had become involved with them at various points. After hearing screaming coming from the Addington household, one neighbor asked another about what had happened.

> I asked my neighbour, Mary Brown, what she was screaming for. She told me she had been in the house and deceased had had a fainting fit.

Several witnesses claimed that Richard Addington was a jealous man who had accused several people of having "wronged" his wife.[102] The night before the murder, he had appeared at a local public house, called Cook's. George Faulkner was present:

> Whilst there, the prisoner came in and demanded of Mrs. Cook to go into the cellar, for he said her husband was down the cellar with his wife. Mrs. Cook held the door. They had a scuffle. I persuaded the prisoner to go away with me. He did.

Addington was also well known to police constable William Clark:

> I consider Richard Addington to be a jealous minded man. When he had a beer, he would often say that people were along with his wife. He challenged me with it two years ago and several others.

After Sarah Marshall's death in 1870, depositions revealed a long history of animosities between her and her murderer, William Bull.[103] Sarah Marshall, for instance, had told several of her neighbors that she was afraid of William Bull and that he had threatened her. Furthermore, others had witnessed Bull's hostility toward her. James Madison, a laborer, deposed the following:

> I had been working before with the prisoner at Bushmead, and, about a month before, the prisoner was talking in my presence with John Handen about her, and the prisoner said, "I'll kill the old B——r." I said, "Gently, gently, if some people were to hear you, you would be taken up and taken care of."

Another witness, Frederick Darlow, had been drinking with Bull and some other men at a local pub. They left together:

> Just before we got to Sarah Marshall's door, the prisoner stopped and picked up a stone. He threw the stone at her door, and she hallowed out "murder!" She said, "D——n you, what do you do there?" He said, "I'll —— you; you old B——r."

In many cases, then, there was a well-grounded community knowledge about the motives for violent acts and the characters of those involved.

Knowledge, of course, is not merely objective, and its meaning was open to debate and interpretation, as Mayhew's description of a "row" he witnessed makes clear:

> From a first-floor window a lady, whose hair sadly wanted brushing, was haranguing a crowd beneath, throwing her arms about like a drowning man, and in her excitement thrusting her body half out of her temporary rostrum as energetically as I have seen Punch lean over his theatre.
>
> "The willin dragged her," she shouted, "by the hair of her head, at least three yards into the court – the willin! And then he kicked her, and the blood was on his boot."
>
> It was a sweep who had been behaving in this cowardly manner; but still he had his defenders in the women around him. One with very shiny hair, and an Indian kerchief round her neck, answered the lady in the window, by calling her a "d——d old cat;" whilst the sweep's wife rushed about, clapping her hands together as quickly as if she was applauding at a theatre, and styled somebody or other "an old wagabones as she wouldn't dirty her hands to fight with."[104]

In another incident he described a row in which a mob of "eager" listeners was discussing the dispute between the two participants.

> One man gave it as his opinion that the disturbers must have earned too much money yesterday; and a woman speaking to another who had just come out, lifting up both hands and laughing, "Here they are – *at it again.*"[105]

Public violence became enmeshed in working-class storytelling and gossip networks, one of the primary agents of information in their communities. Through re-telling, various meanings emerged, and reputations developed as the lives of neighborhood inhabitants were exposed to outside interpretation.[106] One case involving two Irish women, reported by John Paget in his study of the London police courts, highlights the prevalence of such storytelling:

> Another young lady from the sister isle next addressed the magistrate. "It was last June as your worship gave me two months for biting Mrs. Sullivan's finger, and I've served my time for it; and ever since I came out I'm in fear of my life, for Mrs. Sullivan goes up and down raving like a bull-dog in dhrink [*sic*] all over the court, and calling me cannibal Kitty; and it's hard I should be called cannibal Kitty all my life when I've served my time for it."[107]

Reputation could profoundly color the perceptions of an act of violence, and the consequences to be faced by a perpetrator if his or her case reached the courts.[108] Reputations were also established for victims of violence. As we have seen, Sarah Marshall's frequent cries and her reputation as "easily excited" conditioned her neighbors' responses to the sounds they heard on the night of her murder. When James Bacon killed his wife, Sarah, there was much testimony about her character and the state of their marriage.[109] Among some of the witnesses (including her mother and aunt) Sarah's reputation was poor because of her "neglect" of her children and spendthrift ways. "I have thought this led to frequent quarrels between him and her," testified Isabella Stevens, Sarah's aunt, "for he was very fond of his children." The Bacons's neighbor, Emma Price, spoke to another cause of domestic discontent between them:

> The last two months they had lived very unhappy and been quarrelling. They used to quarrel because she put him into debt so…. Last Sunday, I heard some words between them. He had then gone upstairs and found all his clothes gone. I knew from her that she had pawned them.

Even when a violent event did not occur within one's direct experience, knowledge of violent behavior – its form and motivation, the reputations of those involved, its results – became widespread though the storytelling networks of working-class communities. Knowledge gained through direct experience and gossip thus featured prominently in the information gathered by the authorities.[110]

Martha Vicinus has suggested two implications of the ubiquity and "closeness" of violence in working-class communities: they led to either "denial" or an "embracing of the inevitable."[111] Denial was of increasing importance, as sections of the working class began adopting civilized attitudes and "the respectable turned inward to their homes, and separated themselves from street life."[112] More commonly, disputes, quarreling and violence were normalized as a common occurrence. Hammerton has noted that "marital conflict, frequently including violence, was mostly taken for granted in many working-class communities; in itself, it was rarely sufficient to warrant communal censure."[113] The frequency of domestic disputes and their openness to the surrounding community did sometimes lead to neighborly intervention but normally only in extreme cases.[114] The combination of the ubiquity of violence and its tendency to exist not only within the same class but also within groups of people who were closely related through family or neighborhood ties had implications for the meaning of violence: in combination, these factors contributed to the way that violence was a social event at the heart of community life.

Furthermore, divergent spatial environments and cultural forms contributed to different experiences of violence. For the middle class, that experience was limited in the nineteenth century, as spatial demarcation and cultural alienation increased. An expanding commentary on social problems – examined in Chapter 2 – shaped attitudes among a readership that had much less direct experience of violence than did workers. Working-class knowledge of violence was produced in different circumstances: although they increasingly participated in the written discourse of civility, working-class views of violence were also shaped by direct experience (whether as participant, victim or observer) and intra-class oral information networks. Acceptance of the inevitability of violence, furthermore, may suggest a way in which mentalities of violence are influenced by the spatial contexts of knowledge production. Mentalities of violence are shaped according to a kind of spiraling legitimation: a violent act is produced in relation to a particular mentality which also forms the basis on which the act is subsequently evaluated. Individual interpretations vary, since, although a mentality provides norms, there are areas of contestation, and one's reaction to violence will be colored by a variety of factors. However, in general, most interpretations would tend toward reinforcing the original mentality, whether they accept or reject the individual act in question. For example, the disputes that led to fistfights were open to public observation and interacted with attitudes as to which situations legitimated ritualized dispute settlement. Crowds who harassed deviants acted according to notions of acceptable violence for the control of cultural boundaries. Domestic disputes were open to public view and shaped notions that saw conflict and violence as common parts of working-class marriage.[115] The recursive, reinforcing patterns of knowledge of violence perhaps contributed to the resilience of the customary mentality of violence in working-class culture. Finally, the importance of storytelling and direct observation for working-class attitudes to violence continued into the twentieth century; however, these began to compete with other means of knowledge production, particularly as literacy and education opened channels of civilized thought into working-class culture which interfered with traditional legitimating narratives.

Less than a year after his article "Conversion of a Heathen Court," Dickens wrote a companion piece entitled "Wild Court Tamed," in which he highlighted the improvements that had been made to the property.[116] The number of families living in the court had been reduced, "corrupt matter" and filth had been hauled away, the buildings had been whitewashed and a new foundation had been put in. More important than physical improvements, however, was the moral rejuvenation that, Dickens argued, had transformed the inhabitants of Wild Court. Thrift, morality and pacific relationships with their neighbors had replaced decadence, violence and squalor. Along with physical rehabilitation, a new system of inspection and new rules had been instituted:

> Each tenant's room must be scrubbed at least once a week. A superintendent lives upon the spot, who is to have access to all the apartments, and right of interference for protection of the property, and the maintenance of the conditions under which alone it is possible for the houses to continue wholesome.[117]

Outside of the new surveillance regime, "there is no attempt to exercise control." However, such "model" housing did exercise control: a restructuring of space and its use was combined with surveillance to reform behavior. Exterior improvements were accompanied by the internal partitioning of apartments for the maintenance of increased privacy. Such spatial improvements could be referred to as "God's passionless reformers/ Influences that purify, and heal, and are not seen."[118] One reform advocate, speaking of another housing development, asserted that

> not only has the improvement in the physical condition of the occupants of these houses answered the most sanguine expectations of their founders, but it is still more gratifying to know that *moral* improvement has been made. The intemperate have become sober and the disorderly well conducted, since their residence in the beautiful and peaceful abodes.[119]

The connection between physical environment (an important part of which is the use of space) and morality had become a commonplace by the middle of the nineteenth century.[120] From their bastions of relative tranquillity, the middle classes, allied with the growing power of the state, worked to pacify public spaces and to encourage the ideology of domestic life that was reshaping middle-class housing and attitudes. Legislation was used "to create a physical and institutional environment in which undesirable working-class habits and attitudes would be deterred, while private philanthropy could undertake the active propagation of a new moral code," and in this way "the material needs of the poor would then be used as a means toward their moral reformation."[121]

6 "Heave half a brick at a stranger"

Strategies of violence

A whole history remains to be written of *spaces* – which would at the same time be the history of *powers* (both of those terms in the plural) – from the great strategies of geopolitics to the little tactics of the habitat....

Michel Foucault[1]

A very general impression respecting its inhabitants is, that "heave half a brick at a stranger," is the prevailing tone among them.

"In the Black Country," 1869[2]

The preceding chapters have demonstrated the sources and outlines of two mentalities of violence, explored the ways that they shaped violence and suggested some interrelationships between space and violence. Configurations of power also influenced the ways physical force was used. As Foucault has noted, power "is exercised rather than possessed; it is not the 'privilege,' acquired or preserved, of the dominant class, but the overall effect of its strategic positions...."[3] Similarly, mentalities of violence were enacted through a variety of "strategies." The different contexts in which violence occurs contribute to the forms it takes: it can, for instance, take place among social equals or between subordinates and superiors. There are many ways to act violently, but only some will be generally seen as legitimate within a particular set of circumstances. Strategies exist on many cultural and geographical scales, some of them involving dominant political or economic power, others functioning in relatively minute social interstices. For example, the state had for centuries relied upon highly ritualized strategies of publicly displayed physical force. Gallows, pillories and whipping carts organized space in particular ways to maximize their impact and meaning. Under civilizing pressures, judicial punishment changed over the eighteenth and nineteenth centuries, and strategies that directed pain against the body and organized space dramatically – although briefly – were gradually superseded by systems that made less violent but more rigorous uses of space.[4] The civilizing state sought to hide what judicial violence remained from the public gaze, partly because the viewing of pain was seen as having a potentially brutalizing effect on the crowds that witnessed it.[5] The privatization of punishment civilized the public sphere while concurrently giving the state greater control over the popular imagination of judicial violence, denying the condemned convict the possibility of subverting the ritual and eliminating the crowd from its supervisory role.[6] Here, the twin civilizing imperatives of removing violence from the public sphere – of "relocating" violence culturally and spatially – while monopolizing legitimate violence are very clear.

The civilizing offensive proceeded in step with the "pacification" of the public sphere.[7] Pacification included the demarcation of respectable and non-respectable neighborhoods but also aimed at controlling the public spaces of the poor and working class through policing. Moreover, reformers worked to change working-class attitudes that saw streets as legitimate theaters of violence. Increasing numbers of police enforced pacification and limited violence in public spaces. Although the police were an instrument of civilization, policing itself relies upon a strategy of violence, albeit one that is often implicit rather than active.[8] The strategies of policing were, in large measure, exempted from the civilized disdain for public violence. However, policing was always controversial: the state, its agents and its supporters tended to see officially sanctioned physical force as something other than "violence" while the opinions of the policed population ranged from ambivalence to outright hostility.[9] Punishment and policing thus represent two areas in which civilizing thought organized violence in new ways. Customary violence strategies were often different from (and sometimes directly opposed to) civilized ones, particularly in regard to public spaces. These differences reflected fundamental divergences in each mentality's strategies of legitimate force. Two interrelated pairs of themes highlight these differences and, in particular, illuminate customary violence strategies. The first connects the legitimacy of violence to the way it is performed: power brought with it legitimacy to use violence against certain targets in accordance with particular strategies. Equally important, particular ways of performing violence – depending on circumstances – were more legitimate than others. The second pair of themes relates to "exclusion" and "resistance." Exclusion refers to new social and spatial trends in nineteenth-century life as well as to customary notions of community self-policing. Resistance concerns the contestation of power, in particular the power to regulate public spaces. Performance, legitimacy, exclusion and resistance were concepts that shaped the customary mentality and structured its confrontations with the civilizing offensive.

Performance and legitimacy

If mentalities of violence are structured like a language, we might conceive of violent strategies as their spoken form: like any other form of utterance, they take particular forms and follow certain rules. Violence was a prominent way of expressing a wide variety of customary meanings. As the last chapter suggested, working-class life was often lived publicly, in the sense of material as well as imagined geographies. Other aspects of working-class violence could be deliberately public and made use of violent strategies in order to gain legitimacy through the use of space. In some cases, the public, performative nature of customary violence played a key role in structuring the limits of legitimate violence, and many forms of customarily sanctioned violence were at the heart of social life. The coherent "syntax" of some customary violence (a predictable and structured set of rules that gave it meaning) required a public page on which that language could be inscribed. The public structuring of violence kept it transparent to the community and was essential to the expressive functions delegated by custom to violent acts. Spatial strategies were often a vital element in the shaping of rule-based violence. In other words, since participants and observers alike accepted the structural framework of violence, it was a viable medium for the expression of various meanings. Although reasonably clear distinctions between "expressive" and "instrumental" violence have been suggested, the matter is highly ambiguous.[10] Violence was often expressive and at the same time motivated by gain. Power, dominance, authority, masculinity, group solidarity and community disapproval were often expressed in customary violence; however, these messages were also about getting or maintaining "something," even if it were something intangible such as honor or masculinity. Violence usually involved contests over what has been defined as "psychic property," making distinctions between its instrumental and expressive qualities difficult.[11] Thus, on some level, a conversation of sorts was often being carried on among the participants in violence, one which, at times, may have been decidedly unequal. Alternatively, there were situations in which the participants were more evenly matched, either physically or in terms of their social status. In either case, legitimate dynamics for violence could arise in various situations, each with particular strategies appropriate to different power relationships.

Steven C. Caton has usefully analyzed the importance of and differences between different sorts of strategies of violence. In an investigation of an incident of tribal violence in Yemen in 1980, he distinguishes between "violence of community" and "violence of exclusion." The latter will be dealt with in the next section. "Violence of community" in Caton's study "reconstitutes relations among parties": when Yemeni tribesmen believed they had been wronged,

> it was not to the central state that the contending parties turned, or not usually, for the state, it was feared, would jeopardize the region's culturally valued sense of autonomy. Instead, they turned to each other, and would enter into a complex and delicate process of feuding and mediation in the hope of coming to a resolution of their differences.[12]

Through autonomous resolution, tears in the social fabric caused by disputes were repaired, and community authority was reassembled and strengthened. Although Caton's analysis is rooted in a detailed local study, his theoretical approach is applicable to other societies with strong customs of autonomous dispute settlement and community self-policing. As discussed in Chapter 3, the customary mentality accepted a greater amount of physical violence and granted a more diffuse legitimacy in the distribution of violence than did its civilized alternative. In line with traditions of retributive justice and community self-policing, the customary mentality legitimated the use of physical force in response to many situations. Such legitimacy depended upon adherence to community expectations as to the motivations, contents and forms of violence. In order to monitor its legitimacy, customary violence was often "located" – culturally and spatially – at the center of community life and surrounded by a code of assumptions as to its legitimate form. For instance, "violence of community" was shaped by strategies that interacted with imagined space in choosing a particular space (perhaps at a particular time) for the performance of violence. Although often seen as purely "impulsive," the producers of customary violence were often selective about the ways in which they engaged in violence. For example, although the cause of a fight might have been a sudden anger or slight, workers (at least up until the 1860s, as discussed in Chapter 4) were typically scrupulous in taking their fight "outside" and satisfying customary expectations. When workers sought to express disapproval of a community transgressor, they frequently did so in deliberately chosen public spaces. If the transgression took place at work, violence might be performed there in order to emphasize an assertion of control over that space. Strategies were thus, on their most basic level, connected to appropriate places. Ritualized male fighting and the use of force to socially exclude transgressors were two recognizable types of working-class violence shaped by customary spatial strategies. However, more than simply defining, say, "the street" as the legitimate site of a particular type of violent activity, spatial strategies actively chose particular places for performing violence and also used smaller-scale strategies of organizing that space.

These strategies used space in particular ways to shape and channel violence to express certain meanings: enclosing, opening or demarcating spaces in particular ways to bring it maximum visibility and expressive power. "Ridings" and other sorts of "rough music" were one highly performative form of violence, the meanings of which have been subjected to sustained examination by Thompson and others.[13] Although this study is not only concerned with rough music per se, it suggests the spatializing tendencies of customary violence more generally. In 1827, James Tuckfield, a Bristol shipwright, agreed to work in violation of the agreement of the other shipwrights to "stand out" for higher wages. His co-workers expressed their disapproval in a deliberate and particular public use of space. Tuckfield was met by a mob of shipwrights and they "proceeded through various streets of the city carrying him on a pole and at the same time most disgracefully ill using and abusing his person."[14] During a riot in London during the strife surrounding the build up to the Reform Bill of 1832, a factory in London was attacked by a mob. One observer noted,

> The hands employed escaped in the confusion, but death was decreed to the engineer – a stranger to the city, under whose direction the machinery was being fitted. The unfortunate man was caught, placed in a sack with its mouth tied round his neck, laid in a truck, and amid yells and hootings, drawn through the streets.[15]

Although threatened with death and handled violently, he was not killed. In many cases, victims of violence were paraded, dragged or chased through the streets to the accompaniment of shouting and threats. Informers or blacklegs were loudly called out in the street, a public performance that declared the motives of a crowd's violence while potentially attracting more participants.[16] The small crowds who committed these acts made deliberate use of a public space and sought to draw as much attention as possible to their actions; it was a performance, and they were making a point easily legible to observers. There was thus a use of space that was both practical (streets were the most public space) and symbolically resonant (control was asserted over the space in question). To drag someone through the streets while beating them is a type of violent strategy that takes on the qualities of a performance. When Arthur Blatch was beaten and "ducked" by his co-workers in 1882, the "tank" near the stables in their workplace had taken on particular resonances in regard to the enforcement of work-discipline.[17] Binding Blatch with rope, dragging him across the yard (in full view of the other workers) and then dousing him with filth was a performance that expressed a particular meaning not only to Blatch, but also to other workers at the firm. Thus, a well-defined use of space in this situation was tied to the enforcement of workplace discipline. The control of cultural boundaries, the maintenance of group solidarity through force and the assertion of power over a deviant was thus practiced spatially.

Actions sometimes communicated as loudly – and possibly even more clearly – than words. In the customary mentality, violence was a language that conveyed many meanings, and fistfighting was one of its most widely spoken dialects. Fighting was so visible partly because the working class lacked privacy; however, as in other forms of ritual violence, its cultural significance was also shaped by deliberately public strategies. The expressive qualities of fighting derived from the fact that participants and observers alike understood its meanings. One of the most important messages implied in the performative use of violence is the assertion that the act is appropriate, legitimate or "fair." The ritual fight required an audience to witness that the fighters conducted themselves fairly and also to receive the messages expressed in a fight. Ritual fighting could often be simultaneously instrumental and expressive, combining contests for things (money, buying the next round of drinks, a prize) with meanings that were not material. Fights, as I discussed in Chapter 4, often centered on public houses. As a "staging area" for a variety of displays, and under the pressures of economic deprivation, these spaces saw the boiling over of animosities as well as effusions of good-natured sociability.[18] The "ring," the defined arena for fistfighting, was essential to the fair fight, and it was adapted to everyday public spaces. Beyond marking out the boundaries of acceptable violence, the ring deliberately facilitated the crowd's observance of the fighting ritual. The crowd witnessed the fight, and, along with whatever enjoyment or excitement they felt, they ensured that no "foul blows" were struck, that time was kept properly between rounds, that neither man took any "unfair advantage" and that each fighter was given the opportunity to forfeit (and thereby end) the fight. Finally, the crowd recognized the victor, reflecting and receiving the fight's expression of dominance and masculine hierarchy. Within this customary framework, a secretive, non-public fight would have been, in a sense, "speechless," and thus senseless. Ritual fighting suggests a coincidence between received physical spaces (streets), an imagined set of assumptions about those spaces (constructions of "the street" that viewed it as an accepted site of public fighting) and an actively produced spatial strategy (the ring and its internal demarcations) that constituted the legitimacy of a regulated form of violence.[19] More than simply being open to the community's gaze because of the material spaces of working-class life, customary fighting rituals were fundamentally dependent on a structured public arena.

In incidents of spousal violence, either one or both participants sometimes deliberately used public spaces to their own ends. As noted, Mayhew and others witnessed many such incidents in which domestic disturbances were performed publicly, with husband and wife arguing back and forth (often in combination with some violence) about the legitimacy of the dispute. The audience reflected, absorbed and debated the views of the opposing sides. Wives might claim that husbands had overstepped the legitimate boundaries of customarily sanctioned domestic discipline, using public forums as a way to publicize their individual circumstances and gain a moral victory. Husbands might seek community confirmation that their wives had in some way deserved the treatment meted out to them or that it had been within the boundaries of acceptable discipline. It was often uncertain whose claims to legitimacy the crowd would consider stronger.[20] Spousal violence, thus, was often a performance and related to struggles over legitimacy. Although that performance was not conducted in the formalized "ring" of male fistfighting, the nature of working-class spaces facilitated the performative aspects of family violence. Such violence operated according to customary notions of discipline and community surveillance of social relationships. Like other forms of "violence of community," spousal violence sought to repair a perceived imbalance or transgression and to reassert the social economy of power: it patrolled the boundaries of marriage and maintained the hierarchy of the home.[21] Women, working-class women in particular, tended to endure (and expect) frequent domestic assaults, and wife-beaters appear often to have gained some sympathy, or even agreement, from some working-class women, who tended to be well aware of what happened in their neighbors' homes. While neighbors frequently mediated tensions between combative husbands and wives, there was a current of belief, among women as well as men, that abusive and provoking wives were to some degree responsible for the violence that befell them. As Shani D'Cruze has noted, "To late twentieth-century feminist – or humanist – perceptions this sort of violence constitutes abuse. This was not always or unequivocally the case for nineteenth-century working women."[22] The legitimacy of disciplining social transgression through violence was an important foundation of the customary mentality, and that approval functioned in both the public and private spheres.

However, while spousal violence fitted into other imperatives of the customary mentality regarding its motivations and public context, its form was far less restrained than other forms of customary "violence of community." Domestic violence was, as one historian has put it, a "privileged" form of violence in both custom and law.[23] While the disciplinary imperatives of the customary mentality applied to many situations, whether inside or outside the home, and, although spousal violence was part of a more general cultural milieu of violence, the forms and boundaries of that violence were different from other forms of customarily accepted violence, such as ritualized street fights:

> Domestic collisions were far less orderly, and were more dangerous as a result, especially to women who were usually, though not always, the weaker fighters. The fights normally took place at home. Couples did not decorously exchange punches, but wrestled, slapped, kicked, bit and threw household objects, while terrified children looked on or tried to interfere.[24]

The range, tone, and form of domestic fighting did not follow the pattern of male ritual fights, nor were they expected to. Spouses did not fight in rounds, observe rules of "fair" and "foul" blows, or necessarily cease fighting when one of them (usually the wife) wanted to stop. Husbands used implements, kicked, threw things and slammed women against walls and floors, all behavior that would have been viewed as unfair – or even unmanly – in a street fight with another man. For instance, the popular (although mythical) view that the criminal law continued to grant the right "to beat a faulty wife with a stick of the thickness of his thumb" still had some currency in the 1890s.[25] Thus, although constructions of imagined space were as vital to the legitimate production of domestic violence (in "the home") as they were to, for example, male ritualized fighting (in "the street"), spousal violence lacked a strictly defined structure; it was not organized according to a predictable strategy and was devoid of the kind of limits typically placed upon other types of customary violence.

Which is not to say that there were no boundaries on domestic violence's legitimacy. Legitimate spousal violence was to maintain dominance and assert male domestic control, one that the community could be expected to generally accept. Thus, explicitly homicidal violence was not a performative strategy of legitimate violence. As is apparent from the records of the courts, the frontier of legitimacy (and that between homicidal and disciplinary violence) was often very difficult to locate. The benefit of doubt in many cases was to the advantage of husbands, and even fatal violence could be lightly punished if it arose out of provocations that were seen as legitimate. Nevertheless, witnesses and courts appear to have drawn fine distinctions in considering domestic violence's performance. For example, the specific form of a blow might be of interest to the authorities. In a deposition for the trial of Joseph Castle for his wife's murder (he had stabbed her), the victim's mother described a prior violent incident in which Jane Castle appeared at her house exhausted and upset.

> I asked if her husband had ill-treated her. She said he had struck her several times, but with his open hand.[26]

In another case, a shoemaker who witnessed the previously cited row between Mary McCarthy and John Cockering (se Chapters 3 and 5) deposed that at one point,

> she then used very foul language to him whereupon he struck her as I believe with an open hand three separate times upon the head. He hit her as hard as he could and I can't say whether the two last blows were not given with the clenched fist, but the first I believe was with the open hand.[27]

This witness, and others, testified as to how hard Cockering had struck McCarthy. A woman pointed out that some of the blows were given "with violence":

> Some language of an abusive nature was used by the deceased when Cockering kicked her twice on the legs and posterior and hit her once on each side of the head with his fist. The blows were violent and one of them blackened her right eye.

Such detailed considerations were key to evaluating whether or not force had been legitimate. Since Cockering had also kicked McCarthy, beaten her with a stick and repeatedly shoved her head against a wall, determining the closure of his fist might seem irrelevant; however, these distinctions appear to have been crucial in shaping the reaction of witnesses and authorities to violent acts and suggest the connection between performative strategies and legitimacy.

Performance and legitimacy were thus linked in private as well as public violence, though the relationships were different in each case. Customarily, controlling public violence between strangers was seen as a greater social imperative than controlling private violence within families. Moreover, the strategy of ritual fighting reflected the presumed social equality of its participants: the fight must be "fair." However, even "violence of community" sometimes took a relatively unstructured form, notably in instances of spousal violence. Although the aim of domestic violence was to maintain a community-sanctioned balance of power (or, rather, *imbalance* of power), as a "private" matter it was not necessary that the community itself witnessed that violence in order for it to be legitimate. Normally, then, spousal violence did not need to be especially performative. Performative strategies only became necessary when – due to the nature of material spaces or in cases in which a dispute over legitimacy arose – private altercations spilled into the public sphere. Finally, because male dominance of the family featured in both civilized and customary mentalities, public disorder continued to be seen as far more threatening than private conflict. As previous cases have suggested and the next section will explore in greater detail, unequal social power could change the finely calibrated relationship between public performance and legitimacy. In such cases, violence could be more free flowing and the strategies that structured it less limiting.

Exclusion and resistance

Spatial imagination is often structured around notions of belonging. Certain individuals or groups are defined as not fitting into particular areas, either through some quality they possess (for example, their class, ethnicity or gender) or because they have broken a cultural rule and thereby become unwelcome (a situation that might be only temporary). As civilizing pressures and urban demarcation increased, the working-classes became more contained in spaces that excluded them from respectability and power. Space can thus be organized to express power through the ability to exclude. As David Sibley has noted:

> For some, the built environment is to be maintained and reproduced in its existing form if it embodies social values which individuals or groups have both the power and the capacity to retain. For others, the built environment constitutes a landscape of domination. It is alienating, and action on the part of the relatively powerless will register in the dominant vocabulary as deviance, threat or subversion.[28]

However, *within* working-class communities there were also several, overlapping layers of exclusion, and various excluded groups. In Caton's view, just as there is a "violence of community" that seeks to reconstitute social relations, there is a "violence of exclusion":

> By "violence of exclusion" I mean a violence that has the opposite aim, one of driving an opponent out of the community rather than trying to draw him back into it. This may be a violence of brute force, such as open warfare, or of dictat ... but the intention is the same: the removal of the unwanted person or group from the shared space of the community.[29]

Chapter 3 emphasized that the desire for autonomy and the vigorous nature of customary self-policing were parts of the customary mentality of violence. As we have seen, customary notions often shaped violence into limited forms: fist-fighting and "rough music" show ways in which ritual and custom could be mobilized violently but with restraint. Those deemed to be "outsiders" were, generally, likely to be subject to more severe violence, as many of the limits that regulated violence within a community might be relaxed or ignored.[30] There were many varieties of "outsider," simply being unknown in a particular area being perhaps the most common. However, though sometimes "known," soldiers were a common "outsider" presence in many English garrison towns, and there were often clashes between soldiers and local inhabitants, particularly if soldiers were disrespectful towards locals.[31] It is clear that soldiers were perceived by communities as being a threat to their peace, although jurisdictional anomalies probably conceal their contribution to local violence.[32]

While outsiders could be defined by their class, profession or place of residence, ethnicity provided another axis for the highlighting of differences. In particular, the Irish were targets of exclusionary violence. Some English workers believed that the Irish undermined the stability of the labor market and people of all classes saw them as a disruptive and savage outsider group.[33] For instance, James Murray and eight other Irishmen were laboring in a field at harvest time in Woodhurst, Huntingdonshire in 1838 when a group of Englishmen passed and called out to them, "that we were taking the bread out of their mouths and that they would have us."[34] Their employer, William Tyson, locked the men in the barn to protect them after becoming aware of the locals' animosity. A mob broke in and the men were severely punched, kicked and beaten with weapons including bludgeons and a hook mounted on a pole. A farmer deposed that he had heard someone state that he wished to "see the inside of all the Irishmen and those that employ them." The mob asked Tyson to participate with them in their attack and when he refused he was pelted with stones and gravel. One of the participants in the attack, all of whom were laborers, deposed, "the Ramsey men who were at work at Woodhurst said they should drive all the Irishmen out of Woodhurst." He said that he was threatened himself: the attackers told him that if he "did not help them they would throw me in the pond." In London, Mayhew interviewed an Irish rubbish carter, finding that he had been the victim of similar sorts of violence. The man had found work helping a fellow Irishman, making, by his standards, good wages, as Mayhew recounted (in dialect):

> But one Sunday evening I was standing talking with people as lived in the same coort, and I tould how I was helping Tim. And two Englishmen came to find four men as they wanted for work, and ould Ragin (Regan) tould them what I was working for. And one of 'em said I was "a b—— Irish fool," … and words came on, and thin there was a fight, and the pelleece came, and thin the fight was harder.[35]

An Irish laborer in Kent was attacked in his house by a crowd of about twenty who demanded that the "Irish bugger" come out in the street (where they claimed they would kill him), and, when he refused, they threw a "hail" of stones at the house, some of which struck its occupant.[36]

A large mob attacked several Irish laborers and their families on the Isle of Grain, Kent, in April 1864, at the house of Michael and Ellen Ronan.[37] Michael Ronan was employed as a bricklayer's laborer in the building of a fort. Ronan testified that on Saturday, 16 April he saw a large crowd of men, women and boys approaching his house. He fetched a police constable, leaving his wife, three children and four of their lodgers in the house.[38] By the time he returned, his wife and two of the lodgers had been beaten, kicked and bludgeoned with sticks. Ronan stated, "the crowd outside remained a little while shouting that they would 'turn the Irish out of the island,' then they went away." The following morning the crowd returned, entered the house and resumed beating the inhabitants. Michael Ronan was beaten as he left the house with one of his children in his arms, and he sought refuge at the nearby home of the foreman bricklayer. He later escaped. "I was afraid to stop on the island for fear of my life," he recalled, "Timothy Flinn and Bartholomew Sullivan [two lodgers] escaped with me." The crowd may have been angered by the work of the Irish men; however, they took out their anger on Michael Ronan's wife Ellen as well. During the first attack, she had her head cut by a poker, which caused severe bleeding:

> I was then left alone in the house with the children. I begged Charles Pearson and the others to spare me and my children and not to kill the men. Charles Pearson then hit me a blow with a stick just by where the poker struck me. I got four or five blows in one wound on my head. My head bled very much. I begged of the lot standing outside not to kill the men; they were beating my lodgers as fast as they could catch them. Then George Baulkham struck me on the other side of my head with a chopper or something like a hatchet.

She described how the crowd entered the house during the second attack and chased her husband out with one of their children in his arms. Then,

> All the crowd left the house and I was alone except Thomas Keefe and Edward Casey whom I had locked into a room. Thomas Candle came into my bedroom. I followed him into the room where one of my children lay crying and Candle says, "Here lies a kid, I have a good mind to kill it." The crowd had all gone then. I said, "You would not hurt the child would you?" He said, "Yes, hurt all the bloody kit of you."

In the end, the child remained unhurt. A clerk employed at the fortification worksite witnessed the attack and corroborated the Ronans's stories, including the beating of Ellen Ronan. As we can see, when it came to attacking outsiders, customary limitations on acceptable violence weakened, and ideals of fairness and proportionality were far less in evidence than in disputes among English people. There is no sign of the "rules" of fair fighting, and, while domestic violence was common, attacks by men upon women to whom they were not married (let alone using weapons against them) was rarely seen as legitimate.

The customary mentality was adapted to urban environments as the nineteenth century progressed, and the insularity of some communities was at times violently expressed. Andrew Mearns noted the hostility and violence that greeted missionary workers, who were sometimes attacked.[39] Writing of the Black Country, David Woods suggests that

> communities were generally not well disposed to outside interference in their lives. Police, bailiffs, public health inspectors, School Board officials were all unwelcome visitors to the yards, courts and backstreets and were often met with hostile resistance.[40]

Most violence, however, was intra-class. Class differences might engender animosity and hatred (or envy), yet attacks on middle-class outsiders were uncommon unless they were acting as representatives of an agency (whether state or private) perceived to be interfering with local freedom and autonomy. However, in times of exceptional tension, the reluctance to use violence outside of one's class could evaporate, as it did during some labor disputes,[41] periods of political upheaval or during crime panics. For example, in the wake of the Jack the Ripper murders, the assumption that the murderer was a "toff" gave workingmen "license to accuse and intimidate their betters."[42] Other groups of outsiders also found themselves the target of exclusionary violence following the Whitechapel murders, also based upon the various suspicions as to the identity of the Ripper; along with the well-off, Jews and doctors were attacked. Various sorts of "deviants" could, in similar ways, be excluded. In this way, they were subject to kinds of violence often reserved for "outsiders." Exclusionary violence against deviants took two main forms: the exclusion of deviants from public spaces (mainly, the streets) and attacks on their homes. The use of violence to control public spaces and to exclude transgressive individuals from them was, in part, motivated by an assertion of power over the self-policing of public spaces, highlighting further the ways that a "violence of exclusion" was used to assert community control.

The enforcement of labor discipline through the use of violence also had a long history in pre-industrial trade organizations. Violence might be used in response to changes in the structure of work and the power relationships within a given trade.[43] Maintaining unanimity among the workforce was an imperative during a strike; preventing blackleg labor was accomplished through group solidarity, persuasion and, ultimately, through threats and the use of violence. Viewing a labor dispute from the side of employers, Andrew Ure wrote that the workers would set "a watch upon the streets [preventing] us from getting men in, and will abuse anybody that comes, in the most shocking manner, even to taking their lives if it were necessary."[44] Referring to anti-blackleg violence 30 years later, Charles Mackay highlighted the connection between strikes, violence and the surveillance of the streets by workers. If a worker continued his job during a strike, "the machinery of war was set in motion. It became unsafe for such men to show themselves in the streets; they were insulted, beaten, kicked, maimed."[45] We have previously seen examples of the so-called "machinery of war" in action upon workers who defied the authority of their trade, and the performative spectacles that were made of them through ridings and other publicly humiliating assaults. An anonymous laborer's autobiography described some specific incidents that reveal the way that control of public spaces was contested. For example, sabotage had, since at least the early nineteenth century, been a mainstay of the nascent union movement: the Luddites were only the most iconic example of a widespread phenomenon. Machine-breaking was made a capital offense:

By that Act, some executions took place; and a man named Cushman, principal witness in one of these cases, was shortly after assaulted by a mob in Hare Street Fields, and lost his life in a pool of water while endeavouring to escape.[46]

The dangers that informers faced have already been noted. However, the significance of this attack, which is familiar from earlier discussions of anti-deviant violence, became tied to subsequent events linked to the control of the streets. The author continues, writing of another strike some 30 years later:

The weavers union enforced the strike by "sealing" the looms of the workers: running a paper band through the loom sealed by a special wax seal. Thus, if it was used, the weaver would break the seal, forfeit strike pay and become "a marked man."[47]

Soon after this latter strike began, "[the words] 'Remember Cushman' were chalked up on doors and walls in a hundred places."[48] Exclusion was, in this case, physically inscribed into the structures of public space, relying upon both the power of a credible violent threat and the resilience of folk memory for its power.

Other sorts of deviants were treated similarly. A police officer recounting the community ire that would descend upon "bet welchers" (swindlers who would leave race tracks after taking bets) emphasized the typical self-policing mechanisms of the customary mentality. Some "welchers" were able to get away undetected. However,

sometimes there is a little hitch in the arrangements; his line of retreat is cut off, or a goodly number of his clients may have him under observation, and then, if he attempts to get away, the cry of "welcher" is raised, and the miscreant is likely to be almost torn limb from limb by the crowd. Not only is he attacked by those whom he is endeavouring to victimize, but a welcher is always considered "good sport" for all who can get near enough to let fly at him.[49]

More rarely, homes were attacked directly, which signals a different strategy of violence, one involving the "private" sphere of the home. House attacks were often accompanied by a particularly strong fury on the part of crowds. "Pulling down" workhouses was common in riots following the introduction of the New Poor Law in the mid 1830s, and this tradition of protest was clearly adapted to other purposes.[50] As we have seen, the Irish are a notable example of an "outsider" group who were attacked in their homes. However, there might be other motivations for house attacks. In one case, a man fired a gun out of his window at a passing procession. In response, members of the parade began pelting his windows with stones. Some claimed that there was talk of pulling his house down.[51] Other cases were often more symbolic and restrained, falling more in line with the history of "rough music," for example, against men who used excessive violence upon women,[52] or against those who brought disrepute upon a town.[53]

In some cases, "violence of community" and "violence of exclusion" overlapped: some local deviants could be very roughly handled, but then ultimately admitted back into the good graces of the community. Against "outsiders," however, or in times of increased tension, violence could be more sustained and serious. Exclusion could be either short and severe or of longer duration and lesser severity.[54] In considering the fates of blacklegs, informers, welchers, deviants and outsiders, we see various elements of a shared vocabulary of violence for dealing with perceived threats to the community. Mobbing in the streets, calling out their crime to attract a crowd and the resulting beatings were motivated by the customary mentality of violence. The resort to exclusionary force, with the concurrent, implied assertion of the authority to exclude, is a common feature among these disparate motives and contexts for violence. It is in part because these customary actions challenged state authority over public space that they were viewed as so threatening.[55]

The use of exclusionary violence brings us to the related topic of "resistance," a concept with many interpretations. For example, Gatrell has asserted the significance of "resistant mentalities" in reference to attitudes toward death and capital punishment, emphasizing "resistances to change" and the power of "inertia" in cultural attitudes more generally.[56] Resistance is thus conceptualized as a powerful, if rather passive, consequence of tradition, a view which is highly relevant to the customary mentality of violence. Other, more active forms of resistance are also important. Paul Routledge has defined "resistance" as

> any action, imbued with intent, that attempts to challenge, change, or retain particular circumstances relating to societal relations processes or institutions. Resistances are assembled out of the rituals and practices of everyday life, and imply some form of contestation, some juxtaposition of forces.[57]

In this sense, finding spaces *for* resistance and manipulating spaces *as a form of* resistance are both relevant. Sibley takes up the question of awareness and resistance, noting that the socio-spatial contexts of power may not be apparent to the actors within it.[58] The complex nature of resistance is perhaps best expressed by Pile, who argues that

> people are positioned differently in unequal and multiple power relations, that more and less powerful people are active in the constitution of unfolding relationships of authority, meaning and identity, these activities are contingent, ambiguous and awkwardly situated, ... but resistance seeks to occupy, deploy and create alternative spatialities from those defined through oppression and exploitation.[59]

This description of resistance suggests a way of looking at the multiple levels of power and exclusion in working-class communities, the way that violence was an integral part of that social organization and the relevance of the "alternative spatialities" created through resistance.[60] Thus, although the term "resistance" may conjure images of large-scale confrontations against authority and a significant undermining of the processes of hegemonic power, I use the term here to refer to more small-scale, even unconscious resistance and situate it in the practices of everyday life. Within a particular material and imagined space, "innumerable ways of playing and foiling the other's game, that is the space instituted by others, characterizes the subtle, stubborn, resistant activity of groups which, since they lack their own space, have to get along in a network of already established forces and representations."[61] The "spaces of control" carved out by resistance may, in Sibley's words, be "too small to interrupt the reproduction of socio-spatial relations in the interest of the hegemonic power."[62] Resistance, then, challenges a dominant authority, or asserts an alternative authority, without necessarily attempting to overcome it.

In this context, resistance refers both to the general position of the customary mentality in relation to civilizing efforts as well as to specific acts. The prevalence of exclusionary violence highlights one aspect of a spatialized "resistance" in working-class culture: the use of customarily sanctioned violence to make use of and control space outside – or in opposition to – the influence of official law. Some sorts of violence, particularly violent exclusionary practices, were a type of resistance, marking an assertion of the authority to exclude members of the community and to self-police the boundaries of community standards through an appeal to customary rights and legitimacy. Customary assertions of power over public space were confronted by the expansion of state power and efforts to "civilize," "purify" and "pacify" space throughout the nineteenth century. However, this relationship was not only bipolar: resistance may define a counternarrative of power through the creation not only of alternative freedoms, but also by the imposition of new inequalities and exclusions, as I have explored in relation to, for example, domestic violence and deviancy. Violence concerned not a single oppressive power, but multiple levels of exclusion, power and domination. As Foucault has noted,

> power is not exercised simply as an obligation or a prohibition on those who "do not have it"; it invests them, is transmitted by them and through them; it exerts pressure upon them, just as they themselves, in their struggle against it, resist the grip it has on them.[63]

Workers may have lived within an excluded geographic space, but within "their" territory they at times asserted some forms of community control and a degree of freedom (which may, in many cases, have meant limiting the freedom of others). There were preferred sites of resistance – mainly the streets and the other spaces of working-class social life – and there were also preferred representatives of the dominant power to be resisted. The most visible manifestation of new forms of state authority in the nineteenth century in the daily lives of workers were the police, and it is in relations with the police that important aspects of resistance become visible.

Official efforts to clear the streets were often greatly resented. Such innovations as the "moving on" system, in which the police broke up congregations of men on the streets and in front of pubs, "brought the arm of municipal and state authority directly to bear upon key institutions of daily life in working-class neighborhoods," a development that was resisted.[64] Police interference in street disputes often forced a legal proceeding between the participants who were sometimes quickly reconciled between themselves, yet still faced the time and expense of a court case.[65] Police intervention represented an attempted imposition of a new, civilized authority over dispute settlement in conflict with the customary predilection for direct, autonomous action.[66] Storch has given a detailed description of the tense period surrounding the introduction of the New Police and the gradual increase in police interference as a force for the attempted re-shaping of working-class life.[67] There were many explicit disputes over the control of streets, often regarding their use as a site of traditional celebrations. In 1820 a part-time constable, James Millman, was called out to suppress "riotous and disorderly Christmas singing" in Exeter. After repeated urgings from Millman, the crowd began to disperse. They did so, however, with "a great tumult." While Millman was attempting to take someone into custody, the crowd intervened and Millman struck a man with his "mace." Emphasizing the tenuous nature of police authority before the development of local constabularies, Millman was prosecuted by his intended target and convicted of assault.[68] Storch has detailed the changing nature of Guy Fawkes celebrations throughout the nineteenth century, and as the police gradually increased their influence over daily street life, the Fifth of November was marked by attempts to subvert police control of the streets.[69] Street battles were intense in Lewes in 1841, and crowds assaulted several police officers. James Burridge was on duty as a police officer on 5 November,

> and saw a great mob of persons unlawfully assembled together and making a great noise disturbance letting off fireworks and heaving lighted tar barrels through the high street. About ten o'clock I was violently assaulted by the mob who hustled me and threw stones at me and gravel and dirt into my eyes whereby my eyes were much hurt and painful.[70]

Burridge's experience was a common one that night, as many of the police were assaulted with sticks or clubs, punched and kicked. Similar events took place in Lewes in 1847, though these appear to have been somewhat less ferocious.[71] Holidays, in line with customary notions of license, often led to disruption and challenges to official authority, as did elections.[72]

There was another side to working-class attitudes to the law. Although there was great animosity between the working class and the police, especially during the period of their first general introduction, workers' attitudes were often ambivalent rather than purely antagonistic. At times, popular reaction to the police could be actively supportive, particularly as the nineteenth century wore on and the presence of policemen became less of an innovative intrusion and more of an accepted fact of life. Working people frequently used or cooperated with the law, and this acceptance of legal proceedings gradually spread as informal, customary dispute settlement was superseded by formal, civilized means. Grudging respect and acceptance – likely dependent upon the character of individual policemen – is apparent in some instances in the later Victorian period, the time when the image of the "bobby" was taking fuller form. "When an officer does his duty without unnecessary harshness," an observer of the police courts stated, "he is considered as an honourable enemy, to be feared and avoided, to be defeated by stratagem, or if need by force; but he excites no feeling of hatred or malignity; indeed he is not unfrequently appealed to by the man he has just captured to speak a good word on his behalf."[73] There were many occasions in which workers accepted and even assisted the police in their activities, assuming, of course, that those activities met with community approval. If the police interfered with strongly held customary ways of life or crossed a popularly perceived line of fairness (as they did when they assisted employers and blacklegs during labor disputes or violated what workers perceived as "rights") they became the targets of community resentment and, at times, violence.[74] It was only gradually, through a long process of tense negotiation, that the authority of the police became accepted in working-class communities, and, eventually, working-class people were very willing to call upon police assistance.[75] By that point, there had been many decades of civilizing efforts and the increasing importance of respectability among the working class went hand-in-hand with increasing police legitimacy. However, resistance inhered in a variety of actions, many of which were far smaller in scale than the riots noted above and were not as comprehensive in their challenge to authorities. For example, though working-class wives might call on the police for certain needs, such as separation orders and to have summonses enforced against husbands, "their first instinct seems to have been to thwart the police."[76]

The innovations of Peel's police initiatives in the 1820s were much remarked upon, and came in response to heightened fears about crime in the capital. The tradition of part-time, amateur and sometimes unpaid constables was neither appropriate to the increasing urban scale of London nor well-fitted to the imposing of order in working-class neighborhoods. In certain areas, the "old" police were utterly ineffective at stopping violent crime and controlling public spaces.[77] However, the ineptitude of traditional constables and the efficiency of the new police can be overstated.[78] Long after the introduction of modernized police forces, there were certain areas that were avoided by police, effectively ceding control of the streets to their inhabitants, and individual police officers were often willing to not interfere in certain violent situations. Reminiscing about his early experiences as a policeman and detective in mid-century London, Timothy Cavanagh recalled that the police at times allowed street fights to continue, particularly if they involved several people. As one example, he noted a fight that ended as quickly as it began without any interference from a police officer, who had chosen not to intervene.[79] Policemen were often in a precarious position in the streets: their claim to authority could be quickly undermined if they overstepped community acceptance of their legitimate role.[80] The prevalence of attempted rescues of suspects by other workers, and their willingness to assault police officers points to the contested nature of police authority.[81] Policemen often required the assistance of people in the street to effect an arrest if a suspect became unruly or resisted apprehension.[82] Such contestation was a feature throughout the nineteenth century; however, the boundaries of legitimate authority were often unclear and depended upon the individual circumstances of an incident and the character of the officer himself.[83] John Paget noted the complicated nature of popular relations with the police:

> When an officer arrests a prisoner in the very act of committing a felony, or steps in to quell a fray whilst the blood is hot, he not unfrequently gets roughly or even savagely handled … but when a criminal is arrested subsequently, a tap on the shoulder with "I want you, Jack," is generally quietly submitted to.[84]

Although it was a fairly optimistic view of policing, Paget's conclusions ring true for at least a significant portion of arrests, in which suspects often gave themselves up with little struggle, and many officers did, as Paget also noted, speak "a good word" on a criminal's behalf, either at trial or in petitions for mercy.[85] By the time he was writing, in 1875, the police had reached a relatively stable acceptance in working-class communities. Written in the same year, the parliamentary Brutal Assaults Report contains many references to the high number of assaults on the police, though the authorities themselves understood that police actions could at times be provocative. As the Recorder of Abingdon stated:

> The only cases of violent assault with which the justices in session have to deal being assaults on policemen in the execution of their duty; in some cases, I am disposed to think, provoked by the indiscretion of the police themselves.[86]

The mixture of acceptance and resistance that characterized working-class relations with the police was largely concerned with authority over public spaces. As one police historian has suggested of nineteenth-century London:

> Except among persistently antagonistic groups like the costermongers, the police did achieve at least a grumbling working-class acquiescence to their authority. By the 1860s, there was more violence against them in the music halls than on the streets.[87]

The public house was another popular location for negotiation of and resistance to authority. One commentator, his observations directed at the influence of alcohol on the working-class male, hit upon the spatial significance of the pub:

> When there, little or no control is felt either from the law of the land or from loss of employment; unbounded license is taken and the reason of the man is lost in the ferocity of the animal, which too often cannot be excluded from the public eye.[88]

As suggested in accounts of fistfighting in Chapter 4, such "ferocity" was in fact deliberately public and bound by rules rather than strictly "animalistic." However, pubs, as vital institutions in working-class life, did offer a place that connected violence, resistance and masculinity. Occasionally, large-scale riots originated in seemingly minor disputes between workers and police in pubs, particularly if constables attempted to arrest people at beerhouses.[89] In 1832, in Tring, Hertfordshire, Thomas Mullins and Edward Seabrooke started a dispute with a watchman in a pub over his right to hit people with his staff. The resulting brawl drew in some twenty people and required the exertions of several constables to bring the crowd under control.[90]

Thus, the issue of resistance was complex. The police often intervened to protect people who were the victims of customarily sanctioned popular justice: for example, outsiders, informers, "bet welchers" and blacklegs. In these cases, and others, the contesting assertions of authority and justice become visible. A key aspect of the pacification of public spaces was the assertion of a state monopoly on the maintenance of public order. Community violence, in the form of mob attacks on deviants or private violent dispute settlement, offered resistance to the police by contesting local control of the streets and criminality. The police in these cases often intervened to deny the legitimacy of customary forms of retribution and to assert the sole legitimacy of state violence in the public sphere. The nature of the negotiations between mentalities of violence and authority were not always heated.[91] Resistance, violence and exclusion interacted in a context of *competing* powers. The process of "pacification" of public spaces was a difficult affair, one that is obviously related to class, state power and attempts to impose civilized values. The complexities of resistance can also be seen in the state's efforts to suppress prizefighting as part of its efforts to pacify social spaces. This process of exclusion gathered momentum as the police expanded their effectiveness and reach. In response, fight promoters had to find sites further removed from urban and village centers; this customary pastime continued on an expanding geographic margin and used developing modes of transportation (particularly railroads and river travel)[92] to stay one step ahead of the law. While these developments point out the specific, tactical steps taken by fighting enthusiasts, they also point to an adaptive, active strategy. Custom was not simply an inert "tradition," rather it was a flexible set of attitudes that engaged with a developing modernity.

7   Conclusion

> The crimes of GBH and ABH – grievous and actual bodily harm – are to go the way of hanging, transportation to the colonies and penal servitude in an overhaul of the Victorian laws of violence proposed by Home Office ministers yesterday.
>
> *Guardian*, 2 February 1998[1]

> Vigilantes have no place in a civilized society, but there is all the difference between the career criminal who sets out deliberately to burgle a house and the terrified home owner who acts to protect himself and his home.
>
> William Hague, former Conservative Party leader, April 2000[2]

English attitudes toward violence were evolving before the nineteenth century, continued to change during the twentieth and remain unsettled in the twenty-first. The period considered here was neither a decisive leap into "modernity" nor a self-contained period of tension bracketed by placid acceptance of a hegemonic norm. However, in the nineteenth century attitudes toward violence assumed a particular configuration. Prior to the growth of new, civilized attitudes toward violence, there had been periodic tensions regarding the legitimacy of physically injurious force, but these had been defined within the confines of a shared mentality. Similarly, current debates are conducted within a framework that is recognizably rooted in civilizing discourses. In the nineteenth century, however, sustained efforts to change English culture through moral exhortation and changes in legislation, law and policing coalesced into a "civilizing offensive." Civilizing thought was itself internally divided, and while it aimed at a thoroughgoing reformation of manners in all aspects of life, there were particular areas (mainly public spaces) and certain types of behavior (such as "brutal" assaults) in which it was most interested. Civilization was neither a fixed "thing" nor was it defined in isolation. It was a process tied to the creation and maintenance of a refined identity and defined as much by what it *was not* as what it *was*. Violence was identified as working class, and the working class reciprocally identified as violent. The presumed attachment of the working class to savagery was signaled, for instance, by their continuing attachment to public fighting "in defiance of law and public morality," and if there had been a decline in brutal sports, it had not been due to:

a distaste for them on the part of the peasantry or artisans. It has been the advance of public opinion, but, with that section of the public, to whom as a whole such amusements were not congenial.[3]

Curiously, while the number of violent acts appears to have stagnated or declined, the threat of violence seemed to grow dramatically. A new social concern was "invented," primarily by social classes that had relatively little (and decreasing) experience with traditional forms of violence. Gatrell has noted of crime that it

> became (as it remains) the repository of fears which had little to do with its relatively trivial cost to the society and economy at large. It came to be invested with large significance because it provided a convenient vehicle for the expression of fears about social change itself.[4]

Attitudes toward violence were to some extent similar; however, violence, as I hope I have demonstrated, has a social meaning that is not limited to the notion of crime. As discussed in Chapter 2, this "useful" savagery contributed not only to the middle-class social imagination but also to new forms of social organization and state power. Thus, civilization created the "shadows" that were essential to shaping its refined imagination.

However, the customary alternative to civilizing attitudes remained significant throughout the nineteenth century, marking continuities of a once-shared culture of violence in which physical retribution, a relatively wide diffusion of the legitimacy to use force and a higher tolerance for visible suffering had been common. As the source for a mentality of violence that was coherent – and often very practical, however disturbing it appears today – custom helped to script the language of violence in ways that fit community life. As social relations changed and state power increased, customary violence strategies continued to be asserted as a legitimate resource, mainly among the working class, and remained comprehensible to aggressors, witnesses and, frequently, victims. Customary violence was produced according to particular strategies related to power and space. Disputes between men who were social equals were often settled according to a relatively elaborate ritual of violence in which public space was deliberately manipulated to maximize the openness of the fight, while deviants, outsiders, wives and children might find that the language of violence could take far less restrained forms. Spousal violence was shaped by its own geographies and strategies but without predictable, ritualized rules. Customary attitudes to violence often aimed to assert community power over public spaces, but such forms of autonomous, exclusionary violence increasingly functioned in opposition to official law and the agents of legal authority, leading to resistance against the civilizing goals of the state.

The state in question had once agreed with and contributed to the legitimacy of customary violence; however, through the privatization of punishment and pacification of public spaces, it sought to remove violence from the public sphere. Judicial punishment ceased to be an explicit negotiation with the crowds that had structured the old hanging, pillorying or whipping rituals and the customarily expressive language of violence was increasingly denied a legitimate social space. The range of situations within which violence was accepted began to narrow. Where custom had allowed the use of violence to defend honor through the duel and fistfight, civilized male honor could be won and maintained in ways unconnected to violence and physical prowess.[5] However, the "criminalization of men" was an ambiguous, uneven process. Cross-class interest in pugilism (particularly its sporting variety) and its association with a manly variety of Englishness led to some ambivalence in suppressing fighting. Nevertheless, despite a notable appreciation for the fair fight, there was a determined effort to reform fighting for sport and replace customary methods of dispute settlement (impulsive, direct and physical) with institutionalized processes of law. Civilization was thus tied not only to a humanitarian concern with pain, but also to the imperatives of state expansion and the inculcation of new forms of social discipline. Key to this process was the relocation of violence (in both a material and rhetorical sense) "outside" of society: it was increasingly associated with "anti-social" behavior, whereas some forms of legitimized violence had long been located at the heart of society. Previously accepted behavior was redefined as "violence," a degraded, impulsive and animalistic act beyond cultural rules and controls. The view of violence as external to society rested somewhat uneasily with the concurrent notion that it was a product of social forces, a difficulty mediated through the relocation of violence in a social group outside the boundaries of the expanding pacified social sphere.

Pacified social spaces mean that an individual is less likely to be attacked; however, one's own violent urges must also be restrained. Thus civilizing efforts are related to changes in individual psychology. "Social danger" threatens those who cannot control themselves, just as "social rewards" accrue to those who can.[6] "Respectability" was one lever of social reward, and, in combination with new forms of authority, its adoption by a large proportion of workers altered the structures that had sustained the working-class mentality of violence. To the civilized mind, impulsiveness was to be replaced with foresight and the self-controlled individual conjured out of the presumably chaotic mentalities of the lower orders. The courts and the police began to supersede autonomous neighborly violence, the boundaries of acceptable interpersonal violence became narrower and the state assumed a monopoly on legitimate force.[7] Extra-legal community violence became far less tolerated and the state redefined it as a threat to the social order, an affront to its authority and a throwback to a pre-enlightened era. The police were one of the main institutions for the monopolization of force and they had gained a precarious acceptance in working-class communities by the end of the nineteenth century. They were increasingly sought out when violence erupted, and more workers began turning to the authorities rather than to direct, physical retribution.[8] A struggle remained, but it was increasingly played out within the mind of the individual, whose impulsive urges toward violence were kept increasingly in check by patterns of self-restraint: community self-policing gave way to state law and the internal policing of the self.[9] This is not to say, of course, that violence ceased to be a part of English culture. However, the relative pacification of public spaces and the evolution of new patterns of authority were – however grudgingly – accepted. As the customary mentality of violence fractured within working-class culture, customary "resistance" subsided, most notably in the general acceptance of police authority over public spaces. Judging the extent of popular "consent" to the law is a notoriously elusive pastime, and attitudes toward the police remain highly contested and ambivalent.[10] However, the subsidence of overt, daily resistance (outside of various sub-cultural enclaves) was part of a more general alteration in the oppositional nature of working-class culture due to growing political inclusion, more widespread education and twentieth-century changes in consumption.

The relevance of customary attitudes was noticeably fading by the 1870s. A section of the working class sought to distance itself from the negative associations of working-class life and adopted various elements of Victorian respectability, thereby appearing more civilized and contributing to social reform through their disapproval of customary culture. An increasingly broad social consensus defined itself against a variety of newly defined sub-groups, and growing social differentiation relegated customary forms of behavior to the marginalized, "rough" working class.[11] Crime and violence were becoming integrated into a changing social analysis, and they were, in a sense, naturalized as a part of modern life, particularly as a smaller portion of society was associated with anarchic brutality.[12] The customary mentality, after all, had arisen out of an agrarian, pre-industrial society that was increasingly distant. New vocabularies were emerging for the expression of class and cultural differences as a result of the admission of large segments of the working class to the electoral franchise in 1867 and 1884, which allowed the rise of labor-oriented parties and politicized forms of resistance. Conceptually, the history of attitudes to violence within the working class is comparable to changes in certain attitudes to sexuality, another target of the civilizing offensive. "Labour aristocrats," were instrumental in the persecution of prostitutes, who had once been an accepted part of working-class communities. As Walkowitz describes:

> It may well be that the experience of registered women [i.e., prostitutes] was symptomatic of important and long-term changes in working-class life: a growing inflexibility in social norms and habits; a restriction in occupational identities and personal mobility. The isolation of a separate criminal class may have been a necessary corollary to the increasing social and legal pressures placed upon the poor to adhere to a more rigid standard of public respectability.[13]

The civilizing process was tied to the creation of new norms, "by a whole range of degrees of normality indicating membership of a homogeneous social body but also playing a part in classification, hierarchicalization and the distribution of ranks."[14] The creation of new norms structured (and was, in turn, structured by) the demarcation of delinquency through new disciplines that kept criminality "on the fringes of society."[15] Panics regarding social upheaval might still occur, but they were less concerned with the working class as a whole.

By the early twentieth century, labor activists shared many of the civilizing attitudes of middle-class social reformers. In looking back on his working-class upbringing, Labour MP Will Thorne recalled the widespread prevalence of fighting. Although his evaluation was deeply sympathetic, he connected violence to the material conditions of working-class neighborhoods:

> This drinking and fighting should not be magnified or misjudged. We were healthy, normal human beings, fond of fair play; we had little amusement and little opportunity to enjoy the better things in life. If these fights took place, it was no fault of ours, but rather of the system of society we lived under – a system that made us work long hours of brutalizing toil for little money; a system that had no care as to the slums we slept in, the food we ate, or the education we received or tried to give our children.[16]

His suggestion that violence was mainly a product of industrialized society was connected to one strain of civilizing thought and overlooked the pre-industrial traditions that structured customary attitudes long into the nineteenth century. The distancing of respectable laborite opinion from the more violent aspects of working-class culture is also symptomatic of the late nineteenth-century marginalization of custom and violence. As Shani D'Cruze has noted, "Although hard-drinking, physically tough models of masculinities were not erased from working-class culture, the independent artisan of the later nineteenth century was also (for a good deal of the time) a sober and rational family man."[17]

The increased importance of respectability for working-class life had an important spatial component. Not only did some workers leave "unrespectable" or "less respectable" neighborhoods, but they also changed the ways in which they themselves lived.[18] These trends could have a strong impact upon neighboring areas, and one description of a model housing project emphasized the resulting civilizing influence:

> The neighbourhood in which many of the houses are situated has also participated in their ameliorating influence. They appear to act as silent monitors, reproving disorder and encouraging cleanliness and propriety.[19]

Neighborly surveillance was thus enlisted as part of the civilizing cause. In the early twentieth century, social observers noted an improvement in working-class "morality," partly as a result of improvements in housing and environment.[20] Working-class life became increasing "encapsulated," mimicking middle-class developments that had occurred earlier in the nineteenth century.[21] The "threshold" between public and private was emphasized, and "daily life became much less public and less communal, more private and more introverted."[22] The vibrant street life that was a key part of the customary experience, was, in many areas, dramatically changed.[23] Through a combination of policing and the self-adoption by workers of new attitudes to privacy, the role of public spaces was attenuated.[24] Legitimate power over public spaces became more fully associated with state authority, and daily life was increasingly privatized:

> The social life of the street had become a relatively passive affair of women sitting at the front doors talking; the more active forms of the early Victorian city lacked respectability and were ever more controlled, relegated largely to a juvenile subculture.[25]

The increased privatization of everyday life had consequences for a wide variety of behaviors other than violence; however, as customary attitudes to violence had been thoroughly implicated in daily social life, alterations in the structure of that life affected attitudes to self-control, aggression and violence. The production of knowledge about violence also changed: customary knowledge networks remained vitally important, but they faced increasing competition from new media, particularly as literacy increased and direct experience of violence was pushed further toward the margins of social life. As knowledge of violence was produced in new ways, attitudes toward it were more affected by the culture of refinement. Finally, as violence was pushed to the cultural margins, the public strategies of violence fell into varying degrees of desuetude. Since the civilized mentality denied the legitimacy of formerly acceptable types of violence, the particular forms of violence became less performative, more furtive and differently structured.[26]

While the civilizing offensive had its greatest successes in taming public spaces, violence in the private sphere was, in relative terms, untouched and may have been reinforced by the spatial trends in working-class life. Although spousal violence was closely associated with a particular space – the private home – the built environment and vibrant extra-familial networks had located even "private" violence in the public sphere. While neighbors had accepted "disciplinary" male violence within the home, the openness of working-class domestic violence had placed marital conflict in a different context to that of concurrent middle-class violence and had opened domestic violence to the surveillance and policing of the community. The increasing privacy of working-class life and the fortification of the threshold between public and private reduced that openness. It is possible that the strengthening of the private sphere and the resulting enclosure of domestic life from an open community context increased male domination within the home and denied women the extra-familial networks that had monitored violence and perhaps offered some form of support.[27] Domestic violence was structured by ideals of male dominance and female passivity that had strong cross-class agreement, reinforced by liberal notions of non-interference in private life. Thus, in a way perhaps similar to fighting (which also was tied to particular views of masculinity and had enthusiasts among all classes), domestic violence, or at least the ideology of dominance that structured it, enjoyed some amount of cross-class acceptance and resisted change until late in the nineteenth century.[28] Nevertheless, while it is difficult to determine whether or not spousal violence declined in the nineteenth century, it is clear that attitudes toward it and its role began to change. Refined attitudes toward marriage did not provide a necessarily more equal home, but they emphasized affective relationships, cooperation and non-violence.[29] Rather than having a legitimate place at the center of social life, spousal violence was increasingly stigmatized.[30]

The decline of custom was a gradual, partial and far from linear progression. While workers might outwardly signify their respectability through their dress, demeanor and habits, cultural mentalities were difficult to change. In the late nineteenth century, workers could still be "ducked" by their co-workers. Furthermore, retributive arguments never entirely disappeared from "civilized" discourses, highlighting the ways that cross-class cultural agreements increased the longevity of the "old voices" noted by Gatrell.[31] Flogging made a resurgence mid century. In 1882, MPs introduced legislation to reinstate the pillory – that symbol of the old customary punishment order – for wife and child beaters.[32] Children were still frequently beaten at home and at school without much murmur of discontent from working-class neighbors and parents. Working-class communities could still pull together if they felt authorities were interfering with their autonomy, as was increasingly the case as the state expanded its power to enforce school attendance or compulsory vaccination. In the 1890s, for example, enraged working-class communities often set upon authorities that tried to enforce compulsory vaccination.[33] Nevertheless, rather than seeing custom as merely a retrograde anachronism, I think that its coherence and continuing resonance suggest that – at least for a time – it remained a viable counternarrative to middle-class refinement. Peter Bailey has usefully conceptualized a role-based notion of respectability in which working-class people adopted respectable behavior in certain contexts, while also maintaining an alternative culture.[34] Similarly, Jennifer Davis has examined the ambiguities within working-class attitudes toward law and justice: using the courts "did not so much replace informal sanctions as operate in addition to them."[35] However, from the 1870s onward, custom faced a losing battle. Although its subsequent history must await further study, it is clear that it became increasingly marginalized in the social discourses of all classes.

In the course of this examination of attitudes to violence in the nineteenth century, I have applied a variety of theoretical approaches to conceptualize the role of violence in everyday life. Attitudes toward violence are about much more than "crime" or even about violence per se: issues of identity (whether related to class, gender or nation), power, social control, space and individual psychology all impact the role, place and forms of violence. The suggestions I have made about violence in the nineteenth century are intended to suggest openings for further inquiry along these lines, and although I have focused on the English experience, similar patterns and trends (with different chronologies and specific dynamics) could, I believe, be found across Europe. My study of violence has also been informed throughout by an engagement with the theories of Norbert

Elias and Michel Foucault. In particular, I believe that Elias's concepts remain among the most fruitful of conceptual frameworks for the study of violence. However, a variety of complexities were built into the civilizing process. First, although Elias emphasizes the relationship between civilization and impulse as largely conflicted (civilization being at odds with and fundamentally driven by an attempt to overcome impulse), his approach may underestimate the extent to which "impulse" is itself a category defined by civilizing thought. The psychological and sociological theories central to Elias's work were themselves rooted in the new epistemological discourses that Foucault has described growing up around the issue of crime. Labeling a particular form of behavior as the product of "impulse" or "rage" was part of the way refined social commentators drew a boundary between acceptable and unacceptable actions: the self-controlled and rational individual was defined by his or her ability to restrain such affects. Thus, while "civilization" was predicated upon the control of affects (and civilizers certainly saw themselves as engaged in a war with passions and animalistic savagery), "impulsive" action is itself defined as part of the civilizing process rather than existing as an eternal, essentialized "affect structure." Furthermore, mentalities may not only restrain impulsive violence but also create their own imperatives toward violence according to particular configurations of power, identity and legitimate behavior. For instance, were workers who beat deviants or fought each other being "impulsive," or were their acts well-structured responses to a lightly policed society in which the community was granted a great deal of power in maintaining social norms? I do not suggest I have conclusively answered this question; nevertheless, I think that the Victorian emphasis on the restraint of impulsive urges points simultaneously to the utility of Elias's theories as well as the extent to which his analyses were shaped by the enduring imperatives of nineteenth-century European social thought. However, increased "self-restraint" was an undeniable emphasis in the evolution of middle-class identity. "Respectability" – strongly connected to the idealization of the self-controlled individual – became one of the key signifiers of social rank, thus providing an external pressure upon individual conduct that was also experienced through the internal mechanism of "shame."[36] Elias, rightly, emphasizes the ways that behavioral self-control was tied to generalized social processes (such as increasing social interdependence),[37] the growth of state power and the struggle for status among social groups. However, the "civilizing process" was not a unidirectional imposition of new social values by the middle classes upon the working class. First, this would neglect the role that the working class itself played in the adoption of "respectable" values later in the nineteenth century: power in the nineteenth century was exercised through a mixture of imposition, conflict and negotiation. Second, it understates the extent to which workers resisted civilized attitudes toward violence and asserted alternatives. Third, it tends to reify civilization as a well-defined, coherent and progressive trend despite the fact that its advocates were often conflicted about specific goals. The culture of refinement's ability to critique itself points to the ambiguous, contested nature of middle-class identity and attitudes toward violence.

Yet, the nature of interpersonal violence undoubtedly changed. It no longer had the expressive power it had once possessed, since, for any language to be an effective vehicle for communication, its meanings must be coherent and transparent to the community in which it is used. Changes in working-class culture meant that while violence remained, it was conducted according to different rules and had different meanings. Customary violence had originated in a social context very different from that of late nineteenth-century England. As Thompson writes, "rough music," the most ritualized form of community violence,

> belongs to a mode of life in which some part of the law belongs still to the community and is theirs to enforce…. It indicates modes of social self-control and the disciplining of certain kinds of violence and anti-social offence (insults to women, child abuse, wife beating) which in today's cities may be breaking down.[38]

Customarily, violence was highly expressive, and modern interpersonal violence appears relatively impoverished in its ability to express anything other than rage and anger or to serve a variety of more instrumental purposes. This has much to do with our ceasing to see violence (at least certain kinds of violence) as a legitimate vehicle of expression. We have not, of course, ceased to look for some kind of narrative meaning in violence, particularly in its more spectacular or brutal incarnations.[39] Nonetheless, this is rather the exception than the rule. As violence has ceased to be a part of normal daily interaction in Europe, the need to structure it in particular ways has diminished. As a result, it has perhaps become less predictable. Although customary violence was certainly motivated by rage and anger and was at times horrifyingly destructive, it was part of community social life rather than outside of it. Lest this evaluation appear too sanguine, one must always keep in mind Thompson's warning that

> because law belongs to people, and is not alienated, or delegated, it is not thereby made necessarily more "nice" and tolerant, more cosy and folksy. It is only as nice and as tolerant as the prejudices and norms of the folk allow.[40]

It has not been my intention to re-legitimize violence by emphasizing that under the customary mentality it often "made sense" to the people involved. Customary violence was an important tool in maintaining social hierarchies that were profoundly unequal, and, in my eyes, undesirable. However, I have attempted to leave my own civilized prejudices behind in order to accept that there were (and are) alternative mentalities that would view such sensitivities as equally mysterious.

Finally, I have also attempted to draw attention to the way that attitudes to violence remain in a state of constant tension and change. As was noted in 1873, "[t]he apparent number of criminals can be made to appear formidable only by including in it persons guilty of offences which our hard-drinking great-grandfathers would have regarded as merits rather than as faults."[41] For instance, it was in the nineteenth century that the notion of "mental torture" developed.[42] The twentieth century saw a continuing evolution and re-evaluation of attitudes, changing deployments of state policing power, new media depictions of violence and an unceasing attempt to grapple with the question of where English society stood at a given moment in history regarding the state of its violence. Of course, violence has not disappeared from English life; however, the incidence of physical attack is generally far less prevalent today than it was in the nineteenth century. However, in considering our attitudes toward violence, I would argue that "violence" can never disappear, for the mentality of refinement still depends upon its shadows. The dynamic of the civilizing process demands that certain groups continue to be defined as the bearers of some kind of savagery or violent threat to the social order.[43] The discussion about these forms of behavior became increasingly complex over the previous century. Statistical measures of violence have risen and then fallen in recent decades; however, overshadowing these fluctuations is a dramatic decline in violence over the last few centuries. As general social violence has ebbed, ever-finer distinctions regarding the specific nature of violent acts have been made. Particularly when the differences between upper- and lower-class behavior decrease, the "nuances" or varieties of civilized conduct increase.[44] New forms of "violence" are created,[45] interested groups or individuals mobilize narratives of social decay in order to gain political influence or push for new state policies,[46] and increasingly empowered groups might successfully argue for state and legal action to protect them. Concerns about the ability of accepted social institutions to maintain order through their "legitimate" delegated authority might lead to assertions of other powers – be they individual or community – to defend the private and public spheres.[47] The discourse of civility still evolves, connected to questions of individual behavior, standards of public order, the efficacy of judicial punishment and national identity.[48] These issues will continue to shape important patterns in English life, culture and society as they do those in every other country.

Notes

Introduction

1 J. A. Sharpe, "Crime in England: long-term trends and the problem of modernization," in Eric A. Johnson and Eric H. Monkkonen (eds.) *The Civilization of Crime:
 Violence in Town and Country Since the Middle Ages*, Urbana: University of Illinois Press,
 1996, p. 30.

2 Michel Foucault, *Power/Knowledge: Selected Interviews and Other Writings, 1972–1977*,
 Colin Gordon (ed.), Colin Gordon, Leo Marshall, John Mepham and Kate Soper
 (trans.), New York: Pantheon, 1980, p. 61.

3 Carolyn Nordstrom, *A Different Kind of War Story*, Philadelphia: University of
 Pennsylvania Press, 1997, p. 16.

4 Michel Foucault, *Discipline and Punish: The Birth of the Prison*, Alan Sheridan (trans.),
 New York: Vintage Books, 1979, p. 286.

5 The term "economy of violence" comes from Malcolm Greenshields, *An Economy of
 Violence in Early Modern France: Crime and Justice in the Haute Auvergne, 1587–1664*,
 University Park: Pennsylvania State University Press, 1994.

6 T. M. Devine, "Conflict and stability in Scottish society, 1700–1850," *Proceedings of the
 Scottish Historical Studies Seminar, University of Strathclyde, 1988–89*, Edinburgh: John
 Donald Publishers Ltd., 1990; D. J. V. Jones, *Crime in Nineteenth-Century Wales*, Cardiff:
 University of Wales Press, 1992; James Kelly, *'That Damn'd Thing Called Honour'
 Duelling in Ireland 1570–1860*, Cork: Cork University Press, 1995; Carolyn A. Conley,
 Melancholy Accidents: The Meaning of Violence in Post-Famine Ireland, Lanham, MD:
 Lexington Books, 1999.

7 A historiography discussed and extensively cited in E. P. Thompson, *Customs in
 Common*, New York: The New Press, 1991, pp. 185–351.

8 See important discussions and comprehensive citations of this early work in Douglas
 Hay, "War, dearth, and theft in the eighteenth century: the record of the English
 courts," *Past and Present*, 1982, vol. 95, 117–22 and J. M. Beattie, *Crime and the Courts in
 England, 1660–1800*, Princeton: Princeton University Press, 1986, pp. 199–202. Early
 studies that focused on the nineteenth century include V. A. C. Gatrell and T. B.
 Hadden, "Nineteenth-century criminal statistics and their interpretation," in E. A.
 Wrigley (ed.) *Nineteenth Century Society: Essays in the Use of Quantitative Methods for the Study
 of Social Data*, London: Cambridge University Press, 1972, pp. 336–96; David Philips,
 Crime and Authority in Victorian England: The Black Country, 1835–1860, London: Croom
 Helm, 1977; and V. A. C. Gatrell, "The decline of theft and violence in Victorian
 and Edwardian England," in V. A. C. Gatrell, Bruce Lenman and Geoffrey Parker
 (eds.) *Crime and the Law: The Social History of Crime in Western Europe since 1500*, London:
 Europa Publications, 1980, pp. 238–337.

9 Much of this debate centered around the arguments put forth in Douglas Hay, et al.
 (eds.) *Albion's Fatal Tree: Crime and Society in Eighteenth-Century England*, New York:

Pantheon, 1975. For a discussion and citations, see Joanna Innes and John Styles, "'The crime wave': recent writings on crime and criminal justice in eighteenth-century England," *Journal of British Studies*, 1986, vol. 25, 380–435.

10 Alan Macfarlane, *The Justice and the Mare's Ale: Law and Disorder in Seventeenth-Century England*, New York: Cambridge University Press, 1981; T. R. Gurr, "Historical trends in violent crime: a critical review of the evidence," *Crime and Justice: An Annual Review of Research*, 1981, vol. 3, 295–353; Lawrence Stone, "Interpersonal violence in English society, 1300–1980," *Past and Present*, 1983, vol. 101, 22–33; J. A. Sharpe, "The history of violence in England: some observations," *Past and Present*, 1985, vol. 108, 206–15; Lawrence Stone, "A rejoinder," *Past and Present*, 1985, vol. 108, 216–24; David Woods, "Community violence," in John Benson (ed.) *The Working Class in England, 1875–1914*, London: Croom Helm, 1985, pp. 165–205.

11 Sharpe, "History of violence," p. 214. See also: J. S. Cockburn, "Patterns of violence in English society: homicide in Kent, 1560–1985," *Past and Present*, 1991, vol. 130, 70–106 (which is based on a quantitative analysis of homicide rates but points to both the limitations of purely statistical work and the necessity of qualitative considerations) and "Punishment and brutalization in the English Enlightenment," *Law and History Review*, 1994, vol. 12, 155–79; Lucia Zedner, *Women, Crime and Custody in Victorian England*, Oxford: Clarendon Press, 1991; Pieter Spierenburg, "Justice and the mental world," *IAHCCJ Bulletin*, 1991, vol. 14, 38–79; J. A. Sharpe, "Human relations and the history of crime," *IAHCCJ Bulletin*, 1991, vol. 14, 10–32; Eric Dunning, Patrick Murphy and Ivan Waddington, "Violence in the British civilizing process," Leicester University Discussion Papers in Sociology, 1992, no. S92/2; Susan Dwyer Amussen, "Punishment, discipline and power: the social meanings of violence in early modern England," *Journal of British Studies*, 1995, vol. 34, 1–34; the essays in Johnson and Monkkonen, *Civilization of Crime*; Peter King, "Punishing assault: the transformation of attitudes in the English courts," *Journal of Interdisciplinary History*, 1996, vol. 27, 43–74; Shani D'Cruze, *Crimes of Outrage: Sex, Violence and Victorian Working Women*, London: UCL Press, 1998; Martin Wiener, "The Victorian criminalization of men," in Pieter Spierenburg (ed.) *Men and Violence: Gender, Honor and Rituals in Modern Europe and America*, Columbus: Ohio State University Press, 1998, pp. 197–212; Martin Wiener, *Reconstructing the Criminal: Culture, Law and Policy in England, 1830–1914*, Cambridge: Cambridge University Press, 1990; Daniel A. Cohen, "The beautiful female murder victim: literary genres and courtship practices in the origins of a cultural motif, 1590–1850" *Journal of Social History*, 1997, vol. 31, 277–306; Malcolm Gaskill, "Reporting murder: fiction in the archives in early modern England," *Social History*, 1998, vol. 23, 1–30; Shani D'Cruze, *Everyday Violence in Britain, 1850–1950: Gender and Class*, Harlow: Longman-Pearson Education, 2000; Julius R. Ruff, *Violence in Early Modern Europe, 1500–1800*, Cambridge: Cambridge University Press, 2001; J. Carter Wood, "It's a small world after all?: Reflections on violence in comparative perspectives," in Barry Godfrey, Clive Emsley and Graeme Dunstall (eds.) *Comparative Histories of Crime*, Collumpton, Devon: Willan Press, 2003.

12 Spierenburg, "Long-term trends in homicide: theoretical reflections and Dutch evidence, fifteenth to twentieth centuries," in Johnson and Monkkonen, *Civilization of Crime*, p. 68.

13 Richard D. Altick, *Victorian Studies in Scarlet*, New York: W. W. Norton & Co., 1970, pp. 59, 67.

1 "Speakable" violence

1 Nordstrom, *War Story*, p. 17.

2 V. A. C. Gatrell, *The Hanging Tree: Execution and the English People, 1770–1868*, Oxford: Oxford University Press, 1994, p. 236.

3 On wartime violence narratives, see Joanna Bourke, *An Intimate History of Killing: Face-to-Face Killing in Twentieth-Century Warfare*, New York: Basic Books, 1999. On other kinds of violence narratives, see, e.g., Ian Buruma, *The Wages of Guilt: Memories of War in Germany and Japan*, New York: Farrar Strauss Giroux, 1994 and Peter Novick, *The Holocaust in American Life*, New York: Mariner Books, 1999.

4 For an anthropological discussion, see David Riches, "The phenomenon of violence," in David Riches (ed.) *The Anthropology of Violence*, Oxford: Basil Blackwell, 1986; Simon Roberts, *Order and Dispute: An Introduction to Legal Anthropology*, New York: St. Martin's Press, 1979; John Bossy, *Disputes and Settlements: Law and Human Relations in the West*, Cambridge: Cambridge University Press, 1983.

5 Raymond Williams, *Keywords: A Vocabulary of Culture and Society*, New York: Oxford University Press, 1976, p. 278.

6 Riches, "Phenomenon of violence," p. 3.

7 "The structure of the physical world is continuous, but that of mental maps is discontinuous. Reality flows; the ideal is fixed. Maps falsify reality; reality challenges maps. The resulting dialectic leads to maps being changed to fit the world and the world being changed to fit the map. Concern for coherence is a basic engine of human action." John Corbin, "Insurrections in Spain: Casas Viejas 1933 and Madrid 1981," in Riches, *Anthropology of Violence*, p. 29.

8 Margaret Hunt, "Wife beating, domesticity and women's independence in eighteenth-century London," *Gender and History*, 1992, vol. 4, p. 23.

9 Nordstrom, *War Story*, p. 21.

10 "Social imaginaries" are discussed in Patrick Joyce, *Democratic Subjects: The Self and the Social in Nineteenth-Century England*, Cambridge: Cambridge University Press, 1994, pp. 4–5.

11 Riches, "Phenomenon of violence," p. 12.

12 Peter Collett, "The rules of conduct," in Peter Collett (ed.) *Social Rules and Social Behavior*, Oxford: Basil Blackwell, 1977, p. 4. In the same volume, Robin Fox suggests that fighting "is rule-governed in the same way that language is rule-governed, where none of us are aware of the rules of language but where nevertheless we speak according to them. In other words, it is very rare to find fighting that is random, disorderly, totally unstructured." Robin Fox, "The inherent rules of violence," in Collett, *Social Rules*, p. 136.

13 Riches, "Phenomenon of violence," p. 11.

14 Jean-Jacques Lecercle, *The Violence of Language*, London: Routledge, 1990, p. 18.

15 Ibid., p. 30.

16 On "sensibility," see Keith Thomas, *Man and the Natural World: A History of the Modern Sensibility*, New York: Pantheon, 1983; Paul Langford, *A Polite and Commercial People: England 1727–1783*, Oxford: Oxford University Press, 1989, Ch. 10; G. J. Barker-Benfield, *The Culture of Sensibility: Sex and Society in Eighteenth-Century Britain*, Chicago: Chicago University Press, 1992; and Pieter Spierenburg, *The Broken Spell: A Cultural and Anthropological History of Preindustrial Europe*, New Brunswick, NJ: Rutgers University Press, 1991.

17 Karen Halttunen, "Humanitarianism and the pornography of pain in Anglo-American culture," *American Historical Review*, 1995, vol. 100, 303.

18 E.g., Beattie, *Crime and the Courts*, pp. 135–9; see also Robert W. Malcomson, *Popular Recreations in English Society, 1700–1850*, Cambridge: Cambridge University Press, 1973, Ch. 7; Thomas, *Man and the Natural World*, Ch. 4; Barker-Benfield, *Culture of Sensibility*; King "Punishing assault."

19 E.g., Carolyn A. Conley, *The Unwritten Law: Criminal Justice in Victorian Kent*, New York: Oxford University Press, 1991; Gatrell, *Hanging Tree*; A. James Hammerton, *Cruelty and Companionship: Conflict in Nineteenth-Century Married Life*, London: Routledge, 1992. See also D'Cruze, *Crimes of Outrage*, p. 17.

20 Thompson, *Customs in Common*, p. 6.
21 Norbert Elias, *The Civilizing Process*, Edmund Jephcott (trans.), Oxford: Blackwell, 1997. The utility of Elias's work for the history of violence is discussed in Pieter Spierenburg, "Elias and the history of crime and criminal justice: a brief evaluation," *IAHCCJ Bulletin*, 1995, vol. 20, 17–30; Helmut Thome, "Modernization and crime: what is the explanation?" *IAHCCJ Bulletin*, 1995, vol. 20, 31–48; throughout Johnson and Monkkonen, *Civilization of Crime*, particularly the general introduction; Jonathan Fletcher, *Violence and Civilization: An Introduction to the Work of Norbert Elias*, Cambridge: Polity Press, 1997.
22 Elias, *Civilizing Process*, p. 445.
23 Max Weber, *Economy and Society: An Outline of Interpretive Sociology*, Berkeley: University of California Press, 1978, p. 56.
24 Elias, *Civilizing Process*, p. 448; on state power, ibid., pp. 447–51.
25 For Elias, human instincts (their "affect structure") are a unified whole: "We may call particular instincts by different names according to their different directions and functions, we may speak of hunger and the need to spit, of the sexual drive and of aggressive impulses, but in life these different instincts are no more separable than the heart from the stomach or the blood in the brain from the blood in the genitalia." Ibid., pp. 156–7. He also links the infliction of pain to pleasure: referring to the medieval warrior classes, he writes, "Outbursts of cruelty did not exclude one from social life. They were not outlawed. The pleasure in killing and torturing other was great and it was a socially permitted pleasure." Ibid., p. 159. On the connection between increasing "sensibility" and sadomasochistic pornography see Halttunen, "Pornography of pain," pp. 314–18. See also Fox, "Inherent rules of violence," pp. 137–8.
26 Elias, *Civilizing Process*, p. 188.
27 Ibid., p. 213.
28 Ibid., p. 201.
29 Spierenburg, "Elias and the history of crime," p. 19.
30 Dunning, Murphy and Waddington, "British civilizing process," p. 4.
31 Richard Price, *British Society, 1680–1800: Dynamism, Containment and Change*, Cambridge: Cambridge University Press, 1999, p. 37.
32 On the importance, of "new values and new expectations" in the nineteenth century, see David Taylor, *Policing the Victorian Town: The Development of the Police in Middlesbrough, c. 1840–1914*, Basingstoke: Palgrave Macmillan, 2002, p. 5.
33 Spierenburg, "Elias and the history of crime," pp. 20–3; Dunning, Murphy and Waddington, "British civilizing process," pp. 5–9.
34 Elias, *Civilizing Process*, p. 188.
35 Spierenburg, "Long-term trends," pp. 70–1 and "Elias and the history of crime," p. 24.
36 Fox, "Inherent rules of violence," p. 137.
37 Elias, *Civilizing Process*, p. 331. Emphasis in original
38 Spierenburg, "Elias and the history of crime," p. 22; cf., Dunning, Murphy and Waddington, "British civilizing process," p. 8.
39 Michel Foucault, *The History of Sexuality, Volume I: An Introduction*, Robert Hurley (trans.), New York: Vintage Books, 1990.
40 Ibid., p. 17.
41 Of sexuality, "Without question, new rules of propriety screened out some words: there was a policing of statements. A control over enunciations as well: where and when it was not possible to talk about such things became more strictly defined; in which circumstances, among which speakers, and within which social relationships." Ibid., pp. 17–18.
42 Ibid., pp. 32–3.

43 As a roughly applicable point of departure, consider the following quote from
Foucault, mentally replacing the word "sex" with the word "violence": "The society
that emerged in the nineteenth century – bourgeois, capitalist, or industrial society,
call it what you will – did not confront sex with a fundamental refusal of recognition.
On the contrary, it put into operation an entire machinery for producing true
discourses concerning it. Not only did it speak of sex and compel everyone to do so; it
also set out to formulate the uniform truth of sex. As if it suspected sex of harboring
a fundamental secret. As if it needed this production of truth. As if it was essential
that sex be inscribed not only in an economy of pleasure but in an ordered system of
knowledge. Thus sex gradually became an object of great suspicion; the general and
disquieting meaning that pervades our conduct and our existence, in spite of
ourselves; the point of weakness where evil portents reach through to us; the fragment
of darkness that we each carry within us: a general signification, a universal secret, an
omnipresent cause, a fear that never ends." Ibid., p. 69.

44 Foucault, *Discipline and Punish*, p. 77.

45 Foucault discusses the "paradoxical" longevity of bodily punishments in England in
ibid., pp. 14–15. I suggest that rather than being the result of "temporary changes" in
penal practice, the popularity of a punishment such as flogging signals a more significant "resistant mentality" regarding violence. See Gatrell, *Hanging Tree*, pp. 236–41.

46 See, e.g., Spierenburg, "Long-term trends," pp. 67–8; J. A. Sharpe, "Crime in
England," pp. 28–9.

47 Foucault, *Power/Knowledge*, p. 141.

48 Anthropological/historical-anthropological studies exploring the relationship between
custom, ritual and violence are numerous. For this study the works consulted include,
Bossy, *Disputes and Settlements*; Roberts, *Order and Dispute*; Collett, *Social Rules and Social
Behavior*; Steven C. Caton, "'Anger be now thy song': the anthropology of an event,"
The Occasional Papers of the School of Social Science, Harvard University, paper
number 5, Nov. 1999; Nordstrom, *War Story*; and Riches, *Anthropology of Violence*.

49 H. B. Simpson, *Introduction to the Judicial Statistics for England and Wales, 1900*, quoted in
G. R. Chadwick, "Bureaucratic mercy: the Home Office and the treatment of capital
cases in Victorian England," Ph.D. Dissertation, Rice University, 1989, p. 444.

50 Gatrell, "Decline of theft and violence," p. 240.

51 See Howard Taylor, "Rationing crime: the political economy of criminal statistics
since the 1850s," *Economic History Review*, 1998, vol. 51, 569–90, and the discussion in
John E. Archer, "'The violence we have lost'? Body counts, historians and interpersonal violence in England," *Memoria y Civilización*, 1999, vol. 2, 171–90 and Taylor,
Policing the Victorian Town, pp. 9–10.

52 Woods, "Community violence," p. 165. For a nineteenth-century view, see L. O. Pike,
History of Crime in England, London, 1876, vol. 2, p. 481.

53 Geoffrey Pearson, *Hooligan: A History of Respectable Fears*, London: Macmillan
Education, 1983, p. 74; Wiener, *Reconstructing the Criminal*, pp. 337–81.

54 The term comes from Arthur Mitzman, "The civilizing offensive: mentalities, high
culture and individual psyches," *Journal of Social History* 1987, vol. 20, 663–87; cf.,
Wiener, "Victorian criminalization of men," p. 200.

55 V. A. C. Gatrell, "Crime, authority and the policeman-state," in F. M. L. Thompson
(ed.) *The Cambridge Social History of Britain, 1750–1950*, Cambridge: Cambridge
University Press, 1990, vol. 3, p. 249.

56 Wiener, *Reconstructing the Criminal*, p. 11.

57 King, "Punishing assault"; Wiener, *Reconstructing the Criminal*, pp. 47, 78–80 and
"Victorian criminalization of men," pp. 203–4.

58 R. D. Storch, "The policeman as domestic missionary," *Journal of Social History*, 1976,
vol. 9, 481–509; Gatrell, "Policeman-state," pp. 243–310.

59 Hammerton, *Cruelty and Companionship*, p. 3.

60 Report of the Capital Punishment Commission, quoted in Conley, *Unwritten Law*, p. 56.

61 Sharpe, "Human relations," p. 17.

62 Randall McGowen, "Rethinking crime: changing attitudes towards lawbreakers in eighteenth and nineteenth-century England," Ph.D. Dissertation, University of Illinois at Urbana-Champaign, 1979, p. 68.

63 "Murder mania," *Chambers's Edinburgh Journal*, 6 October 1849, vol. 301 n.s., 209.

64 A pitfall that mars Louis Chevalier, *Laboring Classes and Dangerous Classes in Paris During the First Half of the Nineteenth Century*, Frank Jellinek (trans.), New York: Howard Fertig, 1973.

65 Highlighted in an American context in Elijah Anderson, *The Code of the Street: Violence, Decency and the Moral Life of the Inner City*, New York: W. W. Norton, 1999.

66 Rob Sindall, *Street Violence in the Nineteenth Century: Media Panic or Real Danger?* Leicester: Leicester University Press, 1990.

67 Ibid., p. 14.

68 Ibid., p. 13.

69 Ibid., p. 45.

70 Gatrell, "Policeman-state," p. 245. Cf., Foucault, *Power/Knowledge*, p. 47.

71 Clive Emsley, *The English Police: A Political and Social History*, Hemel Hempstead: Harvester Wheatsheaf, 1991.

72 B. J. Davey, *Lawless and Immoral: Policing a Country Town, 1838–1857*, Leicester: Leicester University Press, 1983; Margaret DeLacy, *Prison Reform in Lancashire, 1700–1850*, Stanford: Stanford University Press, 1986.

73 Conley, *Unwritten Law*, p. 3.

74 Jennifer Davis, "A poor man's system of justice: the London police courts in the second half of the nineteenth century," *The Historical Journal*, 1984, vol. 27, 309–35.

75 Price, *British Society*, p. 7.

76 An assumption critiqued in Sharpe, "History of violence," p. 215.

77 E. P. Thompson, *The Making of the English Working Class*, New York: Vintage Books, 1963, p. 12.

78 Price, *British Society*, p. 8.

79 Chadwick, "Bureaucratic mercy," pp. 11, 42.

80 Foucault, *Power/Knowledge*, p. 61.

81 Cockburn, "Punishment and brutalization," p. 177.

82 Dunning, Murphy and Waddington, "British civilizing process," pp. 11–12.

83 Ibid., p. 40.

2 A useful savagery

1 J. H. Elliott, "The increase of material prosperity and of moral agents compared with the state of crime and pauperism," *Journal of the Statistical Society of London*, 1868, vol. 31, 300.

2 Charles Mackay, "Work and murder," *Blackwood's Edinburgh Magazine*, 1867, vol. 102, 448. Emphasis in original.

3 Halttunen, "Pornography of pain," p. 304.

4 Beattie, *Crime and the Courts*, p. 75. See also Spierenburg, *Broken Spell*, p. 195.

5 Amussen, "Punishment, discipline and power," p. 34.

6 Hunt, "Wife beating," p. 14.

7 Amussen, "Punishment, discipline and power," pp. 4–5; King, "Punishing assault," p. 43.

8 Vindictiveness refers to "a conscious intention to hurt someone, regardless of who actually does the injury," and indifference denotes that visible suffering "fails to bother those who inflict it or observe it." Spierenburg, *Broken Spell*, p. 205.

9 On crowd hostility to hanging, see Peter Linebaugh, *The London Hanged: Crime and Civil Society in the Eighteenth Century*, Cambridge: Cambridge University Press, 1992. Cockburn, however, notes that popular culture "endorsed the notion of retributive justice as part of the divine scheme of things." Cockburn, "Punishment and brutalization," p. 163.

10 Sharpe, "History of violence," pp. 214–15.

11 King, "Punishing assault," pp. 68–9. Although King argues, convincingly, for recognizing the importance of eighteenth-century shifts in the treatment of lesser forms of violence, there is little evidence of concern among reformers regarding violence as such. King himself notes that the reforming debates "contained no specific references to assault," although he suggests that "the widespread Essex movement for the reformation of manners may well have had an impact on this area of judicial practice [i.e., assault]." Ibid., p. 69. On eighteenth-century "reformation of manners" movements, see Langford, *Polite and Commercial People*, pp. 266, 499–500.

12 Foucault, *History of Sexuality*, pp. 32–3.

13 On the limitation of capital crimes, see Gatrell, *Hanging Tree*, pp. 570–1.

14 Anna Clark, "Humanity or justice? Wifebeating and the law in the eighteenth and nineteenth centuries," in Carol Smart (ed.) *Regulating Womanhood: Historical Essays on Marriage, Motherhood and Sexuality*, London: Routledge, 1992, p. 196.

15 J. F. Stephen, *History of the Criminal Law of England*, London, 1884, vol. 3, p. 79; "An act for consolidating and amending the statutes in England relative to offences against the person," 9 Geo. IV c.31 (1828).

16 *Gentleman's Magazine*, May 1828, p. 458. For a summary of the act's provisions, see the *Gentleman's Magazine*, June 1828, pp. 636–7. For coverage of some debates on the act, see *The Times*, 19 March 1828, 29 March 1828 and 16 April 1828.

17 Wiener, "Victorian criminalization of men," p. 204.

18 "An act for the better prevention of aggravated assault upon women and children," 16 Vict. c.30 (1853); George K. Behlmer, *Child Abuse and Moral Reform in England, 1870–1908*, Stanford: Stanford University Press, 1982, p. 12.

19 "An act to consolidate and amend the statute law of England and Ireland relating to offences against the person," 24 & 25 Vict. c.100 (1861). This act was part of a series of consolidation acts that also related to larceny, malicious mischief, forgery and coinage. J. F. Stephen subsequently wrote, "About one half of the criminal law is contained in different statutory enactments, and half of this half is comprised in what are known as the Consolidation Acts of 1861. These collectively form the nearest approach that exists in English law to a penal code." J. F. Stephen, *Digest of the Criminal Law*, London, 1877, p. xv.

20 Parliament, *Reports to the Secretary of State for the Home Department on the State of the Law Relating to Brutal Assaults, &c.*, London, 1875.

21 J. F. Stephen, "A sketch of the criminal law," *The Nineteenth Century*, 1882, vol. 11, 644.

22 "The law of murder," *London Quarterly Review*, 1866, vol. 26, 447.

23 "Miscellaneous," *Journal of the Royal Statistical Society*, April 1840, 188.

24 Discussed in the next section of the present chapter, but note P. Gaskell, *Artisans and Machinery: The Moral and Physical Condition of the Manufacturing Population Considered with Reference to Mechanical Substitutes for Human Labour*, London, 1836, in which the spectacular, but rare, crime of vitriol throwing receives attention in the context of "savagery" (p. 268) along with more common "drunken brawls" (pp. 83–4). D. G. Paine, *The Task of the Age; An Enquiry Into the Condition of the Working Classes and the Means of their Moral and Social Elevation*, London, 1850, p. 20, refers to certain pugilistic sports and street-fighting as "brutal" and "savage." Another essay used the term "savagery" to refer to interpersonal assault and murder, particularly stabbing and garroting: John Eagles, "Temperance and teetotal societies," *Blackwood's Edinburgh Magazine*, April 1858, vol. 73, 410.

25 E.g., T. DeQuincey, "On murder considered as one of the fine arts," *Blackwood's Edinburgh Magazine*, February 1827, 199–213. And see later in the century, Leslie Stephen, "The decay of murder," *Cornhill Magazine*, 1869, vol. 20, 722–33.

26 Edward Barry, MD, *Theological, Philosophical and Moral Essays*, London, 1800, p. 275; D. E. Williams, "The crimes of prize fighters," *New Monthly Magazine*, 1834, vol. 42, 326–36

27 E.g., *The Art and Practice of English Boxing*, London, 1815, and Pierce Egan, *Boxiana; or Sketches of Antient [sic] and Modern Pugilism*, London, 1818. William Hazlitt, though he presents an enthusiastic portrait of prizefighting, carefully demarcates the proper behavior that should accompany it: "The fight," *New Monthly Magazine and Literary Journal*, 1822, 102–12. In the 1830s, William Howitt pointed out the "more scientific" and "less savage" forms of sport fighting: *The Rural Life of England*, London, 1838, p. 284. Donald Walker commented upon the various fighting "systems" and also distinguished between "fair" English fighting and the "barbarous contests" fought in other countries, echoing a common refrain in pro-boxing literature: *Defensive Exercises*, London, 1840, pp. 36–7.

28 J. W. Kaye "Outrages on women," *North British Review*, May 1856, vol. 25, 233–56; Hammerton, *Cruelty and Companionship*, pp. 102–33.

29 Barker-Benfield, *Culture of Sensibility*; Halttunen, "Pornography of pain," pp. 305–10.

30 See a letter from a Leicester magistrate to the Home Office, HO 44/18 ff 37–48, 24 March 1828; John Fullarton, "Condition of the labouring classes," *The Quarterly Review*, 1831–2, vol. 46, 349–89; Andrew Ure, MD, *The Philosophy of Manufactures: or, An Exposition of the Scientific, Moral, and Commercial Economy of the Factory System of Great Britain*, London, 1835; Charles Neaves, "Discontents of the working classes," *Blackwood's Edinburgh Magazine*, 1838, vol. 43, 421–36; G. Simmons, *The Working Classes; Their Moral, Social and Intellectual Condition; with Practical Suggestions for their Improvement*, London, 1849.

31 W. C. Taylor, "Moral economy of large towns: crime and punishment," *Bentley's Miscellany*, 1839, vol. 6, 476. This comment matches a statement by the Belgian statistician Alphonse Quetelet in his 1842 *A Treatise on Man*, quoted in Richard F. Wetzell, *Inventing the Criminal: A History of German Criminology, 1880–1914*, Chapel Hill: The University of North Carolina Press, 2000, p. 21.

32 Hammerton, *Cruelty and Companionship*, p. 38. See, e.g., Labourer's Friend Society, *Useful Hints for Labourers*, London, 1834, pp. 26–7.

33 Wiener, *Reconstructing the Criminal*, pp. 46–9.

34 For more detailed sociological studies, see, e.g., Henry Mayhew, *London Labour and the London Poor*, New York: Dover Publications, Inc., 1968; Andrew Mearns, *The Bitter Cry of Outcast London: An Inquiry into the Condition of the Abject Poor*, London, 1883; Charles Booth (ed.) *Life and Labour of the People of London*, London, 1892–7. For critics of social explanations, see Charles B. Tayler, *Social Evils, and their Remedy*, London, 1833, which concentrates upon religious metaphors and individual moral failings. S. A. K. Strahan, "What to do with our habitual criminals," *Westminster Review*, 1895, vol. 143, 660–6 focused upon an inherited "vicious temperament" as an explanation for habitual violent criminals.

35 Foucault, *Discipline and Punish*, p. 78.

36 Cf., Gatrell, "Policeman state," p. 248.

37 Taylor, "Crime and punishment," p. 476.

38 James Hole, *The Homes of the Working Classes, with Suggestions for Their Improvement*, London, 1866, pp. 21, 117; Octavia Hill, *Homes of the London Poor: Four Years' Management of a London Court*, London, 1883, pp. 89–90.

39 Shani D'Cruze, "Unguarded passions: violence, history and the everyday," in D'Cruze, *Everyday Violence*, p. 6.

40 J. F. Stephen, *Essays by a Barrister*, London, 1862, p. 107.

41 "Brief observations on the punishment of the pillory," *Pamphleteer*, 1814, vol. 4, no. 8, 547–8.

42 *Observations on the Offensive and Injurious Effect of Corporal Punishment; On the Unequal Administration of Penal Justice; and on the Pre-Eminent Advantages of the Mild and Reformatory Over the Vindictive System of Punishment*, London, 1827.

43 J. S. Mill, "Civilisation," *London and Westminster Review*, April 1836, in Gertrude Himmelfarb (ed.) *Essays on Politics and Culture: John Stuart Mill*, Garden City, NY: Doubleday & Company, 1962, p. 51. Emphasis in original.

44 Ibid., p. 52.

45 Ibid., pp. 52–3 and 64–5.

46 Cf., Taylor, "Crime and punishment," pp. 476–82.

47 W. C. Taylor, "Moral economy of large towns: Liverpool," *Bentley's Miscellany*, 1840, vol. 8, 131.

48 Simmons, *The Working Classes*, p. 36. See also Gaskell, *Artisans and Machinery*, pp. 129–30.

49 On the uses of imperial imagery in domestic contexts, see Susan Thorne, *Congregational Missions and the Making of an Imperial Culture in Nineteenth-Century England*, Stanford: Stanford University Press, 1999.

50 Referred to as a "fearful multitude of untutored savages" by Lord Ashley, Earl of Shaftesbury, in the House of Commons in 1843. Quoted in Pearson, *Hooligan*, p. 159. See also H. Manning and Benjamin Waugh, "The child of the English savage," *Contemporary Review*, 1886, vol. 49, 687–700.

51 HO 44/18 ff 37–48, 24 March 1828.

52 Kaye, "Outrages on women," p. 235.

53 Rosamond and Florence Davenport-Hill, *A Memoir of Matthew Davenport-Hill*, London, 1878, p. 163.

54 M. S. Crawford, "Maltreatment of wives," *Westminster Review*, 1893, vol. 39, 303.

55 Roger Swift, "Heroes or villains?: The Irish, crime and disorder in Victorian England," *Albion*, 1997, vol. 29, 399.

56 HO 44/11 ff 220–1.

57 Thomas Carlyle, *Chartism* (1839), quoted in Swift, "Heroes or villains?" p. 399; see also Lord Viscount Ingestre, *Meliora; or, Better Times to Come*, London, 1852, p. 164.

58 Sir James Phillips Kay Shuttlesworth, *The Moral and Physical Condition of the Working Classes Employed in the Cotton Manufactures*, London, 1832, pp. 6–7.

59 Gaskell, *Artisans and Machinery*, pp. 83–4.

60 Swift, "Heroes or villains?" pp. 402–3; Frank Neal, *Sectarian Violence: The Liverpool Experience, 1819–1914*, Manchester: Manchester University Press, 1988, pp. 158–67.

61 On rural idealizations, see Martin Wiener, *English Culture and the Decline of the Industrial Spirit, 1850–1980*, Cambridge: Cambridge University Press, 1981, pp. 46–51.

62 Letter from William Cobbold, HO 44/13 f 6, 19 January 1823.

63 Joseph Fletcher, "Moral and educational statistics of England and Wales," *Journal of the Statistical Society of London*, 1849, vol. 12, 171.

64 Ibid., p. 193.

65 Richard H. Horne and Charles Dickens, "Cain in the fields," *Household Words*, 10 May 1851, vol. 3, 147.

66 Horne and Dickens, "Cain in the fields," p. 149. A later literary echo of this statement appears in the Sherlock Holmes story "The copper beeches": "It is my belief, Watson, founded upon my experience, that the lowest and vilest alleys in London do not present a more dreadful record of sin than does the smiling and beautiful country-side." Sir Arthur Conan Doyle, *The Adventures of Sherlock Holmes*, London: Penguin Books, 1994, p. 286.

67 Ure, *Philosophy of Manufactures*, p. 354. Regarding women in rural areas, he claimed that misadministration of the poor laws had created "a race of harpies familiar with extortion, perjury and violence." Ibid., p. 357.
68 Fletcher, "Moral and educational statistics," p. 171.
69 Mill, "Civilisation," p. 51.
70 Rev. Benjamin Waugh, "Cruelty to children," *Good Words*, 1888, vol. 29, 818. Emphasis added. Similarly, new patterns of work and rising industrial wages were frequently linked to an "increase in drunkenness and violence": e.g., *Brutal Assaults Report*, pp. 66, 157, 163, 165.
71 Pearson, *Hooligan*, p. 164.
72 *Liverpool Daily Post*, 4 September 1886, quoted in Sindall, *Street Violence*, p. 7.
73 *Daily Telegraph*, 17 December 1874, quoted in Altick, *Studies in Scarlet*.
74 Mearns, *Outcast London*, p. 2.
75 Paine, *Task of the Age*, p. 41.
76 "Murder mania," *Chambers's Edinburgh Journal*, 6 October 1849, vol. 301 n.s., 209.
77 Philips, *Crime and Authority*, p. 238; Clive Emsley, *Crime and Society in England, 1750–1900*, London: Longman, 1987, p. 246.
78 Leonore Davidoff and Catherine Hall, *Family Fortunes: Men and Women of the English Middle Class, 1780–1850*, Chicago: Chicago University Press, 1987, p. 23.
79 Amanda Vickery, "Golden age to separate spheres? A review of the categories and chronology of English women's history," *The Historical Journal*, 1993, vol. 36, 383–414; Peter Bailey, " 'Will the real Bill Banks please stand up?' Towards a role analysis of mid-Victorian working-class respectability," *Journal of Social History*, 1979, vol. 12, 336–53.
80 Davidoff and Hall, *Family Fortunes*, p. 25.
81 Price, *British Society*, p. 295.
82 Cockburn, "Patterns of violence," p. 77. Sharpe, "Crime in England," pp. 22–5.
83 Barbara Weinberger, "Urban and rural crime rates and their genesis in late nineteenth- and early twentieth-century Britain," in Johnson and Monkkonen, *Civilization of Crime*, p. 207.
84 John E. Archer, " 'Men behaving badly'?: Masculinity and the uses of violence," in D'Cruze, *Everyday Violence*, pp. 41–54.
85 Wiener, "Victorian criminalization of men," p. 20.
86 "Social morality," *Chamber's Edinburgh Journal*, 3 February 1849, vol. 266 n.s., 87; T. H. Yeoman, MD, "On the healthy discipline of the home, No. 2 – The passions," *The People's Journal*, 1849; Simmons, *The Working Classes*, p. 7; Labourer's Friend Society, *Useful Hints*, p. 26.
87 Simmons, *The Working Classes*, pp. 56, 51.
88 Elliott, "Moral agents," p. 301.
89 Clark, "Humanity or justice?" pp. 196–7; see also Anna Clark, "Domesticity and the problem of wifebeating in nineteenth-century Britain: working-class culture, law and politics," in D'Cruze, *Everyday Violence*, pp. 34–6.
90 For a twentieth-century example, see Eric Dunning, Patrick Murphy and John Williams, " 'Casuals,' 'Terrace Crews' and 'Fighting Firms': Towards a sociological explanation of football hooliganism," in Riches, *Anthropology of Violence*, pp. 173–8.
91 "Social morality," p. 87 (which points to but criticizes such efforts); Paine, *Task of the Age*, p. 41; Fletcher, "Moral and educational statistics," pp. 172, 234; Hole, *Homes of the Working Classes*, p. 1; Henry Roberts, *The Physical Condition of the Labouring Classes*, London, 1866, p. 9; Hill, *Homes of the London Poor*, pp. 20, 30–1; Gareth Stedman Jones, *Languages of Class: Studies in English Working-Class History, 1832–1982*, Cambridge: Cambridge University Press, 1983, pp. 189, 190–3; Jacky Burnett, "Exposing 'the inner life': the Women's Co-operative Guild's attitude to cruelty," in D'Cruze, *Everyday Violence*, pp. 136–52.

92 Neil Tranter, *Sport, Economy and Society in Britain 1750–1914*, Cambridge: Cambridge University Press, 1998, p. 16; Dennis Brailsford, *British Sport: A Social History*, Cambridge: The Lutterworth Press, 1992, p. 73; Stan Shipley, "Tom Causer of Bermondsey: a boxer hero of the 1890s," *History Workshop Journal*, 1983, vol. 15, 28–59. On "Lad's Clubs" and their efforts to inculcate respectable values in working-class youths, see Andrew Davies, "Youth gangs, gender and violence, 1870–1900," in D'Cruze, *Everyday Violence*, pp. 70–1.

93 Mill, "Civilisation," p. 51.

94 Gaskell, *Artisans and Machinery*, pp. 77–8.

95 Paine, *Task of the Age*, p. 12.

96 *Observations … Corporal Punishment*, pp. 11, 18.

97 E. G. Wakefield, *Householders in Danger from the Populace*, London, 1832, pp. 2–3, 7–8.

98 A. P. Stanley (ed.), *The Miscellaneous Works of Thomas Arnold*, London, 1845, p. 453.

99 Gaskell, *Artisans and Machinery*, pp. 15, 20.

100 "Social morality," pp. 87–9.

101 Mayhew, *London Labour*, p. 371.

102 Halttunen, "Pornography of pain."

103 For example, the idea that lower-class life "bred" murderers became widespread: Altick, *Studies in Scarlet*, pp. 294–5.

104 Elizabeth A. Stanko, "Challenging the problem of men's individual violence," in Tim Newburn and Elizabeth A. Stanko (eds.) *Just Boys Doing Business? Men, Masculinities and Crime*, New York: Routledge, 1994, pp. 41–2; Chadwick, "Bureaucratic mercy," p. 457.

105 Nordstrom, *War Story*, p. 16.

106 Spierenburg, "Long-term trends," p. 68. Spierenburg warns *against* this assumption.

107 Stanko, "Challenging," pp. 34–5. Cf.; Conley, *Unwritten Law*, p. 67; Gatrell, "Policeman-state," pp. 271, 277.

108 Kaye, "Outrages on women," pp. 235–6.

109 On the claim that violence against children was also common to "well-to-do" families, see Waugh, "Cruelty to children," pp. 818–22; Hammerton, *Cruelty and Companionship*, p. 102.

110 Matilda M. Blake, "Are women protected?" *Westminster Review*, January 1892, vol. 137, 47.

111 W. E. Aytoun, "Banting on corpulence," *Blackwood's Edinburgh Magazine*, November 1864, vol. 96, 602; George H. Savage, "Homicidal mania," *The Fortnightly Review*, 1888, vol. 94 n.s., 448–63; Thomas Holmes, "Obscure causes of crime," *Contemporary Review*, October 1899, vol. 76, 577–88. See also Emsley, *Crime and Society*, p. 65 and Wiener, *Reconstructing the Criminal*, pp. 244–56.

112 Waugh, "Cruelty to children," p. 820.

113 Ibid.

114 Conley, *Unwritten Law*, p. 67; Gatrell, "Policeman-state," p. 297.

115 Blake, "Are women protected?, p. 44.

116 As in Crawford, "Maltreatment of wives," pp. 294–6.

117 Blake, "Are women protected?" p. 47. A view that strikes a similar note to that in Anna Clark, *Women's Silence, Men's Violence: Sexual Assault in England, 1770–1845*, London: Pandora, 1987.

118 Egan, *Boxiana*, vol. 1, p. 4. Emphasis in original.

119 E. L. Bulwer, "On English notions of morality," *New Monthly Magazine*, 1832, vol. 34, 22–5.

120 Mill, "Civilization," p. 65.

121 On the "enervating" qualities of civilization, see Stephen, "The decay of murder," p. 726; Gatrell, *Hanging Tree*, p. 5.

122 Charles Dickens, "The murdered person," *Household Words*, 11 October 1856, vol. 14, 289–91.

123 Elliott, "Moral agents," p. 320.

124 The *Times*, 10 April 1875, cited in Wiener, "Victorian criminalization of men," p. 204.

125 See, for example, the case of James Millman, a constable convicted of assault and imprisoned six months. He had been called out "in consequence of an order from the magistrate on Christmas Eve last for the purpose of suppressing singing, the singers having met in a riotous and disorderly manner." HO 17/2/ Ah 39. See also Clive Emsley, " 'The thump of wood on a swede turnip': police violence in nineteenth-century England," *Criminal Justice History*, 1985, vol. 6, 130–1.

126 Emsley, "Police violence," pp. 135–41.

127 Ibid., pp. 130, 133.

128 David Taylor, *The New Police in the Nineteenth Century: Crime, Conflict and Control*, Manchester, Manchester University Press, 1997, p. 129, n. 19.

129 Men were being whipped publicly as late as 1835, while the public whipping of women was forbidden in 1817 (though it continued privately until 1820), and Cockburn has noted descriptions of executions in the 1830s "in terms almost indistinguishable from those used to describe hangings at Tyburn a century earlier." Cockburn, "Punishment and brutalization," p. 174.

130 Ibid., pp. 155–7.

131 "Brief observations … pillory," p. 546.

132 Pike, *Crime in England*, vol. 2, p. 446.

133 Taylor, "Crime and punishment," p. 477.

134 Davenport-Hill, *Memoir*, p. 182.

135 Strahan, "Habitual criminals," p. 662.

136 "Brief observations … pillory," p. 542.

137 Dickens, "Lying awake," *Household Words*, 1852–3, vol. 6, 147.

138 Ibid.

139 Davenport-Hill, *Memoir*, pp. 201–2.

140 In a letter to the home office, a self-avowed humanitarian generally opposed to "hideous" punishments, for instance, believed that harsh punishment of traitors, including the public display of severed heads, would have a salutary effect on public morality. HO 44/1 f 45, 11 March 1820. Cf., a letter opposing the gibbeting of convict corpses, HO 44/14 f 87, 15 September 1824.

141 At times, the motivation to expand the legitimacy of physical punishment was more prosaic: in 1820, a magistrate wrote to the Home Office suggesting that a magistrate or Justice of the Peace be allowed to whip beggars "on the spot" to save ratepayers the expense of incarcerating them first. HO 44/21 ff 146–7, 24 August 1830.

142 Elliott, "Moral agents," p. 320.

143 Sindall, *Street Violence*, p. 59; cf., "Some thoughts on the connexion of crime and punishment," *Fraser's Magazine*, 1839, vol. 20, 693–4.

144 Hunt, "Wife Beating," p. 23.

145 Wiener, "Victorian criminalization of men," p. 208.

146 26 and 27 Vict., c.44.

147 *Brutal Assaults Report*, 1875.

148 Crawford, "Maltreatment of wives," p. 301.

149 Quoted in Gatrell, *Hanging Tree*, p. 593.

150 W. S. Lilly, "In praise of hanging," *The New Review*, 1894, vol. 11, 198.

151 Ibid., p. 200.

152 Wiener, *Reconstructing the Criminal*, p. 37.

3   "Vigorous passions and decided actions"

1 Stephen, "The decay of murder," p. 726.
2 Elias, *Civilizing Process*, p. 460.
3 Charles Dickens, *Sketches By Boz: Illustrative of Every-Day Life and Every-Day People*, London: Oxford University Press, 1957, pp. 72–3. Emphasis in original.
4 Spierenburg, "Long-term trends," p. 71.
5 Storch, "Domestic missionary," p. 495.
6 On the vendetta, see Thomas W. Gallant, *Experiencing Dominion: Culture, Identity and Power in the British Mediterranean*, Notre Dame, IN: University of Notre Dame Press, 2002, pp. 128–31. English popular culture too "endorsed the notion of retributive justice as part of the divine scheme of things": Cockburn, "Punishment and brutalization," p. 163.
7 Taylor, "Crime and punishment," p. 480.
8 Gatrell, *Hanging Tree*, pp. 5, 326–41.
9 Greenshields, *Economy of Violence*, p. 231.
10 ASSI 36/3 Surrey Lent 1837, *R.* v. *Bayne*.
11 The inspector believed he heard Taylor's party challenge to take on "any three" of the crowd.
12 ASSI 31/28, case #11 at Surrey Lent assizes. Bayne, the accused, was acquitted on murder charges and sentenced to one year in the house of correction with fourteen days solitary confinement for manslaughter.
13 HO 17/85 Pw 32, William Collett, Middlesex sessions, June 1836; ASSI 36/11 Kent Summer 1864, *R.* v. *Thomas Cole, et al.* (the circumstances of the case are also discussed in Conley, *Unwritten Law*, pp. 24–6).
14 Cockburn, "Punishment and brutalization," pp. 172–3; Beattie, *Crime and the Courts*, pp. 466–8. On serious injuries and fatalities at the eighteenth-century pillory see the following issues of *Gentleman's Magazine*: May 1732, p. 774; June 1732, p. 823; April 1751, p. 150; April 1752, p. 190; July 1752, p. 334; May 1755, p. 234; July 1759, p. 344; November 1762, p. 549; May 1780, p. 243; November 1786, p. 992. Cf., The *Times*, 22 November 1786.
15 In response to the death of the "thief-taker" Egan in the pillory, one observer wrote: "I should be extremely sorry to call in the mob as a supplement to the law – because the mob is ever disposed to worry any thing that is thrown into its reach, and find just the same pleasure in battering a malefactor to death, as in the destroying of any unhappy animal." Continuing, he made use of the imagery of savagery that would become commonplace in the nineteenth century: "It is not so truly the greatness of the crime which inflames them [the mob], as the scent of carnage; and now, by one murther [*sic*], they have got a taste for blood, it is high time that they should be considered as dogs of that carnivorous property, and that no more victims should be exposed to their resentment...." *Gentleman's Magazine*, 1756, p. 166.
16 John Paget, "The London police courts," *Blackwood's Edinburgh Magazine*, 1875, vol. 118, 388.
17 CRIM 1/14/1.
18 Thompson, *Customs in Common*, pp. 185–351; Clive Behagg, "Secrecy, ritual and folk violence: the opacity of the workplace in the first half of the nineteenth century," in Robert Storch (ed.) *Popular Culture and Custom in Nineteenth-Century England*, New York: St. Martin's Press, 1982, p. 171.
19 See *The Remarkable Confession and Last Dying Words of Thomas Colley*, London, 1751; *The Tryal of Thomas Colley, at the Assizes at Hertford, on Tuesday the 30th of July, 1751*, London, 1751; and *Gentleman's Magazine*, April 1751, p. 186, for a well-documented case of witch ducking. Other targets included Methodists: see KB 1/11 no. 3, Easter 25 Geo. II, 1752, affidavits of Owen, et al. (Denbighshire). See also, KB 1/11, Hilary 27 Geo.

II, 1754, affidavits of Burd, et al. (Somerset); KB 1/11, Trinity 25 and 26 Geo. II, 1752, affidavits of Duckett et al. (Norfolk); KB 1/11, Hilary 27 Geo. II, 1754, affidavits of Comberback, et al. (Cheshire).

20 Cockburn, "Punishment and brutalization," p. 176; Gatrell, *Hanging Tree*, p. 93.

21 ASSI 36/1 Essex Lent 1828, *R. v. Blenkins, et al.*

22 Taber described that there was "a great riot and I was much beaten" and testified that he was under the care of a surgeon as a result of his injuries: "Two of my ribs were dislocated and my head bruised." Blenkins and Franks received six-month jail terms for assault and riot. ASSI 31/25/376.

23 *The Times*, 25 March 1828.

24 ASSI 36/2 Cambridge Winter 1833, depositions regarding a riot at Switon.

25 ASSI 36/10 Kent Summer 1863, *R. v. Eldridge.*

26 A constable deposed, "The marks of blood extended up the backs of the boot heels and also along the sides of the boots." Hannah Steed deposed that her husband's hair was gray and black.

27 ASSI 31/36/115.

28 Which also appears to have been the motivation for a riotous assault on John and William Polley in Hinston, Cambridgeshire. ASSI 36/2 Cambs. Summer 1833, *R. v. Peachey, et al.*

29 Behagg, "Folk violence," pp. 158, 164.

30 ASSI 36/2 Norfolk Summer 1835, *R. v. Marsham, et al.*

31 Thomas Marsham, James Murrell, and George Sadler were convicted and had the sentence of death recorded against them. ASSI 33/12, Norfolk Summer 1835.

32 HO 17/15 pt. 2, Bm 20, James Bevan. The incident occurred 29 September 1826.

33 On ridings, see Storch, "Domestic missionary," pp. 489–91 and Thompson, *Customs in Common*, pp. 467–538.

34 The argument fell on deaf ears; his petition was not granted and he had to serve out the full term of three months' imprisonment.

35 Storch, "Domestic missionary," p. 490.

36 HO 17/65 Lw 48, William Mayer and John Rush.

37 HO 17/105 pt. 2, Tv 2, John Anderson, Edward Atkinson, Thomas Holmes, George Hunter and Robert McKintosh.

38 Martin Ingram, "Ridings, rough music and the 'reform of popular culture' in early modern England," *Past and Present*, 1984, vol. 105, 92.

39 Hunt, "Wife beating," p. 22.

40 Beattie, *Crime and the Courts*, pp. 36–8.

41 Phil Cohen, "Policing the working-class city," in Mike Fitzgerald, Gregor McLennan and Jennie Pawson (eds.) *Crime and Society: Readings in History and Theory*, London: Routledge, 1981, p. 116; Wilbur Miller, "Police authority in London and New York City," *Journal of Social History*, 1975, vol. 8, 84.

42 ASSI 36/1 Kent Summer 1828, *R. v. Oldfield.*

43 Conley, *Unwritten Law*, pp. 10, 155–7; Cockburn, "Patterns of violence," pp. 87–90.

44 ASSI 36/5 Hunts. Lent 1845, *R. v. Wrightson and Lewis*

45 It appears that the only person who contacted the authorities was unconnected to the events that night, the younger William Lewis deposing that "one Pyett" had left Hall's body in a local beer shop after coming across him lying dead in the lane.

46 HO 17/85 Px 24, Simmons Stammers, Old Bailey, April 1837.

47 HO 17/105 pt. 1, Tt 29, Timothy Cavanaugh, York City assizes 1834.

48 Mayhew, *London Labour*, vol. 2, p. 43.

49 Ibid., p. 29.

50 Shropshire quarter sessions, SRO Q/SB Ea. 1836, quoted in Philips, *Crime and Authority*, pp. 239–40.

51 Chadwick, "Bureaucratic mercy," p. 426.

52 ASSI 36/5 Kent Summer 1846, *R.* v. *Price.*

53 ASSI 31/30/259.

54 HO 17/105 pt. 1, Tw 37.

55 On this trend, see Douglas Hay and Francis Snyder, "Using the criminal law, 1750–1850: policing, private prosecution, and the state," in Douglas Hay and Francis Snyder (eds.) *Policing and Prosecution in Britain, 1750–1850*, Oxford: Oxford University Press, 1989, pp. 36–47.

56 HO 17/115 Wt 38, William Bridges, London sessions, 1834, assault.

57 HO 17/75 pt. 1, Iv 1, Robert Hopton, David Daniel Jackson and Thomas Rattenburg, Gloucester sessions, 1835. The man, William Leviard, had been given in charge to Constable Charles Watts by a "common prostitute of Cheltenham for obtaining money under a false pretence…."

58 E.g., CRIM 1/13/19, 1842, Thomas Shore. Shore's brother refused to testify against him for an assault; cf., Paget, "Police courts," p. 389, for a stabbing between sailors in which the victim was reluctant to prosecute.

59 HO 17/125 pt. 1, Yv 9, George White, Old Bailey sessions, September 1835, assault.

60 Quoted in Sindall, *Street Violence*, p. 96.

61 Stephen, "A sketch of the criminal law," p. 645.

62 Foucault, *Discipline and Punish*, p. 82.

63 D'Cruze, *Crimes of Outrage*, p. 70.

64 Davis, "Police courts," pp. 314–15.

65 D'Cruze, *Crimes of Outrage*, pp. 20–1.

66 Clark, *Women's Silence, Men's Violence*, Introduction.

67 As Hammerton notes, "rough usage" was a commonly accepted part of working-class marriage: *Cruelty and Companionship*, pp. 42–5.

68 Ellen Ross, "'Fierce questions and taunts': married life in working-class London, 1870–1914," *Feminist Studies*, 1982, vol. 8, 592; D'Cruze, *Crimes of Outrage*, pp. 21, 77.

69 Hunt, "Wife beating," p. 22.

70 Amussen, "Punishment, discipline and power," p. 3.

71 Maeve Doggett, *Marriage, Wife-Beating and the Law in Victorian England*, London: Weidenfeld & Nicholson, 1992, pp. 106–7.

72 26 & 27 Vict., c.44, 1863–4.

73 Hammerton, *Cruelty and Companionship*, pp. 63–4.

74 Doggett, *Wife-Beating*, pp. 142–3.

75 Chairman, quarter sessions, North Riding of Yorkshire, *Brutal Assaults Report*, p. 59. In this opinion, he was joined by colleagues from Stafford (ibid., p. 57) and Wolverhampton (ibid., p. 100).

76 Hammerton, *Cruelty and Companionship*, p. 38.

77 Kaye, "Outrages on women," p. 247.

78 D'Cruze, *Crimes of Outrage*, pp. 51–9.

79 Doggett, *Wife-Beating*, pp. 4–6.

80 Matthew Bacon, *A New Abridgement of the Law*, quoted in ibid, p. 10.

81 Ibid.

82 Hammerton, *Cruelty and Companionship*, pp. 34–5.

83 Chief Constable, Westmoreland and Cumberland, *Brutal Assaults Report*, pp. 163–4.

84 HO 17/15 pt. 2, Bm 25, William Carpenter, London sessions, 1827, assault.

85 Conley, *Unwritten Law*, p. 74.

86 ASSI 36/1 Herts. Lent 1830, *R.* v. *Franklin.*

87 Mary revived somewhat before she died, and in that time she and her husband exchanged some words. A surgeon who attended Mary deposed, "She said, 'James, you have stamped on me, you know you have stamped on me.' He made no reply except asking for forgiveness, and said 'You know you aggravated me.' She said afterward she forgave him and they kissed each other. Another surgeon deposed, "I sent

for the prisoner into the room having first asked her if she had any objection to see him. He fell upon his knees and hoped that she and God would forgive him, but he feared the laws of his country would not. ... I understood by her manner that she forgave him. I understood her to say to the prisoner that he had trampled her to death, and added, 'I am a dying woman, what will become of my children?' The prisoner said, 'You are an aggravating woman.'" Despite his fear for the retribution of the "laws of his country," James Franklin was acquitted of all charges.

88 ASSI 36/5 Kent Summer 1844, *R. v. Cockering*; ASSI 31/30/58.
89 ASSI 37/7 Sussex Summer 1853, *R v. Smith*; ASSI 31/33/107.
90 *The Times*, 2 January 1828. Cf., a case in which the *wife* was accused of assault: *The Times*, 3 January 1828.
91 ASSI 36/7 Suffolk Lent 1882, *R. v. Mickleburgh*; ASSI 36/10 Bedford Lent 1860, *R. v. Castle*.
92 "The law of murder," p. 437.
93 Chadwick, "Bureaucratic mercy," p. 457. For similarities with the Greek context, see Gallant, *Experiencing Dominion*, p. 170.
94 Chadwick, "Bureaucratic mercy," pp. 440–1.
95 Ross, "Fierce questions," p. 593.
96 Behlmer, *Child Abuse*, p. 12.
97 Conley, *Unwritten Law*, pp. 109–10. If infanticides are removed from the Victorian figures, the percentage of homicide victims aged under twelve remains a striking 23 percent.
98 Behlmer, *Child Abuse*, pp. 2, 6.
99 Anna Davin, *Growing Up Poor: Home, School and Street in London, 1870–1914*, London: Rivers Oram Press, 1996, p. 60.
100 Behlmer, *Child Abuse*, pp. 5–6.
101 Yeoman "Healthy discipline of the home," p. 221.
102 Labourer's Friend Society, *Useful Hints*, p. 26.
103 "Charity and beating begins at home": John Fletcher (1579–1625), quoted in the *Oxford Dictionary of Quotations*, Oxford: Oxford University Press, 1980, p. 215.
104 *Observations ... Corporal Punishment*. The "barbarous and offensive spectacles" that "outrage the feelings of the best portion of the community and ... aggravate the depravity of the worst," were not suited to the "feelings and judgment of civilized society...." Ibid., p. 1. Cf., a tract on the pillory from 1814: "We have all been taught that the sacred throne of justice should be exalted far above the passions and the ever-fluctuating sympathies of man, that its voice should be as certain as it is awful, and its sentences untainted with any of the grosser particles which move in a lowlier atmosphere." "Brief observations ... pillory," pp. 546–7.
105 Taylor, "Crime and punishment," p. 480.
106 Alfred Jones, "The philosophy of corporal punishment: an investigation into the policy and morality of school coercion. A lecture delivered before the Elementary Teachers' Association, London," London, 1859, p. 7.
107 Ibid.
108 Ibid., p. 8.
109 Mayhew, *London Labour*, vol. 2, p. 312.
110 Ibid., p. 350.
111 Robert Storch, " 'Please to remember the Fifth of November': conflict, solidarity and public order in southern England, 1815–1900," in Storch, *Popular Culture*, p. 73.
112 Thompson, *Customs in Common*, pp. 510–14.
113 William Albery (ed.) *Reminiscences of Horsham: Being Recollections of Henry Burstow, the Celebrated Bellringer and Songsinger*, Norwood, PA: Norwood Editions, 1975, p. 77.
114 For an efficient summary of nineteenth-century "civilizing" activity, see Jones, *Languages of Class*, pp. 191–6.

115 "Physical violence was a common feature of mid-Victorian life among the poor and was widely accepted provided its outcome did not extend beyond a few broken bones." Chadwick, "Bureaucratic mercy," p. 408. See also Johnson and Monkkonen, *Civilization of Crime*, Introduction, for the roots of this behavior in the rural areas and villages of pre-modern European society.

4 "The brave old English custom"

1 Owen Swift, *The Handbook of Boxing; Being a Complete Instructor in the Art of Self Defence*, London, 1840, p. iv.
2 Luby was a sweet-boiler born in Manchester in 1883. John Burnett (ed.) *Useful Toil: Autobiographies of Working People from the 1820s to the 1920s*, London: Routledge, 1994, p. 85.
3 Sir Walter Scott, "The two drovers," in Fred R. Shapiro and Jane Garry (eds.) *Trial and Error: An Oxford Anthology of Legal Stories*, New York: Oxford University Press, 1998.
4 Swift, *Handbook*. Besides Swift, other manuals include *The Art and Practice of English Boxing*, London, 1815; Egan, *Boxiana*; and Walker, *Defensive Exercises*.
5 Tranter, *Sport, Economy and Society*, p. 16; Brailsford, *British Sport*, p. 73. In the nineteenth century, the terms "boxing" and "prizefighting" were used interchangeably, along with other terms such as "pugilism." In this study, post-Queensberry-style fighting will be distinguished by calling it "modern boxing."
6 "Slack's boxing," *Connoisseur* (London), 22 August 1754, vol. 30, quoted in L. S. Wood and H. L. Burrows (eds.) *Sports and Pastimes in English Literature*, London: Thomas Nelson & Sons, 1925, p. 100.
7 Saussure, *Lettres*, p. 184, quoted and translated in Henriette A. Gram Heiny, "Boxing in British sporting art, 1730–1824," Ph.D. Dissertation, University of Oregon, 1987, p. 64.
8 HO 17/15 pt. 1, Bk 35, Shaw; ASSI 36/1 Surrey Lent 1830, *R.* v. *Lambrecht, et al.*
9 Barber Beaumont, Esq., Middlesex magistrate, letter to the *Morning Post*, 18 September 1829, quoted in Swift, *Handbook*, p. 6.
10 Quoted in Shipley, "Tom Causer," p. 35.
11 Walker, *Defensive Exercises*, p. 37. Cf., comments about young street sweepers in Mayhew, *London Labour*, vol. 2, p. 503.
12 Shipley, "Tom Causer," p. 35; Roberts, *Order and Dispute*, p. 35.
13 Cf., Ingram, "Reform of popular culture," pp. 112–13.
14 Elias, *Civilizing Process*, p. 166.
15 ASSI 36/6 Surrey Summer 1851, *R.* v. *Gill.*
16 Swift, *Handbook*, pp. 16–17, lists numerous "schools of boxing" in London's metropolitan area, nearly all of which were associated with pubs.
17 Elias, *Civilizing Process*, p. 166.
18 Ibid., p. 496.
19 Spierenburg, "Long-term trends," p. 74.
20 Ross, "Fierce questions"; Dickens, *Sketches by Boz*, pp. 70–71; Paget, "Police courts," pp. 384–5; Hill, *Homes of the London Poor*, p. 30.
21 Woods, "Community violence," pp. 176–7; Conley, *Unwritten Law*, p. 50; Davies, "Youth gangs," pp. 72, 78–81. Egan, *Boxiana*, p. 300; Frederick Hackwood, *Old English Sports*, London: T. Fisher Unwin, 1907, p. 204.
22 Johnson and Monkkonen, *Civilization of Crime*, Introduction.
23 For such exceptions, see ASSI 36/4 Kent Winter 1843, *R.* v. *Watts*; ASSI 36/1 Surrey Lent 1827, *R.* v. *Rice*; ASSI 36/1 Essex Summer 1825, *R.* v. *Goodday*; ASSI 36/16 Norfolk 1870, *R.* v. *Neave*.
24 E.g., HO 17/65 Lw 33, 1836; HO 17/75 pt. 1, Ny 8, 1838; ASSI 36/1 Sussex Lent 1830, *R.* v. *Hewitt*; ASSI 36/1 Herts. Summer, *R.* v. *Griffiths*.

25 ASSI 36/1 Surrey Lent 1827, *R.* v. *Rice.*

26 Barber Beaumont, letter, quoted in Swift, *Handbook,* p. 6.

27 HO 17/105 pt. 1, Tw 40. Emphasis in original.

28 Quoted in Storch, "Domestic missionary," p. 485.

29 *Brutal Assaults Report,* pp. 12, 17, 157, 160, 165.

30 Chadwick, "Bureaucratic mercy," p. 456.

31 Riches, "Phenomenon of violence," pp. 15–20.

32 Alain Corbin, *The Village of Cannibals: Rage and Murder in France, 1870,* Arthur Goldhammer (trans.), Cambridge, MA: Harvard University Press, 1992, p. 49.

33 See ASSI 36/1 Essex Summer 1825, *R.* v. *Speller* and ASSI 36/1 Herts. Summer 1830, *R.* v. *Owen.* For other instances of serial fighting, see ASSI 36/1 Sussex Lent 1830, *R.* v. *Hewitt* and ASSI 36/12 Northants. 1865, *R.* v. *Cross.*

34 ASSI 36/10 Sussex, Coroner's inquest on the body of John Weeks, 12 December 1863.

35 ASSI 36/11 Bucks. Summer 1864, *R.* v. *Price.*

36 E.g., ASSI 36/7 Kent Lent 1853, depositions on the body of Joseph Wright killed by Richard Sharpe.

37 ASSI 36/5 Kent, coroner's inquest, 9 December 1843, *R.* v. *Ball, et al.*

38 ASSI 36/2 Cambs. Summer 1833, *R.* v. *Munsey.*

39 Riches, "Phenomenon of violence," p. 11.

40 Amussen, "Punishment and discipline," p. 31.

41 ASSI 36/1 Essex Summer 1825, *R.* v. *Payne.* Goodday is spelled "Goody" in some depositions and "Goodday" in the minute book, ASSI 31/24.

42 ASSI 36/2 Cambs. Summer 1833, *R.* v. *Munsey.*

43 HO 17/75 pt. 1, Ny 8, John Latham, cutting and wounding.

44 ASSI 36/1 Herts. Summer 1830, *R.* v. *Owen.*

45 ASSI 36/1 Surrey Lent 1827, *R.* v. *Rice,* William Becket's deposition.

46 HO 17/105 pt. 1, Tw 40, William Penn and Owen Ball, Warrick, May 1836, assaulting a constable.

47 ASSI 36/13 Suffolk Winter 1867, *R.* v. *Martin.*

48 ASSI 36/2 Norfolk Summer 1834, *R.* v. *Seaman.* Waller later died, but Seaman was acquitted of all charges largely because a surgeon's report noted that Waller was prone to "apoplexy" and suggested that it was very easy to provoke a fit of apoplexy in a drunken man.

49 ASSI 36/1 Sussex Lent 1830, *R.* v. *Hewitt;* ASSI 36/2 Essex Lent 1831.

50 ASSI 36/17 Kent Lent 1871, *R.* v. *Sellen.*

51 Cf., the early modern French pattern of "provocation and response" noted in Greenshields, *Economy of Violence,* pp. 232–4. "Escalated showing-off contests" are discussed in Martin Daly and Margot Wilson, *Homicide,* New York: Aldine De Gruyter, 1988, pp. 176–8.

52 ASSI 36/1 Essex Summer 1825, *R.* v. *Payne.*

53 ASSI 36/1 Sussex Lent 1830, *R.* v. *Hewitt.*

54 ASSI 36/7 Kent Lent 1853, *R.* v. *Sharpe.*

55 ASSI 36/16 Norfolk, *R.* v. *Neave.*

56 ASSI 36/6 Surrey Lent 1848, *R.* v. *Pinnion, et al.*

57 ASSI 36/1 Essex Summer 1825, *R.* v. *Speller.*

58 Cf., Fox, "Inherent rules of violence," p. 142.

59 ASSI 36/6 Surrey Lent 1848, *R.* v. *Pinnion, et al.*

60 See a recounting of a fatal fight fought without "quarrel" recounted in Egan, *Boxiana,* vol. 2, pp. 145–55.

61 Letter written by Henry Jex to the Secretary of State, HO 17/65 Lw 33, John Langley, Norfolk Lent assizes March 1836. The petition was denied.

62 ASSI 36/10 Sussex December 1863, *R.* v. *Andrews.*

63 Amussen, "Punishment and discipline," p. 24. See, for example, ASSI 36/6 Surrey Lent 1848, *R. v. Pinnion, et al.*; ASSI 36/4 Kent Winter 1843, *R. v. Watts*; ASSI 36/17 Kent Lent 1871, *R. v. Sellen*; ASSI 36/1 Herts. Summer 1830, *R. v. Owen*. In other circumstances, other drinks, such as coffee, could serve the same purpose: ASSI 36/7 Kent Lent 1853, *R. v. Sharpe*.

64 Stephen, *Digest of the Criminal Law*, 1877, quoted in Chadwick, "Bureaucratic mercy," p. 397.

65 Conley, *Unwritten Law*, p. 49.

66 ASSI 36/5 Surrey Lent 1846, coroner's inquest taken 5 September, depositions of George Bundle and James Brown.

67 See more fights at fairs in ASSI 36/1 Essex Summer 1825, *R. v. Speller* and ASSI 36/2 Bucks. Lent 1836, *R. v. Currell*.

68 ASSI 36/11 Bucks. Summer 1865, *R. v. Price*.

69 ASSI 36/4 Kent Winter 1843, *R. v. Watts*.

70 ASSI 36/1 Herts. Summer 1830, *R. v. Griffiths*. Griffiths is sometimes referred to in the depositions as "Griffin"; in the Crown minute book and other depositions he is called "Griffiths."

71 ASSI 31/26/198

72 "William Speller … came forward and stripped himself to fight and the deceased also stripped himself and they proceeded to fight." ASSI 36/1 Essex Summer 1825, *R. v. Speller*.

73 ASSI 36/2 Surrey Summer 1832, *R. v. Chapman*; "Then Miller, Spencer and Watts went down to the bottom of the field and stripped." ASSI 36/4 Kent Winter 1843, *R. v. Watts*. "We were in the booth a good bit after that when we heard a cry of 'fight, fight' and that caused me to go down the hill and I saw Lynch there stripped…." ASSI 36/5 Surrey 1846, *R. v. Taylor*.

74 ASSI 36/1 Sussex Lent 1830, *R. v. Hewitt*, testimony of William Smithers and William Midmer.

75 ASSI 36/11 Bucks. Summer 1864, coroner's inquest on the death of William Dale, testimony of Cornelius Ridgely.

76 Ibid., testimony of George Berton.

77 ASSI 36/1 Herts. Summer 1830, *R. v. Griffiths*, testimony of James Hosler, William Burr and John Bennett.

78 ASSI 36/3 Surrey Lent 1837, *R. v. Powell*.

79 Swift, *Handbook*, p. 25. Emphasis in original.

80 ASSI 36/5 Kent, coroner's inquest, 9 December 1843, *R. v. Ball, et al.*

81 ASSI 36/2 Cambs. Summer 1833, *R. v. Munsey*.

82 ASSI 36/1 Herts. Summer 1830, *R. v. Owen*.

83 ASSI 36/1 Herts. Summer 1830, *R. v. Griffiths*.

84 Ibid.

85 ASSI 36/5 Kent, coroner's inquest, 9 December 1843, *R. v. Ball, et al.* See comments regarding the importance of keeping the ring clear for the sake of both fairness and safety in Swift, *Handbook*, p. 24.

86 The following cases make note of the presence of seconds and/or discuss in detail the roles they played in the fight: ASSI 36/1 Essex Summer 1825, *R. v. Speller*; ASSI 36/1 Sussex Lent 1830, *R. v. Hewitt*; ASSI 36/1 Herts. Summer 1830, *R. v. Owen*; ASSI 36/1 Herts. Summer, 1830 *R. v. Griffiths*; ASSI 36/2 Bucks. Lent 1836, *R. v. Currell*; ASSI 36/2 Surrey Summer 1832, *R. v. Chapman*; ASSI 36/2 Cambs. Summer 1833, *R. v. Munsey*; ASSI 36/3 Surrey Lent 1837, *R. v. Powell*; ASSI 36/5 Kent Lent 1844, *R. v. Ball*; ASSI 36/6 Surrey Lent 1848, *R. v. Pinnion, et al.*; ASSI 36/6 Surrey Summer 1851, *R. v. Gill*; ASSI 36/10 Sussex Lent 1864, *R. v. Andrews*.

87 Swift, *Handbook*, p. 22.

88 ASSI 36/5 Kent, coroner's inquest, 9 December 1843, *R. v. Ball, et al.*

89 Swift, *Handbook*, p. 22. Emphasis in original.
90 ASSI 36/1 Herts. Summer 1830, *R. v. Griffiths*.
91 Quoted in Swift, *Handbook*, p. 12.
92 Ibid., p. 25.
93 Ibid., p. 22. Emphasis in original.
94 Ibid., p. 23. Emphasis in original. For Swift, the distinction between the second and bottle holder "is almost a distinction without a difference, for both are seconds in every sense of the word. The most responsible part of the duty, however, is entrusted to the active second, who is *not* the bottle holder. Much is done and accomplished by a man being well *nursed* during a fight; the bottle-holder should never fail to provide himself with plenty of water." Ibid., p. 24. Emphasis in original.
95 "Griffiths fell on his back [and] I saw him lifted up by his seconds." ASSI 36/1 Herts. Summer 1830, *R. v. Griffiths*. In ASSI 36/2 Surrey Summer 1832, *R. v. Chapman*, the word "second" is not used, but men picked up the fighters when they fell. "[The seconds] stood by and picked the men up when they fell." ASSI 36/10 Sussex Lent 1864, *R. v. Andrews*. "In the second round, Owen knocked the deceased down. He was immediately picked up and placed on his second's knee and in about two minutes they began fighting again." ASSI 36/1 Herts. Summer 1830, *R. v. Owen*.
96 Swift, *Handbook*, pp. 23, 25.
97 ASSI 36/5 Kent, coroner's inquest, 9 December 1843, *R. v. Ball, et al.*
98 E.g., ASSI 36/10 Sussex Lent 1864, *R. v. Andrews*.
99 E.g., ASSI 36/1 Herts. Summer 1830, *R. v. Griffiths*.
100 ASSI 36/6 Surrey Lent 1848, *R. v. Pinnion, et al.*
101 Swift, *Handbook*, 23. Emphasis in original.
102 In the Griffiths case, "water and gin and water were given to them [by the seconds] to wet their lips." ASSI 36/1 Herts. Summer 1830, *R. v. Griffiths*.
103 ASSI 36/5 Kent, coroner's inquest, 9 December 1843, *R. v. Ball, et al.*, ASSI 36/6 Surrey Lent 1848, *R. v. Pinnion, et al.* (for carrying to assistance and attempts to revive).
104 ASSI 36/1 Herts. Summer 1830, *R. v. Owen*.
105 ASSI 36/10 Sussex Lent 1864, *R. v. Andrews*; for other examples of the identification of seconds, see ASSI 36/1 Herts. Summer 1830, *R. v. Griffiths*, testimony of James Hosler; and ASSI 36/1 Herts. Summer 1830, *R. v. Owen*.
106 ASSI 36/1 Herts. Summer 1830, *R. v. Owen*.
107 ASSI 36/1 Sussex Lent 1830, *R. v. Hewitt*.
108 ASSI 36/10, Sussex Lent 1864, *R. v. Andrews*, for sentencing, see ASSI 31/36/170.
109 ASSI 36/5 Kent, coroner's inquest, 9 December 1843, *R. v. Ball, et al.*
110 ASSI 36/2 Bucks. Lent 1836, *R. v. Currell*, see ASSI 33/12, for sentencing. For other cases, see ASSI 36/3 Surrey Lent 1837, *R. v. Powell*, in which the principal fighter and all seconds were found not guilty of similar charges, and ASSI 36/6 Surrey Summer 1851, *R. v. Gill*, a prizefight in which the identity of the four seconds remained unknown to the court.
111 Shipley, "Tom Causer," p. 37.
112 Swift, *Handbook*, p. 24.
113 ASSI 36/5 Kent, coroner's inquest, 9 December 1843, *R. v. Ball, et al.*
114 ASSI 36/1 Herts. Summer 1830, *R. v. Owen*.
115 ASSI 36/1 Herts. Summer 1830, *R. v. Griffiths.*, testimony of James Hosler, William Burr, John Bennett and William White. For other similar comments see ASSI 36/1 Herts. Summer 1830, *R. v. Owen*.
116 Swift, *Handbook*, pp. 23–4.
117 HO 44/20 ff 274–9, letter from George Moore to Robert Peel, 9 June 1830.

118 Swift, *Handbook*, pp. 28–61; ASSI 36/6 Surrey Summer 1851, *R. v. Gill*; ASSI 36/5 Kent Lent 1844, *R. v. Ball, et al.*, testimony of Alfred Davies.

119 ASSI 36/10 Sussex Lent 1864, *R. v. Andrews*, testimony of Thomas Gasland and Charles Andrews.

120 HO 17/65, Lw 33, John Langley for manslaughter.

121 Quoted in Swift, *Handbook*, p. 12.

122 Ibid., p. 19.

123 Ibid., p. 26.

124 ASSI 36/1 Herts. Summer 1830, *R. v. Owen*.

125 ASSI 36/6 Surrey Lent 1848, *R. v. Pinnion, et al.*

126 Swift, *Handbook*, p. 19.

127 ASSI 36/10 Sussex Lent 1864, *R. v. Andrews*.

128 ASSI 36/12 Northants. 1865, *R. v. Cross*.

129 On street gangs and clogging, see Sindall, *Street Violence*, pp. 61–7. Archer, "Men behaving badly?" p. 9.

130 Barber Beaumont, Esq., quoted in Swift, *Handbook*, p. 6. He also notes, "this, too, is pretty much the case in Ireland…." Similar statements are made in Walker, *Defensive Exercises*, p. 36.

131 See cases in Archer, "Men behaving badly?"

132 ASSI 36/8 Surrey Winter 1855, *R. v. Woods*.

133 Steamboat and railway networks initially helped keep prizefighting alive by extending the range that spectators could travel to outlying districts where the police presence was more sparse. An 1869 article argued that ship and rail operators had not lost their interest in supporting traditional prizefighting. "The decline of the ring," *Tinsley's Magazine*, July 1869, 552. By the time of the "last great rail excursion" to a prizefight in 1860 (for Sayers v. Herman), most railway companies refused bookings for fight excursions. The Regulation of the Railways Act (1868) made the hiring of trains for fight spectators illegal, "and the sport itself was in its long, slow dying." Brailsford, *British Sport*, pp. 84–5.

134 ASSI 36/12 Northants. 1865, *R. v. Cross*.

135 ASSI 36/13 Suffolk Winter 1867, *R. v. Martin*.

136 ASSI 36/14 Leicestershire Summer 1868, *R. v. William Gilley*.

137 ASSI 36/16 Norfolk, *R. v. Neave*, coroner's depositions taken 9 December 1870.

138 ASSI 36/17 Kent Lent 1871, *R. v. Sellen*.

139 ASSI 36/17 Northants. Summer 1871, *R. v. Reedman*.

140 "Illegality of glove fights," *Liverpool Mercury*, 18 November 1878. I thank John E. Archer for bringing this case to my attention.

141 *Brutal Assaults Report*, pp. 13, 24, 87.

142 Davin, *Growing Up Poor*, pp. 36, 70–74.

143 Clarence Rook, *Hooligan Nights: Being the Life and Opinions of a Young and Impenitent Criminal Recounted by Himself and Set Forth by Clarence Rook*, London: Grant Richards, 1899, p. 27.

144 Ibid., p. 205.

145 Burnett, *Useful Toil*, p. 85.

146 Ibid., p. 86.

147 Amussen, "Punishment, discipline and power," p. 33.

148 Barber Beaumont, esq., quoted in Swift, *Handbook*, p. 6. Emphasis in original.

149 On violence as a "resource," see Riches, "Phenomenon of violence," p. 13.

150 Egan, *Boxiana*, vol. 1, pp. 2–3.

151 Ibid., vol. 1, pp. 13–14. Also see the poem, "A boxing we will go" (vol. 1, p. 481) and a description of American fighting methods (vol. 3, p. 594) for similar comments.

152 See also a case quoted in Philips, *Crime and Authority*, pp. 264–5.

153 Walker, *Defensive Exercises*, p. 36. Cf., Elliott J. Gorn, " 'Gouge and bite, pull hair and scratch': the social significance of fighting in the southern backcountry," *American Historical Review*, 1985, vol. 90, 23–41 on American fighting; Chevalier, *Dangerous Classes*, pp. 420–33 on French styles of fighting.

154 Mayhew, *London Labour*, vol. 2, p. 338.

155 "The essential difference between Captain Cilas's system of wrestling and that of the North of England, is this, that in his, the wrestlers catch hold of each other in any way they choose; whereas, in the North, each party has an equal and similar hold before the struggle begins. Who can doubt which is the better system? The Captain's is radically savage and barbarous, and more congenial with the habits and temper of African Negroes than European whites. The other is fair, just and civilized." Walker, *Defensive Exercises*, p. 9.

156 Hazlitt, "The fight," p. 110.

157 Tranter, *Sport, Economy and Society*, p. 19.

158 "There is a certain makebelieve in the glove-business which quite unfits it for comparison with the real thing. With gloves you may indeed close the eyes of your adversary, cause his nose to bleed, and make his head feel unto him considerably larger than his body, yet are the gloves but a miserable compromise with the genuine performance." "Decline of the ring," p. 552.

159 Shipley, "Tom Causer," p. 40. According to some, the traditional form of fighting had also had these qualities. Of course, enthusiasts of the old style had made similar arguments: Swift, *Handbook*, pp. iii, 6.

160 Brailsford, *British Sport*, p. 88.

5   "The wrongdoing of the poor man is as open as day"

1 Hole, *The Homes of the Working Classes*, p. 1.

2 Sibley, *Geographies of Exclusion*, p. 86.

3 ASSI 36/12 Kent Summer 1866, *R. v. Lawrence*.

4 The older child was Lawrence's by another man; the infant was the child of both Lawrence and Highams.

5 ASSI 31/37/56, nos. 69 and 70. Her trial took place over two days. She was sentenced to be hanged "and the lady buried within the precincts of the prison in which she shall be fast confined after conviction."

6 Two weeks before her execution, Lawrence reportedly confessed to the prison chaplain that she had committed the murder while "frenzy mad" over Highams's infidelity. Conley, *Unwritten Law*, p. 108.

7 My thinking on space and violence was greatly influenced by a session at the Royal Geographical Society–Institute of British Geographers conference in Brighton, January 2000, particularly a session in which I participated on "Geographies of fear and violence." I thank Rob Kitchen and James Anderson for organizing the session and for their helpful comments, and Jessica Walsh for her assistance and advice on the paper that served as the basis for this chapter.

8 Jones, *Languages of Class*, pp. 184–6.

9 Ross, "Fierce questions," p. 577.

10 Friedrich Engels, *The Condition of the Working-Class in England*, Moscow, Progress Publishers, 1980, p. 62.

11 Storch, "Domestic missionary," p. 496.

12 Thomas Beames, *The Rookeries of London: Past, Present and Prospective*, London, 1850, p. 7.

13 Hugh MacCallum, *The Distribution of the Poor in London*, London, 1883, p. 4.

14 The portrayal of "defiling" and "threatening" groups is often used to "order society internally and demarcate the boundaries of society, beyond which lie those who do not belong." Sibley, *Geographies of Exclusion*, p. 49.

15 Bailey, "Working-class respectability," p. 340. See also Peter Williams, "Constituting class and gender: a social history of the home, 1700–1901," in Nigel Thrift and Peter Williams (eds.) *Class and Space: The Making of Urban Society*, London: Routledge & Kegan Paul, 1987, p. 188 on the "obliviousness" of the middle-class regarding working-class life and pp. 189–90 on the topic of residential segregation.

16 See, e.g., James Greenwood, *Low Life Deeps: An Account of the Strange Fish to be Found There*, London, 1876 and Clarence Rook, *Hooligan Nights*.

17 Charles Dickens, "Conversion of a heathen court," *Household Words*, 16 December 1854, vol. 10, 409.

18 Dickens was also certain that the project would generate 15 percent profits.

19 Shuttlesworth, *Moral and Physical Condition*, p. 16. Impulsiveness and lack of forethought were key aspects of such immorality. Ibid., p. 7.

20 H. Shimmin, *Liverpool Life: Its Pleasures, Practices and Pastimes*, Liverpool, 1856, p. 66. Cf., Buret's description of Paris in the first half of the nineteenth century provided in Chevalier, *Dangerous Classes*, p. 360.

21 Hole, *Homes of the Working Classes*, pp. 1, 21.

22 Lord Viscount Ingestre, *Social Evils: Their Causes and Their Cure. A Lecture Delivered Before the Bilston Institute in Connection with St. Mary's National Schools*, Wolverhampton, 1853, pp. 7–8.

23 Parliament, *Local Reports on the Sanitary Condition of the Labouring Population of England, In Consequence of an Inquiry Directed to Be Made by the Poor Law Commissioners*, London, 1842, p. 100.

24 Taylor, "Liverpool," p. 131.

25 Roberts, *Physical Condition*, p. 4.

26 Hole, *Homes of the Working Classes*, p. 21. "The existence of this class [the poor] seems almost to be ignored by the legislature, by the respectable portion of society, and by the press itself, except when one of its members attracts attention to it by some act of folly, violence or brutality." Ibid., p. 117.

27 Hill, *Homes of the London Poor*, Preface.

28 Ibid., p. 90.

29 Davidoff and Hall, *Family Fortunes*, pp. 357–96; M. J. Daunton, "Housing," in Thompson, *Cambridge Social History of Britain*, pp. 211–13.

30 M. J. Daunton, "Public space and private space: the Victorian city and the working-class household," in Derek Fraser and Anthony Sutcliffe (eds.) *The Pursuit of Urban History*, London: Edward Arnold, 1983, p. 222.

31 Beames, *Rookeries of London*, p. 177; Gaskell, *Artisans and Machinery*, p. 81. The working class, of course, had their own notions of privacy and the orderly use of space. See, e.g., Davin, *Growing Up Poor*, pp. 45–61.

32 Greenwood, *Low Life Deeps*, p. 73.

33 Mayhew, *London Labour*, vol. 2, p. 153; Mearns, *Outcast London*, p. 18. One study of the parishes of St. John and St. Margaret in London suggested that three-fourths of working families lived in one room: Engels, *Condition*, p. 63.

34 Greenwood, *Low Life Deeps*, pp. 129–30.

35 Gaskell, *Artisans and Machinery*, p. 82. See also Beames, *Rookeries of London*, p. 5.

36 Engels, *Condition*, pp. 59–102. Crowding was also a rural problem. Rural workers often lived in "rows of cottages" in cramped conditions and there was a tendency for agricultural laborers to live in so called "double cottages" – farm houses divided into three or four tenements. Parliament, *Local Reports*, pp. 89, 90–1. When Hubbard Lingley fatally shot Benjamin Black outside a small village in Norfolk, several witnesses knew about Lingley's possession of a gun and at least one had borrowed it

on a previous occasion. One of them "lived under one roof" with Black, "in separate cottages." ASSI 36/13 Norfolk Summer 1867, *R. v. Lingley*.

37 Mearns, *Outcast London*, pp. 18–19.
38 In the assizes, see, e.g., ASSI 36/17 Kent Summer 1872, *R. v. Moore*, and ASSI 36/17 Northants. Summer 1871, *R. v. Addington*.
39 Mearns, *Outcast London*, p. 8. See also, Roberts, *Physical Condition*, p. 3.
40 Mearns, *Outcast London*, p. 7.
41 Behagg, "Folk violence," p. 167.
42 Reminiscing about working in Newcastle in the 1860s, one author noted, "Men are often so much like monkeys and school-boys that they find pleasure in tormenting and ill-using each other. These petty tyrannies, rendering existence intolerable in the case of victims who are capable of defending themselves, are mean and contemptible in the case of helpless and inoffensive companions." W. E. Adams, *Memoirs of a Social Atom*, London, 1903, vol. 2, p. 557. Cf. Burnett, *Useful Toil*, pp. 360–1. For work-related violent incidents, see, e.g., ASSI 36/14 Kent 1868, *R. v. Wells* (supervisor shot and killed at a railway yard); ASSI 36/3 Surrey Lent 1839, *R. v. Fuller* (boy killed by his employer); ASSI 36/2 Cambs. Summer 1833, *R. v. Munsey* (a dispute and fight begun at work); ASSI 36/5 Kent Lent 1844, *R. v. Ball* (dispute that led to a prizefight began at work); CRIM 1/14/1 (worker "ducked" by his co-workers); HO 17/15 pt. 2, Bm 20, James Bevan and HO 17/65, Lw 48, William Mayer and John Rush. For cases of murder between household servants, see ASSI 36/1 Surrey Lent 1828, *R. v. Irons* and ASSI 36/2 Kent Lent 1833, *R. v. Farmer*. When a boy was killed by his employer in 1839 there was an awareness of his history of violence against the child: ASSI 36/3 Surrey Lent 1839, *R. v. Fuller*.
43 See a number of these incidents discussed in Ellen Ross, "Survival networks: women's neighbourhood sharing in London before World War One," *History Workshop*, 1983, vol. 15, 15–16.
44 Hill, *Homes of the London Poor*, pp. 89–90.
45 Ross, "Survival networks," pp. 4–27. See also Davin, *Growing Up Poor*, pp. 57–61.
46 D'Cruze, *Crimes of Outrage*, pp. 50–9.
47 Captain Fulford, "On prison discipline," in Ingestre (ed.) *Meliora*, p. 155. Cf., Booth, *Life and Labour*, vol. 3, pp. 37–42.
48 Hill, *Homes of the London Poor*, p. 20.
49 Ibid., pp. 30–1.
50 Booth, *Life and Labour*, vol. 3, pp. 38–40; Woods, "Community violence," p. 176; Davis, "Police courts," p. 323.
51 Ross, "Fierce questions," p. 578.
52 Judith Walkowitz, "Jack the Ripper and the myth of male violence," *Feminist Studies*, 1982, vol. 8, 554.
53 Martha Vicinus, *The Industrial Muse: A Study of Nineteenth-Century British Working-Class Literature*, London: Croom Helm, 1974, p. 16; Ross, "Fierce questions," p. 592.
54 Kaye, "Outrages on women," p. 236.
55 Ibid.
56 Paine, *Task of the Age*, p. 2.
57 ASSI 36/1 Sussex Lent 1830, *R. v. Hewitt*.
58 Mayhew, *London Labour*, vol. 3, p. 1. Emphasis in original. Cf., Booth's comments regarding disputes at a working-class tenement: "At six o'clock a row in the street calls a crowd of the inhabitants out on to the balconies, where we can look down exactly as from boxes in a theatre on to the stage. The parties to the quarrel are a man and his wife in a distinctly lower walk of life (like all the inhabitants of houses in the street) and any of the tenants of the Buildings. They are eventually separated after much 'old English' on both sides. The general impression among is the spectators is in

favour of the man, but the incident is soon forgotten." Booth, *Life and Labour*, vol. 3, pp. 40–1.

59   Quoted in Ross, "Fierce questions," p. 582.

60   See, for example, ASSI 36/1 Herts. Lent 1830, *R. v. Franklin* (murder of wife); ASSI 36/7 Sussex Summer 1853, *R. v. Smith* (murder of husband); ASSI 36/7 Suffolk Lent 1852, *R. v. Mickleburgh* (murder of female cohabitant); ASSI 36/17 Northants. Summer 1871, *R. v. Addington* (murder of wife). One of Booth's subjects noted that "narrow resounding passages and stairs made domestic disputes and crying children disagreeably prominent." Although she had moved to a new building where she claimed did not have such problems, she gave a very detailed description of her typical day and could, with remarkable precision, recount the movements of her neighbors (and their conversations) by hearing them through the walls. Booth, *Life and Labour*, vol. 3, pp. 38–40.

61   Sibley, *Geographies of Exclusion*, p. 76. See also Thrift and Williams, *Class and Space*, pp. 16–17, for a discussion of "locale," "locality" and "distanciation."

62   Michel de Certeau, *The Practice of Everyday Life*, Steven Rendall (trans.), Berkeley: University of California Press, 1984, pp. 97–8.

63   Nanette Davis and Bo Anderson, *Social Control: The Production of Deviance in the Modern State*, Irvington, NY, 1983, cited in Sibley, *Geographies of Exclusion*, p. 35. High-density networks are related to Durkheim's notion of "mechanical solidarity." In a social identity based upon mechanical solidarity, "society is dominated by the existence of a strongly formed set of sentiments and beliefs shared by all members of the community [so] it follows that there is little scope for differentiation between individuals: each individual is a microcosm of the whole." Anthony Giddens, *Capitalism and Modern Social Theory*, Cambridge: Cambridge University Press, 1971, pp. 75–6.

64   Storch, "Domestic missionary"; Dunning, Murphy and Waddington, "British civilizing process," p. 18; Daunton, "Public space and private space," p. 223.

65   Hall and Davidoff, *Family Fortunes*, p. 358.

66   Women had customarily been active, for example, in rioting and "rough music": See Thompson, *Customs in Common*, pp. 233–4, 305–36.

67   Clark, *Women's Silence, Men's Violence*; Walkowitz, "Jack the Ripper," p. 564.

68   Williams, "Constituting class and gender," p. 155.

69   Price, *British Society*, pp. 205–26.

70   Doggett, "Wife-beating," pp. 90–1.

71   Daunton, "Public space and private space"; Foucault, *Discipline and Punish*, pp. 136–43.

72   Ross, "Fierce questions," p. 576.

73   When they returned home, the husband escalated his violence and beat her to death with a poker. *The Times*, 5 January 1874, quoted in Sindall, *Street Violence*, p. 62.

74   ASSI 36/2 Cambridge Lent 1835, *R. v. Woods*. Woods was found not guilty of murder, but was transported for life for manslaughter. The charges against him note that, other than beating her with the cod, he had struck Harriet several times against a wall and driven her head against the wall and the floor. ASSI 33/12.

75   Crawford, "Maltreatment of wives," p. 297.

76   Horne and Dickens, "Cain in the fields," p. 148.

77   Noted in *Hansards Debates*, 10 March 1853, pp. 1415–16.

78   Hammerton, *Cruelty and Companionship*, p. 26; Nancy Tomes, "A torrent of abuse: crimes of violence between working-class men and women in London, 1840–1875," *Journal of Social History*, 1978, vol. 11, 334–8; Ross, "Fierce questions," pp. 591–2. See a case in which men intervened in violence against women in ASSI 36/1 Kent Summer 1828, *R. v. Oldfield*. Henry Bennett was charged at Bow Street police court with assaulting his wife in December 1852. They were living apart, and upon

meeting her in the streets, he beat her severely. Others intervened, helping her escape from him. Cited in *Hansards Debates*, 10 March 1853, p. 1415.

79   HO 17/55 pt. 2, It 19, Edward Tupman assault on a constable. In the course of his arrest, Tupman accidentally cut Bentley with a knife and was sentenced to nine months' imprisonment. Bentley himself recommended mercy in the case as the cut was unintentional.

80   Chadwick, "Bureaucratic mercy," p. 440.

81   HO 17/15 pt. 2, Bm 25, 1827, William Carpenter.

82   Hammerton, *Cruelty and Companionship*, pp. 34–5.

83   Conley, *Unwritten Law*, p. 78.

84   Ibid., p. 73. For would-be lovers and murder, see ASSI 36/7 Suffolk Lent 1852, *R. v. Mickleburgh*; ASSI 36/1 Kent Lent 1822, *R. v. Hayward*; and ASSI 36/6 Essex Lent 1851 *R. v. Drory*.

85   HO 17/95 Rv 13, 1835, John Cassell.

86   Case discussed in Conley, *Unwritten Law*, p. 79. Cf., "If the institution of marriage, whose purpose was to tame the most powerful and socially destructive characteristic of Victorian man, was destroyed by a woman a provocation had been offered." Chadwick, "Bureaucratic mercy," p. 440.

87   ASSI 36/5 Kent Summer 1844, *R. v. Cockering*; ASSI 31/30/58.

88   Chadwick, "Bureaucratic mercy," pp. 456–7.

89   Clark, "Humanity or justice?" p. 201.

90   Thompson, *Customs in Common*, p. 508. On community reactions to excessive violence, see D'Cruze, *Crimes of Outrage*, pp. 60–1.

91   Mayhew, *London Labour*, vol. 1, p. 153.

92   Ibid., vol. 2, p. 504.

93   E.g., see testimony from the case of Sarah and James Bacon, ASSI 36/13 Essex Summer 1867, *R. v. Bacon*, in which several witnesses commented on the awareness they had of their domestic quarrels, e.g., "I heard him and his wife quarreling on Sunday aft[ernoon] after dinner." Hammerton notes the case of a wife being kicked to death by her husband after neighbors had heard him demanding money from her: *Cruelty and Companionship*, p. 28.

94   ASSI 36/1 Herts. Lent 1830, *R. v. Franklin*.

95   ASSI 36/17 Northants. Summer 1871, *R. v. Addington*.

96   ASSI 36/17 Bedford Lent 1871, *R. v. Bull*. The file contains a map of the area, including references to the site of the murder and the location of the witnesses' houses.

97   Foucault, *Discipline and Punish*, p. 286.

98   One writer described the travails of a working-class couple and the reverberations of their domestic strife throughout the local gossip networks: "His friends were loud in their denunciation of the conduct of his wife, and blamed her for every misfortune that overtook them. Her friends were equally energetic in denouncing the husband's conduct.... This quarrelling among the families and constant bickering between themselves, led to the most disastrous results, and set a barrier between the parents and children, which it was difficult to remove, and still more difficult to overcome." H. Shimmin, *Town Life*, London, 1858, p. 17.

99   Simmons, *Working Classes*, pp. 7–8.

100   Davin, *Growing Up Poor*, p. 60.

101   ASSI 36/13 Essex Summer 1867, *R. v. Bacon*.

102   Cf. ASSI 36/10 Bedford Lent 1860, *R. v. Castle*. Joseph Castle killed his wife, Jane. They had a long history of "wrangling," "jangling" and quarreling, mainly as a result of Joseph Castle's jealousy regarding his wife.

103   ASSI 36/17 Bedford Lent 1871, *R. v. Bull*.

104   Mayhew, *London Labour*, vol. 2, p. 504.

105 Ibid., vol. 3, p. 1. Emphasis in original.
106 On the importance of gossip networks and reputation, see Ross, "Survival networks," pp. 10 and 14, and D'Cruze, *Crimes of Outrage*, pp. 50–1, 59–61. See Behlmer, *Child Abuse*, p. 1, and elsewhere for examples of reputations developed in relationship to child abuse.
107 Paget, "Police courts," p. 385.
108 ASSI 36/14 Herts. Lent 1869, *R. v. Leeton*. Leeton killed his mother and his neighbors testified that he had a history as a "violent man." See also, Conley, *Unwritten Law*, pp. 78–9.
109 ASSI 36/13 Essex Summer 1867, *R. v. Bacon*.
110 For example, testimony about prior violent incidents or knowledge about someone's state of mind were important in deciding whether or not a perpetrator was insane. Sarah Grout killed two of her children in 1848. Her neighbors provided testimony about the way she had been acting in recent months. The trial ended in a verdict of acquittal by reason of insanity: ASSI 36/6 Essex Summer 1848, *R v. Grout*; HO 27/87/293. Cf. ASSI 36/5 Norfolk Summer 1844, *R. v. Frost*.
111 Vicinus, *Industrial Muse*, p. 16.
112 Ibid.
113 Hammerton, *Cruelty and Companionship*, p. 19. See also Hunt, "Wife beating," p. 23.
114 "I went out of my back gate and judging there was some quarrel between the prisoner and his wife, I went at once to his house with a view of pacifying him as I had often done before." ASSI 36/1 Herts. Lent 1830, *R. v. Franklin*, Testimony of Thomas Quilter. Emphasis added.
115 On her deathbed, Mary Franklin forgave her husband for inflicting her fatal injuries within hearing of several witnesses. ASSI 36/1 Herts. Lent 1830, *R. v. Franklin*.
116 Charles Dickens, "Wild Court tamed," *Household Words*, 25 August 1855, 85–7.
117 Ibid., p. 87.
118 Hill, *Homes of the London Poor*, p. 90.
119 Roberts, *Physical Condition*, p. 9. Emphasis in original.
120 Rev. Charles Girdlestone, "Rich and poor," in Ingestre, *Meliora*, p. 23; Paine, *Task of the Age*, and Elliott, "Moral agents," p. 300. This topic is also discussed in Hammerton, *Cruelty and Companionship*, p. 38.
121 Jones, *Languages of Class*, p. 191.

6   "Heave half a brick at a stranger"

1 Foucault, *Power/Knowledge*, p. 149. Emphasis in original.
2 "In the Black Country," *Tinsley's Magazine*, June 1869, 426.
3 Foucault, *Discipline and Punish*, p. 27.
4 Michael Ignatieff, *A Just Measure of Pain*, New York: Pantheon, 1978; Gatrell, *Hanging Tree*; Randall McGowen, "The body and punishment in eighteenth-century England," *Journal of Modern History*, 1987, vol. 59, 651–79.
5 Cockburn, "Punishment and brutalization," pp. 156–7.
6 Gatrell, *Hanging Tree*, p. 590.
7 On the pacification of public spaces, see Elias, *Civilizing Process*, pp. 447–54.
8 "The monopoly organization of physical violence does not usually constrain the individual by a direct threat. A strongly predictable compulsion or pressure mediated in a variety of ways is constantly exerted on the individual." Ibid., p. 450.
9 Emsley, "Police violence"; Dunning, Murphy and Waddington, "British civilizing process," pp. 10–11; David Taylor, *New Police*. Police violence was clearly not always accepted, and the imposition of policing was (as it remains) fraught with debates about the limits of legitimate force. However, state policing is predicated upon

investing a particular group with the ability to use physical force: "public opinion" tends to only reject instances of "excessive" force.

10 See Dunning, Murphy and Waddington, "British civilizing process," pp. 9–10, 17, 21–2; Spierenburg, "Long-term trends," pp. 70–1.

11 Psychic property includes all a person possesses mentally or physically that can be violated, such as "honor dignity, space, possessions, and the physical person." Greenshields, *Economy of Violence*, p. 2.

12 Caton, "Anger be now thy song," p. 4.

13 Thompson, *Customs in Common*, pp. 467–533; Ingram, "Reform of popular culture," pp. 79–113.

14 HO 17/15 pt. 2, Bm 20, 1827, James Bevan.

15 *Scenes from My Life, By A Working Man*, London, 1858, p. 47.

16 E.g., ASSI 36/1 Essex Lent 1828, *R.* v. *Blenkins, et al.*; ASSI 36/2 Cambridge Winter 1833, Switon Riot; HO 17/65, Lw 48, 1836, William Mayer and John Rush.

17 The Blatch case is discussed in detail in Chapter 3.

18 A staging area is a public social space within which public personas are developed and displayed and are particularly important in honor-based cultures (or sub-cultures) within which "campaigns" for respect are waged. Anderson, *Code of the Street*, p. 77.

19 See Fox, "Inherent rules of violence," p. 139, for a discussion of the "principle of ritualisation" and violence among men.

20 Hunt, "Wife beating," p. 23; Hammerton, *Cruelty and Companionship*, p. 21; D'Cruze, *Crimes of Outrage*, p. 76.

21 D'Cruze, *Crimes of Outrage*, pp. 20–1.

22 Ibid., p. 77.

23 Ross, "Fierce questions," p. 591.

24 Ibid., p. 592.

25 Crawford, "Maltreatment of wives"; Clark, "Humanity or justice?" p. 191.

26 ASSI 36/10 Bedford Lent 1860, *R.* v. *Castle*.

27 ASSI 36/5 Kent Summer 1844, *R.* v. *Cockering*.

28 Sibley, *Geographies of Exclusion*, p. 76.

29 Caton, "Anger be now thy song," p. 4.

30 Conley, *Unwritten Law*, pp. 53–8.

31 ASSI 36/1 Kent Summer 1828, *R.* v. *Oldfield*.

32 Cockburn, "Patterns of violence," p. 88.

33 Conley, *Unwritten Law*, pp. 156–66; David Taylor, *Policing the Victorian Town*, p. 63.

34 ASSI 36/3 Hunts. Lent 1838, *R.* v. *Ellsom, et al.*

35 Mayhew, *London Labour*, vol. 2, p. 338. Dialect spelling as in original.

36 ASSI 36/6 Kent Summer 1851, *R.* v. *Chapman, et al.*

37 ASSI 36/11 Kent Summer 1864, *R.* v. *Butler, et al.*

38 From Ellen Ronan's testimony, there were a total of eleven lodgers in the house plus her family.

39 Mearns, *Outcast London*, p. 19.

40 Woods, "Community violence," p. 178.

41 During an especially violent strike, one writer claimed that masters had to arm themselves and "by day, he had to use every precaution to avoid falling into the hands of an infuriated mob." Gaskell, *Artisans and Machinery*, pp. 279–80.

42 Walkowitz, "Jack the Ripper," p. 560.

43 Richard Price, "The other face of respectability: violence in the Manchester brickmaking trade, 1859–1870," *Past and Present*, 1975, vol. 66, 110–32.

44 Ure, *Philosophy of Manufactures*, p. 286. Gaskell, *Artisans and Machinery*, p. 335.

45 Mackay, "Work and murder," p. 491.

46 *Scenes From My Life*, p. 44.

47 Ibid., p. 45.

48 Ibid., p. 46.

49 Fuller, *Recollections of a Detective*, London, 1912, p. 210.
50 See, e.g., ASSI 36/2 Suffolk Lent 1836, *R.* v. *Jerry, et al.* and ASSI 36/2 Bedfordshire Summer 1835, *R.* v. *Burgoyne and Letting*; ASSI 36/2 Sussex Summer 1835, *R.* v. *Springett and Goodsell.*
51 ASSI 36/2 Suffolk Winter 1832, depositions regarding Case.
52 HO 17/85, Pw 32, William Collett.
53 ASSI 36/11 Kent Summer 1864, *R.* v. *Cole, et al.*
54 In the latter category, first, one might find the plight of local drunks, "and in that state, spouting his ribaldry in public-house bars and the open street; pitied by women, jeered by men, and pelted by the boys." *Scenes From My Life*, p. 35. Second, there were other, minor trangressors who were subject to sustained, though relatively minor, violence. A parliamentary investigator for Berkshire noted the lack of window glass on a working-class house, and "subsequent inquiries proved that the windows had been repaired over and over again by the parish authorities, and as frequently broken by the boys of the village throwing stones at the old woman for ill-treating her husband, a practice in which she indulged whenever she was intoxicated." Parliament, *Local Reports*, p. 93.
55 Storch, "Domestic missionary," p. 490.
56 Gatrell, *Hanging Tree*, p. 238.
57 Paul Routledge, "A spatiality of resistance: theory and practice in Nepal's revolution of 1990," in Steve Pile and Michael Keith (eds.) *Geographies of Resistance*, London: Routledge, 1997, p. 69.
58 Sibley, *Geographies of Exclusion*, p. 76.
59 Pile and Keith, *Geographies of Resistance*, p. 3.
60 As Pile and Keith have written, "resistance may reterritorialize space in various ways, in order to transform its meaning, undermine territory as a natural source of power...." Ibid., p. 30.
61 De Certeau, *Practice of Everyday Life*, p. 18.
62 Sibley, *Geographies of Exclusion*, p. 76.
63 Foucault, *Discipline and Punish*, p. 27.
64 Storch, "Domestic missionary," pp. 481–2.
65 See Chapter 3 and, e.g., HO 17/55 pt. 1, Iv 1, 1835; HO 17/115, Wt 38, 1834; and Hill, *Homes of the London Poor*, pp. 30–1. Of course, in some cases the intervention of the police was actively sought out by one or both of the participants.
66 Taylor, *Policing the Victorian Town*, p. 5.
67 R. D. Storch, "The plague of the blue locusts: police reform and popular resistance in northern England 1840–57," *International Review of Social History*, 1975, vol. 20, 61–90.
68 HO 17/2 Ah 39, 1821, James Millman.
69 Storch, "Please to remember"; Conley, *Unwritten Law*, pp. 35–7.
70 See two separate files on Fifth of November celebrations in ASSI 36/4 Sussex 1841.
71 ASSI 36/6 Sussex Lent 1848.
72 E.g., ASSI 36/3 Norwich 1837, *R.* v. *Tunmore, Singer, et al.*; Conley, *Unwritten Law*, pp. 38–41.
73 Paget, "London police courts," p. 388.
74 Taylor, *Policing the Victorian Town*, pp. 79–89.
75 Davin, *Growing Up Poor*, p. 37.
76 Ross, "Survival networks," p. 17.
77 See remarks about Spitalfields in the 1820s in *Scenes From My Life*, p. 30.
78 See Taylor, *New Police*, pp. 1–10, for a cogent summary of "Whig" and "Revisionist" views of the period of the introduction of reformed police forces.
79 Timothy Cavanagh, *Scotland Yard Past and Present: Experiences of 37 Years*, London, 1893, p. 27.
80 Conley, *Unwritten Law*, p. 35.

81 For assaults on police committed in the contexts of rescues of people from police custody, see, e.g., HO 17/2 Ah 39, 1821; HO 17/2 Ah 48, 1828; HO 17/55 pt. 2, It 19, 1834; *The Times*, 25 March 1828.
82 E.g., HO 17/55 pt.1, Iv 1, 1835; HO 17/55 pt. 2, It 18, 1833.
83 Taylor, *New Police*, Ch. 4.
84 Paget, "Police courts," p. 388.
85 HO 17/55 pt.1, Iv 1, 1835; HO 17/55 pt. 2, It 19, 1834.
86 *Brutal Assaults Report*, p. 64
87 Miller, "Police authority," pp. 92–3.
88 Simmons, *The Working Classes*, pp. 57–8.
89 Storch, "Plague of the blue locusts," pp. 73–4.
90 ASSI 36/2 Herts. Summer 1832, *R. v. Mullins and Seabrooke*.
91 Noted in Storch, "Domestic missionary," p. 500.
92 See, e.g., ASSI 36/6 Surrey Summer 1850, *R. v. Gill* and ASSI 36/5 Kent, coroner's inquest, 9 December 1843, *R. v. Ball, et al.*

7 Conclusion

1 "Reform for Victorian assault law," *Guardian*, 2 February 1998. The law in question was the 1861 Offences against the Person Act.
2 "Hague backs right to defend homes," The BBC <http://news.bbc.co.uk/hi/english/uk_politics/newsid_726000/726389.stm> 26 April 2000, accessed 18 August 2003. Hague was criticizing the life sentence handed out to Tony Martin, a Norfolk farmer found guilty of murdering a burglar. The sentence was later reduced, on the ground of diminished responsibility, to manslaughter: "Shotgun farmer wins shorter jail term," *Guardian*, 31 October 2001. He was released from prison in 2003: "Jailed farmer Martin goes free," *Guardian*, 28 July 2003.
3 Paine, *Task of the Age*, p. 20.
4 Gatrell, "Policeman-state," p. 244.
5 Wiener, "Victorian criminalization of men," p. 201.
6 Elias, *Civilizing Process*, pp. 447–8.
7 Ibid., pp. 447–52.
8 E.g., Davin, *Growing Up Poor*, p. 37.
9 For a focused treatment of this topic, see J. Carter Wood, "Self-policing and the policing of the self: violence, protection and the civilizing bargain in Britain," *Crime, Histoire & Sociétés/Crime, History & Societies*, 2003, vol. 7, no. 1, 109–28.
10 Dunning, Waddington and Murphy, "British civilizing process," pp. 40–2.
11 Woods, "Community violence," pp. 195–6; Cohen, "Policing the working-class city," p. 118.
12 Weiner, *Reconstructing the Criminal*, pp. 258, 263.
13 Judith Walkowitz, *Prostitution and Victorian Society: Women, Class and the State*, Cambridge: Cambridge University Press, 1980, p. 210.
14 Foucault, *Discipline and Punish*, p. 184.
15 Ibid., p. 278.
16 Will Thorne, *My Life's Battles*, London, 1925, pp. 45–6.
17 D'Cruze, *Crimes of Outrage*, p. 18.
18 Ross, "Fierce questions," p. 577.
19 Roberts, *Physical Condition*, p. 9.
20 J. Hasloch Potter, *Inasmuch: The Story of the Police Court Mission, 1876–1926*, London: Williams & Norgate, Ltd., 1927.
21 Tarn, *Working-Class Housing in Nineteenth-Century Britain*, Architectural Association Papers, no. 7, London: Lund Humphries, 1971, p. 7.
22 Daunton, "Public space and private space," p. 232.

23 On police emphasis on public space, see Gatrell, "Policeman-state," pp. 267–8.

24 Daunton, "Public space and private space," pp. 219, 224; Cohen, "Policing the working-class city," p. 120.

25 Daunton, "Public space and private space," p. 223; Daunton, "Housing," p. 204.

26 Gatrell, "Policeman-state," p. 289.

27 Hammerton, *Cruelty and Companionship*, p. 33. Hunt argues that there were trends toward this tendency in the eighteenth century: "Wife beating," pp. 25–6.

28 Chadwick suggests that wife killing was perhaps viewed as less socially threatening than other violent crimes, since it was "a domestic event which rarely spilled over into the public domain and it was not one that was likely to be repeated." Chadwick, "Bureaucratic mercy," p. 440.

29 Hammerton, *Cruelty and Companionship*, p. 82.

30 Ibid., p. 38. In 1873, Pike noted that "We have amongst us wife-beaters, and other half-savage ruffians, to whom cruelty is a sport. But the very abhorrence with which we regard them is no less real evidence of the character of the age than the acts of which they are guilty." Pike, *History of Crime*, vol. 2, p. 473.

31 Gatrell, *Hanging Tree*, p. 5.

32 Behlmer, *Child Abuse*, p. 15.

33 *Stroud Journal*, 24 November 1893; *Keen's Bath Journal*, 29 February 1890; *National Anti-Compulsory Vaccination Reporter*, vol. 5, 99, p. 102. I thank Nadja Durbach for these references.

34 Bailey, "Working-class respectability," p. 343.

35 Davis, "Police courts," p. 331.

36 Elias, *Civilizing Process*, pp. 492–4.

37 Ibid., p. 452.

38 Thompson, *Customs in Common*, p. 530.

39 E.g., "The suicide warriors who attacked Washington and New York on September 11th, 2001, did more than kill thousands of civilians and demolish the World Trade Center. They destroyed the West's ruling myth." John Gray, *Al Qaeda and What It Means to Be Modern*, London: Faber & Faber, 2003, p. 1.

40 Thompson, *Customs in Common*, p. 530.

41 Pike, *History of Crime*, vol. 2, p. 480.

42 Doggett, *Wife-Beating*, p. 32.

43 For the early twentieth century, see Jerry White, *The Worst Street in North London: Campbell Bunk, Islington, Between the Wars*, London: Routledge & Kegan Paul, 1986.

44 Elias, *Civilizing Process*, p. 496.

45 A few suggestive examples will have to suffice. In October 1997 a man was charged in Devon with assault and causing actual bodily harm after shouting loudly enough in his wife's ear to cause hearing damage. The following month he was convicted, fined £450 plus £750 costs and ordered to carry out 150 hours of community service: *Guardian*, 24 October 1997 and 22 November 1997. In 1998, the government began a reform of the laws on criminal assault, and included the infection of supermarket goods as a form of violence (*Guardian*, 12 February 1998). A widespread debate about the "right to smack" as part of disciplining children erupted in the late 1990s in reference to the incorporation of European human rights laws. The labeling of certain kinds of activities (both in popular discourse as well as in law) as "hate crimes" is also part of the redefinition of violence.

46 Discussed extensively in Pearson, *Hooligan*. For a recent example, see Peter Hitchens, *A Brief History of Crime: The Decline of Order, Justice and Liberty in Britain*, London: Atlantic, 2003.

47 To take only two examples. First, Tony Martin's conviction and life sentence in April 2000 for the murder of a burglar was widely linked to the issue of whether or not there were sufficient policing resources in rural areas: "Tories warn of rural

vigilantes," BBC News, <http://news.bbc.co.uk/2/hi/uk_news/724702.stm> 24 April 2000, accessed 18 August 2003. Second, a storm of vigilante mob assaults followed the publication of the names of convicted pedophiles in a national tabloid newspaper. Participants in the assaults and acts of property damage often stated that they were convinced that the official punishments were insufficient. "Vigilante mob forces family into hiding," *Guardian*, 8 August 2000.

48 See, e.g., Philip Brownrigg, "Britain: alas, a place apart, where hooligans fit right in," *International Herald Tribune*, 21 August 2000.

Bibliography

Manuscript primary sources

Public Record Office
ASSI (Assizes)
31 Crown and gaol books
35 Indictments, Southeastern (Home) Circuit
36 Home, Norfolk and Southeastern Circuit; depositions: Boxes 1–17 (1820–72)

CRIM (Central Criminal Court)
1 Depositions, 1839–: selected cases
10 Minutes of evidence, 1834–1912: selected cases

HO (Home Office Papers)
17 Petitions for mercy, 1819–39: Boxes 2, 5, 15, 25, 35, 45, 55, 65, 75, 85, 95, 115
44 Domestic correspondence, 1773–1861: selected letters

KB (King's Bench)
10 Indictments and informations: selected boxes

Printed primary sources

Note: author and publication information for articles, when otherwise unavailable, has been provided by E. M. Palmegiano (comp.), *Crime in Victorian Britain: An Annotated Bibliography from Nineteenth-Century British Magazines*, London: Greenwood Press, 1993.

Adams, W. E., *Memoirs of A Social Atom*, London, 1903.
Albery, William (ed.), *Reminiscences of Horsham: Being Recollections of Henry Burstow, the Celebrated Bellringer and Songsinger*, 1911, Norwood, PA: Norwood Editions, 1975.
The Art and Practice of English Boxing: or Scientific Modes of Defence, Displayed in an Easy Manner, Whereby Every Person May Comprehend This Most Useful Art Without the Aid of a Master; To Which is Added, Descriptions of Pugilistic Attitudes, the Art of Attack and Self Defence, as Practiced by the Most Celebrated Boxers of the Present Day, London, 1815.
Aytoun, W. E., "Banting on Corpulence," *Blackwood's Edinburgh Magazine*, November 1864, vol. 96: 607–17.
Barry, Edward, MD, *Theological, Philosophical and Moral Essays*, London, 1800.

Beames, Thomas, *The Rookeries of London: Past, Present, and Prospective*, London, 1850.

Blake, Matilda, "Are Women Protected?" *Westminster Review*, January 1892, vol. 137: 42–8.

Booth, Charles (ed.), *Life and Labour of the People of London*, London, 1892–7.

"Brief Observations on the Punishment of the Pillory," *Pamphleteer*, 1814, vol. 4, no. 8: 533–50.

Bulwer, E. L., "On English Notions of Morality," *New Monthly Magazine*, 1832, vol. 34: 22–5.

Cavanagh, Timothy, *Scotland Yard Past and Present: Experiences of 37 Years*, London, 1893.

Clay, John, Rev., "Annual Report of the Rev. John Clay, Chaplain to the Preston House of Correction. Presented to the Visiting Justices at the October Sessions, 1838," *Journal of the Statistical Society of London*, March 1839: 84–113.

Cobbe, F. P., "Wife Torture in England," *Contemporary Review*, 1878, vol. 32: 55–87.

Crawford, M. S., "Maltreatment of Wives," *Westminster Review*, 1893, vol. 39: 292–303.

Davenport-Hill, Rosamond and Florence, *A Memoir of Matthew Davenport-Hill*, London, 1878.

'The Decline of the Ring," *Tinsley's Magazine*, July 1869: 552–8.

DeQuincey, T., "On Murder Considered as One of the Fine Arts," *Blackwood's Edinburgh Magazine*, February 1827: 199–213.

Dickens, Charles, *Sketches By Boz: Illustrative of Every-Day Life and Every-Day People*, 1839, London: Oxford University Press, 1957.

— "Lying Awake," *Household Words*, 1852–3, vol. 6: 145–8.

— "Conversion of a Heathen Court," *Household Words*, 16 December 1854, vol. 10: 409–13.

— "Wild Court Tamed," *Household Words*, 25 August 1855, vol. 12: 85–7.

— "The Murdered Person," *Household Words*, 11 October 1856, vol. 14: 289–91.

— *The Uncommercial Traveler*, London, 1861.

Doyle, Sir Arthur Conan, *The Adventures of Sherlock Holmes*, 1892, London: Penguin Books, 1994.

Eagles, John, "What Caused the Bristol Riots?' *Blackwood's Edinburgh Magazine*, 1831, vol. 31: 467–84.

— "Temperance and Teetotal Societies," *Blackwood's Edinburgh Magazine*, April 1858, vol. 73: 408–10.

Egan, Pierce, *Boxiana; or Sketches of Antient [sic] and Modern Pugilism*, London, 1818.

Elliot, J. H., "The Increase of Material Prosperity and of Moral Agents, Compared With the State of Crime and Pauperism," *Journal of the Statistical Society of London*, 1868, vol. 31: 299–330.

Engels, Friedrich, *The Condition of the Working Class in England, From Personal Observation and Authentic Sources*, 1845, Moscow: Progress Publishers, 1980.

Fletcher, Joseph, "Moral and Educational Statistics of England and Wales," *Journal of the Statistical Society of London*, 1849, vol. 12: 151–336.

Fonblanque, Albany, "Householders in Danger," *Westminster Review*, 1832, vol. 16: 217–25.

Fullarton, John, "Condition of the Labouring Classes," *The Quarterly Review*, 1831–2, vol. 46: 349–89.

Fuller, Robert A., *Recollections of a Detective*, London, 1912.

Gaskell, P., *Artisans and Machinery: The Moral and Physical Condition of the Manufacturing Population Considered with Reference to Mechanical Substitutes for Human Labour*, London, 1836.

Gilbert, William, "The Dreadful Four Minutes," *Good Words*, 1866, vol. 7: 33–8.

Greenwood, James, *Low Life Deeps: An Account of the Strange Fish to be Found There*, London, 1876.

Hall, A. C., *Crime and Its Relations to Social Progress*, New York, 1902.

Hazlitt, William, "The Fight," *New Monthly Magazine and Literary Journal*, 1822: 102–12.

Hill, Arthur Cleveland, *Crime and Its Relation to Social Progress*, New York, 1902.

Hill, Octavia, *Homes of the London Poor: Four Years' Management of a London Court*. London, 1883.

Hole, James, *The Homes of the Working Classes, with Suggestions for Their Improvement*, London, 1866.

Holmes, Thomas, "Obscure Causes of Crime," *Contemporary Review*, October 1899, vol. 76: 577–88.

Horne, Richard H. and Charles Dickens, "Cain in the Fields," *Household Words*, 10 May 1851, vol. 3: 147–51.

Howitt, William, *The Rural Life of England*, London, 1838.

'In the Black Country," *Tinsley's Magazine*, June 1869: 423–30.

Ingestre, Lord Viscount (ed.), *Meliora; or, Better Times to Come*, London, 1852.

— *Social Evils: Their Causes and their Cure. A Lecture Delivered Before the Bilston Institute in Connection with St. Mary's National Schools*, Wolverhampton, 1853.

Jerdan, William, "A British Nuisance," *Household Words*, 1857–8, vol. 17: 131–2.

Jones, Alfred, "The Philosophy of Corporal Punishment: An Investigation into the Policy and Morality of School Coercion. A Lecture Delivered Before the Elementary Teachers' Association, London," London, 1859.

Justice As It Is and Rulers As They Are in Borough Jurisdictions, in the Nineteenth Century!!! Exemplified in a Full Report of the Trial of Benjamin Stocks Dyson for a Riot and Assault at Doncaster Borough Sessions, Monday, January 7th, 1831, Doncaster, 1831.

Kaye, J. W., "Outrages on Women," *North British Review*, May 1856, vol. 25: 233–56.

Labourer's Friend Society, *Useful Hints for Labourers*, London, 1834.

'The Law of Murder," *London Quarterly Review*, 1846, vol. 26: 428–52.

Lilly, W. S., "In Praise of Hanging," *The New Review*, 1894, vol. 11: 190–200.

MacCallum, Hugh, *The Distribution of the Poor in London*, London, 1883.

Mackay, Charles, "Work and Murder," *Blackwood's Edinburgh Magazine*, 1867, vol. 102: 487–507.

Manning, H. and Benjamin Waugh, "The Child of the English Savage," *Contemporary Review*, 1886, vol. 49: 687–700.

Matthews, William, *A Sketch of the Principal Means Which Have Been Employed to Ameliorate the Intellectual and Moral Condition of the Working Classes at Birmingham*, London, 1830.

Mayhew, Henry, *London Labor and the London Poor*, 1861–2, New York: Dover Publications, Inc., 1968.

Mearns, Andrew, *The Bitter Cry of Outcast London: An Inquiry into the Condition of the Abject Poor*, London, 1883.

Mill, John Stuart, "Civilization," in Gertrude Himmelfarb (ed.), *Essays on Politics and Culture: John Stuart Mill*, Garden City, NY: Doubleday & Company, 1962.

Mingaud, Edward, *The Life and Adventures of James Ward, Viewed as "The Champion" and "The Artist,"* London, 1882.

'Miscellaneous," *Journal of the Royal Statistical Society*, April 1840: 188.

Morley, Henry, "Britannia's Figures," *Household Words*, 1858–9, vol. 19: 13–16.

'Murder Mania," *Chambers' Edinburgh Journal*, 6 October 1849, vol. 301, n.s.: 209–11.

Neaves, Charles, "Discontents of the Working Classes," *Blackwood's Edinburgh Magazine*, 1838, vol. 43: 421–36.

Nugent, Lord, "Crime: How Has It Been Treated? How Should It Be Treated? No. 1," *The People's Journal*, 1847, vol. 3: 233–6.

Observations on the Offensive and Injurious Effect of Corporal Punishment; On the Unequal Administration of Penal Justice; and on the Pre-Eminent Advantages of the Mild and Reformatory Over the Vindictive System of Punishment, London, 1827.

Ormsby, John, "A Day's Pleasure With the Criminal Classes," *Cornhill Magazine*, 1864, vol. 9: 627–40.

Paget, John, "The London Police Courts," *Blackwood's Edinburgh Magazine*, 1875, vol. 118: 379–89.

Paine, D. G., *The Task of the Age; An Enquiry Into the Condition of the Working Classes and the Means of their Moral and Social Elevation*, London, 1850.

Parliament, *Local Reports on the Sanitary Condition of the Labouring Population of England, In Consequence of an Inquiry Directed to Be Made by the Poor Law Commisioners*, London, 1842.

— *Reports to the Secretary of State for the Home Department on the State of the Law Relating to Brutal Assaults*, London, 1875.

Pike, L. O., *History of Crime in England*, London, 1876.

Pulling, S., "What Legislation is Necessary for the Repression of Crimes of Violence?' *Transactions, National Association for the Promotion of Social Science*, 1876: 345–61.

The Remarkable Confession and Last Dying Words of Thomas Colley, London, 1751.

Roberts, Henry, *The Physical Condition of the Labouring Classes, Resulting from the State of Their Dwellings, and the Beneficial Effects of Sanitary Improvements Recently Adopted in England*, London, 1866.

Rook, Clarence, *Hooligan Nights: Being the Life and Opinions of a Young and Impenitent Criminal Recounted by Himself and Set Forth by Clarence Rook*, London, 1899.

Sala, George A., "Open Air Entertainments," *Household Words*, 1852, vol. 5: 165–9.

Savage, George H., "Homicidal Mania," *The Fortnightly Review*, 1888, vol. 94, n.s., 448–63

Scenes from My Life, By A Working Man, London, 1858.

Scott, Sir Walter, "The Two Drovers," 1827, in Fred R. Shapiro and Jane Garry (eds.), *Trial and Error: An Oxford Anthology of Legal Stories*, New York: Oxford University Press, 1998.

Shimmin, H., *Liverpool Life: Its Pleasures, Practices and Pastimes*, Liverpool, 1856.

— *Town Life*, London, 1858.

Shuttlesworth, Sir James Phillips Kay, *The Moral and Physical Condition of the Working Classes Employed in the Cotton Manufactures*, London, 1832.

Simmons, G., *The Working Classes; Their Moral Social and Intellectual Condition; with Practical Suggestions for their Improvement*, London, 1849.

'Social Morality," *Chambers' Edinburgh Journal*, 3 February 1849, vol. 266, n.s.: 87–9.

'Some Thoughts on the Connexion of Crime and Punishment," *Fraser's Magazine*, 1839, vol. 20: 689–96.

Stanley, A. P. (ed.), *The Miscellaneous Works of Thomas Arnold*, London, 1845.

Stephen, J. F., *Essays by a Barrister*, London, 1862.

— *Digest of the Criminal Law*, London, 1877.

— "A Sketch of the Criminal Law," *The Nineteenth Century*, 1882, vol. 11: 626–49.

— *History of the Criminal Law of England*, vol. 3, London, 1884.

Stephen, Leslie, "The Decay of Murder," *Cornhill Magazine*, 1869, vol. 20: 722–33.

Strahan, S. A. K., "What to Do With Our Habitual Criminals," *Westminster Review*, 1895, vol. 143: 660–6.

Swift, Owen, *The Handbook of Boxing; Being a Complete Instructor in the Art of Self Defence*, London, 1840.

Tayler, Charles B., *Social Evils, and their Remedy*, London, 1833.

Taylor, W. C., "Moral Economy of Large Towns: Crime and Punishment," *Bentley's Miscellany*, 1839, vol. 6: 476–82.

—— "Moral Economy of Large Towns: Indigence and Benevolence," *Bentley's Miscellany*, 1839, vol. 6: 575–83.

—— "Moral Economy of Large Towns: Juvenile Delinquency," *Bentley's Miscellany*, 1840, vol. 7: 470–8.

—— "Moral Economy of Large Towns: Manchester," *Bentley's Miscellany*, 1840, vol. 7: 596–604.

—— "Moral Economy of Large Towns: Liverpool," *Bentley's Miscellany*, 1840, vol. 8: 129–36.

Thackeray, W. M., "Going to See A Man Hanged," *Fraser's Magazine*, August 1840, vol. 22: 150–8.

Thorne, Will, *My Life's Battles*, London, 1925.

The Tryal of Thomas Colley, at the Assizes at Hertford, on Tuesday the 30th of July, 1751, London, 1751.

Ure, Andrew, MD, *The Philosophy of Manufactures: or, An Exposition of the Scientific, Moral, and Commercial Economy of the Factory System of Great Britain*, London, 1835.

Wakefield, Edward Gibbon, *Householders in Danger From the Populace*, London, 1832.

—— *The Hangman and the Judge*, London, 1833.

Walker, Donald, *Defensive Exercises; Comprising Wrestling, as in Cumberland, Westmoreland, Cornwall and Devonshire; Boxing, Both in the Usual Mode and in a Simpler One; Defence against Brute Force, By Various Means; Fencing and Broadsword, with Simpler Methods; the Gun and its Exercise; The Rifle and its Exercise, &c.*, London, 1840.

Waugh, Benjamin, "Cruelty to Children," *Good Words*, 1888, vol. 29: 818–22.

Williams, D. E., "The Machinery of Crime in England," *New Monthly Magazine*, 1834, vol. 40: 487–96 and 1834, vol. 41: 77–83.

—— "The Crimes of Prize-Fighters," *New Monthly Magazine*, 1834, vol. 42: 326–36.

Yeoman, T. H., MD, "On the Healthy Discipline of the Home, No. 2 – The Passions," *The People's Journal*, 1849.

Secondary sources

Altick, Richard D., *Victorian Studies in Scarlet*, New York: W. W. Norton & Co., 1970.

Amussen, Susan Dwyer, " 'Being Stirred To Much Unquietness': Violence and Domestic Violence in Early Modern England," *Journal of Women's History*, 1994, vol. 6: 70–89.

—— "Punishment, Discipline and Power: The Social Meanings of Violence in Early Modern England," *Journal of British Studies*, 1995, vol. 34: 1–34.

Anderson, Elijah, *The Code of the Street: Violence, Decency and the Moral Life of the Inner City*, New York: W. W. Norton & Co., 1999.

Archer, John, *Male Violence*, London: Routledge, 1994.

Archer, John E., " 'The Violence We Have Lost'? Body Counts, Historians and Interpersonal Violence in England," *Memoria y Civilización*, 1999, vol. 2: 171–90.

— "Poaching Gangs and Violence: The Urban–Rural Divide in Nineteenth-Century Lancashire," *British Journal of Criminology*, 1999, vol. 39: 25–38.

— "'Men Behaving Badly'?: Masculinity and the Uses of Violence in the Nineteenth Century," in Shani D'Cruze (ed.), *Everyday Violence in Britain, 1850–1950: Gender and Class*, Harlow: Longman-Pearson Education, 2000.

Bailey, Peter, "Will the Real Bill Banks Please Stand Up?' Towards a Role Analysis of Mid-Victorian Working-Class Respectability," *Journal of Social History*, 1979, vol. 12: 336–53.

Bailey, Victor, *Policing and Punishment in Nineteenth-Century Britain*, New Brunswick, NJ: Rutgers University Press, 1981.

Barker-Benfield, G. J., *The Culture of Sensibility: Sex and Society in Eighteenth-Century Britain*, Chicago: Chicago University Press, 1992.

Beattie, J. M., "The Criminality of Women in Eighteenth-Century England," *Journal of Social History*, 1975, vol. 8: 80–116.

— *Crime and the Courts in England, 1660–1800*, Princeton: Princeton University Press, 1986.

Behagg, Clive, "Secrecy, Ritual and Folk Violence: The Opacity of the Workplace in the First Half of the Nineteenth Century," in Robert Storch (ed.), *Popular Culture and Custom in Nineteenth-Century England*, New York: St. Martin's Press, 1982.

Behlmer, G. K., *Child Abuse and Moral Reform in England, 1870–1908*, Stanford: Stanford University Press, 1982.

Beik, William, *Urban Protest in Seventeenth-Century France: The Culture of Retribution*, Cambridge: Cambridge University Press, 1997.

Beresford, M. W., "The Back-to-Back House in Leeds, 1787–1937," in Stanley D. Chapman (ed.), *The History of Working-Class Housing. A Symposium*, Totowa, NJ: Rowan & Littlefield,1971.

Bossy, John (ed.), *Disputes and Settlements: Law and Human Relations in the West*, Cambridge: Cambridge University Press, 1983.

Bourke, Joanna, *An Intimate History of Killing: Face-to-Face Killing in Twentieth-Century Warfare*, New York: Basic Books, 1999.

Brailsford, Dennis, *British Sport: A Social History*, Cambridge: The Lutterworth Press, 1992.

Brewer, John and John Styles (eds.), *An Ungovernable People: The English and Their Law in the Seventeenth and Eighteenth Centuries*, New Brunswick, NJ: Rutgers University Press, 1980.

Briggs, Asa, *The Age of Improvement, 1783–1867*, London: Longman, 1959.

Brownrigg, Philip, "Britain: Alas, A Place Apart, Where Hooligans Fit Right In," *International Herald Tribune*, 21 August 2000.

Burnett, Jacky, "Exposing 'the Inner Life': The Women's Co-operative Guild's Attitude to Cruelty," in Shani D'Cruze (ed.), *Everyday Violence in Britain, 1850–1950: Gender and Class*, Harlow: Longman-Pearson Education, 2000.

Burnett, John (ed.), *Useful Toil: Autobiographies of Working People from the 1820s to the 1920s*, London: Routledge, 1994.

Burnett, John, David Vincent and David Mayall (eds.), *The Autobiography of the Working Class: An Annotated Critical Bibliography*, 3 vols, New York: New York University Press, 1984–9.

Buruma, Ian, *The Wages of Guilt: Memories of War in Germany and Japan*, New York: Farrar Strauss Giroux, 1994.

Caton, Steven C., "'Anger Be Now Thy Song': The Anthropology of an Event," The Occasional Papers of the School of Social Science, Harvard University, Paper No. 5, November 1999.

Chadwick, G. R., "Bureaucratic Mercy: The Home Office and the Treatment of Capital Cases in Victorian England," Ph.D. Dissertation, Rice University, 1989.

Chesney, Kellow, *The Anti-Society: An Account of the Victorian Underworld*, Boston: Gambit, Inc., 1970.

Chevalier, Louis, *Labouring Classes and Dangerous Classes in Paris During the First Half of the Nineteenth Century*, Frank Jellinek (trans.), New York: Howard Fertig, 1973.

Clark, Anna, *Women's Silence, Men's Violence: Sexual Assault in England, 1770–1845*, London: Pandora, 1987.

— "Humanity or Justice? Wifebeating and the Law in the Eighteenth and Nineteenth Centuries," in Carol Smart (ed.), *Regulating Womanhood: Historical Essays on Marriage, Motherhood and Sexuality*, London: Routledge, 1992.

— "Domesticity and the Problem of Wifebeating in Nineteenth-Century Britain: Working-Class Culture, Law and Politics," in Shani D'Cruze (ed.), *Everyday Violence in Britain, 1850–1950: Gender and Class*, Harlow: Longman-Pearson Education, 2000.

Cockburn, J. S., "Patterns of Violence in English Society: Homicide in Kent, 1560–1985," *Past and Present*, 1991, vol. 130: 70–106.

— "Punishment and Brutalization in the English Enlightenment," *Law and History Review*, 1994, vol. 12: 155–79.

Cohen, Daniel A., "The Beautiful Female Murder Victim: Literary Genres and Courtship Practices in the Origins of a Cultural Motif, 1590–1850," *Journal of Social History*, 1997, vol. 31: 277–306.

Cohen, Phil, "Policing the Working-Class City," in Mike Fitzgerald, Gregor McLennan and Jennie Pawson (eds.), *Crime and Society: Readings in History and Theory*, London: Routledge, 1981.

Collett, Peter, "The Rules of Conduct," in Peter Collett (ed.), *Social Rules and Social Behavior*, Oxford: Basil Blackwell, 1977.

Conley, Carolyn A., *The Unwritten Law: Criminal Justice in Victorian Kent*, New York: Oxford University Press, 1991.

— *Melancholy Accidents: The Meaning of Violence in Post-Famine Ireland*, Lanham, MD: Lexington Books, 1999.

Corbin, Alain, *The Village of Cannibals: Rage and Murder in France, 1870*, Arthur Goldhammer (trans.), Cambridge, MA: Harvard University Press, 1992.

Corbin, John, "Insurrections in Spain: Casas Viejas 1933 and Madrid 1981," in David Riches (ed.), *The Anthropology of Violence*, Oxford: Basil Blackwell, 1986

Critchley, T. A., *The Conquest of Violence: Order and Liberty in Britain*, New York: Schocken Books, 1970.

Daly, Martin and Margot Wilson, *Homicide*, New York: Aldine De Gruyter, 1988.

Daunton, M. J., *House and Home in the Victorian City: Working-Class Housing 1850–1914*, London: Edward Arnold, 1983.

— "Public Space and Private Space: The Victorian City and the Working-Class Household," in Derek Fraser and Anthony Sutcliffe (eds.), *The Pursuit of Urban History*, London: Edward Arnold, 1983.

— "Housing," in F. M. L. Thompson (ed.), *The Cambridge Social History of Britain, 1750–1950*, vol. 2, Cambridge: Cambridge University Press, 1990.

Davey, B. J., *Lawless and Immoral: Policing a Country Town, 1838–1857*, Leicester: Leicester University Press, 1983.

Davidoff, Leonore and Catherine Hall, *Family Fortunes: Men and Women of the English Middle Class, 1780–1850*, Chicago: Chicago University Press, 1987.

Davies, Andrew, "Youth Gangs, Masculinity and Violence in Late Victorian Manchester and Salford," *Journal of Social History*, 1998, vol. 32: 349–69.

—— "Youth Gangs, Gender and Violence, 1870–1900," in Shani D'Cruze (ed.), *Everyday Violence in Britain, 1850–1950: Gender and Class*, Harlow: Longman-Pearson Education, 2000, pp. 70–1

Davin, Anna, *Growing Up Poor: Home, School and Street in London, 1870–1914*, London: Rivers Oram Press, 1996.

Davis, Jennifer, "The London Garotting Panic of 1862: A Moral Panic and the Creation of a Criminal Class in Mid-Victorian England," in V. A. C. Gatrell, B. Lenman and G. Parker (eds.), *Crime and the Law: A Social History of Crime in Western Europe Since 1500*, London: Europa Publications, 1980.

— "A Poor Man's System of Justice: The London Police Courts in the Second Half of the Nineteenth Century," *The Historical Journal*, 1984, vol. 27: 309–35.

— "Prosecutions and Their Context: The Use of the Criminal Law in Later Nineteenth-Century London," in Douglas Hay and Francis Snyder (eds.), *Policing and Prosecution in Britain, 1750–1850*, Oxford: Clarendon Press, 1989.

Davison, Lee (ed.), *Stilling the Grumbling Hive: The Response to Social and Economic Problems in England, 1689–1750*, New York: St. Martin's Press, 1992.

D'Cruze, Shani, *Crimes of Outrage: Sex, Violence and Victorian Working Women*, London: UCL Press, 1998.

— (ed.), *Everyday Violence in Britain, 1850–1950: Gender and Class*, Harlow: Longman-Pearson Education, 2000.

— "Unguarded Passions: Violence, History and the Everyday," in Shani D'Cruze (ed.), *Everyday Violence in Britain, 1850–1950: Gender and Class*, Harlow: Longman-Pearson Education, 2000.

de Certeau, Michel, *The Practice of Everyday Life*, Steven Rendall (trans.), Berkeley: University of California Press, 1984.

de Motte, C., "The Dark Side of Town: Crime in Manchester and Salford, 1815–1875," Ph.D. Dissertation, University of Kansas, 1976.

DeLacy, Margaret, *Prison Reform in Lancashire, 1700–1850*, Stanford: Stanford University Press, 1986.

Devine, T. M., "Conflict and Stability in Scottish Society, 1700–1850," *Proceedings of the Scottish Historical Studies Seminar, University of Strathclyde, 1988–89*, Edinburgh: John Donald Publishers Ltd., 1990.

Doggett, Maeve, *Marriage, Wife Beating and the Law in Victorian England*, London: Weidenfeld & Nicholson, 1992.

Dunning, Eric and C. Rojek (eds.), *Sport and Leisure in the Civilizing Process: Critique and Counter-Critique*, London: Macmillan, 1992.

Dunning, Eric, Patrick Murphy and Ivan Waddington, "Violence in the British Civilizing Process," Leicester University Discussion Papers in Sociology, 1992, no. S92/2.

Dunning, Eric, Patrick Murphy and John Williams, "'Casuals,' 'Terrace Crews' and 'Fighting Firms': Towards a Sociological Explanation of Football Hooliganism," in David Riches (ed.), *The Anthropology of Violence*, Oxford: Basil Blackwell, 1986.

Elias, Norbert, *The Civilizing Process: The History of Manners and State Formation and Civilization*. Edmund Jephcott, (trans.), 1939, Oxford: Blackwell, 1994.

— "Violence and Civilization: On the State Monopoly of Physical Violence and Its Infringements," in J. Keane (ed.), *Civil Society and the State: New European Perspectives*, London: Verso, 1988.

Elias, Norbert and Eric Dunning, *Quest for Excitement: Sport and Leisure in the Civilizing Process*, Oxford: Basil Blackwell, 1986.

Emsley, Clive, *Policing and Its Context, 1750–1870*, New York: Schocken Books, 1984.

— "'The Thump of Wood on a Swede Turnip': Police Violence in Nineteenth-Century England," *Criminal Justice History*, 1985, vol. 6: 125–49.

— *Crime and Society in England, 1750–1900*, London: Longman, 1987.

— *The English Police: A Political and Social History*, Hemel Hempstead: Harvester Wheatsheaf, 1991.

Fletcher, Jonathan, *Violence and Civilization: An Introduction to the Work of Norbert Elias*, Cambridge: Polity Press, 1997.

Forbes, Thomas R., "Deadly Parents: Child Homicide in Eighteenth- and Nineteenth-Century England," *Journal of the History of Medicine and Allied Sciences*, 1986, vol. 41: 175–99.

Foucault, Michel, *The History of Sexuality, Volume I: An Introduction*, Robert Hurley (trans.), 1978, New York: Vintage Books, 1990.

— *Discipline and Punish: The Birth of the Prison*, Alan Sheridan (trans.), New York: Vintage Books, 1979.

— *Power/Knowledge: Selected Interviews and Other Writings, 1972–1977*, Colin Gordon (ed.), Colin Gordon, Leo Marshall, John Mepham and Kate Soper (trans.), New York: Pantheon, 1980.

Fox, Robin, "The Inherent Rules of Violence." in Peter Collett (ed.), *Social Rules and Social Behavior*, Oxford: Basil Blackwell, 1977.

Gallant, Thomas W., *Experiencing Dominion: Culture, Identity and Power in the British Mediterranean*, Notre Dame, IN: University of Notre Dame Press, 2002.

Gaskill, Malcolm, "Reporting Murder: Fiction in the Archives in Early-Modern England," *Social History*, 1998, vol. 23: 1–30.

Gatrell, V. A. C., "The Decline of Theft and Violence in Victorian and Edwardian England," in V. A. C. Gatrell, Bruce Lenman and Geoffrey Parker (eds.), *Crime and the Law: The Social History of Crime in Western Europe Since 1500*, London: Europa Publications, 1980.

— "Crime, Authority and the Policeman-State," in F. M. L. Thompson (ed.), *The Cambridge Social History of Britain, 1750–1950*, vol. 3, Cambridge: Cambridge University Press, 1990.

— *The Hanging Tree: Execution and the English People, 1770–1868*, Oxford: Oxford University Press, 1994.

Gatrell, V. A. C. and T. B. Hadden, "Nineteenth-Century Criminal Statistics and Their Interpretation," in E. A. Wrigley (ed.), *Nineteenth Century Society: Essays in the Use of Quantitative Methods for the Study of Social Data*, London: Cambridge University Press, 1972.

Giddens, Anthony, *Capitalism and Modern Social Theory*, Cambridge: Cambridge University Press, 1971.

Golby, John M. and A. W. Purdue, *The Civilization of the Crowd: Popular Culture in England, 1750–1900*, New York: Schocken Books, 1985.

Gorn, Elliott J., "'Gouge and Bite, Pull Hair and Scratch': The Social Significance of Fighting in the Southern Backcountry," *American Historical Review*, 1985, vol. 90: 18–43.

— *The Manly Art: Bare-Knuckle Prizefighting in America*, Ithaca: Cornell University Press, 1986.

Gray, John, *Al Qaeda and What it Means to be Modern*, London: Faber & Faber, 2003.

Greenberg, Kenneth S., "The Nose, the Lie and the Duel in the Antebellum South," *American Historical Review*, 1990, vol. 95: 57–74.

Greenshields, Malcolm, *An Economy of Violence in Early Modern France: Crime and Justice in the Haute Auvergne, 1587–1664*, University Park: Pennsylvania State University Press, 1994.

Gurr, Ted Robert, *Rogues, Rebels and Reformers: A Political History of Urban Crime and Conflict*, Beverly Hills, CA: Sage Publications, 1976.

— "Historical Trends in Violent Crime: A Critical Review of the Evidence," *Crime and Justice: An Annual Review of Research*, 1981, vol. 3: 295–353.

Hackwood, Frederick, *Old English Sports*, London: T. Fisher Unwin, 1907.

Halttunen, Karen. "Humanitarianism and the Pornography of Pain in Anglo-American Culture," *American Historical Review*, 1995, vol. 100: 303–34.

Hammerton, A. James, *Cruelty and Companionship: Conflict in Nineteenth-Century Married Life*, London: Routledge, 1992.

Harris, Tim, *Popular Culture in England, c.1500–1850*, New York: St. Martin's Press, 1995.

Harrison, Brian, *Drink and the Victorians*, London: Faber & Faber, 1971.

Hay, Douglas, "War, Dearth and Theft in the Eighteenth Century: The Record of the English Courts," *Past and Present*, 1982, vol. 95: 117–60.

Hay, Douglas and Francis Snyder, "Using the Criminal Law, 1750–1850: Policing, Private Prosecution, and the State," in Douglas Hay and Francis Snyder (eds.), *Policing and Prosecution in Britain, 1750–1850*, Oxford: Oxford University Press, 1989.

Hay, Douglas, et al. (eds.), *Albion's Fatal Tree: Crime and Society in Eighteenth-Century England*, New York: Pantheon, 1975.

Heiny, Henriette A. Gram, "Boxing in British Sporting Art, 1730–1824," Ph.D. Dissertation, University of Oregon, 1987.

Hitchens, Peter, *A Brief History of Crime: The Decline of Order, Justice and Liberty in Britain*, London: Atlantic, 2003.

Hostettler, John, *The Politics of Criminal Law Reform in the Nineteenth Century*, Chichester: Barry Rose, 1992.

Hunt, Margaret, "Wife Beating, Domesticity and Women's Independence in Eighteenth-Century London," *Gender and History*, 1992, vol. 4: 10–33.

Ignatieff, Michael, *A Just Measure of Pain*, New York: Pantheon, 1978.

Ingram, Martin, "Ridings, Rough Music and the 'Reform of Popular Culture' in Early Modern England," *Past and Present*, 1984, vol. 105: 79–113.

Innes, Joanna and John Styles, "The Crime Wave': Recent Writings on Crime and Criminal Justice in Eighteenth-Century England," *Journal of British Studies*, 1986, vol. 25: 380–435.

Johnson, E. A. and Eric H. Monkkonen (eds.), *The Civilization of Crime: Violence in Town and Country since the Middle Ages*, Urbana: University of Illinois Press, 1996.

Jones, D. J. V., "Crime in London: The Evidence of the Metropolitan Police, 1831–1892," in D. J. V. Jones (ed.), *Crime, Protest, Community and Police in Nineteenth-Century Britain*, London: Routledge, 1982.

— *Crime in Nineteenth-Century Wales*, Cardiff: University of Wales Press, 1992.

Jones, Gareth Stedman, *Languages of Class: Studies in English Working-Class History, 1832–1982*, Cambridge: Cambridge University Press, 1983.

Joyce, Patrick, *Visions of the People: Industrial England and the Question of Class, 1848–1914*, Cambridge: Cambridge University Press, 1991.

— *Democratic Subjects: The Self and the Social in Nineteenth-Century England*, Cambridge: Cambridge University Press, 1994.

Kalikoff, Rita Beth, "Murder and the Erosion of Authority in Victorian Popular Literature," Ph.D. Dissertation, Indiana University, 1983.

Kelker, Signe Jeanette, "Riotous and Disorderly: Policing Shrewsbury, 1820–1860," Ph.D. Dissertation, University of Maryland, College Park, 1993.

Kelly, James, *That Damn'd Thing Called Honour: Dueling in Ireland, 1570–1860*, Cork: Cork University Press, 1995.

King, John E., "We Could Eat the Police': Popular Violence in the North Lancashire Cotton Strike of 1878," *Victorian Studies*, 1985, vol. 28: 439–71.

King, Peter, "Gleaners, Farmers and the Failure of Legal Sanctions in England, 1750–1850," *Past and Present*, 1989, vol. 125: 116–50.

— "Punishing Assault: The Transformation of Attitudes in the English Courts," *Journal of Interdisciplinary History*, 1996, vol. 27: 43–74.

Kitson-Clark, G. S. R., *The Making of Victorian England*, New York: Atheneum, 1967.

Knafla, Louis A. (ed.), *Policing and War in Europe, Criminal Justice History, vol. 16*, London: Greenwood Press, 2002.

Lane, Roger, *Violent Death in the City: Accident and Murder in Nineteenth-Century Philadelphia*, Cambridge, MA: Harvard University Press, 1979.

Langford, Paul, *A Polite and Commercial People: England 1727–1783*, Oxford: Oxford University Press, 1989.

Lecercle, Jean-Jacques, *The Violence of Language*, London: Routledge, 1990.

Linebaugh, Peter, "The Tyburn Riot Against the Surgeons," in Douglas Hay, *et al.* (eds.), *Albion's Fatal Tree: Crime and Society in Eighteenth-Century England*, New York: Pantheon, 1975.

— *The London Hanged: Crime and Civil Society in the Eighteenth Century*, Cambridge: Cambridge University Press, 1992.

Lodhi, A. Q. and C. Tilly, "Urbanization, Crime and Collective Violence in Nineteenth-Century France," *American Journal of Sociology*, 1973, vol. 79: 196–218.

Macfarlane, Alan, *The Justice and the Mare's Ale: Law and Disorder in Seventeenth-Century England*, New York: Cambridge University Press, 1981.

McGowen, Randall, "Rethinking Crime: Changing Attitudes Towards Law-Breakers in Eighteenth- and Nineteenth-Century England," Ph.D. Dissertation, University of Illinois at Urbana-Champaign, 1979.

— "The Body and Punishment in Eighteenth-Century England," *Journal of Modern History*, 1987, vol. 59: 651–79.

Malcomson, Robert W., *Popular Recreations in English Society, 1700–1850*, Cambridge: Cambridge University Press, 1973.

Marx, E., *The Social Context of Violent Behaviour*, London: Routledge & Kegan Paul, 1976.

Mason, Tony (ed.), *Sport in Britain: A Social History*, Cambridge: Cambridge University Press, 1989.

Miller, Wilbur R., "Police Authority in London and New York City, 1830–1870," *Journal of Social History*, 1975, vol. 8: 81–101.

Mitzman, Arthur, "The Civilizing Offensive: Mentalities, High Culture and Individual Psyches," *Journal of Social History*, 1987, vol. 20: 663–87.

Monkonnen, E. H., *The Dangerous Class: Crime and Poverty in Columbus, OH, 1860–1885*, Cambridge, MA: Harvard University Press, 1975.

Morgan, Marjorie, *Manners, Morals and Class in England, 1774–1858*, New York: St. Martin's Press, 1994.

Neal, Frank, *Sectarian Violence: The Liverpool Experience, 1819–1914*, Manchester: Manchester University Press, 1988.

Newburn, Tim and Elizabeth A. Stanko, "Men, Masculinity and Crime," in Tim Newburn and Elizabeth A. Stanko (eds.), *Just Boys Doing Business? Men, Masculinities and Crime*, London: Routledge, 1994.

Nordstrom, Carolyn, *A Different Kind of War Story*, Philadelphia: University of Pennsylvania Press, 1997.

Novick, Peter, *The Holocaust in American Life*, New York: Mariner Books, 1999.

Palmegiano, E. M. (comp.) *Crime in Victorian Britain: An Annotated Bibliography from Nineteenth-Century British Magazines*, London: Greenwood Press, 1993.

Pearson, Geoffrey, *Hooligan: A History of Respectable Fears*, London: Macmillan Education, 1983.

Philips, David, *Crime and Authority in Victorian England: The Black Country, 1835–1860*, London: Croom Helm, 1977.

Pile, Steve and Michael Keith (eds.), *Geographies of Resistance*, London: Routledge, 1997.

Potter, J. Hasloch, *Inasmuch: The Story of the Police Court Mission, 1876–1926*, London: Williams & Norgate, Ltd., 1927.

Price, Richard, "The Other Face of Respectability: Violence in the Manchester Brickmaking Trade, 1859–1870," *Past and Present*, 1975, vol. 66: 110–32.

— *British Society, 1680–1800: Dynamism, Containment and Change*, Cambridge: Cambridge University Press, 1999.

Radzinowicz, Leon, *Ideology and Crime: A Study of Crime in Its Social and Historical Context*, London: Heinemann Educational Books, 1966.

— *The History of the English Criminal Law and Its Administration*, 5 vols, vol. 5 with R. Hood, London: Stevens, 1985.

Reid, J. C., *Bucks and Bruisers: Pierce Egan and Regency England*, London: Routledge, 1971.

Riches, David, "The Phenomenon of Violence," in David Riches (ed.), *The Anthropology of Violence*, Oxford: Basil Blackwell, 1986.

Roberts, Simon, *Order and Dispute: An Introduction to Legal Anthropology*, New York, St. Martin's Press, 1979.

Ross, Ellen, " 'Fierce Questions and Taunts': Married Life in Working-Class London, 1870–1914," *Feminist Studies*, 1982, vol. 8: 575–602.

— "Survival Networks: Women's Neighbourhood Sharing in London before World War One," *History Workshop*, 1983, vol. 15: 4–27.

Routledge, Paul, "A Spatiality of Resistance: Theory and Practice in Nepal's Revolution of 1990," in Steve Pile and Michael Keith, *Geographies of Resistance*, London: Routledge, 1997.

Ruff, Julius R., *Violence in Early Modern Europe, 1500–1800*, Cambridge: Cambridge University Press, 2001.

Sharpe, J. A., "The History of Violence in England: Some Observations," *Past and Present*, 1985, vol. 108: 206–15.

— "Human Relations and the History of Crime," *IAHCCJ Bulletin*, 1991, vol. 14: 10–32.

— "Crime in England: Long-Term Trends and the Problem of Modernization," in E.A. Johnson and Eric H. Monkkonen (eds.), *The Civilization of Crime: Violent Crime in Town and Country since the Middle Ages*, Chicago: University of Illinois Press, 1996.

Shelley, Louise I., *Crime and Modernization: The Impact of Urbanization and Industrialization on Crime*, Carbondale: Southern Illinois University Press, 1981.

Shipley, Stan, "Tom Causer of Bermondsey: A Boxer Hero of the 1890s," *History Workshop*, 1983, vol. 15: 28–59.

Shpayer-Makov, Haia, *The Making of a Policeman: A Social History of a Labour Force in Metropolitan London, 1829–1914*, Aldershot: Ashgate Publishing Ltd., 2002.

Sibley, David, *Geographies of Exclusion: Society and Difference in the West*, London: Routledge, 1984.

Simpson, A. W. B., *Cannibalism and the Common Law: The Story of the Tragic Last Voyage of the Mignonette and the Strange Legal Proceedings to Which It Gave Rise*, Chicago: Chicago University Press, 1984.

Sindall, Rob, *Street Violence in the Nineteenth Century: Media Panic or Real Danger?* Leicester: Leicester University Press, 1990.

Spierenburg, Pieter, *The Broken Spell: A Cultural and Anthropological History of Preindustrial Europe*, New Brunswick, NJ: Rutgers University Press, 1991.

— "Justice and the Mental World: Twelve Years of Research and Interpretation of Criminal Justice Data from the Perspective of Mentalities," *IAHCCJ Newsletter*, 1991, vol. 14: 38–79.

— "Elias and the History of Crime and Criminal Justice: A Brief Evaluation," *IAHCCJ Bulletin*, 1995, vol. 20: 17–30.

— "Long-Term Trends in Homicide: Theoretical Reflections and Dutch Evidence, Fifteenth to Twentieth Centuries," in E. A. Johnson and Eric H. Monkkonen (eds.), *The Civilization of Crime: Violent Crime in Town and Country since the Middle Ages*, Chicago: University of Illinois Press, 1996.

— (ed.), *Men and Violence: Gender, Honor and Rituals in Modern Europe and America*, Columbus: Ohio State University Press, 1998.

Stanko, Elizabeth, "Challenging the Problem of Men's Individual Violence," in Tim Newburn and Elizabeth A. Stanko (eds.), *Just Boys Doing Business? Men, Masculinities and Crime*, New York: Routledge, 1994.

Stone, Lawrence, "Interpersonal Violence in English Society, 1300–1980," *Past and Present*, 1983, vol. 101: 22–33.

— "A Rejoinder," *Past and Present*, 1985, vol. 108: 216–24.

Storch, Robert, "The Plague of the Blue Locusts: Police Reform and Popular Resistance in Northern England, 1840–57," *International Review of Social History*, 1975, vol. 20: 61–90.

— "The Policeman as Domestic Missionary: Urban Discipline and Popular Culture in Northern England, 1850–1880," *Journal of Social History*, 1976, vol. 9: 481–509.

— *Popular Culture and Custom in Nineteenth-Century England*, New York: St. Martin's Press, 1982.

— " 'Please to Remember the Fifth of November': Conflict, Solidarity and Public Order in Southern England, 1815–1900," in Robert Storch (ed.), *Popular Culture and Custom in Nineteenth-Century England*, New York: St. Martin's Press, 1982.

Swift, Roger, "Heroes or Villains? The Irish, Crime and Disorder in Victorian England," *Albion*, 1997, vol. 29: 399–421.

Tambling, Jeremy, *Dickens, Violence and the Modern State: Dreams of the Scaffold*, New York: St. Martin's Press, 1995.

Tarn, John Nelson, *Working-Class Housing in Nineteenth-Century Britain*, Architectural Association Papers, no. 7, London: Lund Humphries, 1971.

— *Five Per Cent Philanthropy: An Account of Housing in Urban Areas Between 1840 and 1914*, Cambridge: Cambridge University Press, 1973.

Taylor, David, *The New Police in Nineteenth-Century England: Crime, Conflict and Control*, Manchester: Manchester University Press, 1997.
— *Policing the Victorian Town: The Development of the Police in Middlesbrough, c. 1840–1914*, Basingstoke: Palgrave Macmillan, 2002.
Taylor, Howard, "Rationing Crime: The Political Economy of Criminal Statistics Since the 1850s," *Economic History Review*, 1998, vol. 51: 569–90.
Thomas, Keith, *Man and the Natural World: A History of the Modern Sensibility*, New York: Pantheon, 1983.
Thome, Helmut, "Modernization and Crime: What is the Explanation?" *IAHCCJ Bulletin*, 1995, vol. 20: 31–48.
Thompson, E. P., *The Making of the English Working Class*, New York: Vintage Books, 1963.
— *Customs in Common*, New York: The New Press, 1991.
Thompson, F. M. L., *The Rise of Respectable Society: A Social History of Victorian Britain, 1830–1900*, Cambridge, MA: Harvard University Press, 1988.
Thorne, Susan, *Congregational Missions and the Making of an Imperial Culture in Nineteenth-Century England*, Stanford: Stanford University Press, 1999.
Thrift, Nigel and Peter Williams (eds.), *Class and Space: The Making of Urban Society*. London: Routledge & Kegan Paul, 1987.
Tobias, J. J., *Crime and Industrial Society in the Nineteenth Century*, New York: Schocken Books, 1967.
— *Urban Crime in Victorian England*, New York: Schocken Books, 1972.
Tomes, Nancy, "A Torrent of Abuse: Crimes of Violence Between Working-Class Men and Women in London, 1840–1875," *Journal of Social History*, 1978, vol. 11: 328–45.
Tranter, Neil, *Sport, Economy and Society in Britain, 1750–1914*, New Studies in Economic and Social History, Cambridge: Cambridge University Press, 1998.
van Krieken, R., "Violence, Self-Discipline and Modernity: Beyond 'The Civilizing Process,'" *The Sociological Review*, 1989, vol. 37: 193–218.
— "The Organization of the Soul: Elias and Foucault on Discipline and the Self," *Archives for European Sociology*, 1990, vol. 31: 353–71.
Vicinus, Martha, *The Industrial Muse: A Study of Nineteenth-Century British Working-Class Literature*, London: Croom Helm, 1974.
Vickery, Amanda, "Golden Age to Separate Spheres? A Review of the Categories and Chronology of English Women's History," *The Historical Journal*, 1993, vol. 36: 383–414.
Walker, Peter N., *Punishment: An Illustrated History*, Newton Abbot: David & Charles, 1972.
Walkowitz, Judith R., *Prostitution and Victorian Society: Women, Class and the State*, Cambridge: Cambridge University Press, 1980.
— "Jack the Ripper and the Myth of Male Violence," *Feminist Studies*, 1982, vol. 8: 542–74.
Weber, Max, *Economy and Society: An Outline of Interpretive Sociology*, Berkeley: University of California Press, 1978.
Weinberger, Barbara, "Urban and Rural Crime Rates and Their Genesis in Late Nineteenth- and Early Twentieth-Century Britain," in E. A. Johnson and Eric H. Monkkonen (eds.), *The Civilization of Crime: Violent Crime in Town and Country since the Middle Ages*, Chicago: University of Illinois Press, 1996.
Wetzell, Richard F., *Inventing the Criminal: A History of German Criminology, 1880–1914*, Chapel Hill: The University of North Carolina Press, 2000.

White, Jerry, *The Worst Street in North London: Campbell Bunk, Islington, Between the Wars*, London: Routledge & Kegan Paul, 1986.

Wiener, Martin, *English Culture and the Decline of the Industrial Spirit, 1850–1980*, Cambridge: Cambridge University Press, 1981.

— *Reconstructing the Criminal: Culture, Law and Policy in England, 1830–1914*, Cambridge: Cambridge University Press, 1990.

— "The Victorian Criminalization of Men," in Pieter Spierenburg (ed.), *Men and Violence: Gender, Honor and Rituals in Modern Europe and America*, Columbus, OH: Ohio State University Press, 1998.

Williams, Peter, "Constituting Class and Gender: A Social History of the Home, 1700–1901," in Nigel Thrift and Peter Williams (eds.), *Class and Space: The Making of Urban Society*, London: Routledge & Kegan Paul, 1987.

Williams, Raymond, *Keywords: A Vocabulary of Culture and Society*, New York: Oxford University Press, 1976, p. 278.

Wood, J. Carter, "Self-Policing and the Policing of the Self: Violence, Protection and the Civilizing Bargain in Britain," *Crime, Histoire & Sociétés/Crime, History and Societies*, 2003, vol. 7, no. 1: 109–28.

— "It's a Small World After All?: Reflections on Violence in Comparative Perspectives," in Barry Godfrey, Clive Emsley and Graeme Dunstall (eds.), *Comparative Histories of Crime*, Collumpton, Devon: Willan Press, 2003.

Wood, L. S. and H. L. Burrows (eds.), *Sports and Pastimes in English Literature*, London: Thomas Nelson & Sons, Ltd., 1925.

Woods, David, "Community Violence," in John Benson (ed.), *The Working Class in England, 1875–1914*, London: Croom Helm, 1985.

Zedner, Lucia, *Women, Crime and Custody in Victorian England*, Oxford: Clarendon Press, 1991.

Index

For Product Safety Concerns and Information please contact our EU
representative GPSR@taylorandfrancis.com
Taylor & Francis Verlag GmbH, Kaufingerstraße 24, 80331 München, Germany